Topaz Eyes

Nancy Jardine

CROOKED CAT

Discover us online:
www.crookedcatpublishing.com

Join us on facebook:
www.facebook.com/crookedcatpublishing

About the Author

An ex-primary teacher, Nancy Jardine lives in the fabulous castle country of Aberdeenshire – Scotland - with her husband who feeds her well. That's just perfect, or they'd both starve. When time permits, ancestry research is an intermittent hobby. Neglecting her large garden in favour of writing, she now grows spectacularly giant thistles. Activity weekends with her extended family are prized since they give her great fodder for new writing.

Teaching historical periods was a joy, and it heavily influences her writing. One historical novel, set in A.D 71 Celtic/Roman Britain, is now available; a sequel to it under construction. Nancy has published two ancestral mysteries and one light-hearted contemporary romance mystery. Whenever possible, Nancy includes her homeland of Scotland in her work, and many of the wonderful cities she has been fortunate to visit. Look out for those clues in her novels and detect which are places she really has visited and those she has only internet knowledge of!

A time-travel adventure has been written for pre-teens and a family saga is a work in progress. Life is now one of travel from the keyboard - in present and past time!

Acknowledgements

Ancestry research can throw up the most amazing details – some very good, and some very naughty. Anyone reading Topaz Eyes will see I've become a devotee of sleuthing out ancestral misdeeds. I love ferreting out details about my own relatives and could not have created the fictitious descendants of Geertje Hoogeveen, for Topaz Eyes, had I not had some prior dabbling with family trees.

I dedicate this book to my paternal cousin, Sandra, and in turn to her maternal cousin, Duncan. If Duncan, a serious amateur ancestry researcher, had not started the ball rolling for my own investigations into our shared distant family tree I would not have learned so much about the black sheep lurking there. To them I give my heartfelt thanks for sparking the idea of creating my totally fabricated family tree for my mystery-Topaz Eyes.

To my editor, Christine McPherson, my thanks for making the editorial process a painless one. To Crooked Cat Publishing – I'm very pleased to be one of your authors.

Topaz Eyes

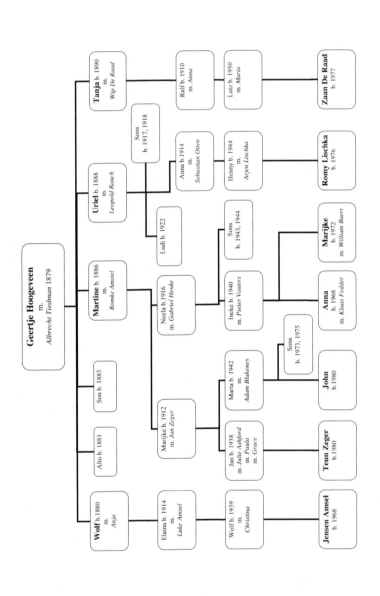

Geertje Hoogeveen
m.
Albrecht Tiedman 1879

Wolf b.1880
m.
Anja

Alto b. 1881

Son b. 1883

Martine b. 1886
m.
Romke Amstel

Uriel b. 1888
m.
Leopold Rauch

Tanja b. 1890
m.
Wip De Raad

Elaina b. 1914
m.
Luke Amsel

Marijke b. 1912
m. *Jan Zeger*

Neela b.1916
m. *Gabriel Henke*

Ludi b. 1922

Sons
b. 1917, 1918

Anna b.1914
m.
Sebastian Otten

Ralf b. 1910
m. *Anna*

Wolf b. 1939
m.
Christina

Jan b. 1938
m. *Julie Ashford*
m. *Paula*
m. *Grace*

Marta b. 1942
m.
Adam Blakeney

Ineke b. 1940
m. *Pieter Vosters*

Sons
b. 1943, 1944

Henny b. 1944
m.
Arjen Lischka

Lutz b. 1950
m. *Maria*

Sons
b. 1973, 1975

Jensen Amsel
b. 1968

Teun Zeger
b.1980

John
b.1980

Anna
b. 1968
m. *Klaas Fedder*

Marijke
b. 1972
m. *William Baert*

Romy Lischka
b. 1976

Zaan De Raad
b. 1977

Chapter One

Keira Drummond had found the bizarre request to return to Heidelberg, Germany, impossible to resist. After almost six years, little had changed on the street named Steingasse as she sat looking down towards the Brückentor – the towers of the old bridge spanning the River Neckar with their distinctive helmeted tops.

Still tremendously busy, Steingasse was too narrow for the clutches of tables adorning both sides. Even in the middle of the street it was difficult to see the cobbles, the pedestrian traffic a constant procession undulating along its length, since it was one of Heidelberg's most popular tourist areas.

Sipping her coffee, she now had great reservations over accepting the strange summons and couldn't fathom the compulsion she'd felt to comply, because caution normally imprinted itself on her forehead. Now she was in Heidelberg, the circumstances surrounding the request were even more nebulous, and so shrouded in secrecy. Apprehension that there was something underhand about it sat heavy in her stomach. She'd yet to meet her host, and presently wasn't convinced she wanted to.

"Frei, or *besetzt?"*

The abrupt question, in halting German, startled a smile from her. Free, or occupied, the tall man beside her was asking? A curve to her lips lingered as he stared, his focus intent. Dull flutters skittered inside her. Something about the man tripped a little switch, yet glued her mouth. Shut. The words free, and occupied, adopted whole new hues.

Her nod was infinitesimal.

Sharing tables in places like this was the norm; in fact, the waiting staff positively encouraged it, liking their tables groaning with potential tips. She already shared with a Norwegian couple who'd been happy for her to take the third seat at the table: the only table in the vicinity with spares. It would be downright mean of her to deny this man the fourth.

"*Danke.*"

His thank you nod encompassed all of them as he glided a small package and an envelope onto the tabletop, before shrugging out of his dark grey jacket.

With no conscious intention of being nosey, it was difficult for Keira to ignore someone who dominated her airspace as he shuffled around in the impossibly tiny gap. She contemplated the swallowing of his throat when his glance alighted on her, and then halted. Interest flared, a widening of his grey eyes accompanied a hint of a smile, just crinkling the corners of his mouth. Blinking a few times, she considered looking away but found she couldn't. It wasn't impossible, she just didn't want to, and it seemed neither did he.

Without breaking eye contact, he fumbled the jacket over the back of the wrought-iron chair and then squeezed in as best he could, a tighter smile coming her way.

Irritability, or perhaps frustration, draped over him as much as his business clothing, the slight pull at his brows not something she could miss. Before tugging her gaze away, she returned his smile. She doubted it was the lack of privacy on the street which bothered the guy, or he'd have moved on to a quieter place.

Alongside her, his fingers idled then tapped on the table edge as he surveyed the area, his head lifting to appreciate the architecture, much as she had done a few moments earlier. Taking stock over his shoulder, by bowing his torso to an uncomfortable angle, he was also able to view the towers, but before Keira could catch it his envelope slipped off the table edge, dislodged by his extended fingers. Bending to grasp it at the same time as he did, she barely avoided a brow collision. Sheer male and a hint of some kind of herb, assailed her nostrils. She savoured it before they both moved; his now smiling mouth within centimetres of hers.

"*Danke.*"

Deep and throaty, the single word of thanks rippled towards her. She answered in English as she held out the envelope. "No problem. Here you go."

"You're English?"

"Scottish. And you're American?"

The man laughed, his teeth bright against the tan of his skin. "I am, though how could you tell my German was non-native?"

One moment of shared amusement was enough. Sitting back in her chair, as he did, they began a casual conversation. Mischief lurked behind her answer. "Mmm. Let's see which might offend the least. Hesitation? The wrong 'a' sound maybe? Or perhaps it's just the fact almost everyone around here isn't a German native, including most of the wait staff."

The raising of his brows stoked a nice little fire. "How can you possibly make such a judgment?"

"I worked at a wine bar, only a couple of streets away, for the best part of eight months, right here in the heart of Heidelberg's tourist areas. Though, it was almost six years ago."

Something about his steel drum gaze, the twinkle perhaps, indicated she'd impressed him.

"No restaurants to wait tables on in Scotland?"

"Oh, sure. I waited on plenty of tables there, too. I attended the university here in Heidelberg, as part of my languages course and, in the nature of things, had to finance my way. But don't get me wrong. A job like that was the best way to improve my fluency."

"Yeah, but how did you manage if most people around were

non-German?"

"Did I forget to say my boss was German?" Memories of the slave driver he'd been brought forth another smirk. "I absorbed a dictionary worth of very nice words from him, I can tell you. And not the German I learned during seminars along at the university."

A slight pause descended, the waiter having arrived at the table. Keira studied the man when his attention moved to their server. His thick hair was mid-brown, short, yet not so cropped she'd be unable to slide her fingers through. A nice idea, but she'd no time for dalliance so why did these errant imaginings even enter her head? Still, she couldn't help notice the polite smile he flashed at the waiter before glancing at her half-full coffee cup. His pointing finger, and questioning glance, she took to mean did she want another: her simple headshake all he needed before he placed his beer order in halting German. Economical with words he, nonetheless, seemed a generous person.

Assessing the character of strangers was a favourite pastime, and it always pleased when her judgment was spot on.

"Are you impressed? I just ordered me a beer."

"I'm guessing your German's limited?"

"How much can anyone learn in transit from London?" Dark laughter rippled down her nerve endings, though there was an abashment that didn't seem to match, because the man oozed masculinity. He flashed a small phrase book taken from his back pocket.

"My German is worse than non-existent, and doubly embarrassing since my father was of Dutch descent. Not the same as German, I know, but I believe some of their words are quite similar. "

Her laugh rang along with his, since it was so easy to join the bandwagon of his mirth. "No lessons in Dutch at your grandma's knee?"

"Not a word. The only thing I've got that's Dutch is my

name."

Keira expected him to introduce himself. Yet, opportune or not, he didn't. His gaze lingered, though, just enough for her to wonder if it was what he expected of her. She chose to resume the topic of his Dutch ancestry. Her own association with Holland went way back, but in many ways her knowledge of the language was no better than his. "You've never visited Holland?"

"Nope. Never visited Holland: never visited Germany before either. Till around midday today, I'd never stepped foot in mainland Europe. The closest I've been across the Atlantic have been visits to London."

"Heidelberg is beautiful, I'm sure you'll enjoy being here." Confidence that he would rang through her tones. It was a fabulous place to visit, especially for a first visit to Europe – the architecture and old world splendour spectacular to view.

The man's smile faltered, his eyes momentarily clouding as he re-pocketed his phrase book. "Nice thought, but I'm not so sure I'm going to be here long enough to see the best of it."

"Your beer, sir!" The waiter's chirrup in English halted their conversation when he appeared at the man's elbow.

The stranger slid his package and envelope towards her, clearing off enough space for his beer stein, since the table was so small. A long pull at the frothy drink brought a satisfied smirk to his face as he appreciated the chill of it. "I needed that."

"Even businessmen are due time off to gallivant just a little, surely?"

A twitch at one side of the man's mouth indicated unease with her statement. As a translator she often had to work one-to-one with people, and though in no way a psychologist, she'd gotten very good at reading expressions, especially when people couldn't formulate the words they needed or were unsure of the meaning of something. Something puzzled the stranger.

"There's the hell of it. I'm not here on business. You?" His personal question sounded as tentative as hers.

"No, I'm not here on business and not for tourist reasons either." Keira's mood dipped, the reminder of her summons spoiling what was proving to be a pleasant interlude with the stranger.

A bit of mystery hung, and hovered, as she sipped her coffee and the man glugged his beer. His thirst appeared great, though he wasn't in the least bit apologetic about being so driven to drink. She wished his tongue wouldn't do that nice little lip-wiping after each sip. Silent sighs did nothing to quell the temptation to lick off the beer froth herself. Hmm. She hadn't been in any kind of relationship for months. Too long, obviously, since she eyed up this stranger with such relish.

The man's head whipped back, a question coming at her in parts, as he again tongued off more beer froth. "If you were a tourist… with only a few hours to spare… what would you do first?"

She laughed at his intent stare. Something lurked in his gaze; most likely nothing to do with a desire to tramp the cobbled streets of Heidelberg. Any innuendo wouldn't embarrass her, though, since she was just as guilty of ogling. "Hmm. I guess that depends on your tastes."

His eyes danced over the rim of his stein as he hesitated, his beer mug held aloft. "Apart from quenching my obvious dehydration, what do you recommend to see in the near vicinity of Heidelberg?"

Keira became an enthusiastic guidebook during the next while as she gave him some pointers – all within a short walk of the Old Bridge.

The American's responses were equally animated until their easy conversation suddenly faltered. Toying with his beer glass in one hand, he reached for his envelope in the other. Concentrating on the white paper with fierce intensity, he fiddled with it as though weighing it up both in his fingers and in his mind. A tense and awkward silence permeated the air around the two of them, which was ridiculous really as the area thronged with noise and busy movements.

Abruptly, he snagged her gaze, his eyebrows a neat little frown. His words rushed out as he set down his beer before wafting the envelope. "Look. I know you don't know me, but… if you're not busy this evening? With friends, or some kind of appointment, or whatever…"

She couldn't look away. Could do nothing but wait. Was this total stranger about to ask her for a date? Or translate for him? Definitely the disappointing one of the two possibilities. Except? Could this be an escape clause from the appointment she did have, and now didn't want to attend?

His words hung in the air. Agitation of some sort held him in a tight grip. Strangely, Keira felt it appealing to witness his hesitation, maybe even vulnerability?

"See, I've been given this invitation right out of the blue, and I wondered if you'd like to accompany me. If you're not busy elsewhere?"

The envelope pinged free of his fingers when a woman at the table behind him stood up, her overstuffed bag bumping his arm, but the plummeting invitation was only one casualty of the collision. In her embarrassment to apologize profusely, in what Keira guessed to be some Eastern European language, the woman grasped the falling envelope and set it awkwardly onto the table, dislodging his beer stein. Keira squirmed as a wash of pale gold liquid sloshed right over the envelope, and headed towards her lap. More apologies, and an even fierier red face, ensued as the woman extricated herself, and flurried off.

Grabbing napkins from the centre stand, Keira swabbed the soggy envelope free of beer, before she swiped the remainder of the flow off the table.

"Don't worry about it." The guy's grunt barked out as he peeled a card free of the saturated wrapping.

Keira's breath hitched when she glanced at the invitation

being uncovered, her eyebrows wincing at the distinctive gilt-edged border and flowery script. This stranger had one of those invitations, too? An invitation which looked exactly like the bizarre one she'd received earlier that afternoon. '... *You will find it to your advantage to attend the opening of the Myer Gallery.*' A request which should have seemed positive, yet lacked so much.

An icy shiver skittered all over her skin, and lodged deep at the base of her spine. Why would a stranger, who'd randomly sat next to her, have a similar invitation? Heidelberg was a large city. It couldn't be good.

Coincidence? She couldn't make herself believe it. The flutters she felt invade her now were nothing like the former desire generated by the stranger; they were of sheer, unadulterated alarm. The invitation she'd been given, less than two hours before, had caused her a lot of disquiet when she'd received it, since it had been handed over in such a peculiar and secretive fashion. That this stranger had a similar card was so weirdly coincidental there had to be something odd going on. Perhaps this American had a sinister motive for revealing it? He could have left it in the soggy wrap. Or was he literally showing his card to lure her into a false sense of security? Her mind ran amok with many possibilities, but all of them alarmed her.

While he stared at the card, her eyes scanned, up and down. She wasn't sure what she was looking for, but relief didn't come to quell her panic. Patrons still exchanged noisy talk, and a steady swarm of people trooped along the potholed cobbles, past her table as before, heading for the riverside. None of them looked furtive, yet she couldn't shake off a feeling of unease.

Why had this American not moved on to another street? Knowing the area from before, it was very likely the next street along would be less crowded. Was it also coincidental he, too, seemed on edge and agitated about something? His concentration was intense on the card as he wiped off the dregs of beer.

The feeling of threat escalated. He didn't seem like a stalker – though she'd never confronted one. Yet, the man must have followed her, and awaited the opportunity to insinuate a meeting. To gain her agreement to accompany him to the evening event. But why? There had been too many unanswered questions – by the third party organizer – even before she'd encountered this American.

His head turned away to catch the attention of the waiter. Grabbing her purse, Keira pulled out a few euros to pay for her coffee, and fumbled them beside her cup. Slipping neatly around the other couple at the table, she sped along Steingasse towards the towers of the Old Bridge, and blended in with the surge of tourists. She ignored the man's plea and shouted apology. Let him believe she'd been annoyed at being drenched with beer, but she wouldn't stay one more minute.

***

Teun's entreaties made not a blind bit of difference. The woman up and ran – make that squeezed – as best one could along the heaving street. He sat down, sending a brief glance of apology to the other couple for startling them, realising his pleas had been loud. What exactly had just happened? Surely the woman hadn't been upset by a little beer? As he reflected on her haste, he knew it wasn't the beer spill that had distressed her, because she'd been smiling as she wiped away the flow.

However, something had.

They'd been getting along quite nicely till she'd taken flight. Maybe he'd been too crass in mentioning the invitation so soon in the conversation, though she hadn't looked to be the type of female who'd be shocked by his fumbling request. Too poised and too assured. Gorgeous didn't describe her. Beautiful seemed too clichéd as well. More appropriate was stunning; exactly how she'd grabbed his attention.

He still felt whacked when he envisioned her face. Eyes, just like the huge imperial topaz he'd seen on his Aunt Marta's finger years ago, had lured him. He'd never forgotten his fascination with the stone, the name having etched itself in his memory banks. The varied golden brown-twinkling facets of the ring were just like the individual hues of the woman's amazing irises, the tiny little diamonds around Aunt Marta's ring like the whites of the Scotswoman's eyes. Her straight dark brown hair matched those drugging eyes since it, too, had many tints, falling as it did from a side parting to well past her shoulders, in a softly uneven cut at the ends. So uniformly uneven, he guessed clever styling created it.

His palms curled around his beer stein, his restless imagination replacing the cold glass with warm soft flesh. He'd wanted to toy with the unusual necklace she'd been fingering, her hand drifting to it, circling sensually around it. There'd been such a temptation to finger the little bunch of golden charms dangling below her throat, her lightly tanned skin below it seeming to beg for his touch. Nothing blunt, or harsh, about her.

He sighed before picking up his now replenished beer, the waiter having lifted the woman's unfinished coffee cup, and the money she'd tucked alongside. She'd been a bright spot in a very odd day.

Gone. Like a will o' the wisp.

Teun fingered the condensation off the side of his beer stein, his focus on it intent. His detour now seemed an unwanted interruption to his carefully planned schedule. Too many things remained unknown, and mysterious, about this invitation to Heidelberg. Fingering the card, he debated whether to collect his luggage from the hotel, which had been booked for him, and disappear as well.

Like the elusive siren he'd just encountered.

***

A new wave of nerves assailed Keira as she stood in a short queue. The venue was in a prestigious part of the old city, the Altstadt, where art studios and galleries dotted themselves around.

After fleeing the American, she'd flashed past the gallery during the late afternoon, needing to check it out. She wasn't entirely sure why, but there had been an urgency to know where it was located, and how to escape it quickly. Then the interior had been almost empty, but now? It burst at the seams, even though she was bang on time.

The queue moved up, vanishing quickly inside, till her turn. Tendering her invitation to the doorman, she greeted him as she scanned around. "*Guten Abend.*"

"Good evening, Miss Drummond," he replied in faultless English. Whipping out his phone, he fingered a brief text. "Herr Amsel will be along shortly to speak to you. Please remain in this front part of the foyer."

She nervously licked off some of her lip gloss. How the hell could the doorman possibly know her name, since the invitation card she'd just handed him bore no name on it? Her confusion must have been worn like a banner, though, because the door attendant made a hasty explanation.

"You haven't noticed the embossed motif on the bottom right here?"

She hadn't, but when she looked closely and fingered the area, she could see what he referred to.

"There are only three guests tonight who have had their invitation stamped with Herr Amsel's special insignia... and only one of them a young woman. That's how I know your name, Miss Drummond."

Accepting his simple explanation, she moved away from the door to allow the next guests to enter. Knowing she was one of three special people didn't make her feel any less vulnerable when she glanced at the surrounding faces. A new fish in a large bowl of established guppies couldn't possibly feel any more out of place. She wondered if the phrasing on the invitations of all the animated guests around her, was just as odd as her own, but then immediately discarded the thought. No-one close by looked insecure as they chatted in little clusters, and pointed, and noisily commented on the displays. There had to be a couple of hundred people crammed into the gallery.

Her host couldn't possibly have given all of these guests the same enticement he'd given her. She'd not only been invited to attend the event, all of her expenses to Heidelberg had been paid. Did it mean the other two special guests had had similar treatment? She wondered if the two special males felt they were in a similar weak position as she did; felt as hesitant about their decision to attend.

Not so for the crowd, though, in her near proximity. All the smiling and nodding, here and there, indicated nothing but pleasure.

Mulling over her situation made her fret even more. If she moved even a few steps away she'd be eddied in the shoal. Yet, cowardice wasn't a familiar trait. Her profession demanded meeting new people. Her inner sister berated her for being such a wimp, urged her to get a grip.

Reaching out, she plucked a champagne flute from the tray of a passing waitress, for liquid courage, before she peered at the intricate detail on a piece of etched glass. Way beyond her disposable funds, nonetheless, it was a work of art she could appreciate. A few sips of champagne drowned some of her disquiet, as she determined she'd make the best of what was the strangest event to happen to her in ages. Maybe even ever.

The door attendant's voice intruded. "Miss Drummond? Herr Amsel won't be available for a while, but I've another of his three special guests with me now. I'll leave you to get to know Meneer De Raad."

Keira looked up at him. Very tall was her immediate impression. Very slim in the way people of Dutch descent often are: not skinny by any manner of means, just a very long drink. An appetizing one if it were the height of summer, since cool elegance radiated from him; though all that Germanic blondness might be chilly in winter time. Her observations grounded her a little more.

"Good evening."

His voice had lightness to it she associated with people very familiar with the meeting and greeting process; assured, confident... and just as assessing as she was. Whiskerless pale skin matched his thatch of streaked blond hair. A strong nose sat above thin lips. The eyes, which displayed a high degree of interest, were an ice-blue behind light lashes.

Though definitely handsome, he packed none of the punch of the stranger on Steingasse. Something about Meneer De Raad spoke of determined ambition. The set of his jaw maybe? Her gaze shifted momentarily while she made a swift check of the faces close by. The American wasn't visible, yet could be anywhere in the throng, if he'd taken up the invitation. She wasn't sure why she seemed to be looking for him... but she did.

"Miss Drummond?" Meneer De Raad's words came after a long pause, as though he carefully considered what to say, yet she surmised it wasn't due to any language impediment.

Her hand was engulfed, small against long, smooth fingers that had nothing roughened about them. The polite smile on her face turned to a grin when she found his handshake as cool as he was. Yet, rather than put her off, it contrarily did the opposite and made her feel more at ease. She felt her tense shoulders relax a little while her hand was released.

"Keira Drummond, and from the introduction, I'm guessing you're Dutch, Meneer De Raad?"

"Yes. My name's Zaan." He waved his invitation. "We are two of a privileged three people here tonight, according to the doorman."

"That's what he told me. Though I wonder why? I've absolutely no idea why I'm here, except I've to meet someone called Jensen Amsel."

When expressed in such fashion, it sounded so simple, so ordinary. She broke off eye contact to gaze around, feeling a dull heat creep over her cheeks. How ridiculous she'd been earlier when the American's invitation had spooked her. Embarrassment deepened further over her silly reactions, making it difficult to resume the conversation and eye contact.

"I, too, have been asked to speak to Jensen Amsel. I've never met him, though I know of him through trade sources."

She allowed Zaan De Raad's ease in the situation to rub off on her. No disquiet or insecurity plagued him, she was sure of it. Rather, there seemed to be a repressed excitement behind those ice-blue eyes when she looked closely. "You're way ahead of me then, since I know nothing. Perhaps you could tell me about him?"

She didn't mean to plead, but it would make her feel less out on a limb if he could tell her something about her host.

"Jensen Amsel is the money man behind this cooperative gallery. He's not an artist, but is an avid collector. He holds investments in galleries and various businesses." Zaan's smile encouraged her to ask questions as he gave her more information. "Amsel's based here in Heidelberg. In addition to this gallery, he has shops in the Altstadt, mainly selling jewellery and crafts; though his jewellery chain extends to other cities in Germany."

"You make it sound as though you're also in the retail market, Meneer De Raad?"

"Yes, I am, but please call me Zaan, and I'll call you Keira?"

"Fine by me." She grinned at the courteous bow of his head. He was definitely a smoothie. "I'm not connected to the retail trade, so that's not why I'm here. I'm a translator but, since almost everyone speaks English, I'm not going to make any money translating tonight."

"If not your profession, have you any other association with Heidelberg which may have drawn you into this intriguing situation?"

"You find it intriguing, too?" She was quick to latch onto that, though Zaan De Raad didn't look as if he believed there was anything fishy about it. A twinkling amusement lurked there in his expression.

"Oh, I've a good idea why I'm here, but till Jensen gives his explanation I must wait in anticipation. I think, perhaps, we need to divulge a little of our backgrounds for this to make any sense to you."

Keira desperately wanted an explanation for the request of her presence in Heidelberg, though she wasn't in the habit of sharing personal information with strangers. Yet, hadn't she done a little of it with the American? If the content of his envelope hadn't been revealed, she was honest enough to admit they might have moved on to even more private disclosures.

She metaphorically kicked herself for being so stupid. Her gut reaction to flee from the guy had been way off base. A degree of anxiety still clenched, but she wasn't so inclined to run off now – especially if Zaan could prepare her for the situation she'd got herself involved in.

She followed the Dutchman to a less crowded space, though still not too far from the entry door if the doorman needed to alert her to Jensen Amsel's arrival. Once there, Zaan had no hesitation about speaking of himself. Cockiness settled on him as comfortably as his pale-cream linen suit, worn with typical European panache. His gaze snagged hers, his concentration absolutely focused. Blunt. A little proud. Yet somehow the attitude suited him, and didn't give the impression of being a negative quality. She couldn't consider him an ally, not quite, though he was, to a certain extent, the best she had at present.

"I'm thirty-four. Born near Den Haag, I've always lived

there. I've two antique shops in Den Haag, another in Amsterdam... and I believe the mystery which brings us together this evening began many years ago with my great-grandmother."

Chapter Two

"Wow! Really? You deduced all that from an invitation to a gallery opening?" His quizzical expression made her grin. "I'm impressed by your sleuthing powers.

"Thank you, but I told you I've some knowledge of Jensen Amsel. Even better is the fact my lawyer spoke to Amsel's lawyer yesterday, so when I went along today for my appointment, I had a belt full of ammunition."

The wink which followed was unexpected. She belatedly realised Zaan awaited her response since she'd been slow to process he'd also had an appointment with Herr Amsel's lawyer, like she'd had earlier that afternoon. She desperately wanted to know if he'd come out as confused as she had, though doubted it.

"You arrived today from The Hague? With your ammunition hanging from a very strong belt, from the sound of it."

Zaan's laughter echoed around and drew interested stares from a stunningly-dressed woman who mingled close by. To Keira's surprise, he turned his shoulder away from the female's blatant interest. She didn't know Zaan, but her quickly-formed opinion was someone as good-looking as he was would pick up a come-on signal right away. But he didn't even blink an eyelash.

"I did. Herr Amsel is looking to add to his already extensive collection. Our invitations to talk with him, I believe, are in regard to something we may have, and which he seeks to own."

Confusion spread. "Me? I don't have a single thing a serious collector might want. Old or new."

"Ah, but as someone who's in the antique business, I know it's not always the obvious which holds the most value. Sometimes people have treasures, but they're not necessarily aware of them."

"I can believe it, though why would I get an invitation? I'm not in your business, and I don't know anyone who deals in antiques, far less collects them. Unless he does need a translator?"

Zaan fingered his sharp-shaven jaw, drawing her attention to his pursed lips. An endearing little quirk hovered there which made him appear younger than his years, and less poised than before.

"No." Zaan sounded categorical. "I don't believe it's your translating skills he's after, Keira. Perhaps your beauty draws him."

She couldn't prevent her inelegant snort. "Now that really is unlikely, Zaan."

"What? You don't believe any man might want you for your beauty?"

Zaan looked so confident she'd accept his easy evaluation of her, but she wouldn't be sidetracked by his smooth tactic. "Let's say, I prefer to believe I've been invited because of some totally different reason. Maybe I do have something after all?"

A little quirk at his lips made her embarrassed by her wording.

"Share your background. We'll work from there. See if we can make a connection."

Keira glanced at the entrance. The queue had dwindled to nothing, and now a young woman attended the door. Herr Amsel had made no appearance at her side, though he could be any one of the many men mingling around the large and overcrowded area, but she didn't feel like hogging just the one space all night.

"Shall we admire what's close to here as I tell you? You must be interested in what the gallery has to offer, I imagine, even if it's just to poach display or merchandise ideas?"

Zaan's quirky grin gave her an idea of what he thought of her assessment.

As they wandered around, servers floated among them with tasty little morsels, inviting the guests to choose from their trays as they passed by. In between nibbles, Keira gave brief details she thought might be relevant.

"Strange though it may seem, I was also born in Holland." She broke off at Zaan's indrawn breath and raised eyebrows, and then hastily resumed. "My father's job took him to Holland, where he worked for about four years. My young sister and I were born there, but we returned to Scotland when I was about three."

"So…" Zaan's expression showed keen interest. "Where were you born? I might know of it."

"If you're a keen sailor, then perhaps you will." She chuckled as Zaan popped down his empty flute and gathered up two full ones, transferring her near-empty one with deft ease. "Do you know the Vinkeveense Plassen, the lake near Vinkeveen?" At his easy nod of recognition, Keira continued. "We lived in a village not far from there."

Zaan clinked his flute to hers, the crystal tinkle like a little bell of attraction since those around them stopped to stare, assuming an announcement of some sort was about to be made. Zaan ignored them and concentrated on her.

"Well, we have the land of our birth in common to celebrate at least. I have distant relatives who still live near Vinkeveen. One of the many ties to this mysterious invitation, perhaps, but not quite the answer yet?"

The strangeness of the summons gave way to an unexpected

21

enjoyment of Zaan's company as they chatted on, yet she focused on trying to make some sort of connection, a reason for her being brought to Heidelberg.

"I've no family connections in Holland, though my parents took us back for holidays. We visited friends, though it stopped some years ago, after they died." Zaan's nod indicated some sympathy, so she ploughed on. "I do have an association with Heidelberg, though, since I spent the best part of a year studying at the university. I knew the city pretty well, but it was almost six years ago."

Zaan's gaze was all encompassing as his gaze roamed top to toe. "Twenty-six?"

"Near enough! I'm twenty-seven, but my time at the university seems immaterial to why I'm here today. I made a lot of friends while I studied here, though none were local."

"What made you accept the invitation to come, Keira?"

Zaan was getting to the heart of the matter, though she truthfully wasn't sure of her answer. "Nostalgia? I had a very happy time here, though it was constant slog. When the opportunity to return on someone else's tab landed in my lap, I was completely mercenary. Although it annoys me, and truthfully the cloak and dagger aspect scares me too, the unknown situation also intrigues, I suppose. I needed a break from work, and Heidelberg is just so tempting. I couldn't refuse."

Zaan had been slowly imbibing his champagne during her monologue, though he looked far from bored. A certain degree of friendly interest, and perhaps a hint of sexual heat, lurked behind his gaze. She had no intention of reciprocating anything sexual, but friendship might be pleasant.

"What made you accept?" It was his turn to talk.

"Insider knowledge. I told you I'm in the antiques business, inherited from my mother."

His smirk engaged more interest till, all of a sudden, Zaan sounded cagey. Almost as if he didn't, now, want to give further information. It occurred that he teased, perhaps withheld something important.

"And?" Keira wouldn't be put off by his mischievous approach as she stared him down. One blond eyebrow lifted before Zaan eventually answered, his tone low, yet not quite a whisper. He deliberately bent closer to her ear, as if about to impart a secret.

"It came to my notice recently, through the grapevine, that Jensen Amsel has added to his collection. And I have something I believe he wants to own."

"You're being deliberately mysterious, Zaan, but you're going to tell me what it is. Aren't you?" Intrigue was one thing, but toying with her quite another. Her tone sharpened. "Why should I be asked here, if you're the one who has something of interest to him?"

Zaan lips moved, again close to her, his body indicating a familiarity too early in their acquaintance as his hand descended lightly on her shoulder. The merest twitch of his expression indicated some sardonic humour she hadn't cottoned on to. "I said he wants to add to his collection. He's not looking for just one single item, Keira. He wants a whole set of related items."

"But I can't possibly have anything he's looking for!"

Zaan's fingers tightened on her upper arm as she looked straight up into his eyes, her body tensing with an inexplicable unease. She didn't hate the contact with him, but it wasn't something she wanted to encourage, her slight squirm indicating she wanted to be free from his hold.

In a heartbeat she felt Zaan's clutch release her, the conversation interrupted by the arrival of two men. One man she didn't know. The other was… familiar. The older of the men offered his hand in introduction.

"Miss Drummond. I'm very pleased to meet you. I'm Jensen Amsel." His words broke off as he wheeled around to introduce the second man. "This is Teun Zeger. Teun has come from California to be with us, and he is the third special guest I invited here tonight." As Jensen Amsel pumped her hand in welcome, her gaze strayed to the other man.

Teun Zeger?

The American from Steingasse. He was another of Jensen Amsel's special guests? Was that why he'd also seemed edgy earlier on Steingasse? Maybe he'd been feeling as vulnerable as she had about the mysterious summons. Heat pooled in her cheeks. What a stupid idiot she'd been!

"Miss Drummond."

Teun Zeger's cool tones assailed her – nothing like his honeyed warmth of the afternoon – his expression forbidding and now distinctly unfriendly. He appeared to be completely ignoring the fact they'd already met, his gaze flashing to Zaan, and then back to her. There was none of his former interest; his mouth tightened as though with distaste. Maybe she had been right to flee him that afternoon, but she couldn't now.

His handshake was brief. Despite his disconnection, her palm tingled from the brief contact. A frisson of awareness started again, trickling down her spine and, in spite of his antipathy, the same desirous warmth of the afternoon pooled low in her torso. She hoped her face didn't appear as flushed as she felt. Though speaking was difficult in the face of his brusque delivery, courtesy ruled her response. And, like him, she chose to ignore their earlier interaction. "Hello, Mr. Zeger."

After a quick introduction to Zaan, who regarded Teun Zeger with undisguised curiosity, Herr Amsel ushered them through the gallery. "I'm so pleased you have all accepted my invitation. If we may talk first, you will be very welcome to browse around the exhibits afterwards?"

An unnecessary question, since they all trooped after Herr Amsel anyway; eager to get on with whatever they were there for. He led them through a door at the back into a small office and indicated three chairs which sat lined up, ready and waiting for them. Teun Zeger politely stood aside to allow Keira to take the middle chair, though didn't acknowledge her nod of thanks, his focus on Zaan sliding onto the chair at her other side.

When all were seated, Jensen Amsel began. "At least one of you has an idea why I've asked you all to come, although I don't believe the other two have any idea at all. Is that correct, Meneer De Raad?"

Keira picked up Zaan's chuckle as he answered.

"Wasting no time?"

Jensen's smile was appreciative, the tiniest nod of acknowledgement moving his head at Zaan's statement. "Indeed. There's no point in being discreet any more, Meneer De Raad. Your identities have all been verified by my lawyer this afternoon, so, if no-one has any objections, we'll use our first names? It'll make things easier."

Keira had no objection. Since there were no howls of protest, Jensen continued.

"Zaan can confirm, I collect many types of artwork. Currently, I want to bring together a complete set of associated objects. I have one article, but I believe all three of you either have missing items from the collection, or have access to them. What I'd like is to amass the set, in its entirety, with your help."

Keira studied Jensen as he clicked his fingers; not a becoming trait, something she always found annoying – even a bit repellent. Somewhere around forty-five, Jensen emanated poise. Polished to the nth degree, this included his bleached-white teeth. Honey-hued, manicured hair had not a short strand out of place, his heavy cologne permeating the air in the small room. Though quite tall, Jensen's height didn't measure up to either of the other two men present. What he projected a lot of was money, self-possession… and purpose.

Regardless of his appearance, Keira didn't believe she had anything this man could possibly want.

Teun Zeger leaned forward in the chair, bracing his palms on his knees. His fingers curled around his kneecaps, demonstrating something of the same disquiet she'd sensed had been his problem on Steingasse, but now, she was sure she was the target of his annoyance as well. Snapped words, and sidelong glances, bore out her evaluation of his mood.

"Would you ditch the mystery, Jensen, and just enlighten me as to what you think I have that interests you? And tell me why you couldn't have asked for it in the letter you sent to me? I came here of my own free will – granted – but I'm not hanging around any longer if you're going to drag this out, for I'm damned sure I've no idea what you're referring to."

Jensen's reply lacked emotion, his face a blank screen, his gaze focused on Teun as Keira regarded the by-play.

"Teun. It may come as a surprise to you, but you actually know more about this invitation than Keira. At least you knew from my letter I had something of family interest you might be glad to take back to the USA with you. Keira had no such suggestion made to her."

Tension rose in the room, which didn't only radiate from Teun.

Keira sat uneasy, also unwilling to be in the dark any longer. "Would you please explain why you think I may have something you want, Herr Amsel?" She found herself reluctant to use his first name, considering the antagonism now mounting.

"All in good time, Keira. And please call me Jensen. I don't set out to be anyone's enemy. I believe each of you can provide access to items belonging to the collection. All the pieces are likely to vary in monetary value but, viewed as a complete entity, it will make an impressive display. It's a historic set... and unique."

Zaan intervened. "Keira and I have shared a little of our backgrounds, Jensen, but nothing, so far, links her with me."

The conspiratorial smile Zaan flashed her way couldn't be

missed before he twisted back to Jensen, and then again, she felt Teun's still bothered gaze.

"You introduced yourself just as I started back through the generations with Keira. I had just informed her I believe what you are looking for, from me, once belonged to my great-grandmother."

Jensen's smile was indulgent. Keira felt that his hazel eyes assessed, perhaps even admired, Zaan's shrewdness.

"To be historically accurate, the collection belonged first to your great-great-grandmother – a woman called Geertje. Reciting the family tree isn't complicated, since there are very few still alive in the branches, but it'll make it easier for Keira, to follow her connection, if I reveal it like a story."

Some head nodding went on. She braced herself, unable to narrate her own family lineage back more than a couple of generations.

Though Keira didn't understand it, a hyper-awareness of Teun's movements persisted when he relaxed back into his chair, seemingly prepared to listen to Jensen for a bit longer.

"In 1879, Geertje Hoogeveen married Albrecht Tiedman. She gave birth to her first son in 1880, and then had two more sons in quick succession. Afterwards came three daughters, the youngest of these born in 1890. For the purposes of our story, two of the sons are of no importance since Geertje only bequeathed her collection to her daughters."

Teun's fingers drummed the chair arm. "I got that. This Geertje woman had six kids. So what?"

Zaan's droll voice grated, as low as he lolled in his chair. "Her daughters were given a fortune."

Jensen carried on as though no disruption had taken place. "The three daughters in order of age – eldest first – were named Martine, Uriel and Tanja. Teun and Keira – you have connections to Martine."

"Teun's connected to Keira? That should please you then, Mr. Zeger." Again, Zaan's dry tones cut short Jensen's explanation.

"Zaan – your link is to Tanja. I am a descendant of Geertje through Wolf, her first-born son."

Jensen wasn't best pleased with how the explanation was going; the interruptions not to his taste, from the tightening of his lips, though it gave Keira an opportunity to question. "I don't have any Dutch relatives. My background goes back generations Scottish on one side, and Irish back two generations on the other. What does your search have to do with me?"

Keira turned first to Teun, to see if he knew what Jensen meant by their connection to the woman named Martine. But Teun wasn't looking at her. His gaze narrowed on Zaan, who now appeared highly amused. Teun might be put out with her because of her earlier abandonment, but it had no bearing on the antipathy he now demonstrated towards Zaan. Though, perhaps some family lore caused it? Some old bad blood she didn't know about, but Teun did?

Or maybe the affable stranger of the afternoon was a figment of her imagination, and bad moods were his norm?

With no idea of those answers, it galled that the awareness of his presence continued to be acute. Zaan merely occupied a physical space on her left: Teun did something quite different on her right. She banished the frown appearing between her eyebrows though, as soon as she felt it forming, determined not to allow this ill-tempered man to affect her equilibrium.

Zaan broke the silence, his smile sardonic. "So, Teun Zeger, we are distant cousins?"

"Guess so. Three ways down the line, or some such relationship?" Teun's attitude didn't soften any as he grilled Jensen for more information. "Where does Keira fit in?"

Teun's gaze lingered on her as he awaited Jensen's answer. She wanted to know the answer, too. The minutest flinch she noticed in Teun's steel grey irises echoed the afternoon's flame of interest.

Jensen painted a family timeline. "We'll take Zaan's relationship first. You were the only child born to your parents?"

"Correct." A secretive smile again sneaked at the corners of Zaan's mouth. Keira felt, yet again, he withheld important information.

"Your father was Lutz De Raad, and your grandfather, Ralf De Raad?" Jensen continued after he had Zaan's agreement. "Ralf De Raad's mother was Tanja Tiedman. Is that correct?"

Zaan's tiniest lift of an eyebrow was confirmation. "My father had no siblings, and my grandfather's two brothers died in World War Two before they had any offspring."

Jensen's gaze scoped to include them all. "Geertje's middle daughter, Uriel, moved to Dresden after her marriage to a German, and established her family there. Romy Lischke, who can't be here today, is the last of Uriel's family line, as most of the offspring didn't survive the Dresden bombings of World War Two. Romy now lives in Vienna and, like all of us here, is unmarried and has no children. Although I've been in contact with Romy, she's currently hospitalized, having been involved in a skiing accident about seventeen months ago. Her most recent surgery has been a hip replacement, which will hopefully restore her to full mobility." Jensen broke off for a second to share his gaze amongst them. "Although Romy is unable to be active in the search, she's given me useful information, and her approval of my plan."

Teun interrupted, as though uninterested in the absent cousin. "My grandmother's name became Marijke Zeger when she married Jan Zeger and went off to Minnesota, way back in the 1930s."

Jensen nodded his acknowledgement. "Yes. Your grandmother, Marijke, was the daughter of Martine, the eldest daughter of our trio. So, like Zaan and me, you are also the great-great-grandson of Geertje. I, too, am your third cousin. Similar to Zaan, Romy and me, you had no siblings and are the last of your branch line."

Keira laughed at their expressions. Curiosity, dismay and doubt lingered in Teun's gaze, yet it was good because it had banished his antipathetic frowns. Zaan looked engrossed, even more animated. Jensen was all cool blandness; given none of it was news to him. But as for her? "Well, that certainly puts me in my place! So, if I'm not your cousin, why am I here?"

Jensen eyes brightened for the first time. "Your link is not through blood, Keira, but through a long lasting friendship."

Pieces of the puzzle fell into place. She leaned toward Jensen, understanding better her role as one of the three special guests. "Are you talking about my *Oma* Neela?"

Zaan's gaze whipped round, the sudden movement pulling her attention away from Jensen, his tone sharpening to accusation. "Your *Oma*? You said you had no Dutch relatives."

"Not my real grandmother. My *Oma* Neela was an acquired granny. Her name was Neela Henke. Does she fit into your puzzle, Jensen?"

Good at interrupting, Teun's tone had gone from prickly to more inquisitive as he slid forwards to confront Zaan. This time, she sat back to observe them.

"You don't know Keira at all, do you?"

Zaan didn't seem to be put off by Teun's abrupt cross-examination. "We've never met each other before tonight, but I find her much friendlier than you, my long-lost American cousin."

After a brief hesitation to gain the attention of the two men, Jensen carried on. "Marijke and Neela were daughters of Martine. Having borne seven children, Martine only had those two daughters who survived infancy."

"Wow! That's amazing. So, Neela was your grandmother's sister, Teun. I guess I am kind of connected to you." Excitement burst free as she scanned her companions in turn, the whole secretive invitation thing less threatening than before. "Neela was the most fabulous person. I loved her a lot."

"So you're definitely not a blood relative of mine?" Teun's question was loaded with something she couldn't quite decipher, since his regard had warmed up – a good bit. "But Jensen believes you've something of interest which originally belonged to Geertje? Which you've acquired from Neela?"

Jensen nodded while Zaan questioned her close association with Neela. "How did you come to call Neela Henke your *Oma*?"

"Neela had retired from nursing before meeting my mother, but our village doctor was happy to have her be a secondary assistant at my birth in Woerden, the town where our nearest hospital was situated. And Neela helped my mother when we got home." She related how the friendship lasted long after her family returned to Scotland. Neela and her husband had visited them often, and vice versa, over the years as she grew up. But, as to her having anything of value from Neela? Absolutely not.

"Neela brought souvenirs but never anything costly: dolls, clogs and typical Delft Blue items."

A slight twitch marred Jensen's brows. "She never gave you any jewellery?"

"Only a pair of tiny Delft Blue and silver ear-rings."

Jensen nodded, absorbing her resume. "And your mother? Would she have received anything from Neela?"

"My mother? Neela brought cases full of edible goodies, but not jewellery. We loved Droste; those Dutch chocolate medallions in the hexagonal boxes." That triggered a surge of remembrance. "If her visit was for my birthday, or my sister's, she'd bring traditional *beschuit*... you know those rusk crackers? We'd spread them with butter, and top with a groaning layer of chocolate *hagelslag* and aniseed *muisjes;* those pink and white sprinkles."

She looked at the men around her, hoping they weren't bored. "Our close relationship with *Oma* Neela wasn't about

31

expensive material things. What she gave us was her time... and her humour. Always cheery, always laughing, she constantly looked on the bright side."

Teun's question was unexpected. "Did Neela have no family of her own?"

"Yes, she had children. Her daughter's called Ineke, and Jan was her son. Jan died in his late teens: a motorbike accident. I've met Ineke, though not since Neela's funeral, a few years ago."

"Ineke has two daughters. Do you know them, too, Keira?" Jensen shuffled the piece of paper he'd been consulting back onto the pile in front of him.

"I met Anna and Marijke when my parents took me to Holland for holidays, and more recently at Neela's funeral. I don't know much about them now, though, since I only trade a brief Christmas card with Ineke."

"If they're also relatives, why aren't they here tonight, Jensen?" Teun was good at grilling, his tone demanding.

Jensen clicked his fingers, making her shudder. "I invited Ineke, but she declined my invitation. I couldn't locate Anna. It seems she's estranged from her mother – at present – and Ineke wouldn't, or couldn't, give me contact details for her."

"And Marijke isn't here, since she lives in New Zealand?"

Jensen's smile showed approval. "Exactly. I invited her but she declined, due to work commitments. However, she's the one who suggested I invite you, Keira, and your sister."

"Really?"

Teun was thorough. "Your sister also declined to come?"

"Isla's a teacher. She only travels during school holidays."

Jensen carried on, "When I told Marijke my reasons for getting us together, she informed me Neela considered you, and your sister, as surrogate grandchildren. Marijke believes she probably has something handed down from Geertje, and wondered if Neela had given you something, too."

"So, Keira, if one of Neela's real granddaughters has a piece of Geertje's jewellery collection, are you very sure you don't have something priceless, too?" Zaan's brusque inquiry and demanding manner startled, since he'd seemed amiable just moments before.

Chapter Three

"No, I don't own any expensive jewellery." Keira's snort was inelegant, a habit she'd have to erase.

Teun went back to prickly tones barbed with exasperation. "Have I been invited here to discuss friggin' women's trinkets?"

He made to take his leave of them, but Jensen's gestures halted his exit. "Wait, please, Teun. Hear the whole story before you wash your hands of what is our family affair."

A grudging Teun retreated back onto the chair. "This had damned well better be good."

"Geertje's extremely rich parents, the Hoogeveens, lived in Amsterdam in the 1870s. They were successful gold merchants. Geertje married Albrecht Tiedman, a silk merchant with no family pedigree. They gave her a set of emerald jewellery – I'm guessing, in the event she could use them to convert to ready cash. "

"Not just an average emerald collection." Zaan's eagerness almost burst from him. "If I'm correct, the jewels originally belonged to Tiru Salana, a Mughal Emperor."

"You have done your homework. Your sources noted I recently acquired one tiny part of this collection?"

Jensen's smirk seemed too manufactured.

Zaan's tone sobered a fraction, though still looked desperate to divulge information. "You now have an emerald, diamond and gold ring of quite spectacular design. When it recently appeared on the market, the uniqueness of it was like a flare in the world of antique jewellery."

Jensen acknowledged Zaan's statement by withdrawing a photograph of the ring in question, handing it over for Keira to view first. Her breath caught in her throat. Incredible. The gold filigree ring was wrought in a shape reminiscent of a tiara which would drop a pendant onto the forehead. A golden snake's head formed the pendant, its eyes sparkling emeralds. Above the head sat an impressive diamond.

Unable to prevent her outburst, she passed the photograph on to Teun. "It has to be worth a bomb! Look at it."

Jensen's reply sounded bland, though there was now banked ardour in his gaze. "I paid ninety thousand euros for it. Zaan, no doubt, already knows this from his astute sources, so I won't waste anyone's time telling you any different. Not all the pieces of the collection will individually rate so highly… but you might now be able to see what they could mean as a whole collection."

Keira slumped back in her chair. Ninety thousand euros was a fortune. How could Jensen think she had anything measuring up to this? It was laughable. Glancing at Teun, his expression indicated he might just be feeling something the same. He, however, did not lack words like she did.

"Are you saying, Jensen, you think we all have something hidden in our sock drawer which looks like this ring?"

"No, I'm not. If it were so easy, I would have contacted you individually and contracted separate deals with you. It is, sadly, not so simple."

Jensen took up the thread of the tale again. "The Mughal Emperors loved elaborate jewellery, but they were inclined to be bored with the pieces after a while. They bestowed them on their wives, or lovers, and Tiru Salana gave away parts of his collection to…"

Jensen fingered his impeccable hair, the tiniest bit hesitant. She understood the German words he muttered and interpreted for him. "Roughly translated, Teun and I would understand it as a religious donation of some sort, I think?"

Jensen looked relieved, the tension which had tightened his cheeks now relaxed. "Exactly, Keira. Tiru Salana had many facets to his nature. Despite being a devout Muslim, he donated jewellery and other gold offerings, to the Hindu faith. The collection I seek originated from a temple donation. Although, it was common practice at the time to reset jewellery on a regular basis, so it's difficult to establish exactly what their original designs were."

Teun's animation heightened as he sought her attention, quirkiness to his gaze which made her suspicious, the tweak at his lip an indicator something now amused him. Was Teun, the pleasant companion of the afternoon, returning? She wasn't sure as she faced him.

"Fancy being bedecked in jewellery once belonging to an Indian princess…" His tone deepened while his grin enticed, eyebrows a mirthful twitch. "…or maybe you'd prefer the gifts to the emperor's concubines?"

Keira had a hard time not answering; his playful words intended to embarrass her. Or maybe the objective was to arouse her, regardless of the other men in the room? For instants, they seemed the only two occupying the office.

Zaan broke the heightened connection between her and Teun. "I think Keira would look spectacular decorated in an emerald necklace. She has the perfect neck for it."

Teun's focus fell from her eyes to the heavy gold chain winding around her neck. The same chain she'd been wearing earlier that day, now minus her charms, looked more sophisticated for the evening's event. It was the only jewellery she'd brought with her and, if truth be told, it was the solitary piece of solid gold she owned. Cheap and cheerful costume jewellery usually enhanced her wardrobe.

"If, and when, Jensen amasses this incredible collection, I'll model it for you guys, gladly… before he hides it away in a safe for the next couple of centuries." Having believed she'd have the last laugh, she found Teun wasn't done.

"You'd model it as an Indian princess, or as a subserviently alluring concubine? I'm fairly sure each woman would have worn the jewellery to gain different responses. "

Zaan's laugh echoed Teun's.

Jensen wasn't so crass in his appraisal of her, though no doubt his thinking wasn't too dissimilar – the twinkle in his eyes a clue before he chided, "I apologize, Keira, for having distant relatives who have no idea of how to treat a lady."

A smile escaped though she was loath to show it. "Thank you, Jensen. Your cousins have had some fun, but their teasing won't solve your problem."

When Teun pulled his warm gaze away from her, levity departed his tone. "And what, exactly, is that, Jensen?"

"I need everyone's help to locate the whole collection. We all, even Keira, have family knowledge which, when shared, might locate the pieces. Without your co-operation, I'm unlikely to uncover everything, especially since I've no idea exactly what the pieces look like."

A pregnant silence ensued as Keira took stock of Jensen's words.

"Wait a damned minute!"

Teun seemed to be itching to get up and walk out again. Keira's fingers gripped his chair arm, a futile gesture since no real contact was involved, though it seemed to work when he slid back down onto the seat pad. However, his expression remained derisive.

"You're expecting us to give up our lives, and go off on some friggin' wild goose chase for this fictitious collection you only have a vague impression exists?"

When Zaan answered, rather than Jensen, the vehemence in his tone surprised her.

"It definitely exists, Teun. When it made its way to Amsterdam, around 1815, it acquired the accolade of being the most fabulous collection to land in the hands of the Amsterdam Gold Merchants. The ring Jensen recently bought featured in a newspaper article of 1815, the description of it a good identifier. That publication states the city burghers of the time wanted it to go on public show, but before it could be enforced, the ring mysteriously disappeared. Nothing more was recorded about any of the collection till a month ago when Jensen bought that most distinctive piece." Zaan pointed to the image of the gold ring.

Keira's attention fixed on it. "The person you bought it from didn't have any other pieces of the collection?"

Jensen shook his head. "No. The seller didn't know its value when he put it up for sale. I paid the market value for the gold, the exceptional cuts of the emeralds and diamond – nothing to do with any history of the piece."

Bluntness seemed to be a trait of Teun's. "But how the hell can you be sure it's from this collection, especially if you don't know how many pieces there are?"

"I didn't say that. What I said was I don't know exactly what they look like. What I do know – and it appears Zaan does, too, from the old newspaper article – is the collection consisted of twenty different items." Jensen opened a file beside him and extracted a plastic wallet.

From inside, he withdrew a stiff-board photograph which he held up to show them all, the edges of the card slightly bent and aged, and the hand-tinted colouring of the photograph a soft blur. Three beautifully bedecked women stood in a typical formal pose, flanked by opulent flower arrangements on high pedestals.

"Meet Geertje Tiedman's daughters – Martine, Uriel and Tanja. This photograph was taken in 1907. Martine was twenty-one, Uriel nineteen, and Tanja seventeen."

Jensen propped the original up and then handed each of them a slightly larger copy of the original.

The sisters were stunning; their elaborate upswept wide hairstyles slightly different, created to enhance the individual beauty of each woman. Keira couldn't help being impressed.

"Your great-grandmothers were all beauties."

"Passed their magnificence down to their great-grandsons, did they, Keira?"

She almost ignored Teun's teasing quip, but she couldn't resist a little jibe. "Zaan and Jensen have definitely got their looks from the sisters. Look at them, Teun, two blonds and a delicate redhead? Not a single dark hair among them! Those locks are tinted on the photographs; nevertheless, I'm sure they were adroit representations of their real hair colours."

Teun's chuckle of appreciation rippled through her, his gaze mirthful. She went for a look of cool dismissal, but knew she'd failed when he winked. Just a minute little flicker, although enough to set her afire. "Brown makes a change though?"

"Have a good look at your photograph, please, and tell me what you can see."

Jensen's request forced her to focus again. The incredibly lavish evening gowns displayed unique designs, tinted in pastel tones of green, peach and cream. The cream gown was a fussy confection of silk with heavily wrought lace trimming. A V-neckline, enhanced by an over-bodice of complicated lace, sat above a fashionably deep satin waistbelt. A breathtaking dress, although even more impressive was the jewellery which abounded on all three women.

"Are you able to put a name to each of them?" Teun's question sounded casual, but she noted both he and Zaan regarded their copy just as keenly as she did.

In answer, Jensen turned around the original photograph for them to view as he read the intricately written inscription. "*Left to right: Martine, Uriel and Tanja on the occasion of Tanja's seventeenth birthday. Their first opportunity to wear the family treasures.*"

"So, the beauty on the right, the birthday girl, is my great-grandmother. Like a little princess, wearing a fortune in jewellery." Zaan's laughter filled the room as he drew Keira's attention away from Martine, the one wearing the cream gown.

Tanja's peach gown was equally striking, though a simpler design. An intricate lace bodice with simple cap sleeves led down to a softly draping narrow skirt of chiffon-covered silk, heavily embroidered near the hem. Focusing her attention on the jewellery, Keira noted the two-strand pearl necklace around the woman's throat settling just above collarbone level. Below it dangled a long, heavily wrought golden chain, so long it hung to just above the waistbelt of the dress. No ordinary chain, it had a painting in a tiny frame draped at the lowest part of the curve, a golden fringe hanging beneath the image.

There was a rustling sound as Jensen opened a box before he presented each of them with a small magnifier. "Take the closest possible look, please."

When magnified, the detail on the jewellery jumped into better focus. Tanja's pendant portrayed a young woman in a Victorian sitting room, the enamelled oval surrounded by an ornate repoussé golden frame.

Zaan sounded quite taken by his great-grandmother as he reamed off her other jewels. "Tanja's not wearing the ring you've just acquired, Jensen, but I can say it definitely is a huge emerald sitting in the scalloped gold setting she is wearing."

A slight throat clearing drew her gaze to Zaan himself, away from the emerald in her copy. Zaan's eyes twinkled, though his expression still assessed, as he absorbed Tanja.

Jensen answered. "Yes, Zaan. I believe the ring you've just described to be in your possession at present. Handed down to your father, I'm sure it's part of the Tiru collection. You may have other items you don't know about, yet, but I'm guessing you're already assiduously trying to have your emerald ring authenticated?"

Zaan's smile sat wide across his cheeks, the twinkle in his eyes a full blown sparkle. "You're absolutely correct, Cousin

Jensen. Your spies must be everywhere."

Zaan's next information was for her and Teun, to bring them up to date with developments.

"Since Jensen made contact with me last week, I've been reassessing the jewellery which belonged to my mother. I always knew about the emerald ring my father gave her as a betrothal ring, although I had no idea it might be from the Tiru Salana collection. I know to a cent the emerald ring's current value." Zaan's pale eyes flashed again. "I'm in the antique business after all. It's presently worth at least seven thousand euros on the open market, but if I can authenticate it as part of the Tiru collection, it'll be worth much more than that amount."

Zaan's anticipation exuded almost palpably in the way he gripped his photograph, his voice increasing in volume and depth. "Now Jensen has revealed the quest, I'd like to draw your attention to the band around Tanja's hair. You'll see a drop pendant pinned there. I believe I've seen the pin before, but it wasn't in my mother's jewellery box after she died. I've a feeling I must have seen it as a child."

Keira used the magnifier to see the intricate detail of the pendant which, according to Zaan, was of the type that could have been hung from a thin chain, or attached as a brooch pin. In Tanja's case, she used it as a hair ornament. The bow motif pin, with a suspended drop, encased three green stones encrusted with what Zaan explained were likely to have been pearls and small diamonds – though he whispered it could only be established if he held the object in his hand, and used a jeweller's loupe. Four bows at the top were each centred by a sizable clear stone, the tails of the centre bow sporting a green stone on each arrow-headed end, another green stone dropping down between. The suspended drop from a small thin chain, redolent of a small cross, held another green stone at the middle. Again Zaan explained the edges of the drop were likely to be encrusted with the tiniest of diamonds.

"Not just a simple little hairpin then?" Teun chuckled into the intense silence as they all feasted on the plethora of jewels bedecking Tanja. "So, potentially, Tanja might be wearing at least two pieces of this collection?"

Jensen's answer came quickly. "I am guessing the ring and the hairpin. The chain with the repoussé framed painting, on the other hand, is of a very European design of the late 1800s and not likely to be from the Tiru collection. The pearl necklace and bracelet she's wearing look like matching items, but aren't likely to be from the Tiru collection either."

The middle sister drew Keira's attention. Uriel wore a pale green confection of embroidered chiffon, the train not as long as Martine's gown, the huge cabbage roses of the embroidery demanding instant attention. Like her sisters, Uriel's tiny waist was highlighted by a wide satin waistbelt, hers having a very large bow set to one side.

"That's a chunky gold choker around her neck," Teun joked as he pointed to it on his photograph.

No simple bauble surrounded her slender neck: a wide, filigree gold collar, studded with sparkling clear stones, centred there with a vertical band of three green stones at the front.

"If the stones are emeralds, it could easily be part of the collection." Jensen stared at the object in question as he spoke.

"It looks like her ring is a part of the set." Zaan's head nodding settled his comment.

Keira took in the detail using her magnifier. A single, heart-shaped, green gem was topped with three good sized, clear stones making a little triangular tiara above the heart. "It's a really sweet ring, but I love her earrings even more."

She chuckled at the expressions of the men beside her after her declaration. Zaan peered at his photograph through his lens; Jensen held his photograph well back from his body for a good look. Teun, on the other hand, Keira found, wasn't looking at the photo at all. He was surveying her, again with the intensity and inscrutability of the afternoon. Only when she felt heat rise to her cheeks did he chuckle and look down at his own photo.

"So, Keira, who I'm glad to find out is my by-proxy relative, what is it we should admire about the earrings?"

Teun excelled at prodding questions. Instead of answering, she studied the detail of the earrings. Three oval green stones sat in the centre of a scrollwork bow –the design surely Indian – a large teardrop gem dangling beneath the tails of the bow. Tiny clear stones sat embedded into the scrollwork. Again, not a simple little pair of ear bobs.

Zaan took up the slack in the conversation, detailing potential Tiru Salana jewels. "Uriel's gold collar, heart-shaped ring and earrings are likely contenders, Jensen?"

"I believe so, but her wristband may also be part of the collection, too."

Keira found it difficult to decide on that one as the chiffon of Uriel's dress obscured her arm. However, a solid gold bracelet, she surmised roughly an inch wide, could be seen.

"Though not clear, I'm guessing there's a very large emerald at the centre of the band." Jensen drew their close attention with their magnifiers.

Viewed carefully, a definite bump lodged at the middle though it was impossible to tell exactly what it was.

"In all, Uriel might be wearing four parts of the set?"

Jensen answered Teun's question with a nod. "Romy Lischke recently sold emerald earrings. We believe them to be the ones in this photograph, but at the time of the sale Romy hadn't seen this photograph and knew nothing of Geertje's legacy. She only knew they had been passed down from her great-grandmother."

"What about the other baubles Uriel is wearing here?" Teun waved his copy.

"Romy says she's never seen any of the other jewels in the photograph."

"When did you discuss this with her?" Zaan still studied his copy, the question probing.

A small smile accompanied Jensen's reply, which Keira again interpreted as an appreciation of astute inquiries.

Only after Zaan raised his head did Jensen answer. "I met Romy for the first and only time last week, just after she had her hip operation. Although she knew Uriel's family had been rich, the only item of jewellery passed down to her mother were the earrings she, herself, had sold to pay for her recent surgery."

"So, a potential part of the collection has just gone into the hands of some unwitting stranger?" Teun's head shook as though to say they had a doomed quest before they'd even started.

"Not a lost cause, Teun. I have the name of the buyer, and I can make an offer for them. An amount which won't be refused."

Jensen looked so deadly serious that Keira shivered, although the room was warm. Tension rose again, unsaid words heralding some kind of mistrust.

Jensen cleared his throat. "We'll move on to Martine."

Focusing on Martine, Keira used the magnifier to inspect the necklace around the young woman's throat. Again, it was spectacular.

Four strands of green beads wound round the back of Martine's neck, the main fastening of the item sitting centrally below her throat. Very Indian in design, a huge white stone was encircled by a row of smaller ones. Because of the type of photograph, Keira could only imagine they were diamonds, but supposed they could have been some other light-coloured stone. Below the central circle lay another two partial circular rows, and below that a teardrop was suspended. The centre of the teardrop was another larger stone, encased by the outer row of smaller ones. The necklace was magnificent.

Dangling from Martine's ears were teardrop earrings matching the necklace.

"I don't believe there's any doubt the necklace is part of the set, and also the earrings. This style of design is commonly known as Mughal, and very Indian in origin."

"But of diamonds, rather than emeralds?" It was Zaan's conclusion, but something Keira also wanted clarified.

Jensen nodded. "It would appear so."

On one wrist, Martine wore the most fabulous gold cameo bangle. Enamelled onto a wide band of smooth gold, the cameo looked like carved ivory, the scrollwork around it delicate gold filigree, standing proud from the main band of gold which widened in the centre and narrowed at the underside of the arm.

"The bracelet?" Teun's question came across hesitant, though he sounded hopeful. Martine, after all, was from his direct line of the family.

The shaking of Zaan's head was very negative. "The design of it looks to be late 19th century. What do you think, Jensen?"

"It could be, but until looked at closely we could never be positive. It's possible the decorative filigree, liked so well during the late Victorian period, may have been added around the cameo after the original band was created."

Teun's lips pursed quickly as Keira looked at him to gain his reaction to the information. He now appeared just as interested in the jewels as the rest of them.

"How could you tell something like that?" Her question sounded lame, but she needed to know. Knowledge of jewellery wasn't her forte.

Zaan jumped in. "The added gold may be of a different karat value, though it would be unlikely. Compatibility would be more usual for a band of this calibre."

Eyes drifting back to the photograph, Keira took in more detail. Martine also wore a very long chain which drooped over her generous chest, hanging all the way to the bottom of her wide waistbelt. Her fingers curled around a delicate fan and it was easy to discern the ring Jensen had recently acquired: the snake-headed, filigree emerald. Keira couldn't prevent her admiring gasp, since the ring looked even more magnificent on the woman's finger.

"From this photograph we can, perhaps, assume Martine was the owner of the ring now in your possession, Jensen. Do you have any idea how many owners there have been since her?" Awe peppered her hushed inquiry.

Jensen shook his head. "No idea yet, Keira, but I'm working on that one."

Her fingers snaked up to lift her own heavy chain. "Is there any way we could tell if a piece of gold jewellery was part of the set? By working out it came from the same source? Same gold mine? Or something?"

Teun's laugh gusted across her neck as he bent to stare at her chain… or maybe it was her skin? She wasn't sure exactly what he looked at as he replied, but she did know his light gusts of breath kick-started her insides again. The darned man only had to lean towards her. During the afternoon it had been a very nice prospect… but now she wasn't so convinced it was a good thing. An association with the dark, misty-eyed Teun might not be a brilliant idea if she had a semi-professional arrangement with him. She huffed as she shifted back in her seat, pulling herself away from his proximity.

"What I know about gold is the higher the number of karats, the more it's likely to blast a hole in my bank balance."

"That's true, Teun." Jensen's smile beamed. "But the answer to your question, Keira, isn't so straightforward. Testing that something is gold is easy, but testing the source isn't a simple business. Though it may be helpful that a member of our little family is an industrial chemist. Is that not so, Teun?"

The flare of acknowledgement in Teun's eyes was impossible to miss as he answered.

"I am that, Jensen, but I'm nobody's jewellery assessor."

Jensen's next words dampened any burgeoning enthusiasm. "Our best way of finding the whole collection won't be to find

46

a few pieces of jewellery. What I need your help with is finding references to authenticate the pieces which belonged to Geertje – and, before that, to Tiru Salana himself. I've researchers looking at the original Indian sources of the collection to determine what they may have looked like when they arrived in Amsterdam. What we, as a family, need to discover are paper trails which still exist within our homes, and which could lead us to find more items."

Teun quickly responded as he slipped his copy onto the table. "You mean like diaries or letters?"

"Could be." Jensen's fingers steepled, the tips tapping his lips. "Or perhaps annotated photographs like this one."

"You've not told us how you acquired that original photograph? How do we know those women are who you say they are?" Teun's tone challenged as he tapped the magnifier against his palm.

Jensen smiled indulgently. "I already told you, I am descended from Wolf Tiedman, the eldest son of Geertje. As the oldest son, it fell to Wolf to deal with the paperwork relating to Geertje and Albrecht after their deaths. Some of the paperwork was passed down to Wolf's daughter, Elaina. Elaina – my grandmother – married a German, like Uriel had also done, and came here to Heidelberg to live. And, as such things happen, my grandmother's effects passed down to my father. Last month when I bought the emerald ring, the sale hit the headlines. My mother called me and told me she suspected it was the ring in one of the old photographs which had belonged to Elaina. This photograph."

"Do we take it your grandmother, Elaina, got a photograph, but none of Geertje's jewels? Was she a bad girl then?" Zaan was back to being droll.

Jensen's laugh was echoed by the others. "The box of photos, which was passed down to my father, included other photos of Geertje and her family. Teun and Zaan, you were given some of those photos today in your package from my lawyer, though none of them relate to the jewellery collection. My father is adamant his mother, Elaina, never got any jewellery from Geertje. Though an old letter he inherited has references to Geertje giving her collection only to her daughters, and not to her sons."

Again Teun interrupted, his attention wholly on Jensen, one eyebrow quirking up. "Did you uncover any other little snippets of information that would help in this investigation?"

"No. The genealogy expert looking at our family history helped me make contact with all of you, but so far I've found nothing else linked with the Tiru collection." Jensen looked disappointed, yet pragmatic about his answer.

"Bills of sale." Zaan drew their attention with his odd interjection. He seemed on a roll. "If an item was sold, it may have been noted somewhere in family memorabilia, or perhaps there's a receipt still around. Some jeweller may even have evidence of a sale."

Teun's abrupt rise from his chair startled Keira as he loped around the small room. "Needle in a haystack. We could be ferreting around forever to get information for twenty items." His just as abrupt stop at Jensen's side was equalled by the snap of his tone. "What the hell makes you think I'll do anything to help you in this quest, my long lost German cousin?"

Chapter Four

"Family loyalty. The kudos which comes from a job well done. Enjoyment of following a paper trail. Take your pick, Teun, of any, or even all of those."

Jensen's smile encompassed them all, but Teun felt it lacked something. There was an anticipatory element, but behind it he detected a quiet scheming. It could just be a form of yearning, or maybe something else more mercenary.

"I would like to mount the collection together as an exhibition for public view... when the items are all found. Naturally, your names will be there alongside mine, since you will be the family members who have helped in the search."

Zaan added weight to Jensen's words. "You have to admit it, Teun; sheer curiosity has drawn us all here this evening. Keira knew nothing about the family aspects of Jensen's invitation, but you did."

"Was your business trip to your London laboratory really necessary yesterday, Teun?" Jensen picked up Zaan's thread. "Or could it have been an excuse to be over in Europe, and close enough to come to this meeting today?"

It would be easy to tell lies. He could easily say he'd only visited his London lab for genuine business reasons, but who would he be kidding? Not himself. Nosiness had led him to change plans when he'd received Jensen's letter; sheer curiosity luring him to Heidelberg. What he wasn't sure of now was why he should get involved in spending the time it might take to ferret out the information Jensen hoped to gain. His business self niggled at him to ditch the quest and leave it all to Jensen... but his gut told him something different.

If he walked away now, he would have no grounds to maintain contact with any of the protagonists in this family quest. No reason to get in touch with the intriguing Keira, who had created an unprecedented effect on him earlier that afternoon, and was still a heavy draw. There was something indefinable about her.

He dropped words into the expectant silence, though centred his gaze on Jensen, the orchestrator of the meeting. "Your plan is to have us find enough family info which will lead to acquiring the rest of the collection? And once you've got all the pieces, you're going to set up this exhibition here in Heidelberg?"

Jensen's laugh approved. "Smart questions."

His German cousin's sarcasm was duly noted, although he kept any further reaction under wraps after the first burst of merriment had passed.

"I think Zaan will agree with me, if we assemble such a magnificent collection, it will be far too important to only be on show in Heidelberg." Jensen's stare invited him to be of the same mind.

"Are you imagining a world tour or something?" Keira's voice dripped with doubting curiosity as she slid forward in her chair, a repressed excitement lighting up her gorgeous eyes.

"Exactly that." Jensen's reply was definite. "There would be a great deal of interest in such a fine spectacle."

Teun's next question probed, as he meant it to. "And after this grand tour? What happens to the collection?"

Almost prayer-like Jensen steepled his fingers, his elbows forming a firm triangle on the desk, his expression enigmatic with a hint of humour lacing his words. "That would depend on who owns the items, of course."

Again there was smoothness to his cousin's answer which Teun felt concealed many jagged edges. His analytical brain wouldn't rest, there was still too much unanswered for him to be in any way satisfied with Jensen's request.

Zaan interrupted. "Are you saying you wouldn't want to purchase all the items we uncover, Jensen?"

"I'm not saying that at all. I would be proud and happy to own the whole collection, but it may be impossible even for me to do that. I have good funding, Zaan, but it's not limitless… and I'm pragmatic enough to know buying all the items might be beyond my means."

"Then, do you mean if we find something, we get to keep it?"

Keira's question echoed in the small room, as though it would be a miracle to find anything at all. Teun was partial to the sound of it though her question met with blank stares from his two European cousins, so much so it made him chuckle. He couldn't resist teasing her. "I don't think the pieces are just going to fall at our feet, Keira."

Jensen sounded patient, maybe too patient. "The first step for all of us will be to agree on a purchasing, and ownership, policy on items which are uncovered."

"You mean they'll all belong to you?" Teun's glib answer was rewarded by a shake of Jensen's head and a small smile he felt was too plastic to be genuine.

Jensen's tolerant voice explained further, "If any of us discover something we can authenticate as being part of the collection, then we need to establish what will be needed for it to be part of an exhibition. For example, the ring I've just bought is owned by me. I can make it available on loan to the exhibition, but it will still be owned by me at the end of any display time."

Teun made no comment since what Jensen had just explained sounded patently obvious.

"If any one of us uncovers a part of the Tiru collection which isn't directly owned by them – for example, if the item hypothetically belongs to your mother, Teun, then your mother can still retain ownership and lend it to the exhibition in the same way as I would do with my ring. But if it's of high value, she may choose to sell it."

Zaan was quick to speak. "We'd want to avoid that if an exhibition were to be mounted."

"Exactly." Jensen's expression was serious. "We need to agree on a policy of buying under such circumstances: to form a consortium."

"A consortium?" Keira sounded bemused, her fingers straying up to fiddle with the chain around her neck. Teun found her fingers mesmerising, wondering what the soft skin below would feel like under his own fingertips.

Unsure how a consortium, such as Jensen had just proposed, would work, he wasn't surprised at Keira's confusion. A deliberate throat clearing by his German cousin pulled back his attention, as Jensen clarified the parameters as he saw them.

"We could agree now that the whole collection is owned by all of the cousins, including Keira and her sister as nominal cousins. As such, each member would get appropriate rewards if the whole collection is eventually sold, since by then some of us may not wish to keep an item."

Keira fidgeted in her seat, clearly on edge. He wanted to curl her restless hands in his own, to soothe her discomfort, maybe even have her on his lap, and nuzzle away her doubts.

"I'm not real family, Jensen. So I don't see how you can include me in your plan, even if I did find something that belonged to Tiru Salana's jewels."

Zaan's gaze slipped admiringly towards Keira, his words not so surprising. "What if you uncover the most valuable piece of the collection, Keira? Would the lure of millions of euros not entice you to want to lay claim to it?"

Keira scoffed at Zaan's supposition, her laugh an embarrassed one as she repeated, "I'm not going to find anything valuable, Zaan, and I'm not a true relative to claim a share of it."

"Please let me continue, Keira, before you re [...]
quickly." Jensen's businesslike demeanour inten[...]
sought everyone's attention. "My reasoning for [...]
together tonight is to establish a family corporation, a way of
agreeing our joint ownership. Tonight was chosen with care as
it was also to give you an idea of how I already have the
expertise to mount such an exhibition – although you have
perhaps not had time to view tonight's gallery selections."

Teun noted the shift from Zaan's earlier relaxed attitude, as
his Dutch cousin's fingertips drummed the armrest of his
chair, his question blunt. "Amassing this collection will be a
very expensive venture, Jensen. Are you suggesting we put
money in to form this company, and reap future rewards
according to our investments?"

"That is one possibility, Zaan."

Jensen sounded amenable, but Teun wasn't convinced. He
observed the others around him. Keira's posture stiffened, her
awkwardness still evident, her words as clipped as her tight
lips.

"My meagre wealth is invested in my own company, Jensen,
so I've nothing to give this venture. Please count me out of
this enterprise right now."

It was easy to admire her poise as she stood to leave. Teun
felt like pulling her down onto his lap rather than have her
disappear; the prospect of her doing another vanishing act
decidedly unappealing.

"Keira? Please sit down again."

Jensen's tone implored, though Teun didn't actually think
his German cousin looked at all ruffled by her intended
departure. He wondered why she'd been invited if Jensen
wasn't too bothered about her being involved. Then again,
maybe it was all part of Jensen's ploy. He wanted to reassure
Keira to stay put for a bit longer, but didn't turn towards her;
he didn't want to miss a single one of Jensen's expressions or

.c nuances. What Jensen was really up to remained an unanswered question.

"My sources have already gleaned information about everyone's financial status. Your limited disposable income isn't the issue here, Keira. It's more about the need to decide on how to divide the assets at a later date."

Zaan's voice reverted to being witty. "How about you put in what you find, and you get that back at the end of the exhibitions?"

The interplay between the other three was fascinating. Keira still looked ready to walk out. Zaan found a lot of amusement in the situation... or appeared to. Jensen's focus disquieted; his gaze penetrating as he again answered his Dutch cousin.

"Again possibly, Zaan, but some of what you uncover may not be in your own home. It may have to be purchased, and someone would have to do that. If I were to buy all those items not found in your immediate family's ownership, I would expect to own them at the end of our partnership. What I'm suggesting is that loan agreements could be made to amass a suitable fund to buy anything we need to acquire. If we find a reasonable amount of Tiru Salana's jewels, then our fund can also cover the cost of mounting an exhibition. I'm suggesting we share any additional costs, and ultimately share the rewards."

Teun's concentration drifted to Keira, who still looked uncomfortable with the financial deal proposed, her response not unexpected given the heat he could see at her cheeks. She had the kind of fair skin that delicately peached, rather than reddened all over.

"Jensen, count me out. It's kind of you to try and include me, but there's no way my bank would advance me a loan of any kind at the moment, and not for such an odd venture as this. And I'll speak for my sister as well. On her teaching salary, she's even poorer than I am."

He imagined the look Jensen threw her way intended to be

reassuring, but what he detected was a very well veiled irritation. Sitting beside Keira and doing nothing no longer remained an option. Rising to his feet, he paced behind the three chairs and then, reversing, he halted behind Keira. Purposely placing his hands on the top rim of her chair, the deep breath he inhaled was infused with the scent of something flowery, the strands of her long hair a fraction away from his skin.

"If you've already had our backgrounds investigated, Jensen, you'll know I do have some disposable income at my fingertips, but that's not the issue here. What makes you so sure I'll put money into your pot on the whim of finding pieces of this collection?"

His German cousin encompassed them all: his tone staying level, his regard unvarying, looking far too comfortable with the whole business. Teun wasn't sure why, but wanted to know even more.

Jensen's focus rested on Keira. "My suggestion is we open an account in the name of the group. I've already established the principle for this at my bank. I have their agreement we would be able to draw funding from them for items we would need to purchase."

Teun wanted those terms clarified before he'd consider further. "Is your bank willing to set up these loans on the basis of each of us having some collateral? Or guaranteed on the basis of individual ownership of an expensive item from the collection?"

Jensen's laugh rang out in the small office as Teun felt the full attention swivel to him. "It's good to know I have astute cousins. You're correct, Teun. My bank will accept my newly purchased ring as an initial guarantee."

Keira's words weren't too surprising. "If your bank is willing to do this, Jensen, why do you need us to form a partnership and sign into this bank agreement?"

"In one way or another, we are all the progeny of Geertje,

and if this collection is mounted, I believe we should all share in the glory of it."

Keira fiddled with her heavy gold chain. Though embarrassment still flooded her cheeks, she looked unwilling to be steamrolled into anything she didn't like the sound of. And that was very good to know: he liked a woman with some backbone. His mind strayed, the rhythmic stroke of her thumb unconsciously stirring. She was a beautiful woman, but something more than her outward appearance called to him, more than her husky voice, and more than her sexy topaz eyes. It was a long time since any woman had such an instant appeal.

Her focus direct, she took up the grilling tone he'd been employing almost the whole time so far. "How long do you imagine it will take us to do this searching? I can't spend much time away from my work, and I'd still be unable to put any money into the venture."

Zaan endorsed her statement. "Much the same conditions apply to me, too, Keira. My financial input is likely to be limited to the market value of my mother's emerald ring."

Keira's breathing evened out; he detected a slight relief that she wasn't the only one without an available fund.

"It could be months, maybe longer, Keira, before we uncover anything. A first step for all of us would be to go home and search our family belongings. Since it's unlikely anyone has looked at family memorabilia, with such a focused intent, we may be surprised at what's uncovered. I've already looked in my parents' home, but I'll be looking again."

Zaan voiced a question that sat on Teun's tongue. "Are you expecting revenue from a successful exhibition to ultimately pay for items that need to be purchased, and to yield some profit?"

Jensen's nod affirmed. "Yes, Zaan, a successful showing will generate healthy income, which will, in turn, recoup the cost of mounting the exhibition. Any profit can then be shared amongst us."

"What about our absent cousins?"

Still sceptical about the whole affair, Teun was intrigued despite his reservations. Any money he would gain wasn't the object: his purpose now was to find out why Jensen had even gathered them together, and bothered to tell them. If they'd been none the wiser Jensen would have recouped all profits.

"I'll investigate anything Marijke Baert has in New Zealand, and continue to make enquiries on Romy's behalf. I'm hoping Keira will have better luck with Ineke and Anna, since Ineke is reluctant to speak further with me… and, as I explained, Anna has yet to be located. They will all be included in the group venture, should they choose to join us."

***

Keira sat in her hotel bar, quite bamboozled, as she pondered over the events of the evening. She'd eventually agreed to be part of the family consortium. Having signed Jensen's bank agreement, she wondered if she'd just made the biggest financial mistake of her life. Yet she wasn't expected to actually hand over any of her own money. Not now, and maybe not ever. She understood what she'd agreed to, but the weirdness of it lingered. Together the cousins had made it seem such a win-win situation for all of them.

Zaan's agitation broke into her musings. "You're going to have to excuse me, Keira. I'm cancelling dinner."

Teun headed towards her, carrying their pre-dinner drinks. The moment Teun handed it to him, Zaan swigged back his genever. She knew the Dutch often drank their country's gin in one go, but had never seen anyone manage it while still speaking.

"I had planned to stay here at the hotel tonight, but I admit I can't wait to get back to Dan Haag and find that hairpin of Tanja's. Since leaving Jensen's gallery, I'm even more convinced it was in my mother's jewellery box not so long ago." Zaan made a hasty farewell with a firm handshake for Teun and typical European air kisses for her, declaring he'd be able to catch a train back to Holland within the next hour.

As she was escorted into the restaurant alongside Teun, the tingles of the afternoon invaded again. A heady anticipation persisted, regardless of any pseudo-business connection. The attractive man of the afternoon had most definitely resurfaced by the time they were presented with their main courses.

Around a mouthful of pork, Teun joked, "If I'd realised the meeting in Heidelberg meant rummaging around for jewels, I'd never have popped over from London."

"And now?" How serious was he, she wondered, since the last part of his negotiation with Jensen had been conducted with such dry humour?

"I'm thinking the effort might be worth it, Keira Drummond." His deep laugh disturbed; his smile conspiratorial. "There's a lot more for us to learn about than jewels, don't you think?"

She couldn't fail to read the sexual consideration in the grey gleam. Her answer intended to tease. "In your dreams, Californian! I think you should keep your mind on the real family jewels and nothing else, Teun Zeger. Let's discuss my plan of action and see if it differs from yours."

"Something about your response makes me think you're saying one thing... yet thinking another. Those beautiful eyes of yours aren't averse to knowing a bit more of me, are they, my acquired cousin?"

Keira didn't want to be a relative of his at all. That would be far too complicated, but friends? Oh, she wanted that. Probably a lot more. "Okay then. I'm your new friend. Tell me about yourself, and maybe I'll tell you a bit about me."

A couple of hours passed easily before they realised they kept the restaurant staff hovering – supposedly solicitously – but she knew how keen the servers would be to close up. Teun requested the staff to deliver a nightcap to the lounge area.

"So, you don't think there's anything your parents have which might have something to do with our quest?"

"I'm sure my mother never had any expensive jewels lying around. But, hey, Keira, I'm just a guy. I wouldn't know paste from an authentic gemstone."

"But your lab could check on something you suspected might be a possibility?"

"Sure, it could, but it would probably be quicker to get the opinion of a reputable jeweller who would be able to put a value on it, something my lab couldn't do."

They'd been discussing a way forward for their enquiries, finding it might be a needle in a haystack, as he'd indicated earlier. His parents had been divorced since he was eight years old, and he rarely visited his father. Although he'd been born in Rochester, Minnesota, after the split his mother had taken him to California, where she'd remarried. "My rearing mostly took place in Sonoma. It was only after I graduated that I moved south to San Francisco."

"Is your mother still alive?"

"Yep. Still lives in Sonoma. I make visits fairly regularly; work them in around my business travel. What about you? Do you travel a lot as a translator?"

"No. Only European travel, if it's necessary, but most contact is now by email."

"What about your father?"

"My dad still lives in Edinburgh." She'd already explained that her family had been devastated the previous year when her mother had died from complications caused by an aneurysm; it had been so unexpected.

"Will you be able to check at your father's house, to see if there are any references to the emerald collection?"

Her laugh was spontaneous since Teun's phrasing sounded so delicate, working hard not to offend. "Sure. My dad will be clueless about Mum's belongings, but there'll be no problem about me browsing around the house. A month or so after Mum died, my sister and I cleared out her clothes, but mostly everything else in the house is as it was when she was alive. Dad hasn't mentioned being ready to have a sweep-clean yet, and we've not pushed him. He's still coming to terms with her loss, but he isn't maudlin."

Sympathy oozed from Teun. "My father's still alive, but lives in a care home in Duluth, at the edge of Lake Superior. He married three times."

She tried to appear impassive, but failed as her eyelids flickered. An ironic chuckle whiffed her way.

"And divorced three times, as well. Alone for the last decade, he now needs constant care. His dementia and heart problems are too serious for him to live by himself. Some days he's okay and will be almost lucid, but if I get him on a bad one there's no way I'd be able to be sure of accurate information."

"He never found anyone to be happy with?" It was nosey, even tactless, to ask, but she did.

His smile was tight. "The marriage to my mother lasted fourteen years, the second less than two years, and the third around six years. I met his second wife a total of ten times, and that was too many experiences of her."

Not sure where the relevance lay, she asked anyway. "The third?"

"Grace is a lovely woman. A much better choice than Paula – his second wife – who was a complete bitch. Grace, at least, tried to get to know me for my dad's sake."

She found the vibes of regret washing over him easy to pick up; she already felt attuned to his moods. "Just not right for your dad?"

His focus slid to the opposite side of the room. "My dad made a mistake, Keira. He didn't forgive my mom, but I'm sure he's never loved anyone like he loved her."

There was a lot unsaid as his eyes drifted back. The breath stifled in her throat, the heat from his attention scorching. She tried hard to back off from the attraction between them, knew she failed, yet contrarily wasn't ready for anything momentous to develop between them.

"I still see Grace from time to time when I visit Dad. Grace's florist shop is the reason he moved his insurance business from Rochester to Duluth. She visits him regularly and gives me updates, but she divorced him knowing he couldn't give her what she wanted."

"His unconditional love?"

Teun's rueful nod signalled she'd got it in one. "Life got too much of a trial for Grace, so she moved out."

"Was he unwell then?"

"No. Dad's just turned seventy-one. He appeared fine until about eighteen months ago, seemed to be getting along with his life, but it turned out he wasn't. Neither Grace, nor I, realised he was well through the early stages of dementia and had managed to cover it up."

Her grandmother had had dementia. Sympathising with his plight, her gentle pat of understanding on his arm felt so natural… even pleasantly exciting. His grey irises deepened, his body shifting closer to her, so close the earlier herb scent of his shampoo now mingled with his more earthy natural cologne. Savouring it, she hoped her tiny sniff didn't come across too obvious while she consoled. "It's difficult to notice these things since they come on so gradually."

Teun's warm fingers clasped hers before he brought their joined hands into his lap to rest comfortably together, his gaze almost daring her to deny them the connection. "My visits being infrequent, I'd noticed a change in him, but I put it down to normal ageing processes. When a mutual friend informed Grace that Dad wandered around a lot, not knowing where he was, we realised how tardy we'd been in getting him checked out. He had home care for a while, but last December a series of strokes meant he needed full time care."

The tension in his fingers made her aware of his guilt, her

squeeze of reassurance met by a gentle shoulder nudge of acknowledgement. Comfortable. Intimate.

"Because of us not knowing of his earlier problems, he's already leapt into the third phase of dementia. Grace and I cleared out his apartment just before Christmas. Both Dad and I spent Christmas Day at her place, and then…" Teun needed to say little more; regret so evident that his father's life had come to where it presently was. Her fingers caressed his palm. "I feel so bloody guilty. I wish now I had done more, kept in touch better over the last fifteen years."

"I'm sure your father appreciated whatever you did." She attempted to reassure in the best way possible, since she couldn't take upon herself any more of his burden of guilt.

She didn't want the night to end, but it looked like they'd arrived at that point. When he asked about her plans for the following day, it was unanticipated.

"My ticket home isn't booked till the day after tomorrow, as I decided to stay another day in Heidelberg, regardless of what the meeting with Jensen was about. I plan to visit some of my old haunts."

"Any chance you'd care to take pity on a poor tourist who's new to Europe?"

It was not difficult at all to decide what to do the following day. As she stood at the door of her room, reluctance went hand-in-hand with her goodnight, yet a strange acceptance flushed since Teun hadn't followed up on the heated glances that had come her way during the last hours. Her contrary feelings annoyed her, convinced he was just as taken with her as she was with him. Yet he, too, held back, for probably the same reasons as she did. They had a pseudo-business relationship, a sort of family connection, and at present it had to set the tone of any liaison between them.

A small peck on the cheek was what she expected when he leaned in to say goodnight. What she got was a settling of his lips on hers, a light kiss which developed in strength when neither pulled out of it. His grip tightened across her shoulders, Teun leaning into the kiss even more, his lips and tongue seeking entrance. Keira had no problem with it, because as soon as his lips descended, the resolution to maintain some distance had already evaporated into thin mist. Her arms snaked around his waist while she lost herself in him, happy to do a bit of exploring herself. Eventually Teun pulled away, his deep sigh one of frustration and firm resolve. Those soft gun-metal eyes of his were intent, telling her a different story from the hands which released her when he stepped a pace back.

"I'm damned sure you know what I'd like to do, Keira of the beautiful topaz eyes, but I've just enough strength to walk along to my room. I'll see you in the breakfast room at eight tomorrow."

After one last searching look, he strode along three doors, popped his key card in the slot and vanished. A swift wave of her trembling fingers was all she could manage as she slid into her own room.

More than a half hour later, Keira still lay awake. Excitement, desire, expectation, heat, promise... there had been such a mixture of feelings created by their shared kisses that she felt she would probably never be able to describe all of them accurately. A giddy smile lingered.

Topaz eyes?

***

Teun had a glass of juice at his elbow while he scanned a newspaper. On her approach he looked up, twinkling a warm appreciation her way.

"You look amazing."

His words warmed her as no real fire ever could. "Ditto. I'm guessing you slept well?"

"Fits and starts." A cheeky smile was all she got on that score

63

as he launched into their plans for the day.

Intensely focused, he encouraged her not to linger over breakfast, desperate to get started on touristy stuff. Laughing along with his almost little-boy eagerness, her chide was soft. "All good things come to he who waits, Teun Zeger. Has nobody ever told you that?"

"Yep! But I've got no patience for too much waiting, Keira Drummond. Never had and probably never will."

The weather played fair; the sun shining in a blue sky only occasionally scudded with wispy white cirrus. She took him at his word that he wanted to see as much as possible in one day and trekked him from their hotel through the cobbled streets to the Kornmarkt, the place of the traditional market. At the Bergbahn – the small funicular railway – they rode the little car to the first stop, up to the castle, Schloss Heidelberg. The breathtakingly huge castle, nestled in the hillside above the city, was a fantastic spot to view the surrounding valley and the city below.

They spent a good chunk of the morning exploring the cobbled-together buildings, each one different from the other, complimentary but from separate historical periods. Tickets were purchased to see inside the remaining rooms of the magnificent building, a fraction of the whole since the majority of the castle had been destroyed by fire in the 1760s.

Though she vaguely remembered a bit of the history, Keira purchased a guidebook to remind her of the exact details as they wandered around. When she scanned through it, her cry of delight brought Teun back to her as he'd wandered away to a nearby parapet to view the panorama below.

"Something you'd forgotten?"

"Oh, yes! I'm pretty sure you'd like to visit the Apothecary Museum, wouldn't you?"

She guessed correctly and they spent time perusing the dispensaries and laboratory of the seventeenth and eighteenth centuries. The pharmacist's office held incredible pharmacopoeias, and had a wide collection of drugs that would have been dispensed. Employing her translating skills, Teun got a glimpse of what the compendium of drug standards had been at the time. Focusing on a particularly difficult explanation to interpret for Teun, it was quite unexpected when someone jostled Keira's shoulder. The pharmacist's office was busy though not packed. By the time she turned to view the person, he was scuttling out the cramped doorway. Sufficiently tall, he needed to bend his head to avoid the low lintel, the ball cap he was wearing set askew in his haste. Not an apology of any kind had passed his lips but Keira wasn't bothered by the interruption; she set to translating again.

After they zoomed through the headily-scented orangery, the water display grotto and the terraces of the gardens, they were ready to descend the mountain again to find somewhere for lunch. Four hours into their tourist pursuits, Keira's feet knew they'd done plenty of hoofing it around Heidelberg.

"If it's still there, I know of just the place to both feed your hunger and quench your thirst." Keira's declaration came as they settled back on the hard bench of the Bergbahn, just in time before the car moved off with a little shudder. "It's not a bistro I worked in myself, but it was a great place to eat on a budget. It had the best local food, frothy beer and super fast service."

"A student haunt?" Teun questioned her casually, taking her hand in his own. The first personal contact he'd initiated that morning, his body was plastered right up next to hers, though the compartment only held the pair of them.

"You could say that, but it's also touristy." She couldn't prevent a huge smile from leaking out; his touch setting her nerve ends sparking again, his big solid frame cosy to snuggle against. "And the best thing is it's not far from the Bergbahn halt. You won't have to walk very far for the beer I'm sure you're looking forward to."

Teun rested his head on the back of the seat and sighed, his sideways gaze intensifying with what she decided was admiration of her plan. An inner heat developed, his thumb drawing arousing circles on her palm. "You were an incredible tour guide this morning, so I know I'm going to enjoy wherever you take me now." His intent stare lingered. She knew her cheeks pinkened, but couldn't help her reactions to him. Her mumble of thanks was rewarded with a wink, before his head slumped back and his eyes closed. She wasn't convinced tiredness gripped him, but appreciated that it gave her time to compose herself again.

The funicular only took minutes and they were soon at the front of the bistro she remembered. "It's possible the management has changed but, from the outside, it looks just the same."

Her fingers still snuggled so naturally in one of his big warm palms, Teun appeared reluctant to relinquish them as he pushed the door open for her to enter.

"I needed that." His announcement complemented a gratified grin a few minutes later when he licked the beer froth from his mouth… as he'd done the previous day. And, like the day before, she wanted to do it for him.

"You said exactly those same words yesterday." She didn't even want to hide her admonitory smirk.

"Yeah, but yesterday I needed a drink for more than just thirst quenching. Yesterday, it wasn't only the sun which had got me heated."

"It wasn't?"

Teun's eyes targeted hers and held. "A two hour delay in my flight from London meant a much later arrival at Frankfurt. As a rookie in Europe, I stumbled through finding the train to Heidelberg, just missed one, and had a frustrating wait for the next. I checked into the hotel with no time to do more than dump my luggage, and arrived a few minutes late for my appointment with Jensen's lawyer. And, after all the hassle, I spent a frustrating half hour with that damned man who gave me a package of photographs which meant nothing to me. He wouldn't explain them; told me precisely zip! Apart from how to walk back to my hotel, how to get to Jensen's gallery... and that Jensen would give me all the details when I met him. I came around the corner to Steingasse wanting to strangle the guy for wasting my time, since he'd been so secretive. Having had no lunch, my stomach protested wildly and I really needed that beer."

Keira's smile slipped; her sigh one of regret. "I'm sorry about my reaction yesterday, Teun."

They'd not spoken at all yet about her hasty escape from him the previous day. "I don't know why I got so spooked." She tried to explain, her brows furrowed, apology dripping. "The minute I clapped eyes on your invitation – which exactly matched the one I'd received that afternoon – I had a moment of sheer panic. It's not like me to react like that, but I felt... I can't explain it. It all seemed too furtive; too coincidental you could be in a similar situation. Then I imagined you were stalking me, or something akin to that, with some ulterior motive."

Teun's face clouded as he processed her words. "I didn't think it was because you'd got beer spilled on your pretty orange dress, Keira. I'm savvy enough to realize it was some other reason which had you running from me."

"Like you, I'd come out of the lawyer's office just as frustrated. Maybe even more so, because I didn't even get a packet of photos. All I got was that cryptic summons. I'd had no direct communication from Jensen. All my contact had been via the lawyer who'd sent on the reservations for flights and the hotel, when I agreed to come. I knew nothing of Jensen until the lawyer mentioned his name yesterday afternoon. The strangeness of the request left me feeling, I can hardly explain it, sort of... open to danger, and... exposed. It was all so secretive and mysterious, it seemed... maybe fraudulent?"

Teun's smile warmed as he squeezed her hand, the reassurance welcome when heat rippled over her fingers. "No matter. As long as you don't still think of me as a predatory stalker."

Ignoring her reactions to his contact, she focused her smile at his inviting eyes. "Stalker? No. Predatory?" She laughed heartily at that point. "I think there's a good chance you might be, but in a very good way." The flicker of his dark eyelashes, the twitch at the corners of his lips, appreciated her comment. "Having that invitation in your hand was just too creepy, given the throngs of people around Steingasse. It made me fearful, about what I'd got myself involved in."

"And now, Keira? Are you still hesitant about this quest?"

"No. All the angst yesterday was so stupid! Now it's been explained, I'm fine with it, although Jensen didn't need to make our invitations so cagey, so clandestine. I accept his explanation about not wanting to publicise our search until we have something to show for it, but I don't condone his mysterious methods. I've never felt so vulnerable like that before this quest, and now I just feel plain stupid!"

Succumbing to the tourist in him, Teun agreed to have what he called "a fun shot" on the Strassenbahn – the tram network – where they rode around the old city areas for an hour or so, Keira pointing out what she could remember as they passed by. The tram was busy, people getting on, and people getting off. Not too many of them stayed on as long as they did but, as well as looking at the sights, she was conscious of those who used the tram. People-watching held great fascination. Her mind went off on a tangent as she contemplated the other travellers.

The Germanic blondness of the bulk of the population always impinged on her consciousness when she journeyed in central Europe, compared to Edinburgh, which ranged with far more variations of brown and black-haired people. Yet, even in central Europe, not many had the seriously pale hair of the man on the along-the-wall seat down near the front of the tram. An ethereal snowy white, it arrested the attention, though Keira reckoned it wasn't because the man was old. Prematurely white was more like it, since the man looked to be in his forties. His fingers idled with a ball cap, tossing it back and forth, intense sidelong glances coming her way, sometimes penetrating when he had to bend past people in the aisle to see. Somewhere at the back of Keira's conscious mind flagged up that the hat was identical to the one worn by the man who'd bumped into her at the castle.

Knowing absolutely nothing of Heidelberg, Teun declared her a mine of information when they got off close to the old bridge, Alte Brücke. Her comfy trainers were so welcome since he was game for the climb up the Philosophenweg, the Philosopher's Walk, which lay on the opposite side of the old bridge. They lingered for a while at the bridge's centre and inhaled the fantastic view along the River Neckar to the next bridge; white, pink and red walls clothing the river sides. The reds, greys and browns of the rooftops flashed a vibrant contrast against the varied greens of the dense bushes and trees smothering the high hills of the valley.

She'd warned him the Philosopher's Walk took a steep climb of roughly two hours, but the rewards were fabulous. What she hadn't told him was the pathways through the woods were local lovers' haunts… though not usually mid-afternoon when thronged with tourists. As they strolled their way along the route and into the woods at the top, their laughter rang out across the copses, stories of their youth and student days entertaining each other. Too soon, it seemed, their hike in the speckled dimness came to a close, their feet zipping along the soft, bark-filled forest paths towards the nearest outlook that edged the hillside.

When Teun stopped to appreciate an exceptionally gnarled

old tree off the main pathway, Keira used the opportunity to undo her shoe: an irritating piece of wood had splintered between her lacing. While she shook it out, some tiny movement drew her attention – a flash of white – but, when she looked around, she detected nothing. The woods hadn't been empty but neither had they been busy, though it had been a good few minutes since she'd seen signs of other walkers. There hadn't been much in the way of woodland creatures either, so she reckoned it must have been some small rodent scurrying through the leafy fronds of the ferny undergrowth. Shoe sorted, she moved on when Teun rejoined her.

Leaning her stomach against the railing at one of the high vista points, before their steep descent, Teun slid in behind her. His hands gripped the railing on either side of her, her breath hitching as his front made direct contact with her back. All afternoon there had been a simmering of desire, and now the simmer no longer flared at a low peep. His lips feathered her neck, his whispered words enough to stir longings.

"I'm very glad to know you're no relative of mine, Keira Drummond. If you were my real cousin, and blood of my blood, I would have a very real dilemma." His arms slowly turned her. "But I think you've guessed that."

The kiss lingered. Teun explored, made angle changes, before his tongue slipped into play and deepened the contact. Though it still held the tentative exploration of first kisses, there was need. She couldn't remember kisses obsessing her before. Future promise. Beyond thinking, it crushed her when the sounds of approaching tourists pulled his lips away. The lookout wasn't the place for indulgence.

"Later."

Just one word. But it set Keira grinning broadly. Mmm.

"Promises!"

"Any promise I make, Keira Drummond, I keep!" This time their shared laughter rang free.

They set off careering down the bark-filled walkway, which zigzagged a steep trek down the hillside, at an exhilarating pace. At the next vantage point Keira took a last glance at the woods above her, again catching a flash of white. A guy leaned over the railing a few levels above them, alongside a woman and a couple of kids. The man who'd been on the tram. As she pondered that thought, the woman gathered her kids in tow and set off on their descent. The man lingered by the railing for a few more seconds, peering down at her, before heading down the path. Keira turned back to Teun and admired his brown hair. Yep! She definitely preferred brown, but couldn't shake the sudden shivers. It just wasn't like her to obsess about anyone. She people-watched often, but not in a way which bothered her. A wry grin spread. What might she do if she went to somewhere like Finland where there might be loads of white blonds? Probably freak all day.

Back down in the Altstadt, Teun surprised her as they passed an expensive jewellery shop. Her hand rested in his, making it easy for him to drag her through the doorway into the chic interior.

"I need to learn something about jewels – emeralds in particular – and what better place than this?"

A graceless scoff huffed as he hauled her toward the back of the shop, to look at the glass cases displaying the more exclusive pieces. "Don't expect me to be your guide this time. I may be female, but I know next to nothing about expensive jewels."

An hour later, after many probing questions, he declared his satisfaction with what he'd learned about settings and gem stones. The assistant had a very good command of English, though a few times Keira had interceded to make something clearer for Teun. She'd learned quite a bit, too, about the names of ring settings. Before, a necklace had just been a necklace. Now she could name styles of chains and pendants.

She fumbled for her own charm chain, but she'd left it in

71

her hotel safe. The worn clasp had been awkward to use for months, so – fearing she might lose the chain before replacing the catch – she'd opted to leave it off that morning.

Teun's eyes followed her restless movements. "You had an interesting thing around your neck yesterday. What would you call it?"

Keira kept her voice low, knowing the assistant tuned into their every word.

"Having learned a bit here, I believe you'd call it a heavily textured, yellow-gold, fancy link chain, with a few dangling charms."

"You don't wear it all the time then?"

"Usually I do but the catch is ancient, like the chain, and is hard to close. I think I bent it a bit this morning when I was in a hurry to go for breakfast." She stopped to savour the flare of pleasure in Teun's eyes when she mentioned her haste. "I left it in my room safe, in case it got loose and I lost it during our tourist walk-about today."

Five minutes later an overjoyed assistant held open the exit door for them, her smile showing delight over her eventual sale as Teun had been adamant about buying a new chain. Though Keira had protested, she'd given in and allowed him to buy her a simple gold link chain, not the more expensive one he'd wanted to purchase. She didn't want to dim her pleasure in his company, but his buying it didn't sit well on her.

"Call it a payment then, for your guided tour today. Hiring a personal guide would have been just as costly."

Keira found nothing funny about his joke. And not his next whisper either. "And I'll be expecting it to pay for helping me to locate the best restaurant to eat real German food tonight, drink some local beer, and have the pleasure of your company."

Chapter Five

"My services are not to be bought like this, Teun Zeger." Her admonishment came as she squirmed out of his grip, more embarrassed by the event than annoyed. "I'll give them for free, or not at all!"

Teun halted her strides and dragged her into his arms, disregarding the stares of the passers-by. His eyes softened; the crinkling at the edges something she found too appealing to resist. His teasing grin dipped away. "I'm not trying to buy services from you in any devious way, Keira. I wanted to buy you something because I like you. I enjoy your company. Can you accept that?"

Moisture stung in her eyes as she melted into his brief kiss, though it was over in an instant since they were in the middle of a very busy thoroughfare. There was no point causing a fuss out in the streets of Heidelberg.

Dinner was fun.

Keira dragged Teun to another of her student haunts, where they munched their way through local-style potatoes, German sausage and sauerkraut, and drank steins of local beer. The bar was a noisy environment. Impromptu singing and dancing often happened there, so it wasn't unexpected when a guy stood up and bawled lustily. Other people sang along when it came to the chorus; the German song almost lifting the roof. Literally breathtaking, dancing feet pounded the wooden floor as diners jigged around the tight floor space, a long line wending in between chairs and tables. When dragged up to join in the revelry, she reassured Teun that not having a clue didn't matter. No finesse was necessary. What mattered was they were happy and having a great time.

As she whirled past, a diner at a corner table snagged her attention. For God's sake! Her head whipped back but she'd moved on too far. That man again? But maybe not him – just someone like him, since she'd jerked past so quickly. Though she didn't remember it from staying here years ago, there must be quite a lot of people with extremely pale colouring in Heidelberg. Taken up in the whirling, she put the white-haired guy to the back of her mind.

While following the line – with Teun clutching tight at her waist, his legs almost glued to hers and his body a cradle around her – there was an affinity she'd never shared with anyone before. It was weird: she couldn't see his face yet she knew exactly what his smile would be like, knew the little laughter crinkles would bracket the edges of his lips, knew his expression would twinkle with gusto. It wasn't the same primal desire she'd felt for other men; a mere physical need which had soon dissipated. Her relationships had been fleeting, none ever lasting more than a couple of months. She wasn't sure that would be the case with Teun, who engendered something else she couldn't put her finger on. But perhaps it was only because they were both now embroiled in the search for Geertje's treasures. Was that extra link making the difference?

After their bout of hectic snaking around the room, a well-earned drink cooled them down, their chat having largely stopped – due, in part, because the noise in the room was so raucous. Gradually, something else prevented their shared camaraderie. Teun answered her occasional question, though now appeared distracted.

"Do you want to leave?" Her shout penetrated the deafening noise around them as she tapped his arm to gain his attention, his focus having drifted away again.

When he pulled his gaze back to her, his face lacked any indication of enjoyment, his words contradicting his introspective expression. "It's fine!"

They drifted into an uneasy silence, Teun toying with his nearly empty beer stein. His gaze kept sliding away to scan the room, a furrow developing at his brow which she couldn't interpret. Was he bored with her? It was disconcerting but, then again, Teun was essentially a stranger. Maybe he wasn't enamoured with the pub. Glad her drink was almost finished, she refused another – no point sitting in an awkward cringe.

Quiet streets met them when they struggled their way out the door, the bar patrons standing so deep they'd had to squeeze a way past them. Once onto the street, Teun's stride quickened. Too quick.

"Where's the fire?" Keira came to an abrupt stop, so annoyed at his manner that being circumspect didn't cross her mind.

An apologetic smile and a quick glance over his shoulder was his answer, as he shoved his hand across his crown, ruffling his short hair. When he turned back, his smile was much more like earlier in the day, yet something lurked. Keira felt his response was far too repressed, too strained.

"Sorry, I didn't realise." His arm drew her into a protective clutch.

Their pace slowed a little, Jensen's quest re-entering the conversation as they tramped the pavements back to their hotel. Avoiding a rut, Teun's arm fell away. The lack was immediate, but Keira had no intention of initiating any close contact again. A subtle tension had been detectable, and she didn't feel like revisiting any awkwardness. Discussing the details of their departures for the following day dampened any last rapport and reminded her of why she'd come to Heidelberg. In getting to know Teun, the reason had hovered in the background. The day had been fun, but now it was over, and she couldn't let their dwindling relationship matter. Still bound by the arrangement she'd made with all the cousins, she needed to remain on reasonable terms with Teun. Any lingering chatter dried up. He appeared perceptive to her mood change as he, too, remained quietly at her side, covering the last cobbles.

"My flight is 11:20 tomorrow morning." Teun pulled his room key card from his pocket. He'd already told her he was flying back from Frankfurt Main to New York.

"8:45 for me, leaving from Frankfurt Hahn."

He held open the entrance door to the foyer of the hotel, his key card fluttering to the ground as she passed by.

"Butterfingers!" Her grin mildly chided, but he didn't seem amused.

He fumbled over picking it up, looked askance before he straightened, then quickly ushered her inside. Any budding togetherness was well gone as they padded over to the lifts, and it wasn't due to any coolness of the night. Keira didn't know if she'd offended him, though it seemed that way. The scowl at his brow matched his determined chin, the muscles of his neck taught, yet his arm hovered protectively at her shoulder.

An even more awkward silence pervaded as they stood awaiting the lift. Her scan of the hotel lobby was a distraction, since the last remnants of the sexual tension that had earlier built between her and Teun appeared to have fizzled back at the beer keller. The uncomfortable hush was timely, though, since she needed to call a halt to the rising feelings for him. In some ways it was a re-run of the evening before, though she didn't expect any sort of kiss this time. From the look on his face, it appeared his thoughts ran along similar lines; there was an edginess she could almost touch. Regret hovered, but she'd gleaned enough of his character to be aware that something else contributed to the detachment now between them.

As the lift doors glided open, she had the sensation of someone scrutinizing her from behind. Teun regarded her, quite blatantly, but he was just behind her shoulder. It was unnerving. She couldn't decide if Teun was annoyed at her, or what? His expression tightened, his brows twisting as he manoeuvred her inside. He couldn't get rid of her quickly enough now, but if that was how he was going to play it, then she'd just suck up her regret and… do the same.

She whipped round after stepping into the lift, a flurry of movement by the entrance door catching her gaze. A figure lingered there, and then swiftly turned to peer through the glass door panel, out to the street – as though searching for someone he awaited. The man was quite tall, casually dressed in a silky-soft, bomber-style jacket. The lift doors closed, but not quickly enough to avoid her noting the shock of hair tucked under a ball cap.

"Bloody hell!" Her words sucked into the closing doors.

"I'm sorry?" Teun's turn was slow, his gaze inquisitive. A jittered shake of her head dismissed his enquiry.

That spooky feeling descended again, coupled with anger. The guy had to be following them. There was no reason for her to even think it, but it was the only conclusion she could come to. She had to get a grip of herself. It was irrational; she knew it, especially as she felt Teun's hand slide over to clasp her fingers again. His touch was both awkward and contrarily comforting. Weird. He retained her hand all the way to her door, though he didn't speak, or attempt any other intimacy.

Focusing on her plans for the following day, she let his hand drift apart to pull out her key-card from her purse. She allowed Teun's brief kiss on her cheek, made a jumpy farewell of her own as his intense, sober stare lingered, like the light grip of his fingertips at her shoulders.

"Keira. I just wish…"

She didn't allow any more as the grating sound of the nearby lift heralded someone arriving at their floor. Not wanting a tearful public scene, she managed to keep it short. Pleasant enough, but swift.

"It's no problem, Teun. We'll keep in touch?"

A few tense words stuttered over, she was into her room. Frustrated. With herself for being so cautious. And, curiously, with Teun as well, because if he'd made more indication he really wanted to get to know her better, she'd have capitulated.

***

The doors of the lift hissed closed, the white head having pulled back sharply on seeing Teun Zeger halt, and wait immobile, at a room near the far end of the corridor. One finger punched the keypad to take the lift to the next floor above. Then back down again. This time the figure disgorged on the ground floor and strode to the concierge desk. It would be useful to find out if Teun Zeger and Keira Drummond were leaving Heidelberg at the same time. Maybe one or other of them had requested a wake-up call or an early taxi?

A few minutes later, Boris Winkelmann whistled his way out of the hotel. The day had been productive enough. He hadn't managed to snatch anything from Keira Drummond's pocket at the castle, but he had other evidence to show for his day's work. His camera had clicked often. A growing rapport had been developing between the American and the Scottish woman. What he had was good enough to report back to his boss. It was far too soon for him to do any real ferreting around, or make big intervention moves on them.

***

Two days later, clutter surrounded Keira in her father's house. There had been mystification on David Drummond's face when she'd related her reason for going to Heidelberg, and her meeting with Jensen. David had assumed work had drawn her there. He became intrigued when he learned about Geertje's emeralds, but could give her no information. He'd no idea if his wife had ever got anything of note from Neela, but didn't imagine so. He wasn't averse to doing a spring clean of his house, though, when she suggested having a rake around.

"You know how much I miss your mother, but it's probably past time for a new look."

That had been enough for them to embark on a major tidy-up. It wasn't a sad time – rather they cherished the memories certain objects brought to them. She cleared her father's bedroom of her mother's bits and bobs, but uncovered nothing at all which showed links to *Oma* Neela. Nothing was being thrown away, though. After some re-organisation, she packed it into containers for storing elsewhere.

Teun phoned that night, his third communication since they'd parted at her hotel room door, their conversations blithe – quite a change from their final words in Heidelberg. His mother had been amused by the whole concept of valuable information, or jewels, having been in the care of her first husband, but had known nothing about any legacy of Geertje Tiedman. Her only advice was for Teun to speak to his father – though how much help Jan Zeger could give was debatable, she'd sourly declared, since he barely knew his own name.

"Your mother still has contact with him?" The notion surprised Keira.

His hearty chuckle vibrated in her ear. "Never. Only what she hears from me. My mother's still very bitter towards my father for not forgiving her, even though she was the one who had the affair which ruined their marriage."

"Are you going to see your father?" Keira's question came hastily, designed to change the touchy subject.

Teun appeared champing at the bit. "I've scheduled a trip to my lab in Boston next Thursday, and while I'm on the Eastern fringes I'll swing past and visit my father in Duluth."

Her laughter peeled out. "You make it sound as if it's on your doorstep, Teun. It's the other side of the continent for you."

An expectant pause made her heartbeat stutter. Was he finding it too awkward now, to chat to her? A gravelly tone eventually reached her.

"How about if you reschedule any work you have, and I organise a ticket for you to meet me in Minneapolis St. Paul? We'll spend a day driving up to Duluth where you can help me talk this through with my father."

"What? You mean I should fly over to the States to visit you and your father?" How on earth she'd even managed to ask the question was a mystery: the suggestion stunned her.

"If I said I enjoyed your company very much in Heidelberg, and I've really missed you these last days, would it be enough, Keira? Enough for you to say that little word, yes?" The lowering tones of his words, and gruffness, left her in no doubt of his sincerity.

"For how long?" She couldn't formulate any more syllables.

"Plan for at least… a week?"

"It's a crazy plan, Teun. All that distance just for a short visit to meet your father? I can't just dump my work and take off; I'd have to bring it with me." Although she gave her answer, desperation gripped. She wanted to agree she'd travel anywhere to meet up with him again – but it was insane. A new translation contract would tie her up for a while; her business made demands on her. She couldn't fly off on a whim. Could she?

His next words clinched it. "Do you realize you knew my father's aunt for years yet I never, ever, got to meet her in person? You can tell my dad lots of things about Neela, because he never actually met her either."

How could she refuse after that?

***

It was Saturday – not a school day – so Keira's sister, Isla, helped do more raking around in their Dad's house. In the kitchen, making a mid-morning cup of coffee, a loud holler had Keira scrambling up to the attic. Isla had unearthed a cardboard box full of bits and pieces. Scarves and gloves, a pair of satin shoes, and something which looked like a boned silk waistband for a dress were all stuffed into a cardboard carton. Isla was sure her mother had never shown her the contents of the box: Keira declared the same.

A fascinating waistband, about five inches deep, it was made of coffee-coloured silk and had a fancy star of embroidered lace stitched to the front. Pleated horizontally with five little folds, each fold was lace-edged. When Keira held it around her waist, she found it impossibly narrow.

"Victorian?" Isla guessed, not known for her historical knowledge. Biology was her subject, and science her passion.

"Maybe a bit later."

"What's later than Victorian?"

"Edwardian, and then some, but you're right – this style could be late Victorian, or early Edwardian."

"Where would mum have got this belt from? This must have felt like a corset! You can feel the bones about every two inches, with heaps of firm support in between. Whoever wore this must have had a minuscule waist, or must have been unable to breathe when it was in place." Isla chuckled as she felt how unyielding it was, though neither of them could answer the questions they posed about it.

Moments later they had a small stash of decorative plates and silver cutlery, which had belonged to their great-grandmother, on the floor beside them. Keira knew they were Victorian items since her mother had often shown them to her, but beyond doubt they hadn't come from Neela. She packed everything away in a cardboard carton large enough to include the clothing items as well.

An old wooden box, quite large and with an open fretwork lid, was the next object to capture their attention. Keira and Isla had certainly seen the box, since their mother had kept knitting patterns in it for years. Amusement rippled as the first pattern on the pile caught Isla's eye.

"Do you remember that cardigan?" Her guffaw rang around the echoing attic. "I had a blue one, and yours was green, to match the kilts we wore back then!"

That was all it took for them to have a sad moment, because they would no longer receive any home-made garments from their mother. No tears were shed, but the patterns engendered bittersweet memories. After a quick rifle, Keira closed and set the box aside.

When they'd checked the whole house, apart from the study, they'd uncovered nothing relating to Neela. Another long day pouring through the shelves of books furnished zero, apart from a couple of postcards her mother had used as bookmarks. The postcards had been sent by Neela, but only with brief greetings scribbled on them to the family.

Isla had been intrigued by the whole quest. Yet, categorically knowing she hadn't been given anything by Neela which could be part of an expensive collection, she wasn't as disappointed as Keira when they called a halt.

"Come on, Sis. Be realistic. Dad's had a good tidy-up done, so we haven't been wasting our time."

***

Keira couldn't contain her excitement when her flight arrived at Minneapolis St. Paul. Her legs felt shaky as she pushed her luggage through the Customs gate and headed towards Teun; a grinning Teun who stood out from the crowd, awaiting her at the closest point for meeting. What if all these pent-up feelings were only one-sided? What if he only flirted with her because of the promise of finding some of Geertje's treasures? What if she was left to deal with her longings for him alone… after they called off the quest?

He grabbed her cart and shoved it aside to keep the walkway

clear, yanked her into his arms and proceeded to almost suffocate her. Stealing a welcome kiss, his arms banded around her. Strength, warmth and the taste of his mouth suffused her. Detaching herself after a few moments to catch her breath, her grinning protest was minimal.

"Glad to see me then?"

Teun caught her into his clasp and bent his forehead to hers. And kept it there, locking them as never before. Completely disregarding the public arena, his voice was husky. "I've missed you these last days, hours, even minutes."

Ages later, her eyes eventually blinked since all she could do was stare when he lifted his head. The bustle around them, the squeals of damaged luggage wheels, the potent mix of stale colognes and strong coffee didn't register as she drank him in – the trembles not only her own as she quivered in his arms. After an enormous indrawn breath, his chin rose to the ceiling and he exhaled again, his expression one of sheer gratitude. Another quick hug and grin later, Teun fisted her luggage and whisked her out of the concourse.

Stuffing her baggage into the boot of his hired car, he caught her to him before she could climb in. The kiss only lasted seconds since, again, it was too public a domain for any development of passion.

"Couldn't wait, Keira. You've no idea how much I've wanted to kiss you." His groan into her lips made her weak, before he reluctantly released her.

Keira grinned a mile wide. "I've a good idea, Teun. I've missed you too."

His gorgeous grey irises deepened to almost black in the dim interior of the car park, the tiny quirk of his lips a tease. "Enough to share a room with me tonight?"

Not sure what to make of his presumptions, she didn't answer. She knew exactly what she wanted, but was that the best thing for them? That's what she still had to figure out.

Teun's fingers caressed her chin and lifted her head up, so

she could see his truth. "I wanted to book one room, Keira, but didn't. We can easily rectify that later, though, if we change our mind."

She shared his honesty. "I guess we could."

They planned to do part of the drive north that night, since her flight had landed around 7pm local time. The whole drive to Duluth, about three hours, was feasible, but Teun explained they'd need to wait till closer to lunchtime the following day before meeting with his father. He'd organised reservations en-route north at Hinckley, roughly halfway to Duluth.

"Don't expect anything like the Heidelberg Ritter." His warning came as they left the lights of Minneapolis St. Paul behind and headed north. "Motels and B&Bs are the norm on this route."

"Are we staying somewhere you've visited before?"

"No. I usually fly to Duluth."

Her tongue never ceased its prattle during their drive through a darkened, and remarkably traffic-free, landscape, as she exchanged information not covered in their daily phone calls of the previous days. Teun's admiring glances promised revisits of the intimacy of their reunion, and she couldn't keep the happy smiles from her face. Even though he made no move to touch her, she felt his presence keenly; she had missed his winks and appreciative looks during their time apart. Mystified by how much she'd grown to like this man in such a short time, she wasn't going to question the fact she wanted their relationship to develop further. That anticipation was again as ardent, her desire heightened. Teun's fleeting glimpses in her direction made her sure his expectation was pretty similar. His mention of one room sounded more appealing as they drove on, though she kept those ideas to herself, their conversation continuing agreeably till she mentioned Zaan.

The buoyant mood nose-dived.

"Zaan called you?" Teun's gaze shifted from the straight stretch of road he was driving on, and he stared at her. His brows knotted, his eyes an annoyed flash in the darkness.

"Yesterday. After your call."

"He's called you at other times?"

It was odd he should ask, since they'd all agreed to keep each other updated.

"Yes. That was his third call."

Jaw firmed, he kept his focus on the road, his clipped words making her feel uncomfortable. His gaze flicked to his rear mirror, and lingered a moment or two before he next spoke.

"Does he have any good news?"

She wondered if he'd been at loggerheads with Zaan over something and accordingly chose her words with some care. "Has he updated you about the brooch?"

His snort worried her, his head whipping round. "Not heard a cheep from him, so how would I know that?"

Discomfort changed to annoyance. "Have you called him?"

He shifted to look back at the road, after another swift glance in his side mirror, his words a grunt. "Why would I call him?"

"We agreed to keep in touch with each other. That can only happen if we talk, or write to each other. Any emails between you?"

Another grumble of derision came heavy in the brief silence after her question. "Nothing to update, so no point in sending trivial emails."

Keira considered the calls and emails which had passed between her and Teun during the last week. Precious few of them had anything to do with Jensen's quest. Why he disliked Zaan so much she didn't know, but she couldn't remain silent over the issue. It just wasn't her style. She was inclined to live by an old adage of her mother's which ran something like – never go to bed on an argument.

Her focus drifted to the side mirror. She wasn't a nervous passenger, but she was always inclined to keep track of what was behind her, even when not the driver. The headlights of the car behind them went dim again in the side mirror as it decelerated, while she pondered exactly what to say next. The road had been fairly quiet for miles in both directions. Cars had overtaken them, but not the one currently behind. It never got really close to them but, even after many opportunities, and many miles, had chosen to lurk behind. She had no clue why, but found it irritating when it came very close to their bumper and then receded again. She wasn't from around these parts so maybe it was fairly normal practice on the straight, largely flat Minnesota road. Or perhaps the car was being driven by another tourist, just like them? At the very least, it wasn't in any kind of hurry, or it would have sped past them long ago since Teun deliberately maintained a very steady pace a little below the speed limit for the road.

Deciding to ditch tact, she got right to the heart of matters regarding his Dutch cousin. "What don't you like about Zaan?"

Her direct question paid off because an answer came immediately. "He's too happy to just follow in with Jensen's plans. It makes me suspicious."

It was only part of his reason, but she stopped probing. Enough was enough. Time to get back to a more even footing.

"Well, I've nothing to be suspicious about, since he's shared everything that's been happening with me. He hasn't got Tanja's emerald pin in his hands yet, but now knows his mother gave a pretty brooch to her sister a few years back when it was approaching his cousin's twenty-first birthday. He's meeting up with his cousin at the weekend to check out the jewellery she was given. Zaan says she moved to Brussels last year, so he has to wait till Sunday to make a quick trip down to visit her."

"A thorough update, then. Good for Zaan." His gaze refocused on the rear mirror.

She decided to ignore the barb as her head turned to the mirror at her side. "You're right. It's good to know someone's

86

having some success, Teun."

A sardonic laugh peeled out as he again snagged her gaze for a few brief moments, the hint of tension dissipating. "You realize these jewels could be all over the world by now?"

"Yep!" She couldn't help grinning; impossible to stay annoyed at him. "That's what so exciting about it. I've got nothing, but just think of all the places Jensen might have had to look if he'd tried to track everything down himself."

Teun's sarcastic humour emerged again. She liked the way his mind turned, but he was so acerbic when it concerned his European cousins.

"Jensen's rich enough to hire private dicks to do the job for him." His words were droll.

"I know that, but then there would be no shared family success at the end of it. I think he's right to have involved all the cousins in this family mission. There are too many ends of the line in your family tree and this, at the very least, has made you aware of the existence of each other."

Teun eased off the accelerator as he approached their Hinckley Motel car park, his flash of humour gone. Checking his rear mirror before flicking on the indicator, a flash of annoyance knotted his brow. As he made the turn, the light-coloured car which had sat behind them for ages idled past. She had no idea why but Teun looked bothered, maybe even a bit grim. When he was able to give her his attention, his words snapped. "Do you really believe Jensen is in this for the joy of a family reunion?"

She thought through his remark as he pulled up at the reception area, engaged the handbrake and released his seat belt with a ping.

"You think he has some other agenda?" She couldn't believe how sceptical he sounded. There was enough light in the car park to illuminate his features, enough light to see the distrust in his eyes.

"He's a very successful, rich businessman." His next words

whiffed out, dissatisfaction evident, a truthful bite she couldn't deny tainting them. "Keira, Jensen's shrewd enough to acquire the whole collection eventually by himself, and has the financial backing to mount an exhibition on his own. He doesn't need us. It's not like any of us knew each other before this, or have any recent pivotal link in our family who kept in touch. Essentially we're strangers – the distantly-shared DNA is irrelevant."

As Teun got out of the car, she pondered his words. Agreeing with him was easy about Jensen being rich enough, but that Jensen wasn't really bothered about the cousinship was too bizarre to conceive. Why would he have gone to the bother of contacting them if he didn't want to reforge the family connections? She got out as well.

"I can't believe Jensen would go to such trouble to contact us if he doesn't need our help."

Teun stopped at the glass door to reception. "You're looking through blinkered eyes, Keira. Be practical and ditch the family glory."

Her stunned look must have been what prompted his next terse words. "Something has stopped Jensen from seeking these things on the open market. I don't know what, or why, but I can't find myself trusting him till I do."

What came next was a blurt without caution, but her words needed an airing. "You don't trust Jensen. You dislike Zaan for no reason I can immediately put my finger on, since you tense up every time I mention him. Am I also in your list of people that you don't trust?"

The look he sent her was an incredible mix of surprise, hurt, irritation and something which just might be doubt. But, underlying all the other emotions, she detected a flare of honesty. It was something she felt instinctively about him – he was sincere, and wasn't someone who would lie his way out of an awkward conversation. He said nothing as he pushed the door open. The dissention over Jensen's intent, and her

88

unanswered question, were enough to blacken the mood between them as he spoke to the reception clerk.

Keira wasn't finished with the conversation. When the clerk excused himself to check something in the office behind them, she pressed on. "Have you spoken to Romy?"

The look he gave her would have intimidated lots of people. He stared, at first, and then slowly released a huffed breath. "No. I haven't. Have you?" His last question challenged.

Her blood boiled. "Yes. As a matter of fact I have." She stood face-up to him. "I used the email address Jensen gave us." Her use of the word *us* was vehement.

"And?" Teun wasn't giving an inch.

"I got a message from her yesterday."

Facedown at High Noon wouldn't have been more fraught.

A whiff eventually escaped her. "She's now out of hospital and is back home. Still undergoing therapy, of course, but she says she's doing well."

Teun waited, his arms now folding across his chest, drawing her attention to the tense muscles at his throat.

"She claims she needs some time to think about any jewellery passed down to her from Uriel."

His attitude was unremitting. "No news then."

Pushing up to him, she was almost chin to chin. "Not exactly. Her words did make me wonder if she's telling us the truth." His blank stare had her adding more. "Her saying she'd need to think further? That, to me, means she's maybe not divulging everything, yet, about Geertje's jewels. She told Jensen she had nothing apart from the earrings, but it doesn't match up with having to do a rethink."

He still said nothing, his arms folded.

"But at least I made contact with your cousin. Which is more than you seem to have done. And, not that you appear interested, I've also made contact with Ineke. The only thing she says Neela ever gave her was an ugly brooch with a brass tassel."

89

Something flickered in his otherwise firm expression. It was just enough for her to continue.

"I told her she shouldn't discount it, just in case the brass she was so scathing about was in fact gold which badly needed cleaned. She's thinking about taking it to a jeweller to have it examined. "

"I get the impression you don't really get on with Ineke?"

It was Keira's turn to feel irritated, rather than just bothered. "I could never believe how different she is from Neela. Ineke's always complaining about something or other. She never favoured Neela in looks, or in temperament, and almost the whole call was taken up with her complaining about Anna having cut herself off from the family."

As they waited for the motel check-in to be finalised, she finished with her Ineke update. "Anna has eventually ditched her good-for-nothing husband, according to Ineke, but has taken up with some other guy who is nearly as bad. Anna and the new lover have bummed off to do some trek around the world."

"Maybe Anna is better off away from Ineke?" Teun was back to being responsive, still circumspect though, a little defensive wall having set up between them.

"Maybe."

Keira was tired. Tired of travelling, and jaded from having zapped the rapture of their reunion at the airport.

Rooms 24 and 25 were not adjacent as she had expected, the motel complex having been built around a series of squares, each of 16 rooms, with a communal lawn area in the centre. Their rooms straddling a corner came as a relief, as there was no way she intended to share a room with the fortification Teun had become, and didn't even want to share a mutual wall. She almost regretted having come.

At her door, he released her luggage and turned to her, making sure he had her attention. He looked as though he'd also had as much as he could take of the stand-off. His fingers did that rifling through his hair thing which she now realised meant agitation of some sort.

"I don't want to fall out with you, Keira. I'm not annoyed at you at all. My gut tells me I trust you…" Her raised eyebrows must have made him rethink the word gut, the tiniest of smiles breaking the tension. "Okay, other parts of me want to trust you as well, but I'm a doubting son-of-a-bitch till I know people better. Call it my self-preservation instinct or something. In my line of business I've had to be hard-nosed to get ahead. I don't go on assumptions, if I can avoid it. I work on facts. And there's just something which isn't adding up properly in this venture we've got ourselves embroiled in."

She was too annoyed with him to pursue what else was bugging him.

***

A half hour later, a bit cleaner if not in a better frame of mind, she stood outside to meet up with Teun. A development of any relationship between them now came secondary to Jensen's quest. She'd come to Minnesota to meet up with a relative of her Oma Neela and, so long as she focused on that, it was good enough reason for being with Teun. Having made up her mind she'd use him as her travel guide, and nothing more, her greeting for him was polite… if cool.

They had a couple of restaurants to choose from. She chose the local diner, a short walk away.

"The food might be better in the other place."

"I don't need anything fancy, and I want to sample what everybody eats around here."

The selection was more extensive than Teun had reckoned it might be, and in typical diner style their meals were delivered very swiftly. That pleased Keira since she'd been on the go for many hours and was ready to keel over onto what had looked to be a comfortable enough bed. Even if it was a board, she knew she'd sleep soundly. Auspiciously, the décor of the eatery intrigued sufficiently to keep their conversation going as they ate. The place wasn't full, by any means, but it was easy to see all the other diners, the walls of the booths at shoulder height of a seated man.

A group of youngsters fed the music machine as they sipped sodas and something Keira guessed were smoothies. The thumping beat might not be quite her style, but it livened the place. A few parents with young families dotted themselves around; other tables were occupied by couples. A few single guys leapt into view; an isolation about them which drew her imagination... and empathy for their solitary state. She often dined alone, knew what a chore it sometimes was, though at other times it could certainly be a blessing when she didn't want company. An auburn-haired guy at the far corner ignored almost everything as he devoured a newspaper, except when he made nervous little eye movements around and about, sometimes staring for longer in their direction before quickly pulling his glance away. Another guy's fingers tapped a cup of coffee as though he impatiently waited for someone who'd stood him up, glaring at anyone, and everyone, who caught his attention. She didn't know what to expect in what was almost rural northern Minnesota, but the pleasant hum around her wasn't it. Her people-watching mellowed her temper.

Keira turned back to Teun, realising she'd ignored him although she hadn't quite meant to. Their chat wasn't stilted and, she was thankful to find, any rancour from earlier had fled. She wondered if that was another thing she'd learned about him. Apart from talk concerning the emerald quest, he appeared positive about pretty well everything else. That attraction of his drew her in again.

"You're exhausted, aren't you?"

Teun's question accompanied a sympathetic hand pat which led to him gently holding her hand as they awaited their bill.

It was the first contact he'd initiated since their arrival. She wanted to welcome it, but wasn't entirely sure. Zigzagging emotions didn't appeal, and not when she'd been on the move for over 24 hours.

"Just a bit." Her smile was watery. "I had to pack a lot into the last days." She'd told him about her newest commission, and the research she'd needed to amass before she'd been able to fly off to meet him.

His arm snaked across her shoulder and kept her close as they left the diner to walk the short distance back to the motel. Companionable? Yes, again it was. She knew it could easily become more if she made any indication it was what she wanted, but she chose not to; unsure if it was only tiredness ruling her actions. The fact that Teun could have reservations about her motives still irked. As they reached her room, he hadn't made any mention of having changed his tune regarding his trust. He still held himself in check: she kept their farewell casual.

"I'll ask for a wake-up call, but if you don't see me arrive at reception you'll maybe need to batter the door down." Her joke was lame as she opened her door.

Teun looked tired, too, and resigned, but added nothing to her farewell. He lightly brushed her lips, and then gave her shoulders a reassuring squeeze before turning away. He glanced all around the courtyard, almost furtively, then headed across the corner to his own room. Since he'd only spent one day at his Boston lab before flying on to Minneapolis St. Paul to meet her, she knew he'd been on the move a lot during the past days as well. Sufficiently aware of him, she noted the tension which locked his brows and neck muscles. Strain sat there, not anger – she was sure of that; not annoyance either, like it had been on their arrival at the motel. Something else had erected a barrier of reserve again.

The door locked, Keira yanked the curtains closed. A flash of shiny dark hair caught her glance in the illumination from the lights dotted around the courtyard. The figure strode past Teun's door, a purposeful gait moving the man quickly along the walkway. She wondered where the guy had appeared from as the little square had been totally empty when she had bid Teun goodnight. It looked like the man in the diner who'd been avidly reading a newspaper, but the figure now carried nothing in his hands. Yet to be in his current position, he must have streaked around the corner really quickly.

Hitting the sheets, a deep disappointment seeped into her bones. Their reunion at the airport had been ecstatic, inherent joy. It should have continued but hadn't, and she knew exactly why; knew what had caused the rift and cooled their relations. Essentially her Minnesota visit was because of the emerald quest, but as she drifted off she knew she had to find a way of discussing the protagonists in their shared mission in such a way as to cause no offence. How, though? Not ever mention Jensen, or Zaan, or Romy? She wasn't sure how it could be achieved, but mention of any of them put the scuppers on any rapport between her and Teun.

The family quest, whether Teun liked it or not, bound them all together.

***

Teun's father, Jan, was delighted to see his son, and even more delighted to see a new face in Keira. She could see where Teun got his good looks from, his father an older version. Similar bone structure delineated their cheeks, although Jan's face was thinner. The older man's hair, a yellowed gray-white was still thick like Teun's. Sadly, though, coupled with Jan's sallow tone, everything indicated a lack of vitality.

Yet, according to Bobby – Jan's assigned nurse – Teun's father was in fine fettle, to Keira's great relief.

"You knew my Aunt Neela?" Jan's voice was thready.

"Dad?" Teun had been painstaking in giving slow details to

94

Jan, explaining why she accompanied him. "Keira can tell you a lot about her."

"I knew of her, son, but didn't ever meet the woman herself. She was my mother's sister, but we lived in different continents, and back then it was impossible to arrange visits. Nobody had money to travel so far."

They spent the next hours with Keira updating Jan on what Neela had been like.

Jan's cackle cheered her soul. "Oh, honey, you know more of my aunt than I do, and you're not even family. Isn't the world a strange place, Teun?"

She had to concur since she'd never expected a flying visit to Heidelberg, and then another following on its heels to Minnesota.

After she'd told Jan another tale about Neela's husband, Gabriel, when he'd made a visit to her family in Edinburgh, Jan's chuckles rang free. His gnarled hand reached out to give her a tender pat before the old man turned to Teun. "She's a real keeper, son."

The fiery face Keira felt she must be radiating would probably warm up the whole residential complex. Her relief was profound when Teun interceded.

"You know I only bring the best to see you, Dad."

The heat at Keira's cheeks receded quickly. How many women had he introduced his dad to?

When it became evident Jan wilted, Teun moved up a gear. The questions became more precise as he told his dad what they might be looking for. Jan's face crinkled, his mouth pursing thoughtfully before speaking.

"My mother only spoke the one time about family wealth, which I remember, son. It was after my sister Marta's second boy died. I think it was diphtheria that time. My mother said no wealth in the world she owned could compare to having healthy children." Jan's tired eyes turned towards Keira, his explanation hushed. "My sister by then had only three boys born, no girls, and two of her three boys had died." A frail smile crinkled his face. "I remember saying to my mother if she had wealth could I have a new car, and she said I should just keep dreaming since her little nest egg could buy me a thousand cars, but she didn't buy them for men who didn't know their manners. It was such an odd thing to say, I never forgot it. Such a joker was my mother."

A tense silence descended as Jan became reflective. A sound which might have been resignation, but to Keira more of a grunt of annoyance, heralded his next words when Jan turned to Teun.

"As you know, son, your own mother had two baby girls die in the womb before you came. And then you became the light of our lives, for that was all we were going to get. Your mother couldn't birth any more babies after you, even though we tried."

Jan's sad smile turned back to Keira. "I loved my wife, honey. There was never any other woman for me and we tried… how we happily tried to have more children. But it wasn't to be. She… I lost her…"

Again Jan's gaze returned to Teun, his voice even more crackled. Tragedy glistened in his eyes, gnarled fingers sliding up to dash at one of them. "And your mother, Teun? She got… disillusioned… and things went badly wrong." After a tiny pause, he nodded. His eyes closed and his chin drooped onto his chest. "Just remember, son. Don't let the love of your life get away from you. Do anything you have to, to keep her."

It was clear they weren't going to get any more useful information from Teun's father when he descended into silence. After sitting for around ten minutes, Teun indicated they should leave, but his father's sudden interjection halted his rise to his feet. Jan's clouded old eyes looked across the room, his words drifting out, his brows puckered as though thinking was an effort.

"Mother had a fine bangle she pulled out on very special

occasions." Jan's voice got fainter. "It was a really wide band at the front, maybe so wide." A trembling hand rose a little; the fingers outspread about three inches. "But it narrowed round the back at the catch." Jan's fingers slowly closed to about one inch.

Keira felt Teun stiffen beside her.

"Right at the front was a white painting of a dancer, set in a fancy sort of frame."

"You saw this bracelet?" Teun whispered, desperate not to break his father's train of thought.

"Mother would ask me to fasten it for her. She declared the catch thing, with a little thin chain on the underside, was too fiddly for her to manage." Jan's eyes closed as though in contemplation, though it was clear to Keira his energy was zapped as his head sloped down to rest on his chest.

"Have you any idea what might have happened to *Oma* Marijke's bangle, Dad?"

"Gave it to Marta for her wedding day. Something old…"

Chapter Six

"I know it's not that old compared to what you're used to, Keira, but it's still pretty good, isn't it?"

The old historic mansion on the Glensheen Estate entranced her, surprisingly not built till the early years of the twentieth century. Teun was reasonably familiar with it and she loved him dragging her around.

"When my dad first moved here to live with Grace, they towed me to all the tourist spots. This is the one I liked the best, probably because Grace is so interested in it. Though, as a born and bred Minnesotan, what is antique to Grace is not necessarily the same as old to you." Teun followed her, patiently waiting at her side as she stepped well back to admire the intricate fascade.

"It's quite a thought that my father's house, near Edinburgh, is a lot older than this, yet this looks more ancient." Keira's neck strained as she scanned the roofline.

"Draughty old place, is it? I mean, your father's house?"

"It certainly can be, but it's lovely and quirky, full of character with low ceilings in parts and awkwardly twisting corridors. Colinton used to be a village, though not for many decades since Edinburgh expanded."

He clutched her hand as they walked along the hallway to keep her from bumping into people, just as well since she was absorbed by the stencilling on the walls. "This Arts and Crafts design work is fabulous, Teun." She allowed him to yank her away when she realised her nose plastered to the wall.

"Philistine!" she gibed as he dragged her into an ornate drawing room, and then her breath stopped in her throat at the stunning décor. "Wow! This is incredible."

"On my last visit, the guide told me the wall covering, upholstery and all furnishings are original, and all the wood trim and panelling in the room exactly matches the wood of the furniture. I hazarded a guess you'd like it even more than the corridor walls." His laugh matched the cheeky twinkle in his eyes as he propelled her forward to look at the gilt leaf decoration, his hands remaining on her shoulders, comfortably squeezing.

"Spectacular. I can imagine the lady of the house sitting on that chair, holding court over the silver tea tray, the china clinking and the chatter ever so polite."

"Are you picturing yourself in the scenario?"

"Absolutely not, but I can picture Geertje's three daughters in a room exactly like this."

"You do have a good imagination. Is this the style you're accustomed to, living at your dad's house?"

His tentative tone made her laugh. "Oh God, no. And I don't live with my dad. I've lived in a flat in downtown Edinburgh for years now. I get on well with my father, and did with my mother too when she was alive, but I've lived on my own since graduation. When my nomadic student days ended, I moved into my own small pad. The place I'm in now is much more central than the first one."

Teun seemed pleasantly amazed that Keira's next tourist choice was the Railroad Museum.

"Indulge me? It's the little kid in me. I've always loved rides on little steam trains and small gauge railway, and I get a kick out of miniature railway set-ups."

"Then you'll adore Depot Square." His gaze alighted on her and lingered for a second, since he was driving, still smiling when he turned away.

"I will?"

"It's a recreation of what Duluth's main streets had to offer way back at the time of... I guess around the time our three Tiedman daughters were photographed."

"Didn't Jensen say 1907?"

"Yeah. The streets in the museum are from around that era."

"Approximately the same time as Glensheen was built?"

"Yeah. There was an expansion of upmarket development back then in Duluth."

Keira loved the museum. The collection of old engines and carriages were interesting, but she valued the old streets in the Depot even more. When she peered in at the goods displayed in the multi-paned glazing of a dressmaker's shop, leaving Teun to have a longer look at the drug store window, a flash of dark red hair caught her attention. The angle of the pane reflected someone off to her right, someone who currently stared in her direction.

How odd.

She shook her head, thinking she must be seeing things. It couldn't be the same guy she'd seen the previous night, but the height, build and hair colour definitely matched. When she turned around for a better view, the figure had vanished.

What the hell was going on? Unease descended again but, since Teun was engrossed in viewing the apothecary equipment, there was no way he'd have seen the guy to corroborate her suspicion.

Teun wrapped her in a tight embrace as they wandered back out to the car park. After he unlocked her door, she noticed his quick scan of the area, realising she wasn't supposed to pick up on it... but she did. It confused her when he caught sight of her open mouth, ready to ask him about it.

"Just making sure no-one is around to see me doing this." His lips descended in a long and thorough exploration. When the kiss ended, she decided she must have imagined he checked for any other purpose. The embrace had been so intense it had made her lose all reality about where they stood.

When possible Teun gazed upon her as he drove back to their hotel, the blaze there matching her own feelings. She wanted more than him only being her tour guide as he pointed out some of Duluth's modern architecture.

As they rode the lift to their floor, back in the hotel, the chirping of a text message had Keira reaching into her bag before she realised it wasn't her phone. Teun's pursed lips indicated it might not be the best news, his small head shakes clarifying it.

"My secretary. Sorry. I guess I've been playing hooky too long." His weak grin showered regret when he ushered her along the corridor.

Disappointment warred with resignation. Teun left her at her room door, declaring she had some time before dinner. He needed to work, check in with his San Francisco and Boston labs. Having fielded a couple of calls during the day, he now needed to do some catch-up.

Three hours of work didn't really appeal but Keira forced herself to focus since she, too, had commitments. She slogged on till she realised eight o'clock loomed. The fastest shower ever, and a rummage in her suitcase for an uncrushable outfit, had her ready with a minute or so to spare. So glad her hair was an easy style, she pulled a brush through it and wiped some lip gloss on, her fingers quivering. Excitement gripped her once again. Containing her anticipation wasn't easy as she met him out in the corridor, deciding that using the connecting door might be too presumptuous.

Once again it had been a magical day – like their day in Heidelberg. They'd laughed, smiled a lot and exchanged lots of personal information. Touches had been continual, fingers, and hands, and occasional body collisions. Only one kiss had entered into the interaction, but the concept, and draw of more of them, had simmered. Maybe even, at times, bubbled. Heat was definitely building now, and it wasn't due to the early June Minnesota warmth.

101

Teun had booked them into the hotel he used when visiting his father, explaining he usually dined at the hotel as well – sometimes because he was too lazy to go elsewhere, but mostly because he really liked having three restaurants to choose from within the hotel complex, and he'd found all were good on past occasions. But they could eat elsewhere, if she preferred? He had shown her their options and let her choose.

Keira felt spoiled. None of her previous boyfriends had been so solicitous of her, but then she wasn't quite sure what she was to Teun. He wasn't actually her boyfriend, or her lover. She hated the idea that his attention might be because he considered her a business acquaintance. Surely that wasn't what drove him?

She rejected the notion. It couldn't possibly be, given the sizzling kisses.

The meal was perfect, the company even more so. Teun didn't have to exert any energy to attract her; he just did. As the evening developed, she became certain he allowed her to set the pace of any relations, though his eyes blazed his intent and his fingers brushed hers at every opportunity. After their coffee was delivered, he took possession of her hand across the table and held on, shifting forward to make it comfortable. Their active day had tired her, but not made her so tired she wanted to finish the night early with a peck on the cheek. Neither Zaan, nor Jensen, had invaded their conversation, except during the explanations to Jan that morning. When Teun suggested a stroll before bedtime, she jumped at the chance to extend their time together.

The late evening was balmy, almost no wind to speak of. Teun didn't need to keep her warm with his arm around her shoulder, but she had no complaints when it settled there and remained. Snuggled into him, she happily let him lead her away from the built-up skyline towards Lake Superior. In minutes they were down onto the Lakewalk, the harbour views quite spectacular as they wandered along, the lights around the Aerial Lift Bridge breathtaking against the darkness. Though it had been fully dark for quite some time, the illumination around the harbour area twinkled and reflected off the calm water of the lake.

"This is amazingly serene, Teun. Did I tell you I love viewing places at night? There's always something so different about the anonymity of dimness." Keira was amazed at how it could be so tranquil, since the walkway was still full of people ambling along the lakeside path even though it was after ten p.m. There was some noise around, music playing quite far off, and the chatter of fellow strollers... and yet it was still paradoxically peaceful.

"If we've got time we'll do a harbour boat tour, I'm sure you'll really enjoy it. I sometimes think the best way to see Duluth is from the water." He pulled her in even tighter to allow a family group to pass them on the opposite side, the path being too narrow for six abreast.

"Aren't we going to visit Grace?"

"Already planned for tomorrow. She's got time organized for us, after lunch, when her cover arrives to help in the shop."

Teun had taken work related calls during the day, but she hadn't realised he'd contacted Grace.

"Do you think she'll be any help?" Keira was keen to meet the woman who'd been married to Jan, and who'd remained his friend despite their inability to stay together.

"I don't expect information or actual jewels from her, but what she does have is the key to my father's storage facility. When we packed up the contents of his apartment before Christmas, we decided it was best she keep hold of the key, just in case Jan decided he needed something."

It startled Keira when Teun pulled to a sudden stop, his arm sliding off her shoulder. He waited a few heartbeats, almost motionless, listening intently before he whipped around. She turned, too, to see what he looked at. A small group of teenagers approached them and then bypassed; their chatter low, yet lively. The kids were the only people in the near vicinity walking in the same direction as they'd just been going in, but the path was well enough illuminated for her to see the man who strode away in the opposite direction. He'd not been pacing towards them moments ago, which must mean he'd abruptly changed direction. Perhaps an odd thing to do, but not impossible. She'd often changed her mind just as quickly and retraced her steps, finding a need to turn back for some reason or other.

The lighting edging the pathway was just sufficient to see the figure. Too familiar.

The angry shiver had nothing to do with a slight breeze building up. Had the guy followed them and turned back to avoid confrontation? She couldn't be sure, didn't want to voice her suspicions, wanted to test Teun out first.

"What's wrong?" Her inquiry broke into their silence.

He looked very thoughtful, that crossing of his brows marring his handsome features, a gesture she now knew meant he wrestled with something.

"What? It's nothing. I just wanted to let that noisy bunch of teens get past us."

It was a cop-out and Keira recognised it for what it was. Did he not level with her because he didn't want to alarm her, or did he still not trust her enough to share his suspicions? His earlier behaviour refuted it, but he was still a stranger to her.

Teun's tone cajoled as he gentled her around again. The smile, she felt, a little too fixed to be casual. "Just a bit more along this way and we can head back to the hotel, or we can walk another three or so miles further up the lakeside. What's your preference?"

They walked back towards the hotel but, instead of heading straight in, Teun led her into a favourite haunt of his. An old-style pub, its long polished bar with traditional gleaming brass footrail was almost obscured by all the occupied tall bar stools along its length. Clearly a popular place, it hummed with vitality. At the end of the long room a duo of musicians played with gusto. The old upright piano had seen better days but was played with reverent delight, the pianist accompanied by something she could only describe as one of those electric fiddle instruments with almost no body to it. Upbeat Irish folk music had the patrons' feet tapping and their hands clapping.

Fingers drummed on the bar alongside Teun as he squeezed in to place an order for them, the guy on the closest bar stool using the polished wood as an improvised drum. By the time Teun was served, Keira had snagged a tiny table in the far corner which had just been vacated.

Squeezed into the corner bench seating, they slotted like sardines packed in a tin. When Teun's arm snaked across to hug her tight to him, she had no objections, leaning in as naturally as though they'd been friends, and more, for years. However, the room wasn't the only thing humming with energy – tension and desire built between them again, escalating even more when Teun leaned closer to whisper in her ear. It was impossible to talk without it but she found she didn't need to be chatting. Being close and enjoying the atmosphere was magic enough. A comfortable familiarity with him juxtaposed the tension – a weird combination, yet undeniable. They sipped their drinks and appreciated the entertainment.

The musicians calling a break had her realising they'd been tight as clams for more than an hour. Guilt crept in and mixed with a strange sort of relief. She'd done only a little work that day but found she wasn't really too fussed; she'd make it up soon. The relief was she'd seen no auburn-haired guy in the pub. She'd been annoyed with herself when she'd found her gaze scanning around after their arrival, deeply thankful there had been no sign of him. Deciding her imagination was way too active, she put the guy out of her mind and concentrated on Teun. What the heck did she need to think about another guy for anyway, when she had such an attentive... friend?

She didn't want him to be just her friend and, from the looks he'd often sent her way that evening, she reckoned Teun didn't want to be just her friend either. He walked her briskly back to the hotel, talking almost non-stop about times spent with his father and Grace, peppered by occasional glimpses over his shoulder. Keira did the same but could see no-one close by who could be following them. The street was long and straight, though, and a lone figure trailed way back, weaving around as though drunk.

To say she was ready for his kiss was an understatement. When he halted her at the door to her room, he didn't do as she expected. After a swift glance up and down the hallway, he plucked the key card from her hand, swiped the door open, and gently pushed her inside. He followed, snicked the door closed, and pulled her into his arms. The lust which had built between them erupted. Keira slid into his embrace as though she'd come home after too long away. She would have combusted if he hadn't come in.

"Don't leave?"

Teun needed no more urging.

"You are so lovely. I wanted to do this the first second I saw you in Steingasse. You drew me like a beacon, Keira Drummond."

Keira came to awareness around dawn, wondering what had just happened to her. Their shattering lovemaking had left her reeling, physically and emotionally. She opened her eyes to find Teun smiling.

"Thought we weren't going to sleep?" His chuckle pre-empted any reply from her.

It took a few hours to be ready to face food, and the outside world. Only the fact she had work to do later that day, and that Teun needed to check in with his laboratories, had them rising from their well-crumpled bed. She wasn't shocked when he unlocked the internal connecting door to make his way straight through to the other room he'd booked, declaring he'd be ready to eat after a quick shower. The knowledge didn't dampen her enthusiasm: she'd have been so disappointed if he'd carried on into his own room the previous night. Crawling from the tumbled bed, her smile was smug.

When Teun reminded Jan that Keira had visited the day before and had talked about Neela, his father nodded as though remembering, but she wasn't convinced he really did. Jan immediately started to talk about his father – and not Neela – making her wonder how Jan's brain made connections. Teun's grandfather had the earmarks of being quite a character, though she'd just learned how he'd also loved a good joke, like his wife, when Bobby interrupted them.

"I'm sorry, Teun. Jan has a chiropodist's appointment, but I'll see if I can arrange a rescheduled time for him." Bobby looked apologetic but not hopeful.

"No, let Dad get his treatment. We're here for a few days. We'll come back tomorrow."

Teun's fingers reaching for her hand felt so natural as they left the care home; now much more familiar.

Their visit to Grace transpired shorter than they'd intended as well.

"I've got the key, here, Teun, but I'll not be able to help you do any of the searching." Grace's cover had called in sick.

She came across as a really nice woman who still cared very much for Jan. "Your father did give me some jewellery, but I was present when he bought the items. He always claimed my being number three wife meant he never wanted to buy something I didn't like. The best way to avoid making a mistake, he said, was to have me choose with him. Birthdays, Christmas, Valentine's – if I got jewellery, you can be sure I chose it myself."

Grace had just enough time to pinpoint a few particular boxes. "The big blue one is where Jan kept important paperwork. It was so neat and tidy when we packed up his apartment that I didn't touch any of the contents, but I did add the loose papers you found in his desk drawer before I taped up the blue box."

As they drove to the storage facility, Teun endorsed Grace's honesty. "I'd never doubt Grace. If she utters anything, you can be sure it's totally truthful."

Keira side-mirrored again. She couldn't prevent those occasional glances, blaming Teun for encouraging her habit since he was continually checking his mirrors, too. The streets of Duluth were busy; the traffic needed constant focus, but perhaps not as often as he looked.

"Is something wrong, Teun?"

His gaze twisted to her for a moment, his weak smile not convincing at all. "No."

Something flashed there she wasn't happy with, before his attention slid back to the road. They'd driven through the centre of the city and now drove in a less populated area where the traffic had thinned out. Fewer houses dotted around as they passed through a mainly industrial landscape. Keira's eyes flicked back to the side mirror.

A gold sedan had been tucked in a few cars behind them for quite some time, holding back in the same manner as the vehicle on the drive north to Duluth had. She wondered if it could be the same car. The one which had passed them at their motel in Hinckley had been light-coloured, but it had been too dark then to say what colour. She berated herself for being stupid. It had to be a fluke. Except, it was now creeping closer to their bumper.

"The stupid bas—"

Teun's sudden turn of the wheel, and rapid acceleration, had them overtaking the truck in front at a speed she felt far too dangerous. Not a manoeuvre she'd have attempted herself. His next wheeling round the approaching corner wasn't something she'd do either, her eyes popping so much she wished she was wearing blinkers. Her fingers clamped around the handrest at the window, for balance and to settle her roiling insides. What the heck was happening?

"Sorry about that."

Teun's apology was feeble, his full concentration on speeding his way along the road. A few more turns and a few streets later, he'd reduced the speed to what she'd have called suitable for a built-up area. By then her breathing had returned to normal. She wasn't too sure about her pulse. She'd only had a small taster of Teun's driving so far, but he hadn't been inclined to be reckless before this. Although he mentioned nothing about the guy following them, he'd been attempting evasive action.

"What was all that about?" She gave him an out.

Teun took time to glance her way. His eyes were dead serious. "Thought you needed a bit of excitement in your life."

"Well, I could do with a bit more notice, please, if my life is going to be so exciting again. Maybe even directions to a public toilet!"

She hoped her levity would ease Teun's strain... but it failed. He also hadn't levelled with her. She couldn't work out, yet, why he made no mention of their pursuer but she let it ride another time. Teun's gaze had flicked back to his mirror.

The gold sedan was a block behind them.

Shit! The tension in the car was almost palpable. Keira sat transfixed, barely breathing, but didn't dare say anything. Teun's fingers compressed the leather cover on the steering wheel, his knuckles white.

"Just around the next corner."

Keira wasn't sure if it was meant to be a warning of a risky manoeuvre, or just a piece of innocent information. Her knuckles were white on the handgrip. When Teun pulled off the road to turn into a car park, the gold car drifted on ahead. She squirmed in her seat. Oh my God! Same guy. She'd expected it would be... but also wished it hadn't.

Teun's voice drew her attention, his throat clearing awkwardly, his voice strained. His hands no longer clutched the steering wheel since he was setting the parking brake and was withdrawing the key from the ignition. His chest heaved. His heart had to be pounding under his thin shirt; his breathing was certainly laboured, but he still didn't trust her. He didn't mention their pursuer at all.

"The papers I found in Dad's desk drawer were related to his car, his bank details and some letters. Since I dealt with selling his car and sorted out his bank papers, Grace must mean she added the letters to his box." Keira noted the tension in his grip as he zinged the car alarm before walking her to the entrance door, his gaze scanning around to encompass the whole car park. His smile remained tight when he pushed the front door open.

"I knew I'd have to come back here someday, but not as soon as this, and not for such strange reasons."

She could relate to any concern he might feel because, in a way, it was similar to how she'd felt about going through her mother's things. The slide of her hand onto his tight fist struck her as not just the right thing to do; it was more that it was necessary she absorb some of his anguish… and stress of the past few minutes. She found she needed his reassurance just as much for herself, selfish though it may be, even if she'd hadn't yet gained his trust. His returning squeeze when he unfolded his hand and linked with hers was exactly what she needed. Apart from the anxiety their pursuer was causing, she was desperate to take on some of his regret, and share his pain regarding his father. In many ways it was much harder to pack up and store belongings before a death occurred.

And right now, to rake through them without Jan's actual permission seemed… discourteous.

For someone who'd lived ten years alone in an apartment, there really was precious little in storage for Jan.

"No point in saving any furnishings." Teun was pragmatic as

they located the particular crates Grace had mentioned. "They were sold, or disposed of. Grace asked to keep some of Jan's photograph albums – ones which recorded vacations they'd taken together – but that was all she wanted."

Keira found that sad.

A while later they came across something interesting. It was an old shoebox Teun remembered seeing in his father's closet when he'd been sent to vacation with Jan – the divorce settlement having given Jan longer visitation access during Teun's school summer breaks.

His tone became reflective as he stripped the tape from the box. "Dad would occasionally visit California for a long weekend to visit me, though mostly his finances didn't lend to it happening more than once a year, but I used to spend a month with him. Coming to Minnesota was a challenge for us both. He always looked forward to the longer summer visit, but the first day hung awkward till he got to grips with how I'd changed in between times."

Keira had no frame of reference to know how that worked out but she sympathised, her palm caress of his tense shoulders intended to soothe out the kinks. He gave her more than just a thank you, though, as his lips settled on hers for a gentle kiss. The fervent passion of the night before wasn't in it, since there was an assistant hovering nearby, but it warmed Keira nonetheless. Restraint lurked as he detached himself and grinned, before whispering in her ear. "How did you know I needed that?"

"My female intuition thing."

His gentle nudge accompanied another quick peck at her lips, before he concentrated on removing the box lid. "This always sat on the top shelf alongside gifts Dad claimed my mother had given him. Scarves, sweaters and such like that he'd kept. He'd point to the shelf and tell me about an item, but I never witnessed him opening this box."

"Were you never curious about it?"

Teun's laughter trilled in her ear as he pulled her into a light clutch. "No, Keira, not really, since I couldn't deal with anything relating to both my parents at the same time." She felt him pull away to look at her from a distance. "Does that make any sense to you?"

"I think so. You had to keep each parent in a separate compartment? And couldn't think of any interaction between them; no memories of them being happily together and in your company?"

His head nodded as he removed a piece of tissue paper wadding. "Close enough."

Inside, they found a pile of photographs. Not as old as the one Jensen had produced, but some dated back to his grandparents' arrival in Minnesota back in the 1930s. There was a formal one they guessed was taken as a mug-shot of Jan senior; one he probably used for identification. The old black and white photo had numbers written on the back, and the name of the studio in Rochester where it had been taken. She knew they wouldn't be random numbers but neither she, nor Teun, had any idea what they meant. Not useful information for them at present.

There was also a formal photograph, dated 1939, of Teun's grandfather and grandmother Marijke – a baby being held in her arms. In pencil on the back, it read: *Jan at five months old.* A few more photos showed his grandparents' growing family, one in particular with three more children. Detailed again on the back were the names and ages of the children. By that time, 1946, Teun's father, Jan, was seven, his sister Marta four, and the two other brothers three, and six months.

"Only my dad and Aunt Marta lived long enough to go to high school. My other two uncles died before they were ten, I think. Children often died during the harsh Minnesota winters. If the weather didn't get them, disease did the trick."

His half-joking tone wasn't really meant to be funny. She let him rifle around in a few other boxes as she spent more time looking at the family photos. Something about the one with Jan at five months niggled. She stared at it, and then put it aside to search though a box of cufflinks and old watches.

"That's it!" Her excited shout almost caused Teun to break a set of crystal glasses he'd uncovered. He laid them down carefully and came to her side as she brandished the photo. "Something niggled about this, and looking at your dad's old watches clinched it."

The way he stared she knew she made no sense. She cleared a space and made him sit beside her at the inspection table. Carefully placing the photo between them, she pointed to his grandmother.

"If you look carefully, Teun, she's not wearing much in the way of jewellery. There's a simple wedding band on her finger." She pointed it out. "No necklace and no earrings of any kind." He agreed with her assessment, his nod solemn… and maybe a little disappointed. "But she is wearing a bangle."

Since Marijke held the baby, the band was almost obscured. They could just see what had the appearance of being a wide bangle.

Keira felt her excitement rise as she gripped Teun's hand, her words not wanting to be wrong. "In Jensen's photo of the three sisters, Martine is wearing that cameo bangle."

"You think this might be the same one?"

She winced, but still wanted to smile her anticipation. His sudden kiss surprised the breath out of her as he whipped her up and whirled her around, whooping along with her screeches. Their euphoria settled though, pretty soon, since all they had was a photograph.

"But at least this might mean the bangle was in your grandmother's house in 1939 – if it was the same one that belonged to Martine. Do you remember what happened to the stuff in your grandparents' house when they died?"

He whirled her around again and gave her another smacking kiss, regardless of who might be watching them. He might not fully trust her, yet he continued to exude an undeniable attraction.

"Yes, I do, you budding Sherlock! My Aunt Marta lived in the family home till she married, after which she and her husband, Adam Blakeney, stayed put in my grandmother's house. By then my grandfather had died and, since it was a big house, it was convenient for Aunt Marta to carry on living there."

Keira liked his update but wanted to clarify what revved his motor so much.

"I'm sorry to say my Aunt Marta died about three years ago, of cancer. That doesn't make me happy, but the fact her husband still lives in the same house does."

"You're hoping there might still be some clues there?"

"Yeah! My uncle's a great old guy, but he's not what you'd call a particular favourite of tidying the place. It might mean he's also not thrown out much over the years."

She chuckled at the face he pulled. "Yes, but not to burst your bubble, it might mean more of the needle in the haystack."

Teun decided to take his father's photos and get copies made of them at a local store. He'd found the old letters Grace had mentioned and made a pile of them as well, since they'd take some time to read. Each had a pile of paperwork in hand when they left the storage lock-up.

It only occurred to Keira to scan the car park after she noted Teun doing exactly that the minute he stepped outside the building. The facility hadn't been busy inside, and there weren't too many cars in the car park. A sigh of relief escaped when she registered it was devoid of people.

***

Across the road, halfway down the block and tucked up into a short driveway, binoculars were dropped down onto the passenger seat after the camera was detached and reverently pocketed. The car fired up, the engine revving a few times echoing Russ Hitchin's satisfied growls. Only paperwork but it should get him a few more dollars. The trick would be to make sure any paper trails that produced the goods weren't missed. Big dollar denominations flashed past in his imaginary scenario as he pulled out into the road. Piece of cake. Though, when he thought about it, Teun Zeger was acting a bit cautious with all those sneaky looks around him, and trying to give him the slip. Russ knew he'd have to play it cool. Wouldn't do for the mark to wise up to him too soon.

***

It couldn't be helped. The minute Teun drove off, Keira went back to mirror scanning. She didn't know quite how she felt when they got back to the hotel without any sign of a gold car... or that man. Relieved. Definitely that, but she also felt annoyingly obsessed.

Teun left her to catch up with work while he headed off to the photo processing store. On his return, she admired the new copies he'd had made, especially the one of his father at five months in a blown-up version. He sat with his arm around her as they studied the detail again. Cosy and intimate.

"You know that might be an emerald on his finger as well." He drew her attention to his grandfather's pinkie finger.

Jan Zeger, senior, definitely did wear a ring with a stone in it but, since the photo was black and white, there was no way they could tell what colour the gemstone was.

"Are you going to visit your Uncle Adam?" Keira closed down the document she'd been working on and awaited his answer.

"We're visiting him tomorrow, Miss Detective, so hold your patience."

"Going to Rochester? How long will it take?"

"It's more than a two hundred and fifty mile drive, so I thought – with you having to work – it would be easier to fly. But if you'd prefer to drive, we could do that."

She looked at him to see if he was in any way joking. He wasn't. It was so easy for him to produce the funding to fly off at a moment's notice. "And how long do you plan to be there for?"

"No idea."

Keira's work could be done anywhere, so she wasn't complaining. And living out of a suitcase in Duluth was just the same as in Rochester. Teun's work situation presently was not so different.

His Uncle Adam's house – and before that his grandfather's – was large, sprawling over two floors in a leafy suburb of Rochester.

"So, you knew my Marta's Aunt Neela?" Adam Blakeney cackled as he welcomed Keira into his house.

The entry door led straight into a large, wood-floored living room, furniture cluttered all around. It wasn't untidy, as Teun had perhaps suggested; it was more that all the pieces of furniture, apart from the seating, had places to store lots of objects. Memorabilia, of many styles, dotted every surface – on tables, cabinets and shelves. An interesting room, definitely, but more interesting to Keira was that Teun was a very welcome visitor in his uncle's house. When their quest was explained, Adam readily assented to them rummaging around.

"I've a woman who comes in to clean for me, so the place isn't too dusty, but there's a ton of stuff here that's been around the house forever. I'd help you look but my breathing isn't up to much these days for getting up and down the stairs."

Keira learned Adam hadn't been upstairs in years, not since his wife died, after which he'd moved into the downstairs bedroom. Arthritis had seeped into his joints; moving around was a torture.

116

"Start anytime you like." Adam's invitation encouraged them to get going immediately.

"Not till after lunch, Uncle Adam. Get your coat. We're going to that favourite place of yours, since Keira likes to eat local. Let's go see what she thinks of your taste." Keira knew Teun was keen to launch in, but liked him all the more when he insisted.

Lunch was good. So was the place. Homely, full of character and noisy, described it to a T. She praised its merits around a mouthful of the best burger, realising why Adam liked coming. More of a pub than a diner, it was filled with lots of the older man's cronies who stopped by their table to get reacquainted with Teun… and to meet her. Chatty and friendly, it was clear Teun was very familiar. He hadn't told her how often he visited his uncle, but she guessed his visits must be reasonably frequent.

On her way back to their table, after popping out to the ladies room, Keira shook her head to clear her vision. Near the doorway of the pub sat a man with his nose almost buried in a newspaper, hair almost buried under a ball cap. A quick glance in her direction confirmed her suspicions.

Him again! But they were in Rochester? Not Duluth. They had to leave. Immediately.

Definitely paranoid. That was what she was. They were now hundreds of miles from Duluth. What was with these men following them? Teun had no idea what her weird mumbling was about as he paid their tab.

She couldn't mirror-watch as they drove to Adam's house, because she sat in the rear of the car, but she did turn round a few times. It was a great relief when they reached the house without her seeing any vehicle which might be tailing them, though the traffic had been heavy, and something could have been missed. She now wanted to share her suspicions with Teun but, since he was chatting away happily to Adam, she didn't want to spoil his enjoyment.

The old guy declared a nap was in order, his three beers having caught up with him. "Pay no mind to me, Teun. Even an earthquake is unlikely to disturb me when I'm sleeping, so you just rake around as you need to."

Teun stared when she suggested the kitchen first.

"My mother kept her rings in a little dish in one of the kitchen cabinets. She claimed it was easier to remember where she'd put them when she stripped them off to do the dishes, or rough cleaning of any kind."

Some fruitless hours later, they sat down with Adam in the living room, the older man having shuffled in a tray loaded with coffee and little cakes he claimed his housekeeper forced upon him. As he munched into the coconut delight, a blissful look spreading across his worn face, Keira laughed at how much obligation had been necessary.

"Don't remember anything, Teun." Adam's head shakes confirmed his belief that his wife had never mentioned any genuine jewels in the house. "We'd no doubt have sold them years ago. Money was real tight at times." After a slight pause, Adam continued his focus on Teun. "Don't suppose you remember much about your grandmother?"

Teun's grin sneaked out and had Keira wondering what caused it.

"I remember some things, though not details like picturing her wearing jewellery."

"Marijke Zeger was a real case, Keira. She didn't allow any kind of nonsense: wasn't averse to lifting her hand and clipping them boys across the ears." Adam's chuckle was echoed by Teun.

"Then she and Neela were very alike. Neela didn't hold truck with nonsense either. She was kind, but firm as well."

Adam continued musing as he blew on his too hot coffee. "Marijke hoarded everything. Most of the damned paraphernalia all over this house belonged to her. Can't junk it though, it meant such a lot to her, and then to my Marta after

118

Marijke was gone. Whole upper floor is covered too, at least used to be. Since I've not ventured up there, I can only assume."

"I don't remember Grandma with anything other than a wedding band on her finger, but I do remember Aunt Marta used to wear a stunning ring." Teun's gaze swung from Adam towards her. His intent stare made her hot with embarrassment since it was so keen, but also because there was sexual heat there he didn't even attempt to hide. "Aunt Marta's ring was the exact shade of Keira's eyes." She was glad when their intense contact was broken, Teun shifting around to look at Adam. "I once asked her what the stone was. She caressed the brown facets and told me in a hushed whisper it was an Imperial topaz."

Adam's guffaw drew her attention. "I'd forgotten about that thing! That was a great big joke, Keira." Adam's gnarled fingers slapped his leg in glee. He was almost doubled over with laughter when his teary eyes came back to her. "I guess you were taken in as well, Teun. So was your cousin, John."

It took a few moments for Adam to sober up. "Told you Marijke was a real case, didn't I?"

Keira didn't know whether to laugh along with him or not, though she wanted to; his mirth was so appealing. She definitely liked Teun's uncle.

"Your grandmother was a practical joker, always finding ways of keeping you and John amused. You remember that?"

Teun's eyes widened as though suddenly remembering things. "Yeah, I do. She used to teach us card tricks!" He, too, laughed heartily. "No cheating though, just stuff for a good giggle. And she knew some really good jokes she'd tell over and over."

Keira was thinking Adam's legs must be sore by now from all his slapping, since he'd become really animated.

"Used to make lots of jokey stuff, too. She once put loads of salt in a fruitcake – on purpose, mind – to teach you lads not to steal her cake without asking first. It sure worked; John never tried it again!"

Teun obviously remembered that too, his grin unabashed. "I learned my lesson as well."

"But that ring thing?" Adam scratched his prickly jaw, the twinkling in his eyes Keira guessed was a precursor to something good. "Marijke used to decorate the Thanksgiving table. She'd make little gifts for everybody and put them down as place markers. Inside her little boxes, or scrolls, or little fuzzy embroidered turkeys, would be a tiny toy or something funny."

Teun moved nearer to Adam. "Was I at these Thanksgivings before Mom took me to California?"

"You were, son. You lived just a couple of streets away till you were six, and you were here every Thanksgiving. Marijke always split you boys up at the table. Claimed her heart would never stand your tomfoolery if you were sitting alongside each other."

Keira felt Adam's full attention on her. "A real pair of mischief-makers those boys were." Adam turned back to Teun, his mood more sombre. "That brown ring came from one of your grandmother's Thanksgiving gifts. She'd got it free in a cereal box, but Marta loved it anyway."

Teun looked marginally disappointed in the news. "Do you think it's still upstairs in the bedroom she used, Uncle Adam?"

"Could be, Teun, but I don't remember seeing it for years."

A thorough search of Marta's room revealed lots of jewellery in small cardboard cartons. Keira could tell she was a woman who'd bought to colour match, and kept in current style with her clothes, but they found nothing of any value. On the dresser, though, was a more formal, leather-covered jewellery case. She handed it to Teun for opening, feeling confident the best of Marta's jewellery would be inside.

"This must be her wedding band." Teun took the gold ring out and carefully set it down as he revealed other bits and pieces. "Do you think this is made of gold?" He laid down a watch beside the ring.

"It's maybe gold-plated, but it looks quite modern. I think it's a bit like the style my mother wore in the nineteen seventies."

There were a few pairs of earrings which looked like gold, but were very simple little studs. Having had their little foray into the world of jewellery in Heidelberg, they discounted all the items they found, sure none of them belonged to the Tiru collection. They'd exhausted all of the little boxes on Marta's dresser except one. A loud sigh of satisfaction cheered her when he pulled a ring out of a twisted mess of broken chains.

"That's the cereal box ring?"

Teun turned to her, his eyes misted. "The very one."

She was embarrassed when he held it up to her eyes. His other hand curved at her cheek as he brought her close. The kiss he gave her was reverent and tender. His voice was a gruff, broken husk when he released her and showed her the ring. "Aunt Marta used to get the pair of us on her knees, and would whisper something…"

He was trying so hard to remember – she was confused about the cousin called John, and made a mental note to ask about him later – but now was not the time to break Teun's train of thought.

"She'd say something like… wish upon this ring, boys, and your lives will take flight. I remember being embarrassed, since I must have been around five, or maybe even six. But I never understood what she meant. John and I would disappear into a corner and laugh about it because he thought his mother too sentimental."

Keira stared at the ring. Dulled with age and dirt, it was still a classy ring; the stone large and flanked by a circle of tiny, little, look-alike diamonds.

Teun pocketed the ring very carefully before they moved on. She laughed at his theatrical groan as they closed the last bedroom door. "I've been dreading this but there's a huge loft area extending the whole width of the house."

"Tomorrow?" She was hopeful Teun would agree to a postponement, as the afternoon had flown and they'd not yet had dinner. "I really need to get some work done tonight, Teun."

He needed to check in at his San Francisco lab as well.

"Great pizza deliveries from this place!" Adam declared, flourishing a brochure when they went down to the kitchen. "Delivery is quick, and they taste good."

Since they were staying at Adam's house, it was a great solution. Keira spread her laptop at one end of the dining table, Teun at the other. Adam was happy to sandwich in between them long enough to eat some pizza then declare he was off to watch his TV shows. Before he disappeared, Teun asked if he could keep Marta's cereal box ring.

"Keep anything you like, son." Adam's declaration was firm. "If you find anything you want, call it yours. Apart from my fishing gear and my architecture books, everything else likely belonged to Marta – and, before her, to Marijke. And in my mind, that means it now belongs to you for there's no-one better to get it."

Keira felt really fuzzy when Teun reached for his Uncle Adam and drew him into a huge bear hug, slapped the old guy gently on the back, and continued to hold him. Maybe it wasn't the manliest thing to do, but she could tell genuine affection bound them together.

Well after midnight, she rubbed her neck. "That's enough for tonight. I'm done in, Teun. So long as I can do about the same tomorrow night, I can search with you during the day."

Two rooms had been prepared by Adam's housekeeper, though they only used the one. Adam had long gone to bed and wasn't going to be fussed over which rooms they used anyway.

Chapter Seven

Clutter abounded.

Cartons and old furniture littered the loft, dotted around in piles as though added to the storage area at strategic times.

"I remember coming up here to play with my cousin, John."

Keira's indrawn breath drew Teun's puzzled glance, but he ploughed on after she shook her head, unwilling for him to stop talking. Again.

"We were both about ten; found this a fantastic place to play. I remember particularly the day after my grandmother's funeral. I'd come here with my dad. John and I came up to the loft to be away from the adults."

She put her question tentatively. "I'm sorry. I'm confused here. Your dad said your cousins died, but last night Adam was talking about John, as well as you."

"John was the only one of Aunt Marta's boys who got past childhood. He died out in Afghanistan. Couldn't wait to get out of Rochester and join the military. He lived through his first tour, but not his second."

No amount of sorry would compensate, so she took his hand and listened.

"I had to go back to California the day after Grandma's funeral, and I remember us sitting down just there." He broke off to point to an old chest. "I'd missed playing with him so much. He'd been my best buddy before I was dragged off by my mother."

She squeezed his hand, led him to the very same chest and

parked down beside him. Lots of memories surfaced. Mostly about escapades he and John had been involved in, and about them as teens.

"I was about fourteen when Dad married Grace. He'd moved to Duluth just before that, but when I came across the continent, on my summer vacation, he always brought me south, to Rochester, to visit with John."

She kept her voice soft so as not to break the mood. "I'm guessing you and John continued to be friends?"

His thumb caressed her palm, his arm a gentle nudge. "We called each other as often as we could. Calls across country were pretty expensive, but we saw each other in the flesh at least once a year. So, I guess, we were still best friends. Our last meeting was around a month before he died. He hadn't been on home leave for ages."

She squeezed his fingers, and then wrapped her arm across his shoulder. Sympathy she could give, but it could never bring John back.

The mood was broken.

Investigating the loft took hours. Piled boxes joined others as they painstakingly opened and closed the next one. Keira worked her way through a large crate which must have belonged to John. It was filled with family board games, jigsaws, painting equipment and old tin boxes. Inside the tins, John had stored worn and dented, miniature metal cars, and trains from a long-gone train set.

"Did you have a car collection, too?" Her sudden question shattered the silence as she held one of them up for him to see.

Teun came over to the corner she worked in, his laughter a delighted sound she was glad to hear again. "Yeah! I traded with him when we were little squirts. What else have you got there?"

They took turns to excavate the huge carton, Teun chuckling away as he unearthed something memorable. Keira pulled out yet another old cookie tin. She prized open the tight lid and shrieked.

"Teun!"

Inside the tin were two long velvet cases.

"You open them!"

His smile was puzzled since she'd been quite happy to do all the investigating before, without any reference to him.

"What is it?" His words faded as he opened the first – a dark crimson velvet box, the plush so stained with dampness it almost looked white. Most of the loft contents were still in good condition, but this looked to be one of the oldest items they'd uncovered so far.

Keira's legs trembled. A cool shiver coursed down her spine, the anticipation making the unveiling seem almost creepy.

His voice was a broken hush. "Is this what I think it is?"

"Good God! Look at that!"

Four strands, made from tiny green stones, joined the most exquisite centrepiece clasp of diamonds, the whole necklace gleaming on the faded cream silk interior. At each end of the box lay two different earrings. All the earrings were pear-shaped; one set made from small sparkling bezel-set diamonds, and the other vibrantly coloured. In place of diamonds, the second pair of earrings was enamelled in red, green and blue on a white background. Teun almost dropped the box as he passed it over for her to have a better look, his arm trembling.

"Oh… shit! I can't believe it!"

Keira was in shock. It was the most intriguing jewellery she'd ever seen, but she was mystified by the extra coloured set of earrings. Although totally gorgeous in themselves, they didn't match the floral cluster of sparkling diamonds. Tentatively lifting the necklace, she realised the significance of two sets of earrings. The whole necklace was double-sided. It could be worn showing a deep centre clasp which was a sunburst of small diamonds, with two additional rows of tiny diamonds set below – and in the ultimate central position was a teardrop pendant of three layers of tiny diamonds. If the necklace was worn in reverse, there lay a masterpiece of red, green, blue and white enamelling.

"This is so amazing! And it looks Indian." Her throat was raspy, her words the tiniest whisper.

They dragged themselves back to the chest and fumbled their way back down onto it, the velvet case in front of them, neither capable of speaking.

She caught Teun's glance. His swallow had been so awkward, a metaphorical boulder lodged in his gullet. Awe. Amazement. Shock. Trepidation. They were all there in his eyes as words eventually seeped out.

"I didn't expect this, Keira. How could my grandmother have hidden these away like this?"

She wasn't sure an answer was needed, but she gave one anyway. "Marijke must have had her reasons for keeping them secret, Teun."

"Secrets? Damn right she had secrets!"

He slowly placed the box down on the floor, and then whipped back up again. His lips on hers were a surprise, his grasp of her shoulders not so light. The kiss lingered and deepened before she realised it wasn't a kiss of exultation, or even happiness. Breaking away from him, she forced eye contact. "What are you not saying here, Teun?"

"You have no idea how this family sometimes struggled for money. Grandfather died before John and his brothers were born, and Uncle Adam was sometimes out of work. My father sent money to Aunt Marta to keep them afloat, since she also looked after my grandmother."

Teun got up and paced between the cartons and furniture which was scattered nearby, his hand rifling through his short hair.

"Don't mistake me. Uncle Adam was never work-shy. He worked in the construction industry, so employment was erratic. Mostly he had contracts, but there were often lulls between those contracts when he had no pay. That's when Dad would help them."

"Do you think maybe, by then, your grandmother had forgotten about the emeralds?" It sounded a bit of a stretch, but his agitation was so great she wanted to soothe him.

"Never. Grandma was sharp as a tack! She forgot nothing."

"Then there must have been another reason."

He grasped her hand and dragged her back to the carton holding John's things. "You open it this time!"

The second box was a similar shape. As she prised open the lid, a loose white bead leapt out and skittered across the wooden floor. She let the stiff lid close again before placing it carefully on the floor. Down on her knees, she opened the box a second time. Very slowly.

Inside was a pile of white, round balls. Not plastic beads as she had first thought when the first had popped out, but pearls. Three strands of thin, hairy thread were strung with a few of the pearls, the rest lying loose. As in the previous necklace, it looked as if the clasp was intended to be worn at the throat, and not at the nape, for it was a work of art in itself. In the centre of the pear-shaped design was a sizable emerald and around it sat rows of tiny diamonds, all set in what looked to be heavy gold. The scrollwork of the clasp alone was enthralling.

"Bloody hell! Would you look at that?" Keira's voice was barely a whisper through the tears freely flowing from her astonished eyes.

Sliding to the loft floor, her knees were unable to support her as she scrabbled for the pearl that had rolled away. Teun dropped down alongside her, trailing his fingertips through the ripple of pearls. "Not only an emerald necklace, but this as well?"

Down in the kitchen, they looked at the jewels with Adam. Teun had been careful to prepare the old guy, in case the sight was too much for his fragile health. To Teun's surprise, and her total admiration, Adam burst into chuckles and found it hard to stop. Teun immediately held Adam's shoulders, fearing his uncle was in trouble.

"I'm fine, son," Adam managed, as he waved his nephew away. Only after she'd handed him a tissue to wipe the happy tears did Adam's heaving shoulders settle. He looked at them both, drawing in as big a breath as his lungs would allow. "That is so like Marijke! There was never such a big joker as that woman."

The next stage, of course, would be to authenticate the emeralds and pearls, since they were convinced they were from the Tiru collection. The velvet boxes were taken through to occupy the centre spot on the dining room table.

She imagined Teun felt just as stunned as she did when they returned to the loft, since they'd not yet opened all the boxes.

"I guess we should be focusing on any paperwork?"

They'd been careful with any found so far and had set aside some old letters to read later, but she agreed a more thorough perusal was necessary during their next searches.

The letters were the only things they took downstairs with them when they'd searched everything. Nothing else seemed relevant. And they'd found no further jewellery. Keira wasn't sure she'd have coped if they had found more.

After a delivery of Mexican food had been devoured, they again set out their work stations, Adam having gone off to his den to catch up with his computer games. He'd already confessed to being both a TV addict and a computer games silver surfer.

A few hours later, Keira needed a break from her work. Teun had long abandoned his laptop and had been engaged in telephone conversations for the last long ages with his staff. Struggling up from the table, she worked the kinks out of her weary shoulder muscles.

"What's on the plan tomorrow?" Her question was mumbled as she plopped down beside him on the couch, seeing he'd just closed his mobile phone.

"I thought we could read those letters tonight. The ones we found upstairs, and those from Dad's place, before we make any decisions."

He looked tired but hopeful she'd agree to his plan.

"A cup of coffee first, maybe? To keep us awake?"

Back in double quick time, he carried a tray of coffee and some biscuits he'd unearthed from a cupboard.

A pile of letters from the loft landed with a soft plop in her lap, while Teun tackled the smaller pile from his dad's stored possessions.

It struck her as being an infringement of privacy to read letters sent to Marta, but Teun decided it was necessary. The first few were from friends: nothing in them about jewellery, or any historical references.

A small pile of carefully folded papers lay on her lap, tied with a faded pink ribbon. Reverently untying the bow, she opened the first one. It wasn't in English. She wasn't familiar with the dialect and reread the first paragraph again before it clicked she wasn't reading German. Of course! It was written in Dutch. Confirmation came when the sender's name was revealed. She just as carefully undid the rest of the pile and laid them flat on her knee: all from the same sender.

Martine!

"Teun!" She nudged him with her knee. "This pile is to Marijke from her mother, Martine." As up in the loft, she couldn't contain her excitement. Surely the letters had to have significant information?

He shifted beside her and lifted the first one, saying nothing till after he'd scanned it. Disappointment wafted from him. "I can read the Martine at the bottom, but nothing else."

Keira absorbed his silent question as his grey eyes deepened, his brows a tight frown.

"I can make a reasonable guess at some of it, but I'd much rather it was properly translated by someone who is Dutch. "

"We can do it later." Teun's voice was clipped. "Let's see what you can come up with first. Are you willing to try?"

They sat in front of Keira's laptop, all six letters smoothed flat. In no time at all she'd downloaded a Dutch dictionary. She then made sure the letters were read in date order of earliest first; thinking that if it was her mother who wrote to her, the first letters would be about more practical things – like settling into a new home in a new country.

That was exactly what Martine's first three letters were like, the letters over a period of three months during 1934. It was a multiplicity of questions which Keira was able to translate; reflections of day-to-day living. Both she and Teun found Martine's writing style amusing as she translated, written Dutch much easier for her to read than she had expected, many words being similar enough to German though the grammatical structure was not alike. In the letters, Martine asked Marijke lots of questions, but also posed what appeared like enquiries about her own exploits. She'd written things like… *I suppose you'll not guess who I met at the Opera last week.* Whether Marijke had been interested or not, the answer followed in a flowing style.

"Look, Teun!" She almost jabbed her finger through the fragile paper. "Martine's talking about Neela bringing Gabriel Henke to their house."

"Don't keep it a secret." He looked amused since she was all but hopping up and down on her chair. "Read it to me."

"Give me a minute." She mumbled at first, focusing on the meaning of a phrase she'd no clue of. A few clicks later, she turned to him. She couldn't stop grinning. "I think she says something like…. *Neela brought this little know-all of a man home and introduced him to us. Marijke? You can have no idea of the dread in my stomach. He clearly adores our Neela, but he's the funniest looking little man. His smile is constantly like the child who has won the only treat from Sinterklaas.*"

"Who?" Teun nudged her to get an answer, since she was

laughing her head off.

"St. Nicholas. Were you never told about *Sinterklaas* coming to little kids on the 5th December and giving the children gifts; sort of early Christmas presents?"

He struggled with an elusive memory. "Grandma told us lots of things. I don't remember anything about this *Sinterklaas* guy, but she did say her Dutch traditions didn't always fit well in Minnesota."

She clapped him on the shoulder in commiseration, her chuckle whispering at his ear. "Ah well, that's maybe because *Sinterklaas* comes up to Holland by boat from Spain, with all his booty in his sack... so maybe your grandmother thought coming across the Atlantic was just a bit too much, too far-fetched? And perhaps it's why she embraced American traditions like Thanksgiving, which is quite close to *Sinterklaas* Day."

They continued with the letter, Teun interrupting occasionally for clarification. "Was Gabriel a weird looking guy?"

"No, he wasn't. He was a very dapper little man. Around five feet seven, or so? I only knew him when he was in his seventies, but he smiled a lot. Quite a funny character. His English wasn't as good as Neela's, so he always made her translate for him."

Keira continued to decipher Martine's droll updates, wondering if Teun's sense of humour had been passed all the way down the DNA line from Martine.

The next letter, the fourth, was full of references to the Holland of the day. Dated 1936, the tone of the letter was not at all chatty, or anecdotal. It stiltedly updated Marijke on family news, but references to the political events in Europe dominated it. Keira interpreted Martine worried about her sister Uriel, who bemoaned living in Dresden.

"Martine writes here Uriel has told her... em... I think she's saying... *letters between us might not happen so often. Uriel's not happy about the area of Dresden where they live, but they can't move since Leopold's clothing business isn't doing so well at present."*

Teun slid closer to the paper even though he was unable to translate himself. She let her finger slip over the next words to show him where she read from, not surprised when his fingers covered her own, as what they were reading was charged with a dangerous tension.

"...I'm very glad you got all the way out of Europe and you're safe in the USA. I fear for the safety of Uriel, and her four children." She stopped and looked around at him. "Did you know Uriel had four children?"

Teun shook his head. "I didn't know anything about her at all till Jensen got us together."

Keira cleared her throat before resuming her reading. "Okay. Martine's writing...*young Anna has just recently got married to Sebastian Otten.*" She stopped reading for a moment to look at his face.

"Did you have a great-aunt Anna, Teun?"

The shaking of his head prompted her to reach for a blank piece of paper.

"I'm confused here. I think before we read any more, we need to make a family tree for you, then if I come across bits that don't make sense in the letters, tracing them on the tree might make it easier to understand."

Teun readily agreed. "Yeah. Especially with all the repeated and almost repeated names."

"Who do you mean?"

His playful nudge had her chuckling. "Well, there's my father, Jan, and his father, Jan, for a start. Not to mention that Martine called her daughter Marijke. Then Marijke goes and calls her daughter Marta. Isn't that similar enough to confuse you?"

Full blown laughter ensued before she answered. "You obviously haven't seen just how much more difficult it is in

132

prolific families with lots of members living in each generation. The names were used and re-used and re-used again. If not as first names, they became middle names!"

They soon had a basic tree sketched out, with the people added they knew about so far. Down Martine's line were Teun's grandmother, Marijke, and her sister Neela. Uriel and Tanja's lines had only the basic information Jensen had given them.

She went back to Marijke's letter from Martine, knowing she must have mistaken something, and a thorough re-reading proved she had. "Okay, I'm backtracking a bit here. This makes more sense. What Martine has written is ...*Uriel's daughter, Anna, has got married to Sebastian Otten and Anna and Sebastian have moved to another part of Dresden so Uriel doesn't see them so often.*"

The next two letters alarmed even more. Dated early 1939, she translated Martine's deepest fears that war was inevitable in Europe. The doom and gloom was unmistakable.

"Oh, this is really sad, Teun. She's written that Uriel's youngest daughter, Ludi, has died of..." She broke off to do a quick search. "Oh. Tuberculosis. She was only seventeen. And Anna has already miscarried two babies."

Reading the last letter was incredibly difficult. Again, Martine had written of her relief Marijke was far away and out of Europe. ...*Neela and Gabriel got married in March, and are living in Den Haag.*

"Oh, listen to this bit, Teun!" She perked up from reading the sad parts and pointed to the family tree. "Get your pencil going again! Martine writes here ...*Neela's husband Gabriel has got a job at my cousin Ralf's clothes shop in Den Haag. It's not Gabriel's trade, since he's a master carpenter, but it's good he's got a job at all since lots of people are...*" She quickly typed in the word and got its translation. "...*unemployed.*"

"The cousin Ralf she's talking about must be Zaan's grandfather." He tapped his pencil at Tanja's line. She found her head leaning on his as they worked their way down each family line from Geertje Tiedman. "Has to be Zaan's line."

She agreed.

"Neela nursed in Woerden during the war. She'd worked in the hospital there for decades and only stopped for a little while when her daughter, Ineke, and son, Jan, were born." He added two more names to the family tree.

"Did Neela speak of any more children?"

She nodded. "They had at least one more during the war years I know of." She bit off a ragged nail as she thought about Teun's question. "Neela said Ineke was born a year after World War Two started, and Jan the year the war ended. There had been another birth in between, but the child only lived a couple of days. I remember being very sad when she spoke of it. I was about 12 and could understand, up to a point. She said she was glad the baby didn't need to starve like Ineke."

"I've read the war years in Holland were horrendous." Teun took her hand and squeezed her fingers, his warmth radiating sympathy.

"I'm remembering something else, too. She said she hardly saw Ineke for four years during the war, since she sent her to Gabriel's parents' house. They lived in the country somewhere, on a small farm, and Neela said they were better fixed to feed a growing child."

"What's Ineke like?"

She rubbed the back of his strong hand, lifting up the fine hairs and smoothing them down again. "I've met Ineke quite a few times over the years, but I actually don't know her at all. She always seems an unhappy person compared to Neela, who was always so positive. Both of Ineke's daughters, Anna and Marijke, are older than me by more than a decade."

The look on his face was comical as he squirmed beside her. "Anna and Marijke?"

She sighed. "Yep! I know. Same family first names used."

Teun wrapped his arm around her and drew her close to his

family tree sketch. Tapping it with his pencil, he joked, "So we call them Anna 1 and 2 and Marijke 1 and 2?"

She shook her head. "Not going to work. We'll probably find more Annas and Marijkes and get totally confused. Ineke's husband is Pieter Vosters. So put their Anna and Marijke down with Vosters as well. Except, they've both been married, so I guess that's another addition on the tree." His pained expression made her laugh.

"Just use the Vosters surname for them."

The names added for Uriel's line were pitifully few. Jensen had only given them the names of Uriel's husband, Leopold Rauch, and their daughter, Anna – though he'd said there had been a number of other children born to the Rauchs.

"Anna married Sebastian Otten, and their offspring – the only one we know of – is Henny. She married Arjen Lischka and they only had one child, Romy. Romy Lischka, who is currently hospitalised."

It was just as well the letters revealed no more family members since she felt they had enough names to contend with at that time.

Before they'd tackled the Dutch letters, Teun hadn't found anything in particular in his dad's correspondence. He picked up the last few papers he hadn't covered. At least his letters were all in English. Burrowing into Teun's side, they scanned them quickly.

"What does that mean?" She looked straight into his bemused eyes.

Jan Zeger had received the letter from his second wife, Paula. The date was 1991, when Teun was 11, and divorce proceedings between his father and Paula were almost finalised. The woman had written about a visit she'd made to Marijke, after she'd split up with Jan.

Teun's reaction was dismissive, his explanation resentful. "Paula was a bitch of the first order. Money driven, she married my dad thinking he was a good bet. Turned out, he wasn't. The harpy probably earned more than my dad back then. He was an insurance agent here in Rochester, but her job as medical secretary to a consultant at the Mayo Clinic earned her a reasonable salary."

The words Paula had written were vicious. "*You're such a loser, Jan Zeger. You think your mother, Marijke, is a good joker? Well, the joke really is on you. That rambling old harridan laughed at me, and told me there was no way she was going to have her legacy pass onto the likes of me – even if my skinny frame did resemble the coldest harlot in history.*"

Keira stopped reading to see how Teun absorbed the sadistic tirade. From the glitter in his eyes, she guessed no love had been lost between him and Paula. She continued on to the even more confusing bit. "*Though it seems, from your stupid mother, the coldest harlot has an eternal place on a chunk of the finest gold.*" The diatribe ended with Paula quoting a huge sum she expected Jan to pay, since he had a fortune at his fingertips if he would just get off his ass and find it!

Teun's grip around her tightened even more as she sat stunned by what she'd just read, unable to prevent the wobble in her voice. "Did your dad have to pay her a fortune to get rid of her?"

"He paid what the court asked him to, which wasn't a whole lot, since his assets didn't run to much. He still gave my mother alimony, covering expenses for me, at that time."

It was nosey but she asked anyway. "Did Paula leave your dad alone after that?"

A tickle was her reward as Teun snuggled her closer. "She married her boss immediately after the divorce. Don't know, and don't care, what has happened to her."

They sat in reflective silence for a minute or two before Teun voiced what she'd just worked out. "Could she have been talking about something of Martine's?"

Wriggling out of Teun's arms, she ferreted around to find her photocopy of the trio of sisters Jensen had given her.

"Could she mean Martine's cameo bracelet?"

Teun pulled out the small magnifier he still had from the visit to Jensen's office. As he used it, she remembered Jensen and Zaan talking about the cameo probably being carved from ivory. When he handed her the magnifier, it was easier to see the details but rather than being a woman's face, it was a stylized dancer of Indian design.

Puzzlement clouded his features. "Dad told us his mother had given a wide golden bangle to Marta for a wedding gift. Maybe it's still here in the house?"

That was confusing since they'd looked everywhere already and hadn't found a bangle like it; though Marijke had been wearing something probably similar in the 1939 photograph. She didn't feel up to starting all over again, yet suggested it anyway.

Teun declined with a tickle at her ribs, followed by more than a peck at her lips. "Not tonight. Definitely not tonight. We've still got two letters of Dad's to look at, and I'm liking that thought a whole lot better than going back up to the loft."

The next missive had been from Teun's mum, updating Jan about the decisions made over Teun's schooling. He put it carefully to one side and picked up the last of the pile. Dated about four years previously, it had come from Marta. Keira again snuggled up close to him as they read it.

"This was written about a month before Marta died."

Marta's words were pragmatic, saying she was sorting out her affairs and had something to return to her brother.

Teun tensed up beside her: Keira felt very strung-out, too, as she scanned. ...*I'm sending on a box to you, Jan. It contains a family heirloom which should have gone to my daughter, except I've never been blessed with one. I've no daughter-in-law either, so I'm sending the treasure back to you since Teun might find a nice bride to give it to...* Teun's shudders rippled onto Keira's arm; she guessed they were reading the same bit. ...*I've sent the box by courier and it should arrive the day after you receive this letter...* The last bit of the letter was another tear-jerker. ... *There maybe should have been a nice necklace and earrings in the box as well, Jan. But you know what our dear mother was like. She told me she hid a box containing Martine's necklace somewhere in the loft, since she didn't want any of your wives to get their hands on it. I looked for it after she died, but I never found anything, so I guess the story was just another of her jokes...*

"No, Aunt Marta." Teun's voice was hushed. "It was no joke at all."

Keira felt his fingers grope for hers. Drawing her close again, he rested his chin on her head as she cuddled in. "We've got the emeralds and pearls, but it appears Dad got the bangle. Is that what you're thinking?"

A few minutes later, Teun pulled her to her feet.

"Let's see if Adam's still awake."

They updated Uncle Adam, who guffawed dangerously again, but apart from being short of breath he was highly amused by the developments. He renewed his insistence anything they uncovered belonged to Teun. What did he need precious jewels for? Or even a whole lot of cash? Money wasn't going to stop old age from creeping up on him, or make his lungs work better. Sure, he could spend a fortune in dollars getting plastic hips but then, he said, he'd need new knees and elbows. And don't forget the fingers. He didn't fancy being an android. He finished off by saying he wasn't even looking for a young chick. His Marta had been all he'd ever wanted.

Keira really liked him even more when he continued in the same vein. "Even if I had a real stash of dollars, son, they only play for plastic matchsticks at my seniors' centre. And it's where I'm due to be tomorrow, by the way. It's my poker day."

Not wanting to dim the euphoria of having found the emerald necklace set and the pearls, and the potential of locating Martine's bracelet, she made a tentative suggestion. "Do you think we should update Jensen? Or Zaan?"

Teun's quick reply was a surprise. "Sure thing. We can do it tonight, but we need to be careful about this, Keira. We've got jewels in those velvet cases. We think they belonged to Martine, but do we know they're real? What if, at sometime over the years, the real ones have been substituted already, and what we have are just very good paste copies? If we tell Jensen just now, he might be a very disappointed man if they're fakes."

She hadn't considered that. She wondered if Teun was actually being nice to Jensen for a change, though somehow thought there had to be more to his intentions. Trust didn't seem a possibility – yet.

"I could go to a Rochester jeweller, but I'd prefer to get them valued in New York. If they're authentic, and we use one of the big name jewellers, it might make it easier when it comes time to add them to the collection. And, if they're as valuable as we hope, they can be safely stored in New York. "

She couldn't fault his reasoning. Big decision time. Go straight to New York and get the emeralds and pearls checked out? Or go to Duluth, where there was a chance Teun's father might remember more about the bangle?

"No. That's not why I want them close by, Teun Zeger!" She fended off Teun's playful chasing as they readied for bed, but made a process of setting the jewellery cases on the nightstand at the side of the bed Teun had occupied the night before. "I'm not coveting these jewels at all, but you need to make a decision on them."

During the night Keira woke, though had no idea what had disturbed her. Teun wasn't in the bed beside her and didn't seem to be in the en suite bathroom either, since the door was open and the light was off. The door to the corridor was open, however, and dim light from the hallway window gave a soft moonlit illumination. As silently as she could, she rose from the bed, yanked on the panties and top lying discarded on the floor, and then tip-toed out into the corridor.

Ignoring the squeaks from loose floorboards, she made her way along to the staircase. There was the faintest sound coming from downstairs, as if someone closed a door down below her. What was Teun doing? The jewels? Was he doing something downstairs with them? Retracing her steps, she scurried back to Teun's side of the bed. Feeling her way across the surface of the nightstand, she located the velvet boxes. For some strange reason a sigh of relief escaped her. Whatever he was doing didn't include the jewels; she knew that, having made sure the jewellery was still inside both boxes, and no stray pearls having dropped on the floor.

Adam? Was it Adam who was unwell and she'd not heard him? Guilt made her embarrassed as she crept back out of the bedroom. How mercenary she'd been thinking of the jewellery before Adam's welfare. Speeding her way down the stairs, the breath whooshed out of her as her foot left the bottom step. A muffled whimper was all she managed as someone tackled her to the floor, before a heavy body pinned her down. What the hell was happening? Face bent onto wooden floorboards, she struggled her way free, kicking her legs wildly. Before she could cry out, a hand cuffed her mouth.

"What are you doing?" Teun whispered in her ear, his arms tightly clasping her, though he did take his hand away from her mouth. He rolled over with her now on top of him, prostrate, his chest heaving into her back, his arms now a protective clutch. His breathing was so loud at her ear, it deafened.

"Teun?"

"What the hell are you doing, Keira?"

"What am I doing?" She forgot to whisper. His hand clamped her mouth again, but not so forcibly.

"Shhh..."

She felt like a punch bag, but realised immediately Teun had thought she was someone else.

"Is Adam okay?"

Instead of answering, he rolled again, immediately releasing her. Jumping up, he put a finger to his lips, reached down and yanked her upright. Hand clamped to her elbow he towed her into the lounge, plonked her down on the settee, and went to the window, where he peeked out from the side of the curtain. There was nothing better designed to alarm her than this sort of behaviour. Creeping over to join him, she stood behind and shivered. Her fingers clenched his boxer shorts, the only clothes he'd pulled on. She murmured in his ear. "You're spooking me out, Teun. What's going on?"

He said nothing at first but led her back to the settee, his arms cradling her as they sat. "It wasn't Adam. I've peeked into his room, and he's fine. There was a noise downstairs, loud enough to wake me up. I came down to see if Adam had got out of bed and had fallen or something."

"Adam's okay?"

"Yeah. I went straight to his room, and he's in there snoring away quite happily."

"What do you think you heard?"

He was silent; thinking deeply in the way she'd already come to know. He seemed to be toying with which words to use, perhaps not to alarm her. "I didn't find anything, but the back door wasn't quite shut."

It hadn't been discussed, she hadn't thought about it since the neighbourhood seemed so nice, but had to ask, "Does Adam usually lock his doors?"

He cuddled her even closer. "I don't even know."

It sounded as though he was blaming himself for being negligent.

"What did you do?"

"No sign of anyone in the kitchen, or the bottom floor, so I went outside into the yard. A cat yowled someplace near, though that was the sum total of any movement – this is a quiet neighbourhood, Keira. I'd just got back in when there

141

was someone on the stairs. But it was you."

He pulled her into a hug. It was caring, arousing, and full of pent-up longing. Yet, most of all, and what she liked best about it, it was proprietorial.

His voice eventually muted into her neck. "I must have hurt you when I wrestled you to the floor."

She was fine. He claimed he didn't believe her, but made sure to check her all over when they went back upstairs... though only after they'd done another search of the downstairs rooms together, and all of the upstairs, including the loft.

Teun wasn't keen to leave Rochester and Adam, but since the old guy had already bailed out to his weekly poker game at the seniors' centre, it was a moot point. Their early walk all around the property hadn't revealed anything untoward. Keira had seen no sign of forced entry into the house, and nothing to prove anyone had lurked outside. Neither of them had the skills to do much in the way of investigating such things, so they'd given up. From their searching around the inside of the house during the previous couple of days, it appeared as though everything was as they'd left it.

Nothing seemed to have been removed, as far as they could tell in a cursory scan.

Teun had tentatively worked security into their talk during the breakfast they'd shared with Adam. What they'd learned hadn't been totally encouraging, but not bad either. A neighbour's cat did have a habit of gaining entry if Adam forgot and left a downstairs window open without screening it. What was clear was that Adam did, customarily, lock his doors. Good news – normally – though it didn't explain why Teun had found it ajar. Still, Keira was relieved to know Teun did nothing, and said nothing, to make the old man feel insecure. To alert the police would alarm Adam unnecessarily, and it was clear Teun wasn't prepared to do that.

They bid Adam goodbye when his lift arrived to ferry him

to his seniors' centre. The bear hug Teun gave the old man was very protective, her own hug one that lingered when Adam stole a cheeky peck at her cheek.

"Now you take good care of this little lady, Teun. She's welcome to visit me anytime." He'd then added for good measure that she could even visit without Teun, if she'd a mind to.

Presently she was keyed up, and she imagined Teun was probably even more so as his fingernails drummed on the armrest of the aeroplane seat when they taxied into a bay for disembarkation at Duluth. To say he was keen to get the issue of the bracelet solved, was an understatement. They'd deliberated carefully that morning over what to do and decided New York should wait till they'd, at least, checked with Jan.

As the unfasten-seat-belt light came on, she breathed more easily, the end of the flight proving to be easier than the beginning. Checking into the flight had been a nerve-wracking experience. The tote she'd carried over her shoulder had unknown value in it. They'd no idea if the jewels were authentic or fake, so Teun had encouraged her to say, if questioned, that her accessories were just paste. She was doing nothing wrong, nothing illegal, since Adam had wholeheartedly given Teun permission to take them.

The old man had, in fact, insisted he sign a hastily drawn up statement that he was giving the jewels to Teun, laughing about the fact he was signing away a fortune! No way did he want to keep them, and if the whole Tiru collection was amassed, he'd jokingly asked – could he have a big name plaque which claimed he was happy to be a philanthropist? He'd always loved the sound of that word.

Keira had nervously checked her side mirror constantly on the way to the airport in Rochester, her tote bag firm in her clutches. She had been glad when they'd arrived at the concourse, there having been no sight of a car following them, or anyone with thick, wavy, auburn hair. Only once when they were standing in the security queue did she look behind and glimpse a dark red head over by the entrance doors, but the figure was too far away to know if it was male or female. Nevertheless, it had made her grip her bag even tighter.

Teun, she was glad to find, was very protective – of her. At least, she thought it was her, but maybe it was just the jewellery he was protecting? Shielding her body everywhere they went, he'd almost glued himself to her back.

The conversation during their flight had been about their success to date, and about what lay around the corner. They'd spoken in hushed whispers, containing their excitement since the authenticity still had to be proved. She was glad of Teun's hand curled around hers as it had kept her nerves at bay. She was convinced they had the real thing, but what did she know? They'd achieved much more than Teun had expected, but the finding of the jewellery was only the beginning. He confessed to being inclined to impatience when it came to a mystery needing to be solved, and now they'd started the ball rolling he wanted all twenty items to be uncovered.

Impatience might be one more thing she learned about him, though what she liked most was that he really cared about his relatives – his dad, and his Uncle Adam.

They picked up another hired car after they arrived at Duluth. Keira was so used to taking taxis when she arrived at a European destination, the novelty of what Teun unconsciously did still amused her. Since it was so close to Jan's lunchtime, Teun suggested they eat first. They'd breakfasted early with Adam, so a quick bite was definitely welcome now.

Arriving at Jan's nursing home, an hour later, was a shocker.

Bobby intercepted them at the entryway, looking upset. "I'm sorry, Teun. Your father's just been sedated. He had another heart attack and needs to rest."

Teun ranted about not phoning to warn the care home

about his visit, as he usually did. It was clear to Keira he blamed himself for not planning properly. She, in turn, felt guilty for distracting him from normal routine.

Bobby led them towards the doctors' station. "Your dad rambled on about someone annoying him after his lunch, asking dumb fool questions. I was listening to him, trying to calm him down, when he had the attack."

Jan's condition wasn't good, yet, though extremely frail, he was stable. Doctor McLaren confirmed they should wait till the following day to make another visit: the attack had taxed Jan's heart.

Keira reached for Teun's hand after he parked outside Grace's shop. Sorrow turned his eyes bleak. She'd made the suggestion they visit the older woman: it seemed kinder, rather than to tell her about Jan's condition in a phone call.

"I know it's the right thing to do. Grace is a strong woman, she takes care of herself very well, but she's still close to Dad. This is going to be difficult."

Grace had nobody to cover the counter, but insisted on locking up before she led them through to her apartment at the back. It was so disheartening to see the woman's distress; her feelings for Jan were still deep. After a few moments to compose herself, she thanked them for keeping her informed, and then admitted she'd not expected them to return so soon.

Teun had no reservations in updating Grace with their progress, and told her about their amazing jewellery findings and about the letters to Jan. Grace blatantly admired the jewels, chuckled merrily and congratulated him. She sobered, though, when Teun spoke of the letters from Paula. It was clear Jan's third wife had known something about his second wife. And those details were not pleasant.

The older woman got up and paced around, a bit stiffly since she was upset, but she said nothing about it as she slowly toured the small living room.

"You've already made a thorough check of your dad's storage?"

Teun nodded. Keira fielded his glance for corroboration. "We're sure we searched his boxes really well, Grace."

Grace did a small tut-tutting sort of thing as she rubbed her lower back before coming to an abrupt halt. "Your dad's apartment was fairly sparse, Teun, when we did the clear out, but I suppose we could have thrown out a small box and not realised it."

As Teun sat down next to her, Keira felt his hand slide along to grasp hers. "I'm hoping that's not the case, Grace, but I'm realistic enough to know it's a possible scenario."

Grace plunked herself down on the single chair which lay alongside the couch where Keira sat. Silence reined for a few moments as Grace pondered the bracelet. She eventually spoke, her voice quite puzzled as she scratched her head, mussing up her neat gray bob. "I'm thinking about something I didn't question at the time, Teun."

Keira felt her interest perk up.

"Jan came to visit me about…" Grace's fingers scratched again. "…maybe two or three years ago? I can't quite remember."

Keira was startled when Grace turned to her, since she'd mostly been maintaining eye contact with Teun.

"Although we were divorced, Jan still came around every other month to make sure things were going well for me. He was always considerate of my welfare, you know? I couldn't live with a man who couldn't give me everything, but that didn't mean he wasn't still my friend."

Keira felt the lack of eye contact with Grace when the older woman turned to look out of the window. It was a few seconds before the woman's head swivelled back again. "Let's just say, once only, I really didn't appreciate a third person in our relationship, in our bed, even when she was only in Jan's mind."

146

Heat flooded Keira's face. It wasn't embarrassment, just a kind of empathetic sadness since she could see how much Grace still loved Teun's father.

"Don't get me wrong, here. Jan loved me, too, in his own way." Grace was wistful. "Just not as much as he hankers after Teun's mother."

Keira wasn't sure how to answer, not knowing if an answer was even appropriate. It moved her even more when Teun slipped from the couch, knelt beside Grace, and put his arms around the woman who had been his dad's wife and loyal friend for years.

Soon Grace found her composure again and shrugged out of Teun's embrace, the clearing of her throat indicating her pragmatic nature.

"Anyway. What I remembered was Jan popped in one day, a few years ago, and asked me to keep something for him, something he claimed was very precious."

Keira felt her heart lurch, but it soon settled down when Grace continued.

"Your dad was slowing down even then, Teun, and I just accepted what he said at the time. He'd had issues with blood pressure for a while and told me he needed to do more walking, more playing golf. What he didn't tell me was that his heart was affected too."

"Yeah. He said he was going to become a new man and get fit on the courses." Teun's laugh was full of happy memories, tinged with regret.

"To do it, he needed to give up the sedentary stuff." Keira felt Grace's smile descend on her. "Came that day and asked me to keep temptation safe; would I store his fishing tackle? Asked me what was more inactive than fishing."

"You've still got his gear?"

Grace looked affronted. "Of course, Teun. Your dad's not dead yet!"

Chapter Eight

"Anyway, you're missing my point. Jan sometimes fished, sure he did, but it wasn't his lifetime passion."

Teun nodded as he rose to his feet and followed Grace out of the room. Keira towed after them.

Grace rummaged, shuffling things around in her hall cupboard before producing the tackle box, and then thrust the plastic crate at Teun.

"You'd best have a look. I'll be in the shop when you're done."

Teun opened the lid of the treasure chest-style box to reveal a jumble of spinners and weights and lines and... Keira wasn't sure what the rest of the stuff was. He took one look at the mess and shut the lid.

Below the lid were four more shelved layers which pulled out, each layer having little compartments for storing feathers and clips and hooks and... other bits and bobs. She'd never been fishing, didn't fancy tearing her fingers to shreds on the sharp-looking metal accessories, but was perfectly happy to watch when he carefully lifted out each layer and checked it thoroughly.

Nothing.

He closed all the shelves and opened the top of the chest again with a cheeky grin and a theatrical sigh. Keira took pity on him and helped to remove the tangle. Soon the lines were re-rolled, the scales set aside, the lures and bait hooks separated. All that remained was a bulky towel lying on the bottom. Teun lifted it and gave it a good shake. A padded posting bag clunked onto the wooden floor.

Keira felt her mouth drying up. Jan Zeger's name and address was written on the front. Teun flicked the bag over. Marta Blakeney's small spidery writing indicated she was the sender.

Keira didn't think either of them breathed for a few moments before Teun gingerly lifted the bag, and held it out as though it had a life of its own.

"Come on."

His other hand towed her through to the shop, Keira almost struck dumb by his consideration. He didn't need to include Grace… yet he was going to.

When her customer had gone, Teun set the bag on the counter, insisting Grace did the opening since she'd harboured the bag for the last few years. Protest did no good at all. He was adamant, so Grace complied.

Inside the padded bag was a velvet box.

"Oh, my goodness, Teun! Is this what you felt like in Adam's loft?"

Grace's hands shook so much she had to lay the box down on her counter before prising up the stiffly sprung lid.

"Wow!" A collective appreciation hushed out.

It was the most fabulous gold bangle Keira had ever laid eyes on, and much more impressive than in the photograph. Weighty and shiny, it was lifted free of its faded cream satin bed by Teun's careful fingers. Leaning over his shoulders, she inched closer. The carved ivory depicted a dancing figure.

"Have you any idea who it's meant to be?" Teun stared hard at the tiny representation.

Keira hadn't a clue.

"Whoever she is, she's got four arms!" Grace sounded quite amused.

Keira clutched the tote even more firmly over her shoulder

when they walked out to the car, nervous perspiration running down the back of her neck. The bag now held probably an even greater fortune… along with two signed pieces of paper. Teun's request that Grace do the same as Adam had been met with similar assent. Though she'd had the bangle in her house for ages, Grace didn't think of it as hers at all. It belonged to Jan but, since Teun had Power of Attorney for his father, she was happy to sign it over into Teun's care.

He looked just as tense as she felt during the drive to the same hotel they'd recently stayed in. Back to mirror watching, she wasn't surprised when Teun suddenly changed lanes on the highway, and unexpectedly veered the car onto the off ramp. She'd noticed the car behind them as well: the driver unmistakeable. Tension gripped her all over, not just the death clutch she had on the bag sitting on her lap. He made no scary manoeuvres, but her breathing needed a bit of damage control, her pulse likewise. Conversation was anathema: Teun's focus totally on driving. It took a little longer to reach the hotel but it didn't matter at all; it was more important that they arrived without a tail. Again he said nothing about his swift change of direction… or about the person following them. She debated whether to broach the subject, but in the end decided not to. She didn't want Teun to feel accountable for her safety as well as guilty; since she was now sure he felt responsible for their shadow and that was why he said nothing about it.

She was more than happy to spend the rest of the day in their hotel suite doing some work, as Teun did. They dined in the bistro down at ground level and, though Teun said nothing, she was happy to have the quickest meal possible and get back up to their suite.

His tense fingers gripped hers as they exited the lift and turned left.

"Hey! You…" His command was ignored by the figure who darted past the last few doors along the corridor to dash down the emergency exit stairwell, Teun in hot pursuit.

Keira dived after him but skidded to a halt at the door of their room. Go after Teun, or check their room? She was in a quandary, her heart hammering. Teun was already through the exit door, screaming like a banshee. It would probably serve no purpose to follow as she was now way behind.

She tentatively pushed at the room door. Oh, shit! Clammy fingers of serious unease crept down her spine. The lock wasn't fully engaged… Pressing a hand to the clenching at her stomach, she wobbled a foot inside, then another. Upheaval abounded. The lounge area was a chaos of papers, as though randomly fallen from a helicopter flyer drop. The racing of her pulse escalated. Nothing had been left untouched, including her laptop case; its contents – cables, connectors, papers, dictionaries – had all been strewn around.

Fumbling her way into the bedroom, the sight was even more frenzied. Sprinkled-out contents from their suitcases littered the bed, the floor and every possible surface: their stalker had been extremely thorough.

"Oh, my God!" Sickness welled. Bile flooded her mouth. Her hand clamped over her face.

Struggling into the bathroom, her recently eaten dinner was desperate for release. Groping for the toilet bowl, she sank to her knees and heaved. It took no time at all for her stomach to empty since the contents had barely settled there. After flushing the toilet, her hand located a wash cloth. Cool water trickled down her neck as she wiped herself free of traces.

"Oh, God! Teun?"

She couldn't believe how selfish she'd just been… although there hadn't been much she could do to prevent herself from being sick.

On rickety legs, she staggered from the bathroom and viewed the lounge again. Where was the room safe?

"Bloody hell!" It was in the bedroom closet.

Back in the bedroom, she took stock. The wardrobe was

wide open, the lower set of drawers randomly yanked out, though they were all empty. There had been no point in properly filling them since she'd an idea their stay in Duluth wouldn't be too long.

Her gaze drifted above the pulled-out drawers to the sturdy safe. A hint of relief suffused her. It looked closed. Trembling fingers pried at sides of the door. Stuck fast. Cool gratitude ran down her spine. It was locked, but had their stalker managed to open it? She couldn't tell as Teun had reset the code before they'd gone to dinner. She'd no idea what he'd keyed in; she'd been in the bathroom at the time.

Another stagger took her out into the corridor. Teun hadn't returned yet. Questions bombarded her brain, her eyes almost not seeing properly. Was he safe? Had their stalker turned attacker? Had Teun fallen down the stairs?

Where the hell was he?

With just sufficient presence of mind to make sure her key card was in her pocket, she snicked the door closed. Stumbling along the wall, her legs still a gelatinous mess, she pried open the heavy door to the emergency stairs.

Noises pounded from somewhere down below: shouts and bellows she couldn't interpret. At first she couldn't tell if someone was going down to lower floors or was coming up. Their room was on the eleventh floor, so there were plenty of floors above and below them.

Stilling her heaving breathing, she listened more carefully. The person was coming back up the stairs but the footsteps no longer powered their way. Edging back to the door, she'd no idea whether to wait or to retreat to her room. Her gaze scanned above, not for divine intervention, but purely because she was too cowardly to look below. There was no problem if it was Teun… but if it was the stalker? Her whole torso plastered against the cold metal, her breath stifled by panic.

A couple more flights by the sounds of the slowing footsteps. That inner sister berated her again, told her to get real and stop wimping. Opening her palms flush against the icy surface behind her, she willed some courage to return. One more flight. Oh God! She could now hear the laboured breathing of someone fighting with their fitness. Taking her unawares, anger roiled inside her and then erupted. Where her gall came from she'd no idea, but she was past caring.

"If you're not Teun, I'm going to beat your head in! I've got a weapon here and the minute you come near me, I'll not hesitate to use it, you thieving… prowler!

The minute the words gushed, Keira's legs almost folded. What the hell had she just done? She gaped at her almost empty palms. A key card wasn't exactly much use.

The gasping came just before Teun's head appeared at the corner of the flight below. "Keira? It's me…"

Her feet flew down the stairs and crushed him to a pulp. Slumping against the wall, his weight overpowered her. And it wasn't lust talking. Teun was staggering worse than she was. Dragging him down onto the lowest step, she looked him over. Blood oozed from a gash at the side of his temple, swelling around the area already egg-shaped.

"What the hell happened?"

Teun lolled on the step, his breath slowly returning. An agonising minute or so later, he was ready to speak. By then she'd mopped the blood from his face with the edge of her top, wincing at how deep the cut looked although she reckoned it probably didn't need stitches. She'd torn off a bit from the edge of the cotton and held the compress firmly against the bleeding.

"Chased him to one floor from ground level. I managed to catch hold of his jacket as he turned onto the last flight, but his wrestling set me off balance. I got one good punch in, though the angle I was coming from was pathetic. One shove from him and I went careering down the steps sideways… and then he jumped over me and made his escape. My skull hit the edge of the step face down and I may have blacked out for a second or two. Took me a little to re-right myself, but by then it was too late. He was out the bottom door, and gone, by the time I hit the fresh air outside."

***

"Bastard!" Groping his way into the hired car, Russ cradled his jaw. His tongue slid around the roof of his mouth, tasting the sharp, coppery tang. A hole gaped where his premolar should have been; a deluge of blood seeping to fill his mouth. It wasn't Zeger's feeble punch that had dislodged the tooth; it was the whack he'd given himself when he'd bludgeoned against the hard wall after jumping over the bastard's legs. His ankle hadn't fared too well either, for it had been the awkward slide on the edge of the bottom step that had smacked him against the wall.

He spat out the window before turning on the ignition. And spat again. The blood tang remained. His mood would have been bad anyway without the injured face – he'd found nothing and couldn't open the friggin' safe.

A few more minutes longer and he'd have cracked it… or been caught. Tentatively cradling his wrecked jaw, his swearing was a mere whisper through the stiffness that was forming, his tongue not fitting his swollen mouth any longer. He felt like jacking it in since the so-called piece of cake job was proving to be a friggin' loser.

He'd almost got caught at that senile old man Zeger's bedside. He hadn't managed to get a single word out of the old guy that made any real sense, except that it was hidden away and nobody would find it. What the hell it was, Russ didn't really care, but it had to be one of the jewels he was after. Zeger burbled on about it not being in his mother's house so much that probably meant it was in that friggin' huge place in Rochester.

He'd not fail next time. He had a plan, but he couldn't go it

154

alone any more, he needed back-up. That meant the profits would have to be split. Not fifty-fifty. He'd get somebody for twenty, or twenty-five, but no more than that.

His eyes blurred as he screeched off to his two-bit motel. A room that had none of the luxury enjoyed by Teun Zeger and Keira Drummond. His sour mood lasted the three blocks he had to drive before a hint of a grimace produced a colourful mumble of curses.

Trashed luxury!

***

Keira pleaded to call a doctor to examine Teun's wound, but he was adamant. No commotion. They couldn't afford to have any investigation made about the break-in. They had to keep the jewels a secret. If the authorities investigated, it would be impossible to conceal them.

After filling a towel with ice from the machine down the corridor – she'd crept warily along for it, scanning frantically the whole time – she'd packed it around the wound and bound it in place with another towel. Refusing to lie down, Teun slumped in the chair next to the wardrobe.

Methodically she keyed in the numbers he relayed to open the safe. Teun was one hundred per cent convinced the intruder had got nothing from their stash, as the guy's hands had been free enough to push him over, yet her heart was still in her mouth as the heavy door creaked open.

Much later he cradled her in the crook of his good side. The ice pack had been refreshed, although the swelling had receded considerably. The gash was held together with butterfly strips and a wide plaster she'd acquired through housekeeping, who fortunately accepted her assurance that Teun's wound wasn't too serious.

"What have we got ourselves into, Keira of the gorgeous topaz eyes?"

Her answer was glib though she was moved by his admission. "Just a bit more of that excitement you promised?"

"Enough of that! You know, I'm not so sure I'd have pursued all this jewellery searching if you hadn't been by my side."

Her chuckle at his ear made him caress her all over again. "You would. You already told me you like nothing better than solving mysteries."

"Yeah? But if you weren't part of this package, I'm sure I'd have ditched the quest and left it all to Jensen."

"So, all I am is part of the package?" Keira knew she was pushing it, even if she was amused by his wording.

"Just to look into your topaz eyes has been worth every second, Keira Drummond. I don't care about the rest of the jewels, but I'm very passionate about a particular golden brown, cereal box ring – because it matches your eyes perfectly."

Visiting Jan the next day was heartrending. Still confined to bed, he had aged years and years, yet it had only been days since they'd seen him. He hadn't a clue who they were, didn't even know Teun. Keira sat hushed beside Teun as he patiently answered the continued refrain. Every few sentences Jan would look at them and say it was lovely to have visitors. He never had visitors. Nobody came, so it was nice they had arrived.

"Who are you?" he asked Teun again.

Keira squeezed Teun's hand which was almost locked in tight, so bad was his tension and... grief. For Keira it was almost as if she was visiting someone entirely new. Jan was not like the same person she'd met days before, and who had been so responsive to her anecdotes about Neela. After a heartbreaking hour or so, where she guessed Teun hoped for a sudden change, he gave in and made movements to go when Bobby said he needed to ready Jan for his lunch.

As they were leaving the care facility, Dr. McLaren stopped Teun, his grim look not a good portent. She fervently hoped it wasn't even more bad news about Jan's condition.

"I'm duty bound to let you know, Mr. Zeger. We've started a full investigation of our security measures. It was logged that your father complained about someone annoying him yesterday lunchtime. After inquiries, the resident in the room next to your father has also complained of someone he didn't know entering his room as well. I'd just like you to be aware that we're treating the matter seriously, and we're having the police check our security tapes. If there's anything to update, I'll advise as necessary. And that goes without saying with regard to your father's condition, since he is still very fragile."

Dr. McLaren was embarrassed, maybe even angry: patient safety had been compromised.

Teun was sitting at the table in their hotel suite a while later, making on-line reservations to New York, when his mobile rang. Looking puzzled at the number displayed, his answer sounded cautious.

"Hello?"

Keira tried not to eavesdrop, but doing some work sitting right next to him made it impossible.

"Yes. I'm Teun Zeger."

Another pause.

"Oh yeah, I remember you now, Dec. How're you doing?"

His greeting to the caller was chirpy, but lasted only seconds before his face drained of all colour. The muscles in his neck tensed up as he swallowed, his free hand slipping up to rifle through his hair. Whatever he was hearing from the caller sent him into an agitated spin of the room. Hearing one-sided conversations was often a disappointment, and this definitely didn't sound a happy one. Teun's responses were one word answers, his anxiety rising with each new one. Yes? Last night? What? The bellowed "what?" put Keira into a spin too, as Teun loped around the small room. What the hell was happening now? Life in Teun Zeger's orbit certainly wasn't boring.

"Yes. Yes. Oh, God, yes, keep me posted. I understand that. Thanks."

Teun fired the closed mobile onto the couch and followed it down. He sat stunned before his head dropped to look at the floor, breathing heavily, palms rising to cradle his ears. She crept down beside him not knowing what to do to console him; it was clear he sorely needed some sort of support.

After a horrible silence, his hands dropped to his knees and he straightened up. His eyes were anguished, the glisten there an indication he barely held strong emotion at bay. His fingers clenched tight across his thighs.

"Adam's dead."

"What?" Keira felt the room spin, just for a second, before she blinked. She groped for his hand, pulled it toward her, and covered it on her lap. Tears hovered on her eyelids but she forced them down. Teun needed more than a wailing woman to get him through this devastating news.

"What… happened?"

His face turned up to the ceiling. It took a few moments before his control returned enough for him to speak.

"There was a fire at his house. Before the Fire Service got him out, he'd succumbed to smoke inhalation. They tried to resuscitate, but he was gone."

The blood drained from her fingers as Teun's eyes squeezed tight, his whole body rigid; not knowing, his strength crushed her bones like fragile, desiccated leaves. Dry tears widened her eyes. It was too difficult to believe. She had spoken to Adam the night before when Teun had updated the old guy about the bangle. Adam's reaction had been the same as when the emeralds and pearls had been found. He'd found it all a bit of a lark. Now he was dead? How could that be? Could it all be a mistake… or a malicious prank… or something? Was the call genuine? She was grasping at straws, she knew it, but needed something to make it seem more real.

158

"Who just phoned?"

"Jane is Adam's older sister." Teun gave her details as though reading them stiltedly from a book. "She lives a couple of blocks away from Adam. That was her son, Declan. He lives nearby as well. He doesn't have details. He's been calling all the Blakeney relatives to tell them the news."

Keira moved even closer, slipping her arm underneath his to draw him in tight. Her fingers soothed his tense fist.

"Jane knew we'd visited recently. She thought I ought to know as soon as possible."

Teun looked gutted. Silence reigned for while, then he paced around their hotel room, and then he ranted about making inquiries himself. The local Rochester police divulged nothing, even though he protested he was Adam's nephew. Any new details would be given to Adam's next of kin – his sister, Jane. After another round of calls, all he could establish was the joint fire and police services weren't satisfied about the circumstances which caused the fire. An investigation was underway.

Keira didn't know what to do. She wanted to console Teun. Wanted to help him – but wasn't sure how.

"Do you want to go back there now?" Her voice was a whisper since he was so distracted.

"Declan said the house didn't burn down. Nobody can access it yet, but the fire guys kept damage to some of the downstairs areas. Declan knows one of the crew. The guy told him, in confidence of course, they're suspicious about the site of the fire in Adam's den."

"What?"

"Some unexplained object caught fire and created almost instantaneous toxic fumes. It was because the smoke was so dense that Adam's neighbour noticed it, and called the emergency services. Their quick response kept the fire contained to the back rooms on the ground floor."

Yet they hadn't been quick enough to save Adam. Keira's

throat was dry as she clutched Teun to her – his stiff body, and dry crying, showing just how much the news affected him.

Teun needed to get back to Rochester.

Leaving him preoccupied on the sofa, she packed their belongings. Then she placed his mobile phone, and his laptop, in front of him.

"Book to Rochester as soon as possible. For two. I'm coming with you."

On automatic, Teun booked.

Their first stop in Rochester was the local police station. Face-to-face they were marginally more informative, but only after they'd contacted Jane first for her approval. Teun was told Adam's body had been removed by the Medical Examiner's Office for further examination as the circumstances surrounding the death were unexplained. The fire authorities were making further investigations. New updates would go directly to Jane.

By the time they reached Jane's house, there was a small gathering of Blakeneys already there. The shock of the sudden death drove the conversation as drinks were handed around. Adam's sister, a tottery old lady, was tearful yet pleased to hear Teun had been to visit her brother just days before he died.

"Adam always liked your visits, Teun. He enjoyed our visits, too," she said, by way of explanation for Keira, "but it cheered him to keep contact with the only young one left from Marta's side of the family."

Funeral details couldn't happen anytime soon, so there was no practical help Teun could give at that moment, though he made sure Declan knew financial help was available from him, if necessary.

Jane attempted to be practical. "I don't know if Adam left a will of any kind, Teun. It was something we never ever talked about, but the house used to belong to your grandparents."

Keira was impressed with Teun's words of reassurance to the

older woman. "We'll talk about the house later, Jane, but keep in mind the people who lived in it for the last forty years. Remember also, your family have been around the corner from Adam for most of those years."

Teun dumped their suitcases at the side of the bed in their hotel room in Rochester as Keira popped her tote bag onto the nightstand, realising she'd carried a fortune around in it for hours. And the jewels hadn't mattered one whit! All she cared about was supporting Teun through such a difficult time. With hindsight she realised she'd not even done the side-mirror watching thing – she'd been too preoccupied. If some auburn-haired miscreant had been following them, she didn't – at that moment – care, but she hadn't been aware of anyone.

Her mobile rang some time later, as she sipped a nightcap in the hotel bar beside a very reflective Teun. Dinner had been necessary to sustain them, though neither of them had done justice to the meal.

"Hello, Zaan."

While she listened, Teun whipped out a pen and pulled a napkin toward him. He scribbled something before pushing the paper back toward her. *Say nothing about the jewels, or about Adam's death.* Looking grim, he stared. Though surprised by his order, his glare had her nodding her head. It was just as well Zaan's monologue still continued since she didn't need to answer at all at that point. That gave her time to compose herself, and try to act as though absolutely nothing untoward had been happening to her. As Zaan burbled on, his call became distraction from her own sad mood.

Zaan hadn't found Tanja's hairpin as easily as he'd first imagined. He'd made the visit to his cousin in Brussels. The woman had clarified the brooch she'd been given did look like the one Tanja wore in the photograph of the three sisters, but she'd sold it. She'd confessed to being surprised by the gift from her aunt – Zaan's mother –but it hadn't been something she felt she'd ever wear; not her style. The good thing was she'd taken it to a reputable jeweller, so chances were high it could be traced. Zaan sounded positive and was pursuing it.

With regard to verification of the Tiru Salana collection, Zaan had news on that front, too. He'd made contact with the descendants of the Amsterdam jewellers, the Koopmans, who'd been named in the 1815 newspapers. Though their company name had changed a number of times, and the business had considerably downsized, they were still trading as jewellers in Amsterdam.

"They have records in one of their premises dating back to the early eighteen hundreds. Jensen has arranged for an archivist from the university to help us trawl through the paperwork in their stores, though it will take her some time. That's my update. Anything new at your end?"

"Not really." Keira hedged an answer but had to tell him something innocuous. "Though, I'm so pleased to have met Teun's dad. He's a lovely man…"

After some general chit-chat about Duluth, she found the conversation difficult to maintain and, at Teun's gesture, she handed her mobile over. He had been absorbing her one-sided conversation with Zaan, and had looked so serious. She still couldn't figure out his mistrust of Zaan, but had come to respect his caution: the person dogging their tail had convinced her of the need for vigilance. Something underhand was going on and they didn't know who had set it up. Till they did, it was right to be watchful. She admired how economical Teun was with the truth.

"Yeah. We're going to New York tomorrow."

Teun's declaration to Zaan came as a surprise since they'd been careful only to mention Duluth. Zaan had no idea they were currently in Rochester, did he?

"I'm hanging around the East Coast for a few days, but Keira's going straight back to Edinburgh."

So, that was it? Teun had used her to find the jewels and she was being packed off home? She seethed quietly while he finished the call. When he gave her the mobile, she couldn't even look at him.

He grabbed her hand and led her out to the bank of lifts, his voice low though there were only a few patrons around and about the foyer. His scan of the area wasn't secretive. She followed his every glance and satisfied herself that she recognised no-one as they stepped into the lift. Tacit silence ruled till they were in their room.

"I'm not fed up with you, Keira. I know it's what you're thinking, but that's not what I'm doing. Listen while I explain, please?" He rifled his fingers through his hair as she turned toward him. "I'm... so bloody furious... about the things that are happening. You have to admit there are too many sinister events happening."

"How do you mean?" She wasn't prepared to forgive him yet. He needed to come clean, about everything.

"Maybe menacing things happen around you every day, Keira, but they don't damn well happen to me. I can't help being bloody suspicious."

"You didn't want Zaan to know about Adam, since you're still not sure if he had anything to do with it?"

"I can't get past the fact we visited Adam a few days ago. I thought someone had been in his house the other night, and, for Christ's sake... now he's dead. We visited my father a few days ago. He has a mysterious visitor who gets him so wound up he has a heart attack. Do those happenings not seem malicious to you? Someone has been trying to get information about the jewels – or even the jewels themselves –and my relatives have been harmed because of it. And I did nothing to prevent it!"

Teun wandered around the confined space, dodging furniture. Keira wasn't stupid. He blamed himself for Adam's death because he hadn't told the police about the suspected break-in. He still wasn't mentioning the fact they'd been followed, and she didn't know why, but she let it go. "So, what's your plan?"

"We go to New York, but don't give anyone else any details. I put the jewels into safe storage, after we verify their worth. After that, I'm not sure."

Keira agreed the plan, up to a point. "I'll come to New York, and do the verification with you, if for no other reason than to be an alibi, as it were, to prove you've done what you say you've done with them. But after that I will go home to Edinburgh, Teun."

Returning home was practical. She couldn't stay around waiting for Adam's funeral. It might take weeks for that, even months – Declan told them that night – if authorities didn't conclude their investigations quickly. Chemical analysis was being done of the materials found where the fire had originated. Declan put them further into gloom by telling them the police had been allowed back to the scene – after the fire was properly out – and had reported the upstairs of the house had been ransacked. They were now classifying the death as robbery-driven.

As soon as Teun finished his call to Declan, his mobile rang again. It was fortunate they could prove where they had been at the time of Adam's death, since the Rochester police asked to verify their whereabouts. Everyone who had seen Adam during his last days was being questioned. Teun gave the police the numbers for the nursing home, and Grace; Keira was shocked they could even be thought as suspects.

"Don't worry about it. Dec said the fire authorities pulled Adam from the building just before two p.m. We were talking to Dad's doctor around that time. Up in Duluth."

That night she held him tight in her arms. Comfort what they both needed, the calls of their bodies not an afterthought, but a poignant declaration of their closeness. She'd only known Teun for such a short time and yet it seemed they been sharing their lives for so much longer. The thought of leaving him behind and going back to Edinburgh was anathema – but it had to happen.

Keira had realised over the days that Teun was a man of action… and a man with resources who could find the correct help when needed. A friend had already recommended a security expert in New York who would counsel on where to have the jewels valued, and where best to store the items. Their plans were made.

At the airport in Rochester, she wondered if security would clamp her in irons because her frantic searching around for an auburn-haired guy must be obvious; must make her appear very suspicious. They'd decided it was still best if she carried the jewels in her tote bag, using the same reasoning as before, if she were questioned. But nothing happened.

It wasn't a long flight to New York though Keira, again, felt susceptible. Exiting the plane at New York, La Guardia, she almost tripped down the gangway, her gait unsteady. So much had happened in such a short time, so many flights over the last few days. It wasn't the flying she was nervous about; it was a more general alarm.

The concourse at La Guardia heaved with a surging mass of travellers, Teun weaving in and out of the throngs. Keira virtually clamped herself at his side, giving him just enough freedom to drag behind a suitcase in each of his hands. One minute she was trailing at his side and the next she sprawled towards the floor. Her crash into the woman in front of her was inevitable as the jostling had come from behind. If her victim hadn't been arm-linked to a very sturdy companion, they'd all have fallen like skittles but, bearing the brunt of the impact, the man managed to keep the three of them from hitting the tiles face first.

Thudding onto her knees, Keira felt the yank on her tote. The weight of it dipped down at her side but, as her fingers still gripped like grim death at the front, she didn't lose it.

"Get away from me!"

Her screech of dismay halted not only Teun but everyone else around them, who cleared the space around her with amazing speed, a little circle forming to watch the spectacle. She'd worn the strap crosswise over her chest and was never more thankful of her caution. As she scrambled back to her feet with Teun's help, her heartbeat pounding in her chest, the bag dangled limply in her fist. Her attacker had sliced the strap at the back, though that was all the success he'd had. Her laptop had been in her other hand but the assailant definitely hadn't been attempting to steal that.

The couple she'd ploughed into were full of concern, wanting to beckon airport security, but it was the last thing they needed. Keira had been the only one of the three to hit the deck, the only one to have suffered any kind of injury.

"I'm so sorry! It was just a mistake. I must have tripped over my own feet!" Her excuse was pathetic even to her own ears, her embarrassment heating her cheeks. How she managed it she'd never know. She persuaded the couple she was perfectly fine and wanted no more fuss. They weren't happy; by then the crowd around had dispersed – just another one-second-wonder in La Guardia.

Persuading Teun she was fine was met with a steel-edged glare. He was spitting fury – although not at her. She could tell he, too, didn't want to draw any more attention to them. Summoning her dignity and a farewell smile for her pleasant co-victims, she crushed the bag to her chest and walked to the concourse doors. She pretended her knees were fine even though she knew she'd given them a ferocious dunt on the hard terrazzo flooring. Almost at the doors, the breath left her chest in a whoosh. A security guard approached them. Someone had pointed them out, having claimed there had been an attempted bag snatch.

Assuring the guard she was fine wasn't easy; it was just as well she played her best ever acting roll, since he wanted to escort her to the medical room to be checked over. Did she want to report the incident? The officer would be happy to point out where she should go. Again, it took some time to assure him she'd no idea what had happened and, since everything was fine, she wanted no fuss about it. She wasn't hurt and she still had her bags. Thankful the officer hadn't asked to see the strap, which was concealed against her chest, she persuaded him she'd just tripped over something. Though he looked doubtful, and was censorious about theft in the airport, he let them go with a warning that, should she change her mind, she should call the airport security office. He needed their names though, as he had to log some kind of incident had happened, having spent time talking to them. After noting down their names, he strode off.

Relief washed over her as they sank onto the back seat of the taxi. By unspoken, tacit agreement, they didn't discuss the incident. Inhaling regular deep breaths, she willed herself to calm down. Teun's fingers secreted themselves in between the edges of the strap she still clung to with ferocious tenacity. The reassuring squeeze, and his weak wink, sustained her through the long nerve-wracking taxi ride.

Teun closed the door on the porter and let out one almighty curse. "Let me see your knees?" It was a half-shout, half-growl as he whipped open the mini-fridge and checked for ice. Seeing none, he grabbed the ice bucket on the counter.

Her attempt at walking normally hadn't fooled him. As she took off her jeans, she assured him it was nothing, though she wasn't surprised to see the bruising already colouring up quite nicely. "It's not so bad, I've had worse bruises before this."

He stomped out of the door to go to the ice machine at the far end of the corridor, demanding she be lying down when he got back. Minutes later she had two ice-filled towels clamped around her knees. What she liked much better was Teun clamped around the rest of her, almost hugging the breath out of her, his face burrowing into her neck.

"The bastard! If I get him I'll wring his f…" What followed was venomously low and controlled, though creatively cursing.

After his outburst was over, she liked his consolation kisses.

It was no hardship to lie prone for a while though she privately thought it was a bit late to expect the cold compresses to have any real effect. The taxi ride to their hotel overlooking the Hudson had taken the best part of an hour, plenty of time for a bit of swelling, but it was only bruising and nothing worse than that.

A few minutes later Teun rolled off the bed.

"I'm going down to get you some painkillers."

A solid thud heralded the jewels were secured in the room safe as the heavy door closed on them.

"Don't open this door to anyone!"

She really didn't need Teun's tirade; he had his key-card.

It was no time at all before he returned, although she'd cat-napped. He'd bought some suitable analgesics and, even better, had anti-inflammatory gel she thought would do the trick. The plastic sack he carried was incredibly large, though, for a couple of small packages. Like a conjuror, he showed why as he revealed a new handbag for her.

"Much sturdier leather straps."

Made of strong leather, the bag had a long strap which could also be worn crosswise over her chest. Very appropriate – very functional, though not a particularly romantic gift – but very easy to forgive him for it, as she'd been wondering how to get the items safely to the jewellers.

When she declared she'd rested enough, she donned a long floating skirt which was much more comfortable.

Teun looked very hesitant… and endearingly protective. "Are you sure about this, Keira? I could arrange for some representative to call here."

"No way! I will not give in to a threat by some bumbling wanna-be snatch thief. We're going, so say no more!"

Teun called in a request for a taxi. He stayed glued to her

side in the corridor and lift, and their taxi was waiting by the time they reached the downstairs lobby. Keira would love to have said she glided out… she tried, but it was more like hobble-wobbled.

Chapter Nine

"Fifty thousand dollars?"

Not only were the jewels all genuine, but the estimated value for each item was much greater than either of them had imagined. If Keira had known in advance, she would never have carried them on her person at all.

"Jesus!" She clutched Teun's fingers like a vice, hoping the jeweller thought she was a very reverent person.

The pearl necklace could be easily restrung and was estimated to fetch around fifty thousand dollars at auction.

Keira almost fainted at the jeweller's next declaration. The pearls, he confirmed, were of superior quality but the diamond and emerald clasp was a plethora of gems of unparalleled excellence.

The double-sided necklace alone was worth at least a hundred thousand dollars – its diamonds, again, of flawless quality. The green stones were not just very nice, clear, green beads. Each one was a tiny but valuable emerald, the cut impeccable. Along with its two matching sets of earrings, the set was worth upwards of one hundred and fifty thousand dollars; the jeweller explaining it was of a type named Moghul, after the Indian design, and though not unique, it would be a well sought after set of jewellery.

It was Teun's gasp this time which echoed around the room. "Oh shit! One hundred and fifty thousand?"

The individuality of the enamelled bracelet, in particular, drew a lot of interest from the jeweller.

"I believe this piece could fetch at least seventy thousand dollars, sir. But, of course the originality of it might bump up the value even more."

The gold was of the highest karat and lots of it, for it was a very heavy piece. Keira could attest to that as she'd clutched its weight for days, along with the other jewels.

Her knees trembled… as well as ached. She'd been trailing around with something like a quarter of a million dollars in her bag? Jesus! A different kind of thumping pulse ensued. The news was scary but also weirdly electrifying. If she hadn't already been seated, Keira knew her legs would have failed her. Her heart thumped, her skin clammy. Her relieved gaze caught Teun's. Thank God the bag snatcher hadn't succeeded!

Teun's expression bothered her greatly, she knew he warred with more than one demon as the jeweller prepared the valuation documentation. The spectre of the wealth Martine had concealed was one major factor, Adam's death and his father's condition was also huge. The thug following them was another, and most of all was the fact they didn't know who had set the man on their tail. He still didn't know who to trust… and neither did she.

However, as it was a privately arranged and a privately paid for evaluation, Teun was quite clear when pointing out he expected total discretion. He was vehement, almost to the point of rudeness, in demanding a written statement to the effect that the jewels could not be publicized in any way as yet. His story about the jewels belonging to his father, and not to him, Keira wasn't sure the jeweller truly accepted, but they left with his signature of confidentiality on the dotted line.

It was dazzling that by five p.m. they'd had the gems valued, and they were already under secure lock and key – the key literally held by Teun. No way were they taking the jewels out of the jeweller's shop by themselves. Teun had called in the security firm recommended by his friend. An agent had arrived at the jeweller's and had escorted the two of them, and the jewels, to a bank storage facility.

Their ride back to the hotel was silent. The enormity of it all swamped her and truth to tell, her legs were weak. Not just from the shock of the wealth she'd been toting around; her legs were literally aching, her bruises stiffening up quite dramatically.

It was pointless to watch out for an auburn-haired stalker, since they no longer carried the gems around with them, but she couldn't help a few glances out of the back window. Hobbling her way into the hotel took all her effort, not even an attempt to look around – though she noted Teun still did his bit of surreptitious glancing.

Together they'd searched Adam's house and Jan's belongings and it was unlikely any more information, or actual jewels, would be forthcoming. They were pretty sure they must have all of Martine's little stash. It still shocked her to know Adam's house had been ransacked but, realistically, it was unlikely it would be targeted again.

It was time for her to go home to Edinburgh.

Teun declared he would remain on East Coast U.S. just in case there was any need for him to go back to Rochester in the coming days. Declan had indicated they might soon be able to have a memorial service for Adam – the actual funeral sometime hence, when the body was released by the authorities. Teun would work at his Boston lab, since there presently was no urgency clawing him back to California.

While Teun made an on-line booking for her for the following day, she couldn't bear to sit and watch him do it. Declaring a bath would help her sore knees, Teun agreed wholeheartedly. She'd not been submerged very long when the bathroom door squeaked open. There was no resistance from her when he offered to do a bit of back scrubbing… and a bit more besides.

Attempting to be jovial during dinner was partially accomplished, yet a strange lament skulked in the background.

They toasted their success with some superior champagne and a wonderful meal, the restaurant they went to close by. They tacitly talked of New York instead of the emerald quest, Teun telling her of all the wonderful things he'd done and seen during his visits. She'd never been to the city before, so she enjoyed his regaling of times past and vowed to come back some day and tour the sights he talked of.

The solace of his fingers gently rubbing hers was in counterpoint to the sadness she felt at their imminent leave-taking. His support as they sauntered along the couple of blocks back to their hotel wasn't just welcomed; she really needed to feel so close to him as she did a sort of hop-skip.

She had an inkling Teun felt it all as unreal as she did when they recapped the fabulous jewels they'd unearthed, once back in their room. Yet he'd been much more practical than she had been. Though she hadn't seen him do it, he'd taken photographs of the jewels with his mobile. When he shared them with her, she couldn't prevent tears from leaking, big fat silent tears which dripped off her chin as she looked again and again at the Moghul necklace and bangle. They really were stunning. Her nervous smile had him cuddling her almost to death.

It wasn't the magnificence of the jewellery that made her cry. Teun believed her explanation that it was relief the jewels were in safe storage, while they awaited their joining with whatever Zaan and Jensen managed to acquire. She cried for Adam, and for Jan who had given the precious bangle to Grace to store. She cried for Grace, too… and for Teun since he now had very few close relatives.

Mostly her tears were because their affair would be over the next day.

Making love that night had a quiet intensity that overwhelmed her. Teun was very attentive to her bruised knees, but it was her bruised heart she was more concerned with.

Their farewell at the airport the next day disturbed her. She wasn't sure now how Teun really felt about her, since he appeared pragmatic over her departure. A last kiss at the barrier was long and searching – yet not desperate – and only broken off when Keira could bear it no longer. One last hug from him was all she could cope with when the last call flashed for her flight. No lingering waves or she'd have sobbed like a baby in distress, though that described to a T how she felt inside.

***

Keira could no longer be seen in the long queue leading to the security scanners. Teun's mobile chimed the arrival of a text message which he ignored, his gaze still riveted on the line. Glad she'd not turned back to him, he wasn't convinced he wouldn't have hauled her back out. He didn't want her to go – though he was sure she thought the opposite. Keeping their loving almost detached the night before, not loving her with all his heart like he wanted to, had almost unmanned him. It had been partly in deference to her bruising, but more because he needed to steel himself against their parting. Keira was special; but it wasn't the right time to make any declarations.

She needed to be safe.

Sending her home was the best option for that. It wasn't just the dire events that had happened to his dad and Uncle Adam. The auburn-haired guy who had been dogging their footsteps for days now, had followed them back from the restaurant the previous night. Why the friggin' hell the bastard was still doing that was impossible to work out. The tail had followed them from the jeweller's to the bank storage facility. The bastard would have worked out the jewels had been offloaded, so why the need to still track them after that?

Teun was taking no more chances. Keira was better away

from his presence, as he was sure he was the one attracting the shadow. Murder was part of the guy's handiwork, but he still didn't have a clue who he worked for.

He was relieved that Keira had found nothing at her father's house which had been handed down from Neela. He rode on the hope it would keep her, and her sister, safe from harm. Jensen, and Zaan, had known that bit of information for days. It was debatable which of those men he mistrusted most. Jensen was held suspect for the reasons he'd explained to Keira, but he just plain didn't like the idea of Zaan getting too friendly with her, the woman who was now the best lover he'd ever had. He didn't want their affair to end. He vowed to contrive more UK visits, but only after he'd settled things with Adam's Blakeney relatives.

Another text chimed. Declan. An intriguing message.

The phone call which followed was even more so. Remarkable news, though deeply disturbing. Dec's fire services buddy had given him a piece of paper which had been in Adam's hand when they'd gained access to the house. Only after the shift was over had Dec's pal realised he still had the paper tucked into his suit pocket, having removed it when Adam's body had been checked for signs of life. The slip of paper had letters scribbled on it which didn't make any sense. The entire piece of evidence should have been immediately logged, but the part with writing on it had been passed on to Dec before being filed. It wasn't usual procedure but was done on the understanding it would be quickly returned. Did the name "Dan" mean anything to Teun? Teun didn't think so but he asked Declan to courier the paper to his Boston lab. He'd examine it there, and get it to the authorities if he thought it was important.

***

Russ kept Teun Zeger in his sight as the guy crossed the concourse at a fast trot. Something about the call Zeger had just received had put some spark in him: a big difference from a few moments before when the stupid bastard had looked like the sky was falling in. He could see his point, though. Keira Drummond was a good-looking bit of flesh he'd like to get his own hands on. He had two things in mind for the bitch – he'd spend his own bit of time with her, and then he'd see she didn't live to tell the tale. He'd almost had her damn bag at the airport. If she hadn't had a grim death clutch on it, he'd have been off with big dollar signs.

How much he'd no idea, but hiring that security clown to escort them to the bank storage meant serious money could be collected on the jewels they'd found. If only he'd managed to get into that friggin' house in Rochester the first time. Tripping over the damned cat in the dark had sent him careering into the kitchen table, making enough noise to waken Zeger.

His tongue worried the gap in his gum. And Seth, the klutz that he'd hired, had been friggin' useless. Stupid bastard was already a squealer: wanted out, wanted his cut for having done nothing. There was no way Russ was giving him a dime, but he'd have to keep his eye on Seth, since the numbskull had seen him clock the old guy before he could get out his front door.

At least he was only following Zeger now. He had to get back that half-ripped bit of evidence stupid Seth hadn't managed to snatch properly. Russ picked up his pace. Zeger was flagging a taxi. Where was he headed now? Didn't matter, he wasn't going to lose the guy.

***

Keira was in the middle of some awkward translation, finding concentration difficult to maintain, constantly wondering what Teun was doing. When her phone rang she jumped for it, keen to hear his voice, since he'd called her at odd times during the incredibly long three days they'd been apart.

"Zaan! Hello." She hoped disappointment didn't ring over the line, because there was something in his tone that sounded quite – she couldn't explain it exactly – like repressed excitement. "Any success yet?"

She could swear his smile seeped out of her mobile, though it wasn't a camera link-up.

"I have really excellent news. My mother's emerald ring has been given a much higher value than I'd imagined. Ten thousand euros."

"That's wonderful!"

"The news gets even better. Naatje, my cousin who sold Tanja's hairpin, was pretty sure my mother had given our other female cousin something around the same time." Again Keira could easily imagine Zaan's happy smile from the chuckles in her ear. "She was right. I've just made a visit to Berhta, who lives nearby. She still has the bracelet my mother gave her. It's a four strand pearl bracelet with an emerald embedded in the catch. I've got it in for valuation just now. What are the chances of it not being significant?"

Jensen hadn't made much progress, according to Zaan. Inquiries regarding the donation of Tiru Salana's jewels, in India, were still ongoing. His update was thorough, which pleased Keira but also made her feel guilty because Zaan accepted, without question, that Teun was busy with work concerns and had given her no updates.

Keira closed her mobile wondering if he'd accepted her excuses too readily. Yet she just couldn't believe he was anything but perfectly open about the whole search. Her gut feeling about his honesty hadn't changed.

But her reciprocal honesty had.

Concern mounted as the following day waned. There had been no word from Teun for ages. Fretting for someone wasn't usual; it made her jumpy as she checked her email and phone yet again. He was thousands of miles away. Had some other incident happened to him that she didn't know about?

Worse still was the possibility he wasn't so bothered about keeping in touch, now that Martine's legacy had been uncovered. Those depressing thoughts pulled her into gloom. Was Teun now regretting their affair? Or did he still not fully trust her with anything that might be happening to him in her absence?

The chirp of an incoming message jolted her from her introspection.

A positive update from Zaan had been copied to Jensen, Teun and Romy. A paper trail had been uncovered at the Koopman's stockroom in Amsterdam, referring to a shipment of considerable value which was due to arrive from India, though no details were given on the consignment contents. It was dated May 1815. The year matched the local newspaper entry of June 1815, which referred to the Burghers wanting Tiru Salana's collection to be put on public display. The archivist Jensen had employed was looking at sales records of that year.

Even better news was that the hairpin worn by Tanja had been traced, and the owner prepared to negotiate a good price for it without being told the importance of the Tiru collection. Jensen was procuring it for the group, as per their agreement.

The ringtone of her mobile only a few moments later had Keira's heart pumping again, but caller ID identified an unknown number. She was surprised when she learned the caller was Romy Lischka.

Romy spoke in halting English at first but when she lapsed into German, Keira assured her she understood. She was only at home for a short period before undergoing her next scheduled treatment, and admitted she'd called Keira first, even though she wasn't a blood cousin. Her news wasn't exactly inspiring. She'd been selling off inherited items to finance various operations as her insurance cover was not adequate for all she needed.

Keira empathized with the woman who'd been through a lot over the last couple of years, yet Romy seemed such a sunny and positive person.

"My mother, Henny, lived all her years in Dresden. I lived there until I was twenty-five, but I can give you more of my family background another day."

The call wasn't long yet, by the end of it Keira found herself making promises. Before speaking to Romy she'd had no intentions of visiting Vienna, but – like going to Heidelberg – it was an impulsive decision. Meeting Romy sounded like the right thing to do, but since the woman was due back to hospital in six days, the best visiting time was sooner, rather than later.

"If I can clear off the current work I'm translating in the next couple of days, I'd love to visit you after that," she told Romy.

A few more hours passed. Silently. Though now she had a valid reason for calling Teun. Her call went to voicemail. She left a brief message saying she had information he should hear.

An apologetic Teun called as she readied herself for bed. A bit stilted at first, he told her there had been difficulties at his Boston lab.

"Data from an important test has been erased from the computers."

Keira wasn't sure how to console him since he sounded angry... and frustrated. "Can you get it back somehow?

"Yeah, but only if I re-run that test!"

Although the call started off stilted, it swiftly warmed up. He soon squashed Keira's regret for badgering him with calls.

"No. Don't think that! I wanted to break off to call you, to just hear your voice, but I had to sort out the mess." Pent-up longings burst down the airwaves. "Do you know how much I've missed you these last days, Keira?"

She assured Teun she felt just the same. As she updated him on Romy's call, he groaned.

"She must be the unknown caller who's left me a message on voicemail. I need to go and check on the test re-run just now, but I'll call her as soon as I'm free."

Keira only had a couple of days before Romy had to go back into hospital, but it would be enough to get to know the woman. Vienna was a brand new city for her; the urge to be a happy tourist was high, but she wished Teun could be with her. She'd love to see the sights with him, knowing they'd have so much fun together.

A taxi sped her from Vienna's Schwechat International Airport directly to Romy's house. Her flight connections hadn't gone smoothly, and she was a couple of hours later than she'd expected to arrive. Eight-thirty in the evening was too late really to be visiting an invalid, but Romy had put aside her misgivings, telling Keira she was desperate to meet her. As the taxi headed toward Josefstadt, an area of the city which was just outside the central core of old Vienna, Keira absorbed her surroundings. She didn't know what Romy's house would be like, but didn't expect the quaint row of cottages the driver pointed out to her as he drew to a halt at the end of an alleyway, off a busy main street. Leading down to a leafy, tree-filled inner courtyard, Keira had a hunch the rows of very old cottages would be expensive to buy, even though space inside them would be restricted. They were in too affluent an area to be otherwise. At the driver's urging, she took her case and started off down the path to the number Romy had given her.

She stepped through an arch onto wide grey flagstones which marked a pedestrian path between the rows of cottages. There was just enough room for one person on the irregular stone paving, scrubby patches of grass sitting below the windows of the single storey houses. Her case bounced along behind her as she scanned the numbers.

The door was opened by a teenage girl. Explaining she was the daughter of a neighbour, she welcomed Keira and ushered her in. By the time Keira stepped into the small sitting room, Romy had struggled up from her chair.

"Thank you, Therese. I'll be fine now."

"I'll pour your coffee first. Will you need me tomorrow, Romy?"

A side table was spread with cakes and sandwiches, even though it was late evening. Keira hadn't stopped to eat on arrival and eyed the feast with admiration.

Romy's smile was kind. "Thanks, Therese. If I do, I'll give you a call."

Romy needed no urging for Keira to delve in.

"My grandmother, Anna, told me stories about Uriel and her wealthy family, but, of course, I never met any of them. I have a couple of Lischka cousins on my father's side, back in Dresden, but apart from them I have no other family." Romy's smile widened, a delight there that made Keira smile, too. "I'm going to enjoy having more cousins now, even if they are more distant."

After a short visit, Keira left to get checked in to her hotel in central Vienna, promising to be back early the following morning. It was clear that even the brief time spent together had tired Romy, but they'd been so busy trading stories of living in Vienna and Edinburgh. Discussion of any jewels which Romy might possibly still have would be for another day.

Preparing to set off for Romy's house the following morning, Keira noticed the red light flashing on her hotel phone. The caller was Therese.

"Romy's been rushed back into hospital. I don't know what happened to her. She managed to send my mother a text

181

message before she collapsed. She's still unconscious, though the nurse says she's stable. I knew you were staying at this hotel, from a conversation with Romy before you arrived yesterday. I thought you'd want to know."

Feeling sick herself, Keira noted down the hospital details then flopped flat down on the bed. Romy had looked tired the night before, but she hadn't looked seriously ill. What could have changed the woman's state of health so drastically?

She'd learned Romy's life had centred on being a Vienna Tour Guide during the summer months, and a skiing instructor throughout the winter months. The skiing accident had put paid to that, though. Many attempts at corrective surgery had been made now to restore Romy's health. The hip replacement over, the next was for a small tarsal reconstruction.

What had gone wrong during the last hours?

Memories of Adam's death and the fire at his house made Keira frantic. Had something menacing also happened to Romy? That insidious creepy sensation that something was amiss again took hold. It wasn't rational to make links, but too many incidents had occurred since the emerald quest began. She still couldn't believe Jensen and Zaan were suspect; and now it was clearly not Romy. Though, what if the incidents had been caused by someone else looking for the jewellery collection? Someone neither she nor Teun had met? It was a new thought which hadn't occurred to her before.

She called Teun. After keying in his number, she hesitated. What if he thought she panicked over nothing? Thought she overreacted over every last thing? It went to voicemail. Maybe Teun was avoiding her? Berating herself for being paranoid, like before, she left a message asking him to contact her as soon as possible.

On arrival at the hospital, the reactions of the medical staff were predictable... and unhelpful. She couldn't prove her relationship to Romy, therefore all she got was a very basic report from the reception desk. Romy was stable.

On the point of giving up, she felt a tap at her shoulder.

"Therese? You don't know how glad I am to see you!"

Even better was the fact Therese's mother, Elise, was with her. As Elise was noted as a replacement next-of-kin, they gained access to Romy's bedside.

Though tubes and wires monitored vital statistics, the news was good. Romy was no longer unconscious. Her current sleep was medically induced; a procedure which would continue for a few more hours. It would likely be late in the evening, or the following day, before Romy would be capable of normal conversation. Fortunately the new hip bone had not been dislodged; a scan having clarified the surgery was intact. The only other damage she'd incurred was a blow to her cheek, though that was consistent with her fall – the emergency response team had noted a small table had been overset alongside Romy when they'd gained access to her.

Keira swallowed. Her imagination was far too vivid. What if Romy hadn't just fallen as the medical personnel were surmising? What if the blow to her head had been deliberate? She didn't want to think someone had maliciously harmed Romy... yet what if they had? That worm of suspicion wouldn't slither away.

Under the circumstances – Keira having come all the way from Edinburgh – the hospital authorities agreed to call her as soon as Romy was stable enough to have her visit.

Keira thanked Therese and Elise, but declined their offer of company.

"I'm going to wander around the old city centre."

"We'll show you where the nearest taxi rank is then."

"That's kind of you, Elise, but I'd much rather go by tram."

Keira knew little about Vienna, but she did know there was an extensive tram system.

"You'll have to take two trams to get right into the Hofburg." Elise worried she'd get lost.

Keira assured them she had no demands on her time so she'd enjoy the challenge. As they wended past many hospital and research buildings, she learned more about Romy from her neighbours.

"Romy's only lived in the cottage for about three years, but we can always depend on her to help us." Elise was clearly happy to have Romy as a neighbour… and very concerned about her welfare. "Romy answered a text from Therese, about seven-thirty this morning. She was fine then."

Therese continued. "It was about half past eight when another message came through. Well, only the beginning of one, a few letters, which made us suspicious something was wrong. I found her on the hall floor, near the door."

"You had a key to get in?"

"Romy gave us one after her skiing accident. We looked after the house, and her mail, and took her clothes and such, when she was hospitalized. We've had the key ever since."

Keira knew she really had no right to ask, but she did anyway. "Is there anyone else who would have a house key? Maybe some other friend of Romy?"

Elise explained Romy had been in a long term relationship before her skiing accident, but it had fizzled out during her recovery time. Romy hadn't talked of any new boyfriend during the last months and they didn't think anyone else would have a spare key.

Keira boarded the second tram with no particular destination in mind, glad to just enjoy the ride. It gave her time to plan. She'd come to talk with Romy but if it wasn't possible, what should she do? Wait a bit to see if Romy recovered? In the light of the woman's accident, Keira didn't know if the hospital would now cancel Romy's planned ankle surgery, or if they would keep her in till she was medically fit for the operation. Stay in Vienna? Or go home? Unsure of what was best, her mind churned over the possibilities as the tram glided past building after tall white building in the

University area and made its way into the old city.

What had been the purpose of her visit that might not be possible now? She'd wanted to get to know Romy's background, and to tell Romy about Neela. She'd wanted to ferret out any jewels Romy might still have in her possession, or which she may have sold in the past. Mercenary details, yet the crux of the matter.

Magnificent buildings caught some of her attention as the tram hummed along busy streets. Needing to get her bearings, she pulled out the tourist leaflets she'd grabbed up from a stand in the hotel foyer before she'd scurried off to the hospital. A glance at the easily read street names confirmed she was near the Ringstrasse. The circular boulevard had many tourist spots dotted along its length, but also enclosed the old heart of the city, jam-packed with places of interest and showcasing fabulous architecture of different periods.

Another leaflet indicated she could ride the Ring-tram, on a hop-on hop-off basis, as it wound around a large area of the inner city – the Innerstadt. Perfect. The Ring-tram was similar to hop on-hop off City Tour Buses. She wouldn't return to Edinburgh quite yet, wouldn't abandon Romy, but she could see some of Vienna meantime.

She bought a flexible ticket – one allowing her to use the Ring-tram, but also some of the old city trams, as many times as she wanted to over a 24-hour period. During her first journey around the Ringstrasse, about a half hour's duration, she earmarked the places she'd stop at on her next circuit, though determined to buy a better map and guidebook for she was sure she'd want to see a lot more places in the Innerstadt. Her tram had already passed alongside the Danube Canal – the Donaukanal – and was headed back toward the University area when she realised the time. Close to 12:30p.m. Hunger had caught up on her.

Disembarking at the next halt, she wandered along the street leading down to the Hofburg – an area of the old city. At one of the many bookstores she rifled through the city guides and maps. Her choices bought, she picked a nearby restaurant, the menu perfect for her needs. Only just seated at a free table, her mobile rang.

Teun?

Excitement, relief, pleasure… she didn't know quite what else, but she was so pleased to hear his voice.

"I just picked up your message, Keira. What's up?"

Teun must be at work; she could hear someone mumbling in the background. She gave an update on Romy, trying hard to keep anxiety from her voice, but knew she hadn't managed it when his deep sigh came to her ear.

"Where are you just now?"

"I've just got seated at a bistro for lunch." Her plan for the afternoon was decided on the hoof, her rifling through the guidebook as quiet as possible.

"I wish I was with you right now, you know that, don't you?"

She made sure her response left him in no doubt of her preferences as she told him the places she'd glimpsed so far. Teun was agitated; she couldn't put her finger on it, but felt he was.

"Be careful around the tourist areas, Keira. I've read Vienna is supposed to be a pretty safe place, but just watch out for sneak thieves… and…"

"I will, Teun." She reassured him. "I'm a tourist, but at least I can speak the language, give or take some heavy local dialects."

"Yeah. Well, you can't be too careful." What sounded like an overhead PA system intoning some sort of tinny message was in the background before Teun bid her a hasty farewell. "I'll call you again soon, okay, but it won't be for a few hours. Got to go."

She closed her mobile and sat staring at it. The call had been so short they'd not talked about any of his progress, or lack of it, during the last days.

As she tackled her Eierspeise – a variation of an omelette served in the pan –she planned her first visit. She was on the street called Herrengasse. A good walk down would take her to the museum quarter, and she'd be able to see lots of architectural detail along the route. Since she'd no idea how long she'd stay in Vienna, she decided to head for one of the larger museums with many different collections. The Kunsthistorisches Museum, the Art History Museum, was back down at the Ringstrasse – back to the trams if she wanted to use them later.

While paying for her meal, unease crept upon her; as though someone had been staring at her. The restaurant was busy; plenty of people were scanning around, just as she did, though no-one in particular appeared to be staring now. Teun's warnings had spooked her. God! It was ridiculous how much she missed his company. She was used to being a lone traveller, had done it a lot when establishing her business. Solo wandering had never been an issue with her. Now it seemed it was.

Exploring Vienna would have been so much nicer with company, special company.

Every single building needed time to savour. One fabulous piece of architecture led to the next… and the next. Speed-walking the last part of the Hofburg didn't do it justice. She muttered a vow to explore it more thoroughly the following day as her neck craned to the top of a particularly ornate rooftop on the corner building, before she emerged out into the boulevard. Finding the pedestrian crossing at the Ringstrasse was in her favour, she scooted over the road.

After she crossed, she looked back to enjoy the view.

"What the hell?" Her mouth gaped… her eyes, too.

At the far side of the wide stretch of road someone ducked down to tie his shoelace, the whiteness of the hair grabbing Keira's attention before a steady stream of traffic flowed in

187

front of her as the traffic lights changed.

"Not again!"

Anger built, the little frisson of initial fear became a heat of annoyance. Why was the bastard still following her? She'd no jewels to protect any more, so what the hell did he think he'd get from her? She squinted in the strong sunlight, cars and vans creating a stroboscopic effect. When the traffic ceased to flow, the lights red again, she faced an empty space.

A quick stomp along the pathway banished her misgivings. Spooking herself wasn't to be encouraged. That inner sister of hers told her, yet again, to get a grip!

She stood and drank in the facade of the Kunsthistorisches Museum, impressive against the clear blue sky, breathing deeply to regulate her pulse rate before she headed for the ticket office. Incredibly ornate, the long rectangular frontage boasted two storeys of arched windows; the stonework of the upper levels slightly-paler blonde sandstone than the lower. The dark gray dome of the high cupola above the central entrance contrasted well with its intricately carved stonework, the four smaller domes around the cupola just as eye-catching. Each small dome contained a statue, the detail of which was too high to see from ground level. Keira was sure they'd each be worth a good look, but consoled herself with the knowledge that an official guidebook would cover their details. Her long perusal was exactly what she needed. Feeling grounded again, no longer spooked or angry, she trod the steps up to the ticket office.

There was no preference for the media she liked to view in a museum or gallery. Scanning the leaflet she collected along with her ticket from the front entrance hall, the art work in the Kunsthistorisches Museum was stunning. It housed the painting collections of the imperial Hapsburg rulers, but was by no means the only art gallery in Vienna.

Egyptian antiquities were her first port of call. Sculptures and artefacts from different dynasties were dotted around the rooms of the collection. Huge sarcophagi and large canopic jars – used in the funerary mummification processes – were viewed with the backdrop of original wall friezes acquired from ancient temples.

Hours later, Keira wished she'd worn trainers. Her sandals were comfortable, but not for all the standing around necessary to absorb details of the many paintings. By six p.m. she'd only viewed a fraction of the huge museum, but it was time to call it a day.

She'd kept her mobile on vibrate, but there had been no messages. Not from the hospital, and not from Teun.

Hunger gnawed, but phoning Therese was her first priority. It took only a few sentences to ascertain they'd had no contact from the hospital either. Elise didn't advise calling the hospital: in her experience it was best to wait, since Romy was not in a life-threatening situation. Though it might be best, it was frustrating. Keira had thoroughly enjoyed the museum, but it wasn't why she'd come to Vienna.

Instead of walking back to her hotel, she hopped onto the Ring-tram as it squeaked to a halt outside the impressive museum frontage. Entering through the middle doors, she punched her ticket and squeezed her way to the rear of the car. It was jam-packed, but she found an empty seat when a couple made an impromptu late choice to get off at the stop, jumping up in a flurry. As she settled down, her gaze drifted to the front of the tram. Just before the doors closed and the car slid into motion, a man forced his way through the closing space at the front doors.

Oh God! That shit again?

Panic set in. She stared out the window for guidance, from who knows what, or whom. The grip on her bag threatened to break the leather strap, her fingers trembling against her chest.

Rat in a trap.

Not absorbing a thing outside, she willed calm to descend. She was being ridiculous again. The back of one hand snaked up to towel her sweaty brow. The tram was packed full of people, the man trailing her couldn't do anything to her while she was on... but when she got off? Her eyes tracked her surroundings. Wide open. Squelching down her fear, she made plans. Exit really quickly, so fast her hunter would be unable to follow her. He was still wedged down near the front and that was a good thing. Wasn't it?

Oh God! Why was the tram so hot? The window close to her was open, but she felt as if she was a tasty bit of meat on a spit... just ready for the picking. Or more like the meat in amongst all the vegetables on a plate: her pursuer the fork, poised and ready.

Having got on at the Museumsplatz area, she guessed the tram might get less busy by the time it reached the University quarter. That was a good few stops ahead. She had to get off before then to lose her shadow. Once she lost him, she could do normal things like... find somewhere to eat? She felt nauseous already. Drawing on reserves of strength, she fought back the bile threatening to erupt and concentrated on the elusive being-normal thing.

According to her guidebook, there were plenty of good restaurants around the area called Schottenkirche, and it wasn't too far from her hotel. She yanked open her map so fast a split screeched down the middle. Her eye movements were feverish as she blinked to a clear vision, one finger tracing her route. When her tram passed along the Rathaus Park, she could get off and walk down the street named Schottengasse, and stop at some place when she was sure the man wasn't following her.

She avidly scanned to confirm her bearings. When the car hissed to a halt at the next stop, lots of people around her were exiting. Finding no street name, she swallowed her alarm. She must be on Schottengasse already! How did that happen? Scrambling from the seat, she ducked down as low as she could and followed the queue. When she was almost out of the door, she leaned to the side to track her snowy-haired follower.

Her stomach almost heaved up its contents. He'd forced his way to the nearest doors. Panic overtook her; her foot froze on the lowest step, her body fully out of the vehicle. In slow freeze frames, her pursuer got off. A pile of travellers surged behind him and forced him to move further onto the pavement.

Keira's chin whipped around. No-one exited behind her. Zipping back inside, the doors hissed to a close before the tram wheezed into motion. Thumping down onto the nearest seat, her eyes gravitated to the window. Her stalker speed-walked alongside the tram. She was terrified. He looked furious. Now he wasn't just a white head as his features imprinted on her memory banks. An aquiline nose sat above tightly-drawn thin lips. Strong blue eyes flared his anger.

Keira shut her eyes tight. She couldn't look out the window any more. Her hand willed the rapid pulse at her neck to still. Involuntarily, her lips curled up in a nervous smile. Her nerves were still a jingle, but she also felt exhilaration, a heady excitement. She'd lost him. Steeling herself to be braver, she scanned the street up ahead. He'd have to run much faster to keep up since the stretch they were travelling on moved alongside the edges of the Rathaus Park, now a greater distance between the tram stops.

That was confusing.

Pulling up her map, she checked again. A genuine smile of delight split her face; her body slid even further down the vinyl seat, beginning to relax a little. All those people had exited at the Burgtheatre, the city theatre, and there was still a bit of park to pass along before the next stop. She wasn't near Schottengasse yet. Relief flooded as the tram clicked into an even faster pace. No-one got off or entered at the next stop. Keira heaved a sigh of relief when there was no sign of her shadow alongside.

Her legs trembled like mad when she got off at Schottengasse. As she walked down the fairly major thoroughfare, she willed her nerves to calm. She sporadically scanned back on her speed-walk, relieved there was no sign of her pursuer. After a few long blocks, she slowed her pace and regained her breath. She couldn't truly appreciate the marvellous architecture around her, though she tried. When she was close to the Schottenkirche, the local parish church, she selected a place to eat.

The restaurant wasn't too busy but she sat in towards the back, in a seat facing the entrance. By the time she'd ordered, she'd gained some equilibrium, though why her stalker was still on her tail in Vienna eluded her. It was the same guy as in Heidelberg, but why was he following her? Did the guy think she could lead him to more jewels? She certainly wasn't carrying any around on her person. The thought of another bag snatch truly alarmed her!

She nervously fiddled with her cutlery. Did Teun suspect someone was following her? Was that why he'd been persistent about her being careful as she wandered around Vienna? If so, why could he not just trust her with his suspicions?

That last thought made her seethe.

Her Rindsgulasch, a very traditional dish of beef stew with dumplings, was almost eaten when her mobile chirped. Teun!

"Hello, Keira. What are you doing now?"

Forking up a little of her soft dumpling, she savoured it as she absorbed Teun's greeting. "Mmm. I'm just finishing my first sampling of Austrian dumpling."

Teun's tones rumbled at her ear. "And is the dessert tasty?"

"Very tasty, but it's not dessert. I'm eating a paprika beef stew with dumplings. I guess maybe it's more of a Hungarian dish originally, but it's still quite popular here. My guidebook tells me restaurants now have a tendency to cater towards worldwide tastes, but I fancied something old-fashioned with dumplings. Dumplings also used to be popular in soups, apparently, but I'll sample those another day."

The conversation seemed inane, so Keira let Teun do the

talking. He asked about Romy.

"Nothing yet. Therese sent a text a few minutes ago saying Romy had wakened naturally, but can't have visitors till tomorrow morning."

The hum of a car was in the background. "Wait for that dessert, Keira, please?"

The plea in Teun's voice was unmistakable, but puzzling.

"Wait dessert? I don't understand."

Teun gave no answer; instead a question. "Where are you just now?"

What a strange conversation. Odd, yet intriguing. "I'm in a small restaurant near Schottenkirche. Why are you asking?"

"Are you close to your hotel?" Another odd question.

"It's a short walk away, or a very quick taxi ride."

Teun sighed. Then he chuckled. "How soon would you like dessert?"

"Teun. I can tell you're in a playful mood, but why all these odd questions?"

"Would you like to share dessert with me, Keira?"

Now it was almost too much. Keira set aside her cutlery and caught the eye of the hovering waiter, indicating she'd like her bill. Her tone dropped a few octaves, regret humming through it. "You know I would."

"Flag a taxi. Please?"

Keira's breath hitched. "Why would you want me back at my hotel so quickly, Teun?" Was there something she needed to know about? "Should I be worried about my safety?"

"Your hotel looks nice, Keira."

"How would you know that?"

Teun was really in full teasing mode. "How about, because my taxi has just pulled up outside it?"

Keira's squeal of delight startled the waiter who presented her with the bill.

A little over five minutes later Keira was outside her hotel. She'd not even waited for a taxi since it was a straight route

193

along the road. Out of breath, she opened the entrance door and almost fell over Teun who stood just inside the reception area.

The downstairs foyer wasn't the venue for too ecstatic a welcome. It took an agitated minute or so for the lift to ascend to her floor, then Keira opened her room door and they tumbled inside in a flurry. Teun dumped his case and dragged her into his arms.

"Oh, God! I've missed you, Keira."

She could scarcely gasp a response. "Me, too."

A while later Keira peeled herself away from Teun, a rumble having deafened her.

"You're starving."

The flare of heat in his eyes matched his words. "I'm probably always going to be starving."

Keira nudged him. "Food. I'm talking food, Teun."

His chuckling mellowed into a hearty laugh as he teased her even more. "Yeah. Food." His arms banded around her. Only another starving growl made him release her.

Teun swivelled up from the bed, dragging her with him. "A quick shower, then we'll go fill me up." She ignored the teasing wink.

They were pushing it, since it was now late in the evening. However, a little conference with the front desk clerk solved the problem. They didn't have far to walk to reach the recommended restaurant. While Teun got stuck into a main course, Keira sipped a fine glass of wine.

"There's something you're not telling me, Teun," Keira persisted, since she knew he'd been evasive.

Chapter Ten

Keira was right. He had been withholding information she needed to know. The problem was more how to tell her without being too alarmist, rather than him wanting to keep secrets.

"I didn't want you to worry, but you can't be kept in the dark any longer."

"I knew it."

He launched in, not wanting her to get any more annoyed. "Call me a suspicious bastard, if you like, but after Adam's death I decided it wouldn't go amiss to get some help regarding our safety."

Keira's expressive eyebrows hitched up. "Our safety?"

He made sure his nod wasn't mistaken. "I called the security agency I hired to help me store the emeralds, and requested them to dig up all the information they could get on Jensen." He broke off at Keira's huffed gasp. "I know what you're probably going to say – he's my relative, or something."

One of the things he liked best about Keira was she could surprise him. She didn't fail this time either as she encouraged him to continue, wasting no time berating him for his family mistrust. "And Zaan... and Romy."

Keira's gaze was serious, her bottom lip being gnawed. Nibbling her lip himself came to mind, but that would have to wait till later.

"Jensen had us checked out, so you reciprocated?"

He loved how Keira's brain assessed. "Pretty much, though

by the end of that first call to them, I also asked the agency to ensure our personal safety."

He had a hard time veiling the truth from his gaze, Keira's focus was so intent.

"You're obviously not happy with what they have to report? Is it something about Jensen? Or about the people who have been following us?"

Teun reeled back in his chair. She was quick but he hadn't expected this for a question. "Both."

Keira looked askance, as though collecting her thoughts before she spoke. "Can I go first? I'll tell you what I think?"

He nodded, watching every nuance of her expressive face.

"There's a man with silvery white hair who's been tailing me. Not an old man. He's probably early forties, wears a black bomber jacket. He tailed us in Heidelberg, and now he's doing the same, tailing me here in Vienna. He's got close enough to me, but hasn't tried to harm me. I'm thinking he's just following me in the hope that I lead him to more jewels."

Teun didn't refute her suspicions. "You've seen him again?"

She nodded, quite deliberately, before taking a deep breath. "Today. Just before I went into the Kunsthistorisches Museum. I told myself I was hallucinating; I was paranoid; or becoming fixated by the notion of having a white-blond lover."

Teun's throat seized up. "Really?"

The serious look on her face was replaced with a wry grin. "No. I prefer my men dark-haired."

"Men?"

They were getting off track but she humoured him by answering, her topaz eyes twinkling. "Man. One man to be precise."

"You saw this guy just the one time?"

Keira's head shook, sending a cascade of dark brown hair to ripple across her shoulders. "He got onto my Ring-tram after I finished at the museum."

Teun wasn't deluded. Her pretence of being proud of how she handled her escape from her stalker on the Ring-tram was tinged with the real fear she'd felt. He almost crushed her fingers, so glad she was safe. After apologising profusely, he absorbed to the rest of her update.

"I'm fine, Teun. He could have grabbed me anytime at the museum. I was so engrossed I wouldn't have noticed him following me at that point. I can't work out why he's still tailing me, except that he may think Romy gave me information the night I arrived in Vienna."

"So, because of this guy… when you knew I was here, you ran all the way to the hotel to meet me?"

"Yes." Her deeply rich tone warmed him right to his core.

"You may have shaken him off on the Ringstrasse, but I'm sure he knows, by now, which hotel you booked into."

Brows knotted, she demanded his answer. "How did you know which hotel I'd booked into? I don't remember telling you."

"You can work it out, I'm sure?"

A tweak of her lip and sideways look confirmed it. "Your private dick company?"

They needed to talk, but in more secure surroundings. On the walk back to the hotel, he stopped often to look in shop windows. Not because he liked looking at darkened merchandise. Sampling Keira's lips was a fine temptation, but it also meant he could have a good scan around to see if they were being followed. He didn't detect anyone, but it didn't mean it wasn't happening.

Back in the hotel room, they sat in two chairs flanking a small table. He cradled his glass of wine, and began.

"The fire at Adam's house is confirmed as arson. Forensic testing proved Adam had no traces on his fingers of the plastic wrap which was set on fire, and no traces of any kind of fire-inducing materials. He did not make that fire happen."

Keira looked ready to cry. He deposited his glass on the

table and took her hand. Still not close enough, he pulled his chair around, knee to knee.

"Police investigations established the upstairs had been ransacked, so burglary is now also confirmed. Unfortunately, there's no-one who can tell what might be missing. Neither Jane, nor Declan, have been upstairs for years, and Adam's housekeeper can't be certain. She was the only one who was ever upstairs to clean. The place is such a mess she's not sure if small items have been taken. Although she is adamant nothing large has been removed."

"The intruders were looking for Geertje's collection?"

"Most likely."

"They'd been following us, so they decided to strip out Adam's house. We'd stayed long enough to do some serious looking ourselves, but they wanted to be sure we didn't miss anything?"

Keira was astute. The next bit was going to be a shock though.

"Dad's nursing home called me a couple of days ago."

Keira flinched, her fingers trembling within his grasp. He could drown in the sympathy radiating from her gorgeous eyes. "Is he okay?"

"Much the same. Stable. Though very frail. Not responding to anyone now."

Her fingers reassured him, her little smile for him momentarily replacing concern for his father.

"Remember the day Dad said someone had been pestering him?" After her brief nod, he carried on. "The security cameras had been compromised. Those outside the main entrance doors had been disabled, but the one on the corridor, leading down to Dad's room, was still operating. The police have footage of an unknown person gaining access to Dad's neighbour's room first. The man didn't stay long in there before going into Dad's room."

"What can the police do?"

"Not a whole lot at the moment, about catching the person, however, they have promised better security for Dad in the future. The director of the nursing home has already upgraded their security system. There's no way they can be negligent again – Dad's only one of their many patients."

"The guy sneaked in and tried to get Jan to give him information?" He waited till she finished her thought processes. "Do you think the guy knew Jan has dementia, and his information can't exactly be..?"

He finished her sentence for her. "Trusted?"

Her cheeks pinkened. "You know I don't mean anything horrible."

She needed cheering up again. Unfortunately he wasn't nearly done. He squeezed her fingers and leaned into a light kiss, pulling away sooner than he wanted. He had to finish what he'd started. "In New York…"

Keira finished his sentence. "The same dark-red haired guy who'd tailed us up in Duluth and in Rochester, followed us that night?"

He jumped up and paced around, rifling his fingers through his hair. "For Christ's sake, Keira. Why didn't you tell me you'd seen that guy?"

"Why didn't you say anything to me? You didn't trust me!"

She faced him down, her anger bristling. Antagonism flared between them. He tamped down his tone accordingly, not wanting her more upset than she had to be. "I sent you home since I was too damned scared to have you around me. I thought it would be safer if you were back in Edinburgh. I was pretty sure it was me who was being tailed, and all the time you knew the guy was creeping after us?"

Again Keira was full of surprises. She smiled at him. Smiled? She didn't harangue, or complain, or wail in horror.

"You sent me away so I wouldn't be in danger?"

He couldn't resist any longer. Pulling her into his arms, he gorged on her beaming smile. The silky top she wore slipped up and over her head with the most infinitesimal interruption. The pile of clothes grew when he stripped everything off them both.

"Just where I want to be."

It was only a couple of hours since they'd made love, but he couldn't do without her. She was all he'd ever wanted in a woman. He'd never had such a fit as Keira. Hectic minutes later she lay exhausted, could probably have slipped into sleep, but he knew she wanted more details. He hadn't yet divulged all. Stroking her arm, he drew her in tight.

"After we parted at the airport in New York, I was gutted at having banished you."

Her chuckle whiffed against his chest, the muscles of her cheek tickling his skin. "Banished? I thought you'd had enough of me."

He squeezed her closer; it didn't seem possible, but she shifted enough to fit him even better. "Never. It nearly killed me to send you home, Keira."

Her sleepy, but smiley, voice encouraged him to continue. "Go on."

"I went straight to my Boston lab. Declan's couriers had bust a gut, and had got the package there before I arrived."

"Package?"

He hadn't yet mentioned that news. Her eyes shadowed as he told her about the scrap of paper Adam had been clutching when he died. The name "Dan" didn't mean anything to Keira either, but her arms tightened even more around him.

"What if it wasn't meant to be a name? What if it was only the beginning of a word?"

Teun had thought of that as well but hadn't wanted to influence her in any way. "You think Adam was writing the word 'danger' as well?"

"What if he had written the whole word but had been interrupted, and the rest of the paper got ripped from his grip?"

This was exactly what he had been surmising. "I ran tests on the paper that first day in Boston. I couldn't find any traces of a fire accelerant, but there were definitely fingerprints on it. My lab isn't in a position to name fingerprints, so I kept the sample, suitably sealed, in my pocket that night when I went back to the hotel, while I worked out the best way of getting the evidence to the police."

"You phoned me indicating you'd had a problem at your Boston lab. Was it a break-in?"

"Yeah. Overnight. The intruders mucked up data on my main computer, and smashed up the samples taken from the paper – the ones which proved no traces of chemical accelerants. While I waited for the Boston police to arrive, I took further samples from the scrap of paper, to re-do the tests, and then I handed over the scrap of paper to them when they conducted their investigation. The Boston cops are liaising with the force in Rochester."

"So, the Boston police are treating the break-in seriously?"

Teun assured her they were, especially when he'd told them about the jewellery hoard they'd removed from Adam's house.

"So, now the Boston and Rochester police forces know about Geertje's jewels?"

"I'd no option, Keira. Adam's dead. A major crime, arson, has been committed as well as housebreaking and burglary to my lab. I had to tell them about me tackling our pursuer on the stairwell, and the bag snatch. They know everything we know."

Keira's relief looked total. "So, what now?"

Teun updated the last of his information. The Rochester and Boston police forces considered their investigations internal US matters but would liaise with Interpol, if requested, regarding the man tailing them in Europe. The police were satisfied the jewellery was safely stored in New York. It would remain there, while investigations were pending.

"What do we tell Jensen?"

Keira's plea stirred his heart. He guessed she'd avoided any confrontational talk involving his cousins.

"The truth. Everything that's happened so far."

"Does that mean you now think he's done nothing suspect?"

Teun didn't think that at all. He hadn't a clue about his cousins' honesty, but the time had come to share. And to flush out the perpetrator.

***

Keira called the hospital a little after eight a.m. to inquire after Romy. Responding well, she could have visitors for a brief time.

A groggy-looking Romy looked up when Keira approached her bed. The bruise on her cheek was spectacularly colourful, though the swelling had gone down. Most of the tubes were gone: a single probe alone monitoring something. A smile tweaked on her wan face when she recognized her. Keira was relieved as she'd no idea what she'd do if Romy didn't know her. The weak smile was replaced by a flash of alarm when her gaze alighted on Teun.

Hastening to calm her, Keira greeted Romy in German, and then introduced Teun in English.

"It's nice to meet you, Teun, though I wish I was not lying in a hospital bed."

Romy tired quickly after a few minutes of general chit-chat. The small amount of colour she'd started with visibly drained away, but she appeared desperate to tell them something. Her question, in German, shocked Keira.

"Do you trust this man?"

Keira made no hesitation, her glance at Teun meant to reassure him as he understood nothing. "Absolutely!"

Romy then told them in a mixture of English and German about the incident. It had been no accident. She'd been out of bed for a while, had been getting her breakfast when someone knocked at her front door. Knowing it wasn't Therese or her mother, who would have used their key, she'd gone to the door.

Keira had a feeling she wasn't going to like the next bit.

Romy had no peephole on her door, but she hadn't opened it right away. She'd called through the wood asking for the person's identity. The caller had told her he was Jensen Amsel, and he'd important information he needed to discuss with her. Romy had been in recent email and telephone contact with Jensen and didn't hesitate to open her door. Although she thought it was early for him to visit, he was family so it was the natural thing to open up for him.

"When I opened the door a crack, I immediately knew it wasn't Jensen. I'd looked him up on the internet and had seen a publicity photograph of him. My attacker tried to force his way into the house as I pushed the door closed again, but he was too strong for me."

Romy's weak smile broke free. Keira reached for her hand, gently squeezing to give support.

"In good health it wouldn't have been a problem. I used to be a very fit woman, but he overpowered me. When he thrust the door open, I screamed and fell back from him. As I toppled over, I picked up a book that lay on my little table and threw it at his head, but he caught it and whacked me on the face with it. I'm sure I screamed again when I hit the floor."

Romy was agitated, yet determined to finish. Sympathy radiated from Teun as he drew closer.

"We can hear your story later, Romy. You need to rest now."

"No, no. You must listen. He would have been inside my house if the little dog from the end house hadn't come scurrying up to the doorway. My attacker must have realised my neighbour was coming. He shoved me further inside the hallway and then ran off, but he closed the door first."

Keira finished for her. "The neighbour with the dog didn't realise what had happened? Because the door was closed, the person had no idea you'd been attacked."

Romy told them she'd blacked out for a while. When she came to she remembered trying to text Therese, but then nothing till she wakened in the hospital.

"He must have been trying to get me to give him the jewels."

Keira caught the tiniest flare in Teun's eyes, and was very careful with her next question. "Didn't you sell the earrings which might have been from Geertje's collection?"

Moisture formed and hovered on Romy's eyelids, distraught tears that soon dripped. "Yes. But I lied to Jensen. I didn't tell him I have other things that came to me from Uriel." The tears ran in full flow down her cheeks.

"Romy. Don't distress yourself! It doesn't matter."

Romy's head nodded on the pillow. "It does matter. The man who broke into my house said he'd get them later, no matter what he had to do. He knows about the other jewels."

"Would you be able to describe him to the police, Romy?"

A puzzled look on Romy's face was followed by a slight nod as she processed Teun's question. "I think so. I expected it to be Jensen so I probably looked more closely than normal. Jensen's light-haired, but not like that guy was. He had a sports cap on, but it covered snowy white hair. "

Keira exchanged a glance with Teun. Romy's eyes were closed as though picturing the person in her memory banks.

"He had light-coloured eyes, but I'm not sure if they were blue or green. Much taller than me, and I'm quite tall for a woman. His voice was rough, sort of hoarse."

Keira knew from her visit Romy was probably five nine, or even five ten. The guy definitely matched a description of the one who had been following her.

"You need to tell the police about your attacker, Romy. Have you told the doctor who examined you?" Keira was pretty sure she knew the answer from the guilty look on Romy's face.

"No. The doctor asked questions about how I fell. I told him someone had come to the door. He assumed I overbalanced and then called Therese for help."

Romy looked so distressed Keira put her arm around the other woman's shoulders.

"Most of that was true."

"The police need to know you were attacked, Romy." Teun sounded sympathetic, but firm.

Romy started to cry again. "I know. I just wanted to talk to you first, and to get you to tell Jensen about my other jewels."

"You still have other jewels in your house, Romy?" Teun's tone was low, worried.

Romy sighed, her tears drying up, though her lip wobbled. "I didn't want to tell Jensen about the other three things I've got." Her eyes implored. Keira felt the woman's emotional pain as she explained. "You know I sold the earrings to pay for my hip operation, but I'm still in debt for other medical expenses. I wasn't thinking straight, I don't suppose. I thought if I told Jensen about my other jewels, I wouldn't be able to sell them. Although they might still technically belong to me, while they were part of an exhibition I'd not be able to get money for them."

Keira wasn't sure what she'd have done if she'd faced the same dilemma.

Romy was adamant. "You must tell Jensen for me. He must get someone to collect them and put them somewhere safe."

Teun repeated his earlier question. "Where are they, Romy?"

"My bank. They're in a safety deposit box."

Nursing a cup of coffee, after a quick lunch at a bistro near the hospital, Keira made plans with Teun. Romy was fairly sure the gold choker was the one in the photograph Jensen had sent. She couldn't be sure about the gold bangle, but the fact that the heart-shaped gold ring had a huge emerald at its centre meant she was confident it had also once belonged to the Tiru jewels.

"I'm not happy about telling Jensen in a phone call. I think we need to tell him in person."

Keira was surprised at Teun's declaration. "Go to Heidelberg?"

He nodded, his answer interrupted by her mobile chiming a message.

"It's Therese. Oh, my God! She says Romy's house has been broken into."

When they arrived at Romy's cottage, Therese stood outside her own door. Beckoning them inside, she told them the police were still inside Romy's house, doing whatever they do after a break-in. Romy's cottage was a mess. The place had been turned over, every nook and cranny.

Elise was in tears. They hadn't heard anything at all, and couldn't understand how someone could do such a dreadful thing. Romy had enough to think about with the state of her health, without having this happen to her as well. If they hadn't gone into Romy's house to gather some clothes to deliver to the hospital that afternoon, they wouldn't have known it had happened. They'd not been in Romy's house since the morning before, and had no idea when the culprits had been inside.

Keira could tell Teun itched to leave, his whisper insistent. "We need to get out of here before the police question us, Keira."

At first she was shocked, since Teun was so law abiding in the US. Catching sight of his imploring glimpse, without betraying anything to Therese or Elise, she made haste to leave, making sure her next words sounded casual.

"We'll go now, Elise. Unless? You don't think the police will need to speak to us, do you?"

Elise tut-tutted. "They might want to speak to us again, but I don't see why they'd want to talk to you."

Promising to call later, she and Teun zipped through the

arch to the main street where they flagged a taxi.

Relief flooded when she was back at their hotel room, yet it was a quandary what to do next. Romy's jewels were safe. Teun had managed to establish that no-one would be allowed to access the box except Romy herself.

Teun revisited the plan of visiting Jensen. He thought it even more imperative now they spoke face-to-face with Jensen, since the police might soon contact him. If the Vienna police questioned Romy, as they no doubt would, they'd find out about Jensen's quest for the Tiru jewels.

"We might have a little window of time," Teun told her. "It all depends on how quickly the Austrian police contact the German authorities."

They hadn't done anything illegal, but Teun wanted to confront Jensen before the establishment did.

***

Four hours later, Teun sat in Jensen's house, Keira plastered at his side. Everything had timed in perfectly. Their dash to the airport had been worth it as they'd managed to catch an immediate flight to Frankfurt.

Jensen supplied well-needed coffee. Though they'd turned up unannounced at his house, he was delighted to see them. Nevertheless, Teun wasn't yet convinced about his honesty. His German cousin would have to do more for that to happen.

"Jensen, we're here with both good news and bad. Have you had any contact with the police today?" He went on the attack.

"No, should I have?"

Surprise raised Jensen's brows, the measure of shock in his voice and expression just plausible, though absolutely no sign of panic. Teun considered him a very good actor, or he really was genuine.

Keira fidgeted with the charms at her neck. He knew by

now it was a sure sign of her unease since he'd seen her do it so often. Sidling his body closer to her on the couch, he hoped it gave her some reassurance. He was aware she became more and more spooked by the whole affair, as incident after incident happened. Where she'd not doubted Jensen's, or Zaan's, motives initially, he was sure she had misgivings now.

She'd told him right outside Jensen's doorstep she was anxious, worried about what they were about to do. She'd challenged his decision to confront Jensen. The argument she'd put up had been good, and almost had him agreeing to go straight to the local police. A messy confrontation unquestionably wasn't what she wanted, they'd already discussed that. Nonetheless, it wasn't Teun's way to avoid nasty stuff if it cleared the air.

Jensen merely looked enquiring, so he decided questions about the police could wait till later. Changing the topic to the good news, he watched every nuance on Jensen's face. Appropriate flickers of astonishment appeared when he revealed finding what they suspected was Tiru jewellery at Adam's house, and then the bangle at Grace's. Jensen's initial surprise led to sheer delight. Again, it seemed genuine delight. It wasn't sufficient confirmation, though; Teun's instinct told him Jensen still wasn't totally truthful.

"But that's wonderful news. We've now got quite a few pieces of the jewellery already."

"We have?" Keira asked.

Teun liked how Keira's brain worked when her question sounded so innocent. She was an amazing woman, her enquiry filled with suitable incredulity and skill, given he knew she hated something underhand was going on. He rested his hand proprietarily on her thigh, to help settle the minute trembles he could feel transferring to his own leg, welded as they were together on the sofa. His eyes clashed with hers for a second, her answering smile relaying her intention to persist, regardless. In spite of the tense situation, a smile creased the corners of his mouth.

"What have we got?"

Jensen looked truly pleased as he related the items, but Teun wasn't giving an inch yet.

"First we've got the ring I acquired. Zaan's mother's ring is also very likely as a second thing. I've located the buyer of Romy's earrings, and have put in a purchase bid for them. The sale will go through as soon as they are authenticated. That's three items."

Teun admired Keira's dexterity was spot on as she encouraged Jensen to confide. "Did Zaan contact you about the hair pendant?"

Jensen became more animated, eyes aglow and the most excited Teun had yet seen, a broad smile accompanying a ticking off on his fingers to number four. "Yes. The pendant was easily traced. Zaan's cousin, Naatje, had sold it to a local jeweller who had details about the buyer. Zaan called me last night to say he's having it valued and has also made a purchase deal with the buyer, should it be valid."

"I take it the buyers of Romy's earrings and Naatje's pin are happy to sell?" Teun was still sceptical over how easy it seemed to be, though he refused to feel guilty when Jensen's smile dipped and disappointment of some sort replaced his earlier elation.

"We've offered both of those people twenty-five percent over the valuation price. They're happy to sell, Teun. Though you're not happy about something else, and that's got me confused. None of what's just been discussed is negative." Jensen's tone hardened, now concerned.

Teun wasn't quite ready to divulge the rest that had happened in the US – not yet – and was relieved when Keira chipped in, still looking perky, though he knew better how she really felt. Although nothing so far would have eased her anxiety, she still came across positively.

"That's four items. Added to what Teun has found in the

US, makes nine altogether when we account for the two sets of earrings matching the Moghul necklace."

Jensen's focus was on Keira as he replied, returning her beam. Teun understood that; he wasn't able to resist Keira's smile either.

"I've been talking again to Marijke Baert in New Zealand. She emailed me a photo of the ring Neela gave her. Excuse me for a moment while I bring in some paperwork from next door."

He broke off to go through glazed dividing doors separating his lounge from the next room. Teun could see him rifling around a cluttered desk. On his return, Jensen passed Keira a printout which she shared.

"Very impressive!"

Her declaration was genuine but brief, her grin engaging as she leaned in closer. He pretended interest in the ring; it was a wide gold band set with three large emeralds, divided by two large pearls. Although pretty enough, it was nothing compared to Keira's topaz eyes sparkling alongside him. Realising his attention had strayed from the topic, he dropped his gaze to the photograph once more. Try as he did, he just couldn't see Keira choosing that type of ring for herself. What he knew of her already indicated her preference for more simple styles of jewellery. A simple setting with a simple stone; he filed the thought.

"It's been valued in Wellington, equivalent to nine thousand euros. Marijke Baert is perfectly happy to be part of the group if we authenticate all items, and will be delighted to include it in an exhibition – though she has no intention of selling the ring at present."

Teun kept it light as he determined further good news from Jensen. "Any advance on ten items?"

Another beam from Jensen preceded his next update. "You also know Teun's cousin, Behrta, has a bracelet? It's beautiful too." Another printout was handed over.

"Number eleven. The list is rising." Teun was more impressed with the delicate bracelet he now looked at. His first thought was it would decorate Keira's slender wrist very well, but it was a digression he couldn't afford. It was time to tell Jensen about Romy's other jewellery, Keira picking up his minutest nod, so in tune with him it was in some ways alarming

"We've just been to visit Romy. Did you know she was back in hospital?"

Jensen was astonished. He slipped forward in his chair, an unconscious movement inviting more details. "I thought her next surgery wasn't for a few more days, sometime next week?"

"That was her plan, yes." Keira was careful with her next words but he almost felt her stress. Before arriving at Jensen's, they'd decided she should give the information about Romy's assault if possible, since she'd visited Romy the evening before her fall.

Teun scrutinized his German cousin's reactions as Keira filled him in.

"Romy's not in hospital early due to any of her surgeries, planned or just completed. She was assaulted yesterday morning."

To give him his due, Jensen appeared genuinely upset. "What happened?"

"Someone claiming to be you attacked her."

Jensen was appalled, his jump to his feet instant, his walk about the room an agitation that didn't appear false. "I would never have just turned up at her doorstep unannounced. I would have made an appointment. She was still recovering from her hip operation."

Belatedly, Jensen asked after her welfare.

Teun's answer was about as informative as the hospital would have been.

"We visited her this morning. Her cheek is badly bruised; her hip is swollen and delicate; but at least she's not unconscious, as she was yesterday."

He still couldn't put a finger on it. Jensen looked truly concerned for Romy, and had shared his findings regarding the quest. The next news about Adam was going to be hard to talk about, but he really needed to gauge Jensen's reactions to the dire events in Minnesota. Yet, he was only prepared to divulge piece by piece.

Jensen was completely shaken on hearing about the fire at Adam's house and of his subsequent death, his grope to sit down an awkward slump. Teun left the details ambiguous enough for Jensen to deduce the death had been as a result of the fire. Jensen's pallor increased, about on par with the tension in his fingers which strangled the arms of his chair. Increasingly more alarmed, he was even more anxious when Teun related that an uninvited visitor to his dad's nursing home had caused Jan's serious decline. Grave was too easy a word to describe how Jensen looked when Teun also revealed how he and Keira had regularly been tailed.

"Someone has been following you as well?"

Keira was quick to answer, as focused on Jensen as he was. "Definitely following us."

Teun laid his cards firmly on the table. "If you know anything about this, Jensen, you'd friggin' well better tell us now, because the police are going to be battering your door down sometime soon."

Jensen's palm did a compulsive face wipe of his jaw area, his gaze frantic. "I don't know who has been following you, Teun, and I'm appalled your family has had such dreadful things happening to them."

Teun couldn't contain his temper. Sloping around the room, he attacked. "My family? A few days ago you claimed my family was your family."

Jensen looked abashed, but he had to give the guy some credit since his focus didn't shy away from the virulent outburst berating him. Jensen's voice was a plea.

"We are all family. I don't know who has attacked Romy either. I never meant for any of this to happen when I dreamt of having the Tiru collection brought together again."

Keira had been sitting in stunned silence, her features tight with worry. Teun sat down beside her, and cradled the hand she'd been using to fret the gold chain and the charms dangling from it. He sensed how perturbed she was about the whole undertaking and guessed she was reverting back to her earliest view of Jensen, back to believing in him – which gave her the same problem as he had. If Jensen was totally honest, then who the hell was harassing his family... and who was paying the bastard goons to follow Keira?

Teun again cut the guy some slack since Jensen had waited till he had his full attention.

"There are only a few other details I know, and you don't."

Teun's ears pricked up. His cousin was eventually going to level with him?

"It surprised me when the seller of the snake ring approached me directly. He came to my shop in Cologne and asked for me by name. I wasn't in the shop, of course, as I'm mostly here in Heidelberg. My manager made contact with me, and we arranged an appointment. I went the next day. The seller told me he was sure I'd be interested in the ring."

"Did you get the name of the person?"

"Of course. The ring was valued at ninety thousand euros, and this is what I paid into his bank account. Though we made a private deal, during the valuation process by a secondary jeweller, the news leaked out I had acquired something quite spectacular."

"I don't understand these processes yet. Why did you have to have another jeweller involved?"

Jensen's laugh was regretful. "Though I realised I had a highly valuable piece, I wanted to make sure I wasn't paying over the odds. It's not completely unknown in my profession to have a second opinion. A seller will sometimes request it themselves but, I suppose, I just had to have another estimate. My colleague agreed with my assessment of value, but he also inadvertently let it leak to the jewellery world – though it was actually one of his assistants who spread the word."

"What other details do you know, and we don't?"

Keira's breath made the tiniest hitch, but he was proud of the way she kept her cool.

"After the sale, the word spread like wildfire. The internet is such an amazing thing these days, almost nothing is private. A very astute gemology student in Amsterdam read about it in a social network, saw the photo of my newly-acquired snake ring, and matched it up with the newspaper article of 1815. She contacted me with her suspicions that what I had just bought was a part of the Tiru Salana collection."

"Is that how Zaan knew about it?" Teun asked.

"Yes. The gemologist wasn't alone when she'd made the connection. Her friend put an article on her blog, and that was all it took for it to become public knowledge."

Keira's breath exhaled loudly, right beside him, as she grabbed his elbow. He curled her in closer. "That's amazing."

"I, naturally, got a security agency to find out more, since the ring did match the description in the old newspaper. I also asked them to investigate the seller of the ring. What I failed to tell you is I now know it was sold to me by the ex-husband of Anna Vosters."

"Neela's granddaughter?"

"Yes."

Teun felt he'd been in a bubble and it had just burst, the energy from it kick-starting his brain. "Do you know how long it is since their divorce?"

"It's only six months since their official divorce signing. They had been estranged for two years before that, and had been married for about twelve years."

"Could it have been part of the divorce settlement?" Keira seemed doubtful about the answer to her question.

Jensen's shoulders shrugged. "I don't think so. My sources could find nothing much in their settlement. They never had any children, so it appeared to have been a fairly simple divorce procedure, with little or no property needing divided."

"I met him at Neela's funeral." Keira's words were hushed, her expression disdainful. "He was the sort of guy who was all bluster. All talk and not much action."

Teun thought back to days before, something about Jensen's words not quite matching up. "When you first told us about the ring, you said the guy didn't know what he was selling. Have you changed your mind?"

Quick shakes of Jensen's head negated that. "No. He knew it was made of gold. He guessed the emeralds to be worth a little, but he had no idea that, along with the diamonds, the item would be so valuable."

Keira looked puzzled, that little nibbling of her lower lip a quirk he'd already worked out meant she was deep in thought. "He asked for you in particular? He went to your shop in Cologne, and not the nearest shop to him in Holland?" After Jensen nodded agreement, she continued. "He must have known about your family relationship?"

"I haven't talked to him about it, but yes, I'm sure he must know who I am. I'm guessing he'd done a little genealogy homework, too, knowing Neela had given the ring to his ex-wife."

Chapter Eleven

"He stole it from Anna?"

Teun knew there was probably no other reasonable conclusion they could come to till they located Anna, and spoke to her about it.

"My agents have tried to locate Anna but so far they've come up with nothing. There's no way I can prove he stole it, though that was what had occurred to me, too." Jensen's thoughts on it looked far from happy.

Teun had other questions needing answers regarding Jensen's agents. He tightened his arm around Keira, including her in his question, but felt a need to shelter her as well. "Did you set your guard dogs on us, as well as finding out our financial status?"

Jensen had the decency to look ashamed, though Teun noticed that again his cousin didn't avoid eye contact. "I already told you it was to satisfy my bank. I could then indicate who might be able to put up collateral, if insisted on. But that's all I asked the security company to do."

"You didn't set those goons to follow us?"

Jensen was furious. "Absolutely not! What would be the point in that?"

"To know how successful we were at finding Tiru jewels?"

The colour drained from Jensen's livid face, his answer cold and precise. "You agreed to be part of the group, Teun. That was sufficient for me to trust you would inform me of your progress, as Zaan has, and Marijke. Though I now know you failed to give me your trust."

Teun's focus shifted to Keira. Fiddling with the charms, her gaze anywhere but on him, her embarrassment was palpable. He felt only partially guilty – he was the one who had forced distrust between Jensen and Keira – but the whole story wasn't revealed yet. Jensen's outrage had dissipated to a dull flush but his eyes still withheld. Something. Teun's gut knew it.

"Why do I still have trust issues regarding you, Jensen? My intuition is usually spot-on, and it's telling me you're still shielding information we should know about."

Jensen paced about, agitated and stressed. Teun had an inkling what was coming wouldn't be good, but he needed Jensen to divulge everything before he told him the rest of what had happened in the US.

"I know something sinister has happened, but I don't know why. I know it's got to be something to do with the Tiru jewels, but I can't see how."

Jensen again disappeared into his study, returning with a photograph. It displayed a beaming Jensen with his arm around a stunning woman. Zelda had been his girlfriend for a couple of years, but the relationship had floundered.

"She's in the jewellery trade, like me, with a larger shop in Amsterdam and a small boutique here in Heidelberg. Our relationship was of the on-off variety. On, when she visited here or when I went to Amsterdam. Off, a lot of the time in between. We called a halt to our affair about a year ago. At first I'd been enthralled by her, flattered, since she had pursued me after we met at a jewellery convention."

Jensen was embarrassed. Teun didn't know the guy, but he could tell divulging a past relationship wasn't easy for his cousin to do. "The first flush of lust passed quickly?" His comment was accompanied by what he hoped looked like genuine commiseration.

A nod confirmed before Jensen picked up the threads of his story. "Yes, except the affair lingered over a couple of years. I

217

was surprised when she called me the day after the first press release hit the newssheets about the snake-headed ring. She congratulated me on a spectacular acquisition and asked if she could come and see it."

Teun couldn't help it. "Not interested in you, but highly drawn to your ring?" Keira nudged him, an indication he should behave. When he looked at her, those expressive topaz eyes of hers chided even more. Smiling, he softened the blow for Jensen. "Or, maybe she had been missing you?"

Jensen actually chuckled, his expression wry as one side of his lip curled a little. "I don't think she was ever interested in me, not really."

"Did you show the ring to her?" Keira sounded sceptical.

"Yes. She was in Heidelberg that day, visiting her shop."

"Very convenient, don't you think?" Teun was having some fun at his gullible cousin's expense. He didn't know why the naïveté bothered him, but it did.

Jensen smoothed down his hair, returning it to pristine tidiness. "She was very impressed, wanted to know who I'd bought it from."

Keira's voice was soft and caring – even though he knew she was pulling the answers from Jensen as much as he was. "As a jeweller, she'd be interested in the history of the piece?"

"Absolutely. It's so original every jeweller in central Europe wants to have a look at it."

Keira got her question in before Teun had time to formulate it tactfully. "But what makes you think there's anything sinister going on? As your ex-girlfriend, what would be wrong in her contacting you?"

Jensen sat down heavily on the opposite chair. "Our break-up was accelerated by me buying a particularly nice, antique china clock we both bid for. Both wanted it… but I was the one who got it. Zelda is a very competitive lady in the auction room, and she doesn't forgive easily. I was confident we'd never speak again after I refused to give it to her."

"But she did contact you. Perhaps she wanted to heal the rift between you?" Keira was still being nice.

"Good of you to say so, but I'm not so sure. I'd been storing the Tiru ring in the usual safe in my Heidelberg shop for the few nights after I bought it, but the evening of Zelda's visit, I decided to bring it home. It was an impulse I was very glad of. My shop was broken into that night."

"What happened?"

Teun was so impressed with Keira as her compassion flooded the room.

"The safe was breached. A small amount of cash was taken, and a diamond necklace which was in for repair to the catch. Nothing was stolen from the shop itself; the robbers had to flee having set off the alarms. The police have nothing so far on the culprits, except they know from CCTV footage that two people were involved."

"Have you kept the ring here?" Keira got the question in first.

"No. I took it to my bank for storage. It was during that visit I thought up the whole exhibition venture, since by then I'd read the articles which had appeared in the Amsterdam papers of 1815, and my mother had given me the photograph of the trio of sisters. "

"Are you saying Zelda had something to do with the robbery at your shop?" Teun monitored his cousin's reactions.

Jensen looked as though he fought with his conscience and no-one was winning. "My shop has never been broken into before. I have good security measures in place, yet someone knew how to stall the alarm system long enough for them to enter by the rear door. It was only thwarted because a secondary alarm system went off; a system I'd recently installed. The new alarm alerted the authorities quickly, but not swiftly enough to catch the thieves."

Keira was thoughtful, as though choosing the least offensive way of making her inquiry. "Are you saying Zelda would have known about your old system but not this new one?"

Jensen looked torn, and exasperated, at one and the same time. "Only my shop manager and I knew about the new system and how to operate it. My manager is not the culprit; the police have proved it already."

It was time to tell Jensen absolutely everything that had occurred in the U.S.

"We must inform the police – and leave nothing out. I will not be responsible for anyone else being harmed."

Teun had no objection to doing that, but he first wanted to know who might still be a victim. Keira stiffened at his side before she jumped to her feet.

"I need to call my father, and my sister." Grasping her mobile, she retreated to the next room.

Jensen's voice was muted, as though still considering who else might be a victim. "Zaan called me last night, and everything seemed fine with him. The only other family members are Ineke and her daughters. I am assuming Marijke is well, since she emailed me the photo of her ring yesterday."

Keira returned looking relieved.

"They're both well. My sister called Dad just a little while ago to cancel dinner tonight. She eats with him about once a week, but she'd forgotten to tell him of a teacher meeting this evening, so she'll be busy at school for a few hours yet. The only thing wrong with Dad just now is his temper. He's been having a lot of hang-up calls; they really irritate him."

When they talked things over, they weren't sure what to tell the Heidelberg police. The break-in at Jensen's shop had been weeks before, and none of the other dire events had occurred in Heidelberg.

Mulling through everything at their hotel after dinner, Keira slid back to counting again. "We now have fourteen of a possible twenty items probably accounted for. We need to find out if Zaan has any more details from the Koopmans."

Teun surprised himself. Whipping out his mobile, he wanted to be the one talking to Zaan.

Zaan was at the Koopman's stockroom, poring over documents with the archivist, Fenna.

"Fenna's found something relevant in the Goods In ledger for 1815."

Teun flicked the speaker as high as it could go, sharing the call with Keira. They could hear the rustle of paper as though Zaan moved between pages before he continued. "They received a shipment of assorted items from India, among which is the set said to have belonged to Tiru Salana. There's an additional note below stating the Tiru collection is being evaluated and recorded separately from the other goods in the consignment."

"So, they didn't record the items in the ledger you're reading from?" Teun couldn't help feeling disappointed, though Keira's squeeze of encouragement around his torso was a nice compensation. Those gorgeous eyes of hers were sad, but not defeated. Before he could say any more, Zaan's hearty laugh echoed around them.

"I'm not finished yet, Teun. You're an impatient guy, aren't you?"

Keira smiled mischievously. "He definitely is Zaan but, you know, I'm getting used to it."

"I'm reading from only one of the ledgers that this amazing archivist next to me has uncovered."

Zaan sounded like he was getting along very well with said archivist. Teun grinned, even though he knew Zaan couldn't see it. "You've got even better information?"

"I do. There's a smaller notebook someone, a family member or an employee, has made notations in. There's no name on it so we can't identify who wrote it, but there's a fabulous list explaining what is in the Tiru collection."

Keira's squeal deafened. "It tells you what everything was like? That's incredible."

"It's just a list, Keira. In itself it's not enough to authenticate an item, though it should help with the next paper trails. Fenna is now pouring through the sales ledgers for July to December of 1815 to see if anything turns up. I'll get a copy translated – of what I've just told you about – and email it as soon as I can. I'm going to call Jensen now to update him."

"You might not get him till later this evening."

Teun warned Zaan they'd seen Jensen a few hours earlier, told him they were in Heidelberg.

Keira could hardly wait for the email. The descriptions given should go a long way towards authenticating the jewellery they suspected was from the Tiru collection.

Teun cautioned. "I'm no expert, Keira, but the list Zaan has won't be enough to prove the items, or to show who actually owned them. Remember, way back Zaan told us the newspapers claimed the jewels vanished, and the first new mention was when Jensen bought the snake ring. The photo of Geertje's three daughters wearing them is significant, but it also opens another can of worms."

Her grin was wide. "You mean your great-grandmother and her sisters were proudly decked out in potentially stolen jewels?"

Teun ruffled his hair, feeling a bit sheepish. "Yeah. I'm beginning to find it very strange, aren't you?"

"Geertje wouldn't have thought them stolen, surely? She got them as a gift from her parents."

Teun reflected as he paced around. "I think she was an innocent in all this. What I'm thinking is her parents gave her the jewels, with some conditions attached. Remember, they were jewellers of long standing. I'm thinking they told her to use them if Albrecht got into financial difficulties, perhaps breaking up the pieces to use the diamonds, emeralds or pearls separately, so they weren't obvious. Maybe told her to keep them secret otherwise? Or perhaps they fobbed her off with part of the secret: told her they were from a very special collection and she had to guard them safely?"

Good thinking, maybe, but he couldn't prove any of it.

"Why would Geertje have allowed her daughters to be photographed with most of the collection dangling around them?"

He couldn't think of any reason at all for such a public display – except maybe it hadn't been quite so public. He suggested maybe they wore them to a more intimate gathering of Tiedman friends and relatives? It was one possibility. But why have the photograph taken? That could have been a damning piece of evidence if it got into the hands of an unscrupulous person.

"Do you think any of the three girls had an idea they might be wearing stolen goods?"

"No. I suspect Geertje told them they were precious heirlooms, and they had to guard them safely. Remember how my grandmother, Marijke, had kept them a huge secret even as late as the 1970s."

"You don't think your grandmother had any idea of their stolen background?"

Teun was amused. "Having known what Marijke was like, I think if she knew she'd been harbouring stolen jewels she'd have found it hilarious. She was the joker Adam said she was. I can easily see my grandmother deciding if they'd been kept a dirty secret for nearly a century, then a few more years wouldn't make any difference. She probably thought nobody in the US would be bothered about something stolen so long ago in Amsterdam, but selling them would have been a problem. Somebody as poor as she was would have drawn a lot of suspicion if she suddenly had a fortune to offload."

"Maybe it's why she never sold any of the jewellery. Although, if the pearls we found in the loft had been broken ages ago, it would have been easier to sell single pearls."

Teun pulled her up into a swinging hug which took them full circle around the room. The smacking kiss preceding his answer he thoroughly enjoyed. "Maybe she did sell one or two pearls on the sly. Maybe she kept the family afloat while waiting for my dad to bail them out when Adam was out of work."

"I suppose when the pearls are re-stranded the jeweller will be able to tell if some are missing from the original threads?"

He hoped to know that answer soon. The thought that some of the pearls might have helped his grandmother and aunt keep the wolf from the door, appealed. If it had been the case, then some good had come from them.

The prospect of an exhibition was becoming more of a reality. Six more items needed to be found – but it had to happen without the awful consequences that had bedevilled them so far. He sensed Keira was thinking the exact same thing. It wasn't telepathy, yet they were so in tune. Her twinkling eyes were so excited he came to an immediate decision, before his lips touched down for a lingering kiss.

"Don't unpack too much, Keira. I'm in the mood to have a little peek at Amsterdam."

"You want to go now?"

Teun's answer was a tackle. This time not to the floor as he'd done in Adam's house, but a sideways sweep landing her onto the bed she'd been ogling.

"Tomorrow. I've a few other priorities right now."

"Good railway connections here, Keira, but I'm glad you're steering me in the right direction."

Teun towed along behind her when they descended at their terminal in Frankfurt Main Airport. Her knowledge of the language had made their travel much faster: Teun would have taken much longer to work out where to go.

"They're great, but you'd have coped."

On the flight to Amsterdam, Keira shared what she remembered.

"You'll love the Netherlands, Teun. The canals are fabulous, all over the place, some larger for boats and some smaller for irrigation and drainage. They call them different names according to their size and purpose, but don't ask me for details. I think the bigger ones are called *grachten* – like the *Keisersgracht* in Amsterdam. In Amsterdam the houses are tightly packed together, all jostling for a peek at the sky, tall and thin. Some of them look as though they're being propped up by the neighbouring one, and in some cases they are, since their foundations are sinking. There are different colours of stonework; some dark, others light; contrasting with white painted window frames. They have different roof top shapes as well: some are flatter; some steeply shaped; others are a typical style called mansard. I'll point it out when we see it."

One of Teun's palms caressed her arm, his other fingers gently squeezing hers, their bodies resting companionably against each other. "You obviously love coming back to Holland?"

Her sigh was deep and heartfelt. On an excited roll, she burbled. "I do. Every time. It's weird knowing I was born in a country I don't live in. I love Scotland, but I also love knowing I've shared some of my growing-up time in such a wonderful country as Holland."

When the plane descended, Teun got a better glimpse of rural Holland as it swept down in a wide curve. The flat countryside of regular-shaped fields, bordered by small waterways, gave way to the built-up areas around Schiphol Airport.

"Schiphol's an interesting name. Makes me think of ships, but they're miles away, aren't they? Any idea why it's called that?"

Keira had to think. "I've a feeling it was Neela's husband, Gabriel, who told me something about it, but it was a long time ago. All I remember is the whole area of land around here used to be under water, a few centuries ago. The Haarlemmermeer – a sort of lake with sea access – used to be here before the land was reclaimed for use by the people to live and farm on. When the water was still here, ships were driven up to a corner of it by wild storms, and were shipwrecked. The "hol" bit at the end of Schiphol means a sort of grave – the whole thing meaning the grave of the ships. I'd have to get a history book to be sure of those facts, but that's how I remember it from Gabriel."

Teun was full of questions as they taxied from the airport north to Amsterdam. Some Keira could answer, but many she couldn't. It wasn't a problem, though, because the taxi driver gave the answers. Teun was definitely impressed, holding none of his admiration back as they drove through the streets of Amsterdam to their hotel, on Damrak. He'd taken up her suggestion that if their hotel was in a central location, they could do lots of sightseeing on foot around the old city centre. After checking in, Teun left a message on Zaan's mobile, telling him they'd just arrived in Amsterdam and would like to meet up with him. She could tell Teun wasn't too fussed about any delay over meeting Zaan; going walkabout appealed more.

The last time she'd been in central Amsterdam had been in her mid-teens, when she'd done touristy things with her parents and sister. Her visits to Holland after that had been to see the aging Neela, and then for Neela's funeral. Not trusting her memory, she picked up a map in the foyer before they set off. Their saunter took them across Dam Square, Keira assuring Teun she was leading him somewhere he'd love.

"Another museum?"

"Tomorrow. We can visit the Rijksmuseum, the State museum, tomorrow. We can spend all day there if you want, but it's too late now to do justice to any museum. I'm taking you shopping!"

Teun's groan was so loud the Dam Square gulls flapped off in protest.

"Don't worry! You'll like where we're going."

She dragged him into the pedestrian-only street called

Kalverstraat. It was lined with shops of almost every imaginable kind, though she gave him no time to window shop. She had a destination in mind. They passed jewellers and clothes shops, coffee bars and music shops, small cinemas and household goods stores. Approaching halfway down the Kalverstraat, Keira came to a dead halt. Her disappointment was crushing.

"It's not there!"

Teun pulled her to the fringes of the street, making sure other shoppers didn't mow her down as she'd halted so abruptly and now stood stock still.

"What were you looking for?"

Keira didn't answer, just stared around her, and then headed for a little bakery on the corner of one of the many side streets. She left Teun to trail after her.

"Wait!" Putting her outspread hand to his chest, she entreated him to listen. "Please stay here for moment? I just need to go in here and ask about something?"

A few moments later she rejoined a bemused Teun, who'd drifted to look at the next door shop window.

"I want you to just accept that what we're going to do is a bit odd. Nothing sinister."

Teun's gaze was amused, and a little concerned. She knew him well enough now to note the difference.

"I'm the tourist here. I'll just follow where you lead. You said I'd love it and… I will."

"Yes. Well, I thought I only had to bring you to this spot. Not the case now, since this street has changed since my last visit. Ten years has brought a few alterations." She took his hand and led him along one of the very narrow lanes running perpendicular to Kalverstraat.

After a short, but very slow taxi ride, it disgorged them in an area of Amsterdam Keira didn't recall having been to before, just out of the old city centre. She stood and sniffed to get her bearings, loud enough to amuse Teun.

"Okay, now I'm wondering what's going on, Keira. I don't mind the taxi ride. I enjoyed travelling those streets, but what's got you into such a tizzy? Care to enlighten me?"

"There it is!"

Grabbing his arm, she pulled him along at a trot before halting at a café. Pushing the door open, she wished and prayed this really was what she sought for Teun.

"Yes!" Her elated shout drew his smiles. Her inhalation of the sweet smell of vanilla, and icing sugar, and baking, made him smile even more as he looked around.

"You brought me here to see photographs of carousels?"

His question was accurate, if confused. The walls of the café were decorated with huge photographs of brightly bedecked carts, like those you'd find at traditional fairgrounds.

"This is a *poffertjes* house. They make those tiny Dutch pancakes here."

Teun was already nose-up to the nearest photograph, his eyes scanning furiously. He turned to her and just looked, said nothing, just stared at her, his grey eyes molten. Then he let out a whoop and whipped her up into his arms. The cafe was busy, but he didn't care a button as he whirled her around and gave her a smacking great kiss, before releasing her.

"My grandmother used to make *poffertjes*. I'd forgotten all about them, since I've not had them for years and years."

Shown to a table, Keira explained her odd behaviour.

"There used to be one of those carousel carts selling *poffertjes* right where I came to a sudden halt on Kalverstraat. It was the thing we always wanted to do first when we returned to Amsterdam; it became a family tradition. That particular stall sat in a nice little space between buildings and had a cute little picket fence around it, so that when you parked down at the tiny tables it was like being in a fanciful little garden. The area was bedecked with colourful pennants and was... just magic when I was a child. I wanted to give you that same coming-back-to-Holland experience we loved, but the woman in the baker's shop told me it stopped trading there years ago and a building sprouted up in the space."

"Sounds like what happens in every city centre. It's called progress."

Teun's tone sounded wry but he was busy looking at the counter where the *poffertje* baker plied his skills. Looking at overhead options, Teun did a lot of sniffing for himself.

"*Oma* Marijke never gave us any choice, and I don't remember any fruit being added. Though, maybe we had that on the side?" He reminisced, sniffing the sweet scented air, his eyes closed. "She'd put the little pancakes onto the plate, put knobs of butter on top, and then she'd sprinkle the top with powdered sugar which had vanilla added."

Keira laughed at his dreamy look, his excitement making him appear the little boy he was describing. Boy and man – she found she liked both very much indeed.

"Hold that thought!" His exclamation was loud enough to draw interested stares. "I forgot the lemon. She'd squeeze lemon on at some point as well." His deep chuckles echoed around.

Keira prompted him, her grin a cheeky interruption. "Having remembered all that, what would you like on your order?" She pointed to the waitress who awaited their decisions.

Teun decided to stick to as close as his grandma had made, while she chose additional strawberries and a dollop of whipped cream. Totally decadent, and totally delicious. They traded tastes as they ploughed their way through the scrumptiously sweet desserts.

Teun declared he was in heaven. "God, these are so good. *Oma's* always seemed really tasty when I was a kid, but these are fabulous. Thank you for bringing me here and for sharing something so precious."

Keira knew he didn't refer to the fact they'd shared their pancakes. For a while they'd forgotten the realities of why they were in Amsterdam.

They rode the Amsterdam tram system back to their hotel, by way of a long route, enjoying travelling through the busy thoroughfares. Interruptions to the pleasure had come, though nothing to do with Amsterdam commuter traffic or anyone following them. A couple of work-related texts had come through for Teun; he needed to do some work, and so did she.

Hours later, Teun asked about dining options.

"Indonesian? My father used to like having Ristafel meals in Holland."

It took little persuasion when she explained Ristafel was a feast of many little dishes – some quite spicy if she remembered correctly. With a little help from a friendly hotel concierge, they headed to the street called Rembrantsplein.

"Taxi this time?"

Teun disagreed; he wanted to ride a tram again since there was a direct one they could pick up just a short walk away. What she'd forgotten about a Ristafel was just how much food was brought to the table. Small dish, after small dish, appeared to tempt them. After a few, she gave up counting. Teun made a valiant attempt to finish everything, but in the end gave up.

His phone chirped as they strolled back to their hotel. Though it was a good distance, they'd already covered about half, enjoying the saunter up the still busy wide street. The pavements were a melee of pedestrians, parked bicycles and *bromfiets* – the mopeds used by old and young alike. Some of the *bromfiets* were now powered by electricity – plugged in to chargers – something she didn't remember seeing during her last visit. Trams swished past them at regular intervals up the middle of the road. When Teun flipped his mobile open and scanned, his winces informed her their tourist break was again over.

"We need to get back to our hotel right away."

Teun pulled her to a stop as he scanned the message again, and then passed it to her before he searched down the street.

The text was brief and had come from Fenna, the woman archivist Zaan had been working with the previous day. Zaan was in trouble? Fenna awaited them at their hotel? That heartbeat of hers started a merry thumping again.

The tram approaching soon had two more passengers. When they entered the hotel foyer a young woman stood at the concierge's desk chatting to the employee who'd given them directions to the restaurant. She hurried over to them, her eyes filling with tears.

"Remko over there says you are Teun Zeger?"

There had been an incident involving Zaan. Fenna sobbed as she told them Zaan was being held at a local police station. Keira was shocked, Teun disbelieving.

"What's happened to my cousin?"

Though the circumstances were disturbing, Keira was heartened to hear a kinship in Teun's voice, rather than his former censure. That was a big sea change from his prior attitude.

"There has been a very bad accident. Zaan was walking along the Prinsengracht to turn onto Brouwersgracht." Fenna stopped, sounding flustered. "Do you know Amsterdam?"

At Keira's head-shake, the Dutch woman tried to visualize it for them, making sweeping motions with her hands as she described the area. "The Prinsengracht is the outside one in the girdle of canals winding around the city centre. There are many streets across it and Zaan was making his way to the Central Station. It is a good walk, but sometimes walking in Amsterdam is more convenient. As he crossed the bridge at Brouwersgracht, someone grabbed him from behind and tried to steal the bag he was carrying. There are always lots of bikes parked at the little railings, and the guy pushed Zaan into one of those, but it wasn't... you know, locked up?"

"Oh, God! Was Zaan hurt?"

Fenna smiled for the first time, but it was a nervous smile. "Zaan is a large man, and his attacker was smaller. The guy tussled to steal the bag, but Zaan wouldn't let him take it. There was a fight, and they struggled and fell onto the railings. The bike slipped and fell on top of Zaan, but the mugger? He fell into the canal."

Relief washed through Keira, it wasn't Zaan who'd tumbled into the water.

Teun looked amused, even admiring. "It serves the bastard right, but why is Zaan still at the police station?"

Tears leaked from Fenna's eyes and drifted down to her chin. Her lips wobbled as she found the words to answer. "When the robber fell over the railing, there was a boat going under the bridge. He landed badly on it, his head hitting the front, and then he fell into Prinsengracht."

Keira barely knew what to say. "What happened then?"

"The people in the boat, they tried to find the man, but, you know, he was under the boat, under the water. The ambulance services came, and the police. They got him out, but the man was dead. The police took Zaan to their headquarters to ask him questions. He was allowed to call me, and asked me to let you know. He'd picked up your message earlier and knew you were trying to meet him. "

Even though it was very late, Teun insisted on going to the police station. Keira couldn't exactly follow the spoken Dutch, it was too quick, but she suppressed a grin when she guessed what Fenna told the officer at the front desk – she claimed to be Zaan's girlfriend.

"I'm Zaan's cousin," Teun blurted out alongside her, his fingers gripping her arm, his tension evident.

Keira hoped such an association would get them news of what was happening to Zaan, but let the other two do the talking. In a mixture of English and Dutch, Fenna explained that Teun was a second cousin of Zaan, from the US, who didn't speak Dutch. Keira was his girlfriend. Though not exactly true, it wasn't a lie either. Zaan was being held in custody till the police interviewed some witnesses who had viewed the incident. The front desk officer waved them off to the nearby waiting room where they were able to talk freely since they were the only occupants.

"Did you just claim to be Zaan's girlfriend?"

Fenna grinned. "They'd have chased us away otherwise. It was a bit of a stretch but we've had dinner two times now. Does that count enough for you?"

Keira had no problem at all with it. Teun remarked he'd a feeling Zaan had been doing more than consulting with her. Fenna's cheeks pinkened, but she revealed no more.

Fenna had spent the late afternoon and early evening with Zaan, initially at the Koopman's stockroom and then at dinner. With some translating help, she updated them.

"This morning I inspected the purchase ledgers for 1814, thinking I might find some information about the sale of the Tiru jewels in India. An entry of late December, 1814, authorized a sum of money – a huge amount at the time – to be delivered to a shipping agent based in Amsterdam. The goods paid for were expected to arrive in the spring of 1815. Two signatures in the ledger authorize the money to be delivered to the ship's captain, who was headed for Calcutta on the first favourable tide."

Fenna looked more excited now. Keira wasn't sure what to expect but was glad they had the time to hear the new developments.

"The first signature is Joop Koopman, who was the head of the family business back then, and the second signature is of Hendrick, his brother."

"Do these signatures prove the Koopmans were the owners of the shipment? Even before it arrived?"

"It is very admissible, but we must still look for more evidence."

Keira shared a moment of elation with Teun. This was the closest they'd come to prove anyone's ownership so far.

"I called Zaan immediately, asked him to come to

Amsterdam and read for himself. I deciphered the references in the margin, for they are quite difficult to understand. Sometimes it is very small writing, or the ink is faded."

"Do you mean a sort-of cross-referencing system?" Keira was unsure what Fenna referred to.

"Only sometimes are there actual numbers involved. The clerk who wrote up the entries has jotted some notes at various times throughout the register. When they have been added, I cannot tell, but they mention things like who was dispatched to do collecting of goods, or delivering things. They are mostly a sort-of check of who moved important merchandise around. Sometimes it is the Koopman family members who are named, other times it is people who worked for them."

"What did the margins tell you?"

"Hendrick Koopman delivered the money to the captain himself."

"And that's important?"

Teun sounded impatient. Keira wasn't sure if it was because he thought the information useless, or if it was because he was concerned about Zaan.

"Oh, yes. But it is not simple to explain the significance. I searched the ledgers for other instances of either of the two Koopman brothers ferrying large amounts of money around when making purchases directly. There were quite a few of these, since the Koopmans were very successful gold merchants. I pulled out boxes of receipt slips signed by the brothers, and those matched sums of money which had been mentioned in the ledgers. What was odd was there was not a single receipt for the Tiru jewels."

"That's definitely strange," Teun agreed. Keira knew the look on his face meant he was considering as many angles as he could think of.

"Zaan came after lunch time and I showed him what I'd found. The Koopman descendant who owns the shop just now told Zaan he could borrow anything, if it helped in the search for the Tiru jewels."

Teun muttered alongside. Keira felt his small nudge. Was he back to distrusting Zaan?

"So they know about Jensen's quest?"

Fenna's smile was reassuring. "Zaan had to tell them, otherwise they would not have allowed me to poke around in their documentation."

Keira wondered why they had given permission, but Teun got in first with the question.

"Why do you think they did that?"

"They are having my services free, since Jensen is paying my fees. The Koopmans are happy enough to have their historical evidence documented properly. And I might just find something that is important to them, too?"

Teun was scathing as he got up and paced the small room. "Like them proving ownership of the Tiru jewels?"

"I never thought of that. They might be the real owners. Jensen will be furious if it's the case." Keira knew her gasp was loud.

Fenna's grin was conspiratorial. "I don't think it will come to that, but who knows?"

Zaan had decided to take the ledger proving the money transfer, to have it copied. He'd put it into a plastic carrier before they went to eat at a nearby restaurant. After dinner, she'd headed off to a late seminar at the university while Zaan made for the Central Station, intending to return to Den Haag. He hadn't got far along his route when he was attacked.

She and Teun learned a bit more about Fenna's investigations while they waited, giving them a better idea of what she would have to uncover to prove ownership of the Tiru collection. Eventually, Zaan was released. From witness statements it had been made clear the robber had attacked Zaan first and, though he had fought back, Zaan was not blamed for the man tipping over the railing into the canal. Witnesses had declared Zaan had been struggling free of the bike handlebars which had twisted around him and wasn't even in body contact with the mugger when he'd gone into the canal.

Chapter Twelve

Zaan nursed a cognac. He'd checked in to their hotel, since the police were likely to talk to him again in an all too short few hours. At 3:30a.m. there were still quite a few people around, still a bit of bustle.

"It was definitely the bag he was after. Muggers generally target cameras, or women's bags, or waist pouches for cards and money. I don't see how he could have known what I had in my bag was valuable."

He was answering Teun's question but didn't look entirely convinced of his own answer.

"What if he had been following you? What if he didn't know exactly what you had in the bag, but had guessed it might be to do with the Tiru collection and was, therefore, important?" Keira inched her way through some scenarios. "What if he'd seen you go into the Koopman's storeroom empty-handed, but had later watched you come out with the bag?"

"Why would someone have been following me?"

Keira looked to Teun to enlighten his cousin. Whatever reason had changed his mind, she didn't know but she was now sure Teun no longer suspected his Dutch cousin of anything untoward.

Teun told of the man who'd followed them in the US, and of the silvery white-haired guy who'd tailed her in Heidelberg, and in Vienna.

Zaan was appalled. "You suspect Jensen?"

"No. Jensen's not the one who's paying them."

Keira was relieved Teun was quick to dissuade Zaan of the idea. A slight colouring flushed across Teun's face. She appreciated what it took for him to admit his earlier suspicions.

"At first I thought it was either Jensen, or you. Now I don't have a damned clue who paid the cretins to follow us."

Zaan laughed. It was good to see him relaxing, since he'd been justifiably wound up over his own ordeal. "Cretins?"

"I don't think they can have been the best at their job since both Teun and I noticed them quite quickly."

For a moment they wondered if it had been intended till Teun put the scuppers on the theory. "Just inept."

She swished the Cointreau around in her glass as Teun gave Zaan updates on everything, including Jensen's shop break-in. In between the elation over the finding of Tiru jewels, Zaan was appalled to hear of Adam's death and of Jan's poor condition. When Teun told him about his tussle with their stalker in the US, and of Keira's own experience with the bag-snatcher, he was even more visibly upset. His hand reached out to pat Keira reassuringly before his gaze lasered once again on Teun.

"Anything else I should know?"

Zaan didn't seem as angry as she felt he could have been, given their lack of information sharing: rather, his sympathy abounded, unreserved. He told them he hadn't even dreamed that anyone might have been following him before the incident on Brouwersgracht and certainly hadn't noticed anyone, but also confessed to being a bit taken by Fenna and therefore quite preoccupied.

Like them, he believed it necessary they share all details with the police, especially about the men dogging their tails, though none fit the description of Zaan's mugger.

Before ten a.m. Zaan called their room saying he was

requested to return to the police station. Would they go with him? It wasn't that he needed someone to hold his hand – far from it – but he made a good case for more of the cousins lending weight to the strange tale of the Tiru jewels. Zaan had a hunch the police already knew something about the jewels, although nothing had been asked the previous evening. They only had time to snatch a coffee as they got ready.

Being escorted into an interview room was the strangest experience. For twenty-seven years Keira had never had any contact with the police, but during the last two weeks police forces all over the place had been hovering in the background too many times.

In English, the lead detective, Detective Golder, didn't waste any time. His questions were succinct as he established their relationship to Zaan, his younger colleague scribbling away alongside. Teun explained they hadn't known each other till recently, but that a family reunion had brought them together during the last weeks. Keira wasn't sure how plausible it sounded, since the policeman's expression gave nothing away. The colleague contributed very little, and continued to write in between searching glances. Detective Golder then double-checked what had been in the bag the mugger had been trying to steal.

That was like opening Pandora's Box. Keira was glad she wasn't addressed directly; she wouldn't have known where to start. Beside her, she could sense Teun's tension, though he volunteered nothing.

In Dutch, Zaan explained it was an ancient ledger which had potentially great value to a recent search the family had been making regarding family heirlooms – then translated in English for them. Keira understood enough of it to know what he'd just said, but appreciated Zaan's consideration of Teun's lack of language.

Keira faced Detective Golder, his mood sombre and his eyes assessing. The policeman flicked the folder which lay alongside

239

his notebook, and questioned in English.

Did any of them know someone called Christian Drost? Keira turned toward Teun, her eyes asking a silent question, not sure how to respond.

"Jensen told us his ex-girlfriend is called Zelda Drost."

Teun's answer was cautious as he explained who Jensen was, the detectives scribbling away.

"And this cousin, Jensen, has a jewellery shop?"

Keira thought it an odd question coming out of the blue, since no mention had so far been made about jewellery shops. The officer pinned a glare on Teun, who answered it was true, though Jensen's shops weren't in Holland but in Germany. Again lots of scribbling went on as silence reigned for moments before contact numbers and an address were requested.

"When did you last have communication with Jensen Amsel?"

The officer's eyebrows twitched very minutely when Teun explained he'd been with him the day before in Heidelberg.

"All three of you?" Detective Golder wanted to know.

Keira wasn't convinced the police were happy with them when Teun related their movements during the last week. It appeared they'd been constantly on the move, which, of course, they had been. She didn't like the way she was being assessed by the second officer, as though something was suspect about their travels. The detective wound back to where she and Teun had been last evening when Zaan had been attacked.

They could probably prove they had been in the restaurant, but not when they were out walking back up the street called Rokin, though Keira wondered why it should be necessary. The questions continued. Yes, Fenna had called them and they'd immediately returned to their hotel. The officer then returned to question them about the mugger. Were they sure they didn't know the man?

240

Keira wasn't surprised when Teun tuned up, his tone sounding placid; she'd an idea he wasn't feeling like that inside. "Is this man connected to Zelda?"

Detective Golder excused himself in English then spoke to Zaan, very quickly and very precisely in Dutch. Keira understood enough to know he was asking what Zaan knew about Zelda. Since they'd relayed to him what they'd learned about Zelda, during their nightcap in the hotel bar, Zaan was able to tell the officer the little he knew of her.

The conversation reverted to English, she and Teun being asked to relate what they knew of Zelda. Naturally their information was the same as Zaan's. Detective Golder studied his notebook before his head lifted to encompass them all, his gaze sweeping across the three of them. Keira realised they were seated exactly as they been many days before in Jensen's office, on the night of their first meeting. This time was vastly different, though. Teun now regarded Zaan as an ally, rather than an enemy.

Detective Golder's mobile bleeped. He nodded to his colleague. Excusing themselves, saying they'd only be a minute, they stepped outside the door

"What's going on, Zaan?" Keira was feeling unnerved now.

He didn't know, but suspected the police wanted to check out their relationship to Jensen. A tense and fairly silent few minutes passed before the officers returned. No-one wanted to rehash anything and, in truth, Keira wasn't sure their conversation wasn't still being taped.

Detective Golder referred to the mugger again. He'd been identified as Christian Drost, initially by contact information in his wallet, and now by someone who knew him.

"Christian Drost was also a jeweller." The officer eventually parted with his information, Keira sensed very reluctantly. "As is his sister, Zelda. They both have businesses here in Amsterdam."

Zaan assured the detectives he had never ever had any

dealings with them. It was easy for Keira and Teun to assure the policemen of the same thing – they'd never met either of them in person. Enquiries would continue, the detective droned, and would they all please remain in Amsterdam, as they would most likely be needed again soon.

Zaan declared he'd like to head home to Den Haag to clean up, but could be back in a couple of hours. That was no problem, the officers said; they had his mobile number if they wanted to contact him.

Keira felt stunned as they all left the police station and found the nearest coffee shop. What was the relevance of the mugger being Zelda's brother? And the fact that the officers were fixated that both Drosts had been jewellers. The police definitely knew more about the Drosts, but weren't telling them yet. She realised the questioning had been so focused none of them had made any mention at all about having men following them, or about the Tiru jewels.

What should they tell Jensen?

"I think Jensen didn't want to believe Zelda could have been responsible for the break-in at his shop."

Teun made the call to Jensen, who was horrified by the latest development. Keira thought at first he was overly concerned about the death of Christian Drost, but then realised it was Zaan's welfare he worried about.

"Jensen, did you ever meet Christian Drost?" Zaan wanted to know.

"No. I knew Zelda had a brother who was also a jeweller, but the information I learned about the man did not endear him to me. I did not think too much of Christian Drost's buying methods." Jensen was scathing.

Teun asked the question Keira would have asked herself had he not jumped in first. "Was there something shady about him?"

Jensen again sounded sorry, apologetic as though blaming himself. "Let's just say the way he did business was not how I work. I don't cheat people, or undercut, but I suspect he did."

Jensen promised to come to Amsterdam as soon as possible if they thought he could help in any way. Zaan made them all laugh when he declared it might be sooner than Jensen thought if the police forces got their acts together and wanted them all in for questioning. Privately, Keira thought it had to happen soon. She wasn't forgetting the threat from whoever had been following them.

When Zaan went off home, she turned her thoughts to how they'd spend the afternoon. So many events had happened to make life appear unreal. It was difficult to play tourist, but the police had asked them to stay on in Amsterdam and work didn't appeal. Teun hadn't had any urgent calls from his labs so there was no urgency for him to be glued to his laptop.

Keira remembered lots of tourist spots which either her parents or *Oma* Neela had taken her to. However, they needed something relaxing, something which would take their interest yet wouldn't be demanding. Passing on the plethora of museums they could visit, she suggested they go on a waterbus tour: to see Amsterdam from the canals. Teun's hug and long kiss told her he approved.

"Sounds perfect. I really don't care, so long as we're tourists together."

They chose the hop-on, hop-off boat tour since they didn't want to be far from a taxi if they needed to be somewhere quickly – like the police station again. It wasn't that Keira was desperate to return there, but she'd a gut feeling the summons wouldn't be too long in coming. It was great to be with Teun, but the recent sinister events lurked at the back of Keira's mind. It was hard not to check every other second to see if either of their former pursuers – or someone else – tailed them. Her eyes scanned the small queue waiting for the tour boat, happy to see no known threat, and happy those who were waiting all looked like typical tourists.

Very relaxing. That was Keira's immediate thought as she

slipped further down in the surprisingly comfortable, bucket-shaped plastic seat. The sun beat warmly through the clear plastic glass of the roofing, the seat pad was comfortable underneath, and Teun held her hand. It remained relaxing till they came to the first bridge they needed to go under.

"Oh, my God! I didn't think..." She screwed her eyes up tight.

"Don't think. We're just having a boat trip." Teun's hug reassured, though he made her face the ramparts of the bridge.

Once she'd got over the horror of visualizing a body hurtling over the railings and bumping into the water, she relaxed again. Teun remarked on almost everything they bypassed: the amazing amount of houseboats, as the guide gave the demographics of those who lived on the water. From those few feet below street level, everything appeared so leafy and dappled in the sunshine. As the boat glided along the smaller canals, the flickering sun-to-shade appeared almost stroboscopic. The late night, and precious little sleep, had caught up with Keira. Her eyes were closing when her mobile vibrated in her jeans pocket.

Zaan? She amazed herself that she was so concerned about someone she barely knew, but in a weird way he had become family already.

It wasn't Zaan. She passed the brief text over to Teun to read.

"*You were wrong. Pin is worth very little.*" The text was from Ineke and the tone of the sentence typical.

"Call her back and ask for details."

She wasn't sure if Teun was back to distrusting mode, but the shake of his head and small grin told her it wasn't his aim. "Maybe she's not gone to a reputable jeweller? You said she was very negative about even getting it valued."

She didn't want to call on a busy tour boat, so texted instead, promising to call back as soon as they got off at the next stop – the guide having warned them which one was coming up. Given the tour boats came along every fifteen minutes or so, they'd not have long to wait for the next one.

Climbing up onto the street, they used Teun's mobile.

A grumbling Ineke answered. "I took it to a friend who knows a jeweller in Uithoorn," she said, naming a town in central Holland. "He says the gold is real, the pearls are real, but the diamonds and the emeralds are fakes."

"How much does he say it's worth, Ineke?"

"He'll give me a thousand euros for it."

Keira thought a thousand euros wasn't to be sneezed at, when Ineke had been so scathing about it being worthless. "So, it's not made of brass, but real gold?"

Eighteen karat gold, Ineke told them, but it was still an ugly pin. Keira smiled at Teun's ear. He was being so careful not to offend this difficult new cousin. "How about we ask Zaan to suggest someone to give you a second opinion, Ineke?"

Ineke wasn't interested in the pin at all, wasn't bothered it had come to her through Neela. She was quite happy to let Teun, or Jensen, buy it from her for a thousand euros. At Teun's tactful insistence, she grudgingly agreed to have Zaan's help. On the other hand, Teun's casual invitation to dinner that evening was accepted with alacrity, especially when Ineke was told which hotel they were booked into. She'd be quite happy to dine there, but she could suggest a few other places to eat if Teun wanted her to.

Keira fought hard to keep a straight face when he closed the phone with a grunt. She hugged his arm as she dragged him down the street, having checked the map to locate them. It would be a nice walk skirting a few of the narrower canals and would bring them to another boat halt. "I told you she was a difficult person to get on with. Though you can charm the birds off the trees, Teun Zeger."

"Yeah, maybe I can, but we need to update her properly on everything that's happened, especially the most recent of our incidents. I mean the attack on Zaan, and a phone call on an

Amsterdam street isn't the place to do it. I don't want to alarm her unnecessarily, either."

Keira was ashamed. Teun had reminded her there were other legitimate cousins in the loop who could be in jeopardy just as much as they were, and she hadn't even considered it. On the opposite end of the scale, it was now so lovely to have him be solicitous of his cousins, rather than be suspicious of them. He might not realise it, or even acknowledge it yet, but he'd mellowed towards his fellow descendants of Geertje Tiedman.

During the last part of their boat tour, Teun fielded texts from his labs and needed to make longer return calls and emails. Keira had almost forgotten what it was to work. What she had lined up had no urgent deadlines to meet, but it was good to join Teun at the table in their room and work alongside him. Quiet, when he wasn't on the phone, but definitely companionable. She could learn to like his company, a lot…

"I'm free to come and meet Ineke, but I'll be bringing Fenna."

Since Zaan had already asked Fenna to dine with him, it wasn't a problem, and it wasn't unexpected. Fenna now knew as much about the emerald quest as the rest of them, so there were no family secrets to keep from her. Dinner turned out to be very pleasant, Ineke having agreed on an upscale restaurant Zaan approved of, too.

Keira dreamed of how lovely it would be to have an early night while they were at their after-dinner coffee stage. Tiredness and the stress of the last days, not to mention the constant travel, had caught up with a vengeance.

The moment a mobile rang, she knew sleep wasn't lined up; though it was Zaan who flicked open his cell. He relayed to the assembled company bit by bit.

"The police have been questioning Zelda all day."

Zaan was requested back to the police station and, although

it was late, the police would rather it happened that evening than wait till the next morning. Detective Golder was delighted to know the cousins were together – including Ineke.

"Golder says any more cousins who are involved should come too, since he'll not have to repeat himself."

Zaan laughed as he closed his phone, claiming it was the first evidence that the police officers were human.

It was a full room when they all trooped in – two officers, three cousins, Keira and Fenna. After establishing who the newest cousin was, the police told them there was a lot they needed to talk about. Disclosures left Keira reeling. Their fraud squad had been monitoring Christian Drost's nefarious activities for some time.

"We had reasons to believe Drost had been involved in resetting stolen property, but we didn't have sufficient evidence to charge him."

Keira thought Detective Golder sounded quite pleased the death meant they needn't keep pursuing that case.

The police had found nothing to link Zelda directly to her brother's unlawful dealings, though her activities had also been monitored for some time. As his next-of-kin, they'd had legitimate reason to summon her to identify Christian's body. It transpired she was annoyed, as much as distressed, over Christian's death. She'd admitted to knowing Jensen Amsel. She knew of Zaan De Raad, but had never met him, and knew nothing about the bag snatch.

Golder's tone was so controlled, Keira wondered at his real feelings. "Zelda Drost claimed the bag snatch must have been her brother's idea – she wasn't to blame for him bungling the attempt to get the ledger. I then asked her: What ledger?"

Further clever questioning by the police uncovered Zelda had surmised the details Fenna had found in the ledger were likely to be important. Important to what, Golder had probed? Zelda had been a hard nut to crack though, and had only admitted, after hours of questioning, to getting to know Jensen in order to find out about the shipment of jewels referred to in the ledger. Why did she want to know about these particular jewels, Golder had asked?

It had got complicated at that point. The police had asked Zelda what Jensen knew about the shipment referred to in the ledger of 1815.

"Miss Drost got very derisive. Told me Jensen Amsel was a moron who knew nothing."

Keira's hackles rose at this part of the retell. She'd not known Jensen long, but he was far from being an idiot.

Zelda had eventually given the detectives enough information for them to link the ledger details to the Tiru collection, and to the ring which Jensen had recently bought. The two officers looked at each of them in turn: slowly and deliberately.

"We need you all to tell us everything you know about this Tiru collection. This incident, the death of Christian Drost, is not the whole affair. We still have many questions to ask, and we believe you can give us plenty of answers."

The whole story of Geertje's jewels dribbled out. No details were left unexplained. Keira felt the Amsterdam police force were suitably aggrieved that the cousins hadn't divulged the whole story earlier in the investigation. After a couple of hours, they were dismissed. Detective Golder said it was late, and he and his colleagues needed to investigate further. They'd want them all back in the following day for further talks – Golder stressed – after they'd made contact with the police in Vienna, Heidelberg and Rochester; probably even Duluth. Keira sat feeling as if her knuckles had just been rapped.

Zaan and Fenna went off together. Teun put Ineke into a taxi. No matter her protests, she could take a bus, Teun insisted, filling the driver's hand with a bunch of euro notes to cover it. He was not having his cousin wandering the streets alone. Ineke had capitulated after Teun reminded her what had just happened to Zaan. None of them could be sure the malicious incidents were over. Not till the police had the culprit, or culprits, under lock and key.

On the way back to the hotel, Teun ventured a guess. "Interpol will have some hot lines jangling just now?"

Keira definitely agreed, glad the local authorities now knew the full details.

"I'm stunned Zelda manipulated Jensen so much." Keira turned to Teun in the dimness of the bedroom, faint street lighting filtering in through the curtain edges.

Teun's answer came as he whispered kisses at her neck, while slowly removing her clothes. "For nearly two years she groomed him for information, you mean?"

Her reply was the merest murmur as she explored a little herself. "Yes. Just to learn about Geertje's jewels."

Keira had worked out Zelda must have secrets the police didn't know about yet, Teun agreeing wholeheartedly. Zelda was knee-deep in muck. How had she known about the Tiru collection in the first place? Had it just been chance, perhaps having studied the old Amsterdam newspapers? And how had she known Jensen was connected to it?

Teun's attentions zapped any further pondering of Zelda.

Teun chose to catch up with some work the next morning instead of enjoying tourist ventures, with Keira happy to do likewise. He wasn't prepared to be hauled away from somewhere fascinating like the Rijksmuseum to go back to the police station. That instinct of his was working overtime. Detective Golder had appeared very competent: he was positive more details wouldn't take long to be uncovered, especially since liaising with foreign police departments was so much faster with internet communications.

He knew Keira's work wasn't urgent, but it still needed to be done. They were able to recharge their physical batteries, working alongside each other at the table in their suite sitting room. He'd never been in a similar situation before. It was… calming… even though they were both working. A weird combination. Keira was a very focused woman when she got stuck into her work, only responding to his occasional questions or to his offers of ordering coffee. Not a babbler was something more to admire about her. Lust plagued him again, though it shouldn't, since their early lovemaking had been pleasurable and energetically satisfying. But, back to the calming thing? Sitting alongside, he found it possible to suppress those urges, just knowing she was right next to him and they would have plenty of time to explore each other sometime soon. Since he had a ton of work to do, he ploughed in, though at break points his attention strayed. He couldn't help it. No prizes knowing where the target was. Restraint was a real bind.

Their work session lasted till gone 2p.m. when the police asked them to come back in again: just as well they'd stopped working long enough to eat the club sandwich he'd ordered. Jensen had been contacted that morning, his presence also requested. He'd now arrived at the Amsterdam police station and awaited the arrival of the rest of his cousins.

"Are Ineke and Zaan requested to come too?" Teun wanted to know.

"Already organized," Detective Golder told him. "We've also requested Fenna, since she may be able to help with our investigation."

They used a larger room this time. Zelda had been held in police custody overnight, possible charges of harassment, and much worse, were hanging over her head.

"Zelda Drost gave us some interesting information early this morning."

Teun could see Golder's long list upside down: he had a lot to tell them about. The officer's gaze swung first to Jensen.

"I have no wish to distress anyone, but some of Zelda

Drost's information may do exactly that. We'll start with more recent events. Zelda did not just target you, Herr Amsel. She told us that while she was your lover, she also had a sporadic lover here in Holland. She groomed the man in precisely the same way as she used you – for information gathering."

Jensen's curse was ignored by most in the room. Detective Golder merely made some eye gestures indicating the interview room was not the place for it. He carried on.

"What may be distressing is her lover in Holland was Klaas Fedder."

Ineke slumped in her chair, her breath catching in her throat. Alongside her, Jensen looked mystified as he quietly repeated the name, something clearly puzzling him.

"My ex-son-in-law? She was having an affair with that piece of trash?" Ineke held none of her rancour back.

Developments were certainly convoluted. Zelda had been conducting affairs with both Jensen and this person called Klaas, at the same time? Teun found the whole situation quite bizarre.

Detective Golder continued. "Zelda meeting up with Klaas Fedder was not random either. She targeted him to find out more about the Tiru jewels."

Teun guessed Jensen wanted to say something, the shakes of his head telling some other kind of story. He, however, couldn't keep silent. "How did Zelda know about the jewels?"

"That is quite surprising information."

Teun was sure Detective Golder enjoyed himself as he consulted his notes. Zelda had known all her life about a collection of fabulous jewels; her mother having always claimed her pearls were part of a larger set.

Teun looked at his cousins to see if any of them understood what Golder referred to, but they looked as baffled as he felt. Who was Zelda's mother?

Detective Golder opened a file and extracted a photograph. Teun looked at the string of pearls. He was still no expert, but he was sure the ones in the photo weren't of the same calibre as those he'd found in Adam's house. He looked at the catch in particular – no emeralds and, as far as he could see, only one possible diamond involved in the setting which looked like silver, rather than gold. It was a simple two-strand set of pearls, of probably an average length.

"These pearls have been in Zelda's possession since the death of her mother some three years ago. They had been passed down in the family in the same way as the jewels from the Tiru collection had been handed down in yours." Detective Golder's baleful gaze took in all of them before he carried on.

Teun slid his chair closer to Keira, just to be nearer, sensing her anticipation that a great denouement was about to take place.

Detective Golder lifted his notepad and scanned it again. "My colleague will keep me right on these facts, though I suspect you would be able to help me if I make any errors. Zelda's great-grandfather was Alto Tiedman."

Tiedman was familiar, but who was the Alto person? Teun didn't remember anyone being named Alto. His eyes sidled to Keira, whose lips pursed as though she had no clue either, her eyebrows raised.

Jensen got the question in first. "My ancestry researcher told me Alto never married."

"That's correct, he never married, but he did have at least one child we know of. He had a long-time married lover, who bore him a daughter. That lover was also the best friend of Martine Tiedman. He could not publicly claim the child, but it seems he did acknowledge her sufficiently on his death. He gave her a jewellery box which held the pearls in this photo, but also a very special list."

Teun felt Keira almost leap out of the chair beside him. "A list of the Tiru collection?"

"Exactly that. And years later Zelda's mother got the pearls and the list, but by then she'd also inherited a set of letters from Martine Tiedman. The letters were sufficiently detailed for Zelda to know Geertje had divided the jewels between her three daughters – but her sons had received none."

Teun needed some clarification. "If Geertje gave the items to Martine, Uriel and Tanja, how did Alto manage to give those pearls to his illegitimate daughter?"

Detective Golder smiled. "Zelda isn't committing herself, but she suspects her great-grandfather stole them from his mother."

The collective gasp of censure around the room made Teun feel a lot less conspicuous. Rogues abounded, from the sound of it, in Zelda's line of the family.

Detective Golder looked to Jensen again. "It appears Alto Tiedman, as second son, was the only one of Geertje's children to go into the jewellery trade with his grandparent, Jan Hoogeveens. As the eldest son, your great-grandfather Wolf went into the Tiedman silk merchant business?"

Jensen nodded his agreement as Golder continued to check with his notes, his voice staccato as he read the details. "I believe the only reason your father, Wolf Amsel, went into the jewellery trade was after he married your mother? Since he'd been in the silk business before that? Your jewellery business in Heidelberg had originally belonged to your maternal grandparents?"

Jensen's polite nod looked full of admiration for the facts Golder had uncovered so swiftly.

Teun sat smirking and realised Keira wasn't looking much different. There wasn't actually anything funny about the declarations, but it was amazing how things worked over the decades. He hadn't even thought about how Jensen had come to be in the jewellery trade; it had been so easy to assume direct connection to the trade through Geertje. He knew in usual circumstances he'd be annoyed his deduction skills had been less than thorough, but put his lack of good reasoning down to the distractions of recent days – the lovely Keira in particular. Fortunately, not having worked out how Jensen was in the jewellery trade, wasn't life-threatening. He focused back on the explanation being given by Golder, to find Zaan was now interrupting.

"Alto was the only son who would have had any working knowledge of jewels, then?"

"Yes. According to Zelda and her family stories, Alto was not best pleased Geertje was adamant about dividing the collection amongst his sisters, and took matters into his own hands. Why he acquired these particular pearls is unknown. The list Zelda had in her possession seems to indicate quite a spectacular set of gems, and these pearls…" He waved the photograph. "Are likely to be more insignificant than most of the pieces."

Teun definitely agreed with it, having seen the ones he'd put into safe storage. Detective Golder continued to check off his own list, reeling off the strategies Zelda had used to access more of the jewels.

"After her mother's death, she learned the Tiedman family name from the letters, and like your researcher – Herr Amsel – she did her own family tree. She traced her way down the lines and hired someone to check everyone out. Sadly, her contacts do not belong to the security firms who advertise their services widely; hers are definitely of the underworld. She engineered the meeting with you, Herr Amsel, at the jewellery convention, and likewise with Klaas Fedder. Klaas very kindly told her of the jewellery his wife had." Golder looked to his colleague to confirm the items.

The colleague, who had been largely the silent partner, flicked his pad and recited, "An emerald brooch…"

Ineke huffed. "My mother, Neela, gave Anna a better-looking pin than mine, and Marijke got a ring."

Detective Golder almost smiled. "It seems your mother also gave your daughter, Anna, something else."

"I didn't know that!" Again, Ineke harrumphed.

Detective Golder gazed around, ensuring he had everyone's attention, and nodded again to his colleague to give the information.

"Neela gave Anna an unusual-looking ring."

At Teun's side, Keira gasped. "The snake-head ring Jensen bought?"

Detective Golder and his colleague looked to Jensen to clarify.

"I bought the ring, but I had no idea of any family connection at that time. It was only after the newspaper reports of 1815 identified it, I realised what I, potentially, had in my hands."

Teun put a few bits of the story together and voiced them into the small silence that had developed.

"So. Zelda grooms Klaas for information about the jewels, knowing he was married to Anna. Klaas tells her about the brooch and the ring. How did he know to go to Jensen directly, though, and ask for a private sale?"

Detective Golder patiently explained, "Zelda persuaded Klaas to steal the ring from Anna, and gave him details for approaching Jensen to organize a cash sale, saying Jensen would give him a very good deal. But she hadn't told Klaas anything about exactly how valuable it was, or Jensen's family link. Zelda's theory was that if Jensen got the ring, and made the connection to the Tiru jewels, he'd start to do exactly what he did do."

Keira beamed at Jensen. "You'd start a search for the rest of the family, and flush out the jewels?"

Zaan chuckled. "I know she's a devious woman, but in a way that's quite clever."

Detective Golder made no comment.

Teun still had quite a few loose ends. "Zelda sets up the buying of the ring, Jensen takes the bait and Klaas gets the cash. Where is Klaas Fedder now?"

Detective Golder consulted his colleague.

"Location unsure, but thought to be somewhere in the Caribbean."

Teun couldn't help it, his laughter broke free. A ripple followed till Detective Golder read his notes. "We have an arrest warrant out for him: for stealing property from his ex-wife and some other incidents not relevant to this case. Extradition will not be a problem."

Teun was then told the Amsterdam police force had been in touch with Rochester, who had some new information on the case there. Zelda, through her network of dubious contacts, had hired a thug to follow Teun around in the US. Her cohort, and an associate, had been the ones who'd gained access to Adam's house. The next details left Teun feeling both miserable and gratified concurrently.

"Rochester Police Department had the perpetrator in custody when we made contact last night. He was already on their fingerprint register, and had been identified as having been in the house. The associate, likewise."

Detective Golder turned to Teun. "We believe you helped with that identification?" There was admiration in the policeman's tone, but also a hint of – You didn't tell us that during our investigations.

Teun nodded.

"The fingerprints on the piece of paper you forwarded to them, and other prints taken from the upstairs areas of the house – the flush handle of the toilet in particular – matched up with those in the police database."

Detective Golder waited for a few seconds till the sheer incredulity had passed.

"Stupid bastards!" Teun couldn't help his grin, inappropriate or not, but he noticed he wasn't the only one thinking the goons were exactly that – completely feckless.

Golder resumed. "From their questioning, the US authorities have the facts down as follows." He nodded once again to his junior colleague who recited from his notes.

"The assailants entered the property from the rear. The owner, Adam Blakeney, became alerted that something odd and suspicious was occurring. Realising someone was entering his house, he tried to make his way to the front door. It seems Adam Blakeney was almost at his front door when one of the assailants, Russ Hitchin, hit him over the head and knocked him down before Adam could leave, or call for help. The assailants then did a thorough search of the property, inadvertently leaving some prints in the upstairs bathroom. Finding nothing, they returned downstairs to find Adam had a piece of paper in his grip. One assailant ripped the paper when attempting to remove it from the man he presumed already dead. The assailants then went into the den and set alight a cardboard carton, having added a newspaper which was lying close by. They didn't seem to pay any attention to the fact the carton also contained some plastic wrap which would create toxic fumes. Satisfied the room was alight, the assailants left by the rear door."

Chapter Thirteen

Teun left the police station, his arm across Keira's shoulders – exactly where he wanted it to be – his cousins in his wake. They all made their way to his hotel, some time needed to ponder the list given to them by Detective Golder, even though it had already been pored over in the police station.

In the downstairs lounge, they occupied a large table and laid down their copy of the list.

"We've twenty items on the list to check off." Zaan was unofficial spokesperson and translator.

According to information given by Zelda – gleaned from the letters between Martine and Zelda's great-grandmother – the list had been compiled by Alto himself. As a jeweller, he was very descriptive, much more than in the notebook Fenna had uncovered.

One by one, they ticked off who had what, and what still needed to be uncovered. All of the items Teun had uncovered in the US matched exactly against the descriptions written down by Alto Tiedman. That numbered five pieces: the Moghul necklace and two sets of earrings to match, the enamelled bangle with the Indian dancer, and the three strand pearl necklace.

Jensen's ring definitely fit the description, and Romy's four items made a total of ten. Adding on Zaan's mother's ring, his cousin's hairpin and the other cousin's pearl bracelet, made thirteen. Marijke in New Zealand's ring, Anna and Ineke's brooch pins made sixteen items. The pearls Zelda had made seventeen.

They still had three items to uncover.

Zaan read the descriptions again, translating them very carefully. "This item is said to be contrary to the rest of the stones in the collection. Alto has written the ring has a dark golden stone which does not match the emeralds, but it was genuinely part of the Tiru jewels bought from the Temple agent. The diamonds flanking the stone are very small, but are of impeccable clarity and, as such, the ring is therefore a very important part of the set."

Zaan looked up at everybody after translating.

"Read the exact description again, please," Keira urged Zaan, looking as though she was about to pass out from excitement.

"The ring is of the same quality of gold as the bangle."

Teun knew what that was. "Twenty-two karats."

Zaan nodded then read on. "The stone is exceptionally large and of superior quality, its golden facets a myriad of colours. The setting is the strongest possible to hold such a large stone safely along with its circle of diamonds."

Keira gasped and grabbed Teun's hand. "It is the cereal box ring!"

Zaan continued to translate. "On the skin-side of the ring is the sign of the blessing from Rama to his wife, Sita, on the value of true love. From one love to another."

Unbelievable, if true. Teun startled them all by delving into his wallet. From inside, he produced the cereal box ring he'd been carrying around all the time. The other jewellery he'd put under lock and key, but he'd carried this ring for purely sentimental reasons, and because for him it was now like a little bit of Keira that was close to him.

On the inside band of gold, there was a stamp of some kind.

Keira was the one who produced a magnifier from her bag, the one Jensen had provided for her.

Unbelievable wasn't descriptive enough. Everyone around

the table marvelled at the tiny symbols etched onto the underside of the band, even though Teun had no way of really knowing if it was the sign of Rama till he enlisted the services of an expert. In his heart, though, he knew it belonged to the Tiru collection. The others agreed when he told them the story about his Aunt Marta and what she'd said about the ring.

That left two items to identify. One was a gold ring with a small emerald at its centre. The band was of twisted gold, wider at the stone and narrow at the rear. None of them had seen anything of that description.

Zaan translated the description for the last one. It was a gold chain of exceptional length, finely wrought with an enamelled tassel, the painting of a dancing Lakshmi.

Teun felt Keira nudge him. "Tanja's long chain, with the miniature painting?"

Zaan wasn't sure and re-read the description slowly. He consulted with Jensen who agreed Tanja's enamelled brooch looked typical of the end of the nineteenth century, the painting being what they would have termed a Victorian drawing room.

"What if it was the same chain, but the painting had been changed to a more modern one?" Teun asked.

Jensen and Zaan, who had most knowledge of jewellery, both agreed it was worth considering, since they had no other ideas or leads.

Time had sped by. It was already well past a normal bedtime, though they hadn't experienced that for nights. They decided to sleep on their findings. Decisions could wait till breakfast. Jensen had checked in to the hotel when they'd arrived, so only Ineke had to taxi home. Zaan grinned that he was staying with Fenna in Amsterdam, and that came as no surprise to Teun since his Dutch cousin had been plastered to her side.

A lunchtime get-together was arranged, though not too early.

Upstairs in their room, Teun grappled Keira onto their bed. His lips feathered all along her jaw, his words like punctuation marks between kisses.

"Do you realise a month ago I didn't know you existed?"

Keira's answer was muffled as her lips snatched whenever she could. "And the significance is?"

"If my cousin, Jensen, hadn't bought a very special ring, I wouldn't know you."

Keira's chuckle tickled his now bare chest, her clever lips teasing him into a frenzy. "Can you be sure of that? I think life works in very mysterious ways, Teun Zeger."

For a while, no words at all were uttered.

"Mmm, touch me just like that," Keira moaned. "I'm sure fate would have introduced us sometime…"

"You're sure?"

"I'm sure." Keira's answer was to his same rhythm.

"More?"

"More?"

"Like this?"

"Like that."

"I'm so glad…"

"Me, too…"

Too busy to answer, some part of his brain agreed with that statement.

Next morning, Keira woke in a muddle. So much to think about. Her eyes still closed, she reflected over recent events, a satisfied smile leaking to brighten her dozy expression.

They only had two items to find, but it looked impossible now. She supposed it was inevitable that out of twenty items, something would have been lost. The previous night Jensen had been buoyant about the amount they'd found, certain any exhibition they mounted would still be a resounding success. He'd agreed to make arrangements to buy the few pieces which required to be purchased. The cousins were all in

261

agreement to put their own finds into an exhibition – even Ineke – who had decided she wanted to keep her ugly pin, Jensen having given her a truer valuation at five thousand euros. The diamonds and emeralds were genuine, but all the items would get a second opinion; an unbiased assessment.

A rustling of bedcovers indicated Teun was waking up. No more time for thinking about jewels. Who needed jewels anyway? Her tiny smile morphed into a full blown smirk as she pretended to evade his marauding fingers.

A while later they rose and did some work.

"I need to go home, Teun." The prospect of leaving him again didn't appeal, but she needed to be practical. The weird merry-go-round of the quest was slowing to a halt. Their affair had to halt, too.

She was surprised and delighted when Teun made an unexpected suggestion.

"I've never been to Scotland. How about I come and see what Edinburgh is like?"

Before they could make those plans, Teun's mobile rang. Oh, God! Detective Golder. He'd like to speak to them. Again?

Jensen was still in Amsterdam, so by mid-afternoon there was another assembly of the cousins, their lunch date having been postponed.

Detective Golder wasted no time. "Klaas Fedder is now in custody. He had an emerald brooch in his possession, which belongs to his wife. He hadn't sold it, yet, since he still had some of Jensen's cash left."

More important was new evidence the police had gleaned from Zelda's letters and paperwork.

"We now believe, from this particular letter, that Alto Tiedman was involved in at least one other theft. This missive from Martine, to Zelda's great-grandmother, refers to Martine knowing her brother was implicated in a larceny. The same letter indicates she took steps to hide the evidence, to protect her brother. The letter states that Geertje's jewels are priceless, but the stolen object is even more so."

The policeman's glare scanned them all. "Do any of you have any ideas about this?"

None of them did. They'd been so focused on amassing the jewels it had never occurred to them something else was to be found. Keira wasn't sure she wanted to even be involved in looking for yet another mystery object.

"Can you read what it says to us? Perhaps one of us will recognize something about it?" Keira asked.

The younger officer gave some explanation first. "The batch of letters from Martine, which were passed down to Zelda, has been written over a number of years. This one is dated years later than the others, and not long before Martine died. Martine says: *I still have the infernal problem of hiding the little dabbling, and I must change its location. The size of the lady in question is about the same as Tanja's dancing lady. I have recently persuaded Tanja to give her chain and dancing lady to Neela, since Tanja has no daughter, and Ralf has only produced sons.*"

Zaan intervened. "That's correct. My great-grandparents only had sons. Four of them, but only my grandfather lived after WW1, and the dreadful 'flu of 1918."

The young detective read on, "*I have lived with this secret too long. It preys on my conscience. I must conceal it elsewhere, yet I do not want my daughter to be burdened with it. The jewels are not much different, of course. Neela will have to know she has something of value to keep safe, but not what. I will tell her to keep my wedding gown, and all my accessories, for her own daughter, but that will be all she'll know.*"

Detective Golder had on his baleful stare, directed in particular at Ineke. "Do you have any idea what she might be referring to?"

Ineke was on her high horse. "I know nothing about a wedding dress, or accessories. I still have a box of photos which came to me from my mother, but I don't remember if

263

there is a photograph of Martine in it. I haven't looked at the box in decades."

Detective Golder was grave. "Thank you. We'll send a uniformed officer to collect it."

Keira sensed Teun's restlessness as he sat next to her, and knew he'd been chewing over the new facts.

"Do we assume Zelda wanted to flush out this item as well?"

Detective Golder nodded agreement, flicking to another page in his notebook. "She told us she doesn't know what the item actually is, but it was even more important to uncover. From the statement, we questioned further. She has now admitted she had her hired hands following all of the cousins, Keira included. Their assignment was to ascertain if anyone had found anything, and then to acquire it from the receiver, by any method necessary."

"Even murder?" Keira had to ask it, though she knew the details would hurt more than Teun.

"They were to be paid according to the deeds they'd actually done. You need to understand these felons are not professional assassins, but it appears they were prepared to do anything for money."

Jensen had been sitting quietly but that changed. He looked furious. "How many of these people did she hire?"

The younger detective flicked his pad. "She contracted one felon in the US and hired him – Russ Hitchin, who worked with another accomplice." The young policeman turned to a new page. "Zelda Drost also hired someone to follow Teun and Keira in Heidelberg and Vienna – Boris Winkelmann. That same felon, Boris Winkelmann, attacked Romy Lischka, and broke into Jensen's shop. Another followed Zaan and Fenna in Amsterdam. He was the one who passed on the information to Christian Drost that it looked as though Fenna had uncovered something important." Another page was flicked over. "A fifth tailed Ineke, but that one gave up after Ineke visited the jeweller in Woerden. When that felon wormed out the information that Ineke had left a brooch in the jeweller's care, he gave up the chase, awaiting further orders. And a sixth was hired in Edinburgh."

"Edinburgh? Has anything happened to my father, or to my sister?" Keira slid forward, her insides churning. She'd not talked to them for a while.

"That offender has not been arrested yet, although the police in Edinburgh are pursuing him at present. Zelda claims he broke into your father's house but found nothing."

Keira felt Teun's hand slip around hers, giving her support. "When did this break-in happen?"

A moment passed before the detective answered, having flipped open yet another page of his pad. "She claimed it happened one week ago."

Keira turned to Teun. "Why didn't my father say anything?"

Teun's gaze was reassuring. "We'll call as soon as we're done here." He turned to Detective Golder. "You're sure the Drummonds haven't been harmed?"

"Not according to Zelda's accomplice. The Edinburgh police have given no indication any damage has been done to people, or property." Detective Golder wound up the interview. "This case is not yet closed, although we now have a number of people under arrest in different countries, including Zelda Drost and Klaas Fedder. Most important: we still have to clear up the matter of the original Tiedman thefts."

Keira was stunned. Her own family hadn't been harmed, but they'd been targeted as well. With regard to the Tiedman thefts, all those sat around were affected. They'd been under the impression their heritage was a noble one and that was now in grave doubt.

Zaan broached a question Keira wanted to know the answer to as well. "Who actually owns this mystery item, and, in fact, who owns the Tiru collection?"

Detective Golder wasn't sure. It would take time to establish that, since so many years had passed. The Tiru collection had left India in 1815, but no-one had any idea how old this other precious item was.

Perhaps it had come to Amsterdam in the same shipment, Jensen suggested. They only had ideas, no evidence.

Golder wanted all of the Tiru items to be in safe storage in Amsterdam while the inquiry was still ongoing. Since more than one police department was currently involved, there would have to be liaison between them before movement of some of the jewels. Teun's hoard would remain in New York till further notice. All the other items would be amassed in Amsterdam.

To start Golder's hoard of jewels, Teun reluctantly handed over the cereal box ring from his pocket. His explanation of why he still had it actually made Detective Golder smile. The man was human after all.

After the ring left Teun's fingers, Keira felt his stare for many moments, his focus on her eyes. In front of so many other people, she was embarrassed. Her hand went automatically to fidget with her chains, since she was now always wearing the one Teun bought for her intertwined with her original one for safety. She wasn't sure what was in his deep regard but wanted it to continue.

***

A nearby café had an influx of patrons as the group sipped a well needed drink. Jensen wasn't the only cousin looking glum. The Tiru collection was being amassed together but not in the way Jensen had envisaged. Locked up in a police safe was not what he'd wanted for such a wonderful set of jewels.

"Maybe it won't take too long to have them released, Jensen." Keira knew it wasn't very likely, yet hoped it would be so.

Zaan cheered them up. "How about we have a little contest? There are still two items on the list not accounted for: a ring and a tasselled chain. And, of course, this mystery object which is the size of Tanja's enamelled painting. How about the cousin who discovers the first of them is declared the winner of our family quest?"

"And the winner gets what reward? Those items won't immediately belong to the finder either." Teun's laugh was echoed by pretty well all of them since the items would join Golder's hoard.

"He, or she, gets to pick a nice restaurant, and we'll all get together again to celebrate."

Jensen lifted up his beer. "I'll drink to that, and I'll even foot the bill for the meal, although you can pay your own hotel bills next time." General laughter echoed around the room.

The deal was done.

Keira always liked going home, but she was even more excited this time since Teun was seated beside her as the plane taxied into a bay at Edinburgh Airport. They hadn't hung around Amsterdam, because Golder declared he didn't need their presence in Amsterdam any longer. He was confident any updates could be done at a distance.

"Is your dad going to approve of me then?" Teun's eyes twinkled in the dusty sunshine filtering in the small window of the aeroplane.

"Does he have to approve of you?" Keira teased, yet she did want her father to like Teun as much as she did. "I think I'm more concerned with whether my sister will leave you in peace."

Teun nudged her. "Really? What's she going to like the most about me?"

Keira pretended to assess him, though she knew every single bit of him by heart. "She'll like your manners."

Teun's laughter made the woman across the aisle stare at him. "My manners?"

"Yes. You hold open doors for me, and take my arm to help

me get from place to place. Isla's impressed by that sort of thing."

Teun sounded more serious. "Keira, it's because I can't stop myself from touching you. All the time I want to touch your lovely body, and any bit of it will do."

"What? Any bit will do?" She laughed along with him when his face scrunched up. "You're telling me you don't have bits you prefer?"

Their conversation was halted when everyone bustled themselves up the aisle to disembark. Just as well, since Keira was beginning to overheat. Teun still packed that punch; he could set desire to spread around her at the mere flick of an eyelash.

Keira always loved her dad's welcomes, especially if he met her at the airport. He grabbed her in a big bear hug and, as usual, gave her a smacking kiss on the cheek. She was glad she'd mentioned her father's enthusiasm to Teun, or her embarrassment might have been acute. Teun, she was glad to see, got a hearty handshake and a welcome clap on the back, their heights nearly matching.

Back at David Drummond's house, they sat down to dinner with Isla.

"You have had an adventurous time, big sister. While I get to educate the grungy youth of today, you get all this travel and danger. Not to mention meeting this lovely man."

Teun caught Keira's glance, acknowledging what she'd warned him about, regarding her sister's approach.

"I'm the lucky one." Keira blushed hearing him make his intentions clear to all. "It's thanks to Jensen I got to meet Keira."

A thorough update followed, since during phone calls to her father and sister, she'd tried not to be too alarming. "Are you sure neither of you noticed anything strange happening here?"

"Did you tell Keira about the day I went on my golfing spree?"

Keira looked at her sister; sure she hadn't missed Isla telling her anything odd.

"Maybe I didn't." Isla was concentrating hard, remembering events. "It was early last week, wasn't it, Dad?" When David nodded, she carried on. "Dad was off to Gleneagles for a round of golf with his friends. I stayed the night before since he was meeting his buddies at 5a.m. I got up as well to drive him to the mini-bus. When I went downstairs, I found the back door was unlocked."

Keira felt Teun grip her hand across the table. It was like *déjà vu*. The events at Adam's house came to mind so disturbingly.

"I thought I'd locked it the night before, but guessed I must have meant to and had forgotten. I'd gone into the kitchen to check it when Dad shouted to me, asking for a drink of water. Anyway, in the morning the door was closed, but not locked. I put the kettle on, laid out our breakfast stuff, and then went to confirm the weather report on the TV for Dad. When I was in the lounge, I thought there was a noise somewhere downstairs. Dad was up in the shower so I knew it wasn't him."

Keira reached for her sister's hand. "I'm so glad you weren't hurt; neither of you."

Isla looked confused. "What do you mean?"

"You finish first, and then we'll tell you." Keira knew it was irrational to be scared for them, since it had happened more than a week ago, but she couldn't help it.

"When I went back to the kitchen, there was a blur of movement outside the window, yet when I went out into the garden I noticed nothing. There was no-one on the driveway either. Nothing looked different in the house, so I thought I must have imagined it, though I did tell Dad about it as we were driving to meet his buddies."

David Drummond asked Keira to explain her comment, his expression wary. The story of the hired accomplice tumbled

269

out.

"This guy claimed he rifled through the house? And found nothing?"

It was an incredible thought but Isla couldn't discount it. "I popped back to my flat that morning, and then onto school. Dad was out till late on that evening. If the intruder got back in again, he could have spent all day looking. If he'd been watching us leave, he'd have known Dad would be out for hours golfing."

Glad no-one had come to any harm, Isla and David were thoroughly updated about the search for the Tiru jewels, the last thing mentioned being the mystery item.

"That's amazing, all but two of the twenty items have been identified," Isla enthused. "Though I've forgotten what they were already."

Teun had the description learned by rote and proceeded to reel off the details. "You're sure you didn't get a nice little ring from Neela, with a little emerald?"

Isla laughed. "Nope. And I didn't get a nice long chain with a picture on it either. Neela was fond of us, but obviously not too fond."

The next day Teun picked up an email from the Amsterdam Police Department, with attachments for them to study. Ineke had rummaged around and had given over her box of photographs to the police for inspection. There were three different photographs of Martine; two formal ones with her sisters, but different from the one Jensen had. Although the females were all well dressed, they were not dripping with jewels. The third photograph was of Martine's wedding. Forwarding the email to Keira was the fastest way to get a printout, since they'd stayed at her apartment. He didn't quite match Keira's enthusiasm as she studied the wedding photo.

"Very pretty." He knew his comment was lukewarm but he wasn't exactly into women's fashion of 1910.

"It's more than pretty, Teun Zeger; it looks like it might be a spectacular Paris original."

He knew Keira was teasing him and loved her for it. Actually, he was beginning to think he loved everything about the woman, when she gasped alongside him.

"My God! I've got to phone my sister." Keira scurried off for her phone.

"Are you ill? What's wrong?" He hated the idea of Keira being sick: she'd seemed fine just a couple of seconds before. He couldn't understand her reactions.

She ran back to him, looking at her watch. "No, I'm fine but I must go to Dad's house right now."

Teun was really mystified now. "You just said you need to talk to your sister, but you're going to your dad's?"

Keira paced around after keying in Isla's number. "We have to see this together."

He wanted to stop her pacing, calm her agitation, though didn't know how. "What do we have to see together?"

"Not you! I need to be with my sister."

Teun was feeling very concerned. Was Keira rejecting him? "Stop pacing and tell me what I've done to put you in such a tizzy?"

"You've not. Oh hello, Isla. I know school's not long finished but can you get to Dad's as soon as possible. I really need you to be there."

Teun wondered if she had some sort of telepathy with her dad and knew he was ill. Her call didn't last long, though, since she closed her phone and turned to him with a huge smile splitting her face. The phone sailed down onto the couch, followed by a euphoric Keira, who laughed so hard he really thought she'd flipped her lid.

"Okay. I'm pretty spooked here. What's going on, Keira?"

She yanked him down so hard he feared he'd flattened her ribs. Her arms snaked around him and crushed him to her. He warmed up to this behaviour a lot better than her weirdness.

He found she wasn't finished, though, for she proceeded to kiss the breath out of him. Teun was more than happy to oblige and reciprocated, a few more times. Yes, she'd calmed down, but he wanted to be sure she was mentally stable; the outburst had been so unlike her.

"You've got to tell me just one thing, Keira Drummond. Sane, or insane?"

Her smile warmed him to his toenails, her eyes still teasing him, a secret hovering there. "Sane-ish. I can't say anything else till we get to my dad's and until Isla is with me." Struggling free of his grip, she slid off the couch, thrust out her hand to pull him up, and towed him off to the door.

Darting back, she collected up the newly-printed photograph, and the one Jensen had given her. She searched around her purse for something but guessed she wasn't finding it.

"Darn it. I'm going to need a magnifier."

Teun went to his jacket pocket and produced the one Jensen had given him weeks ago. "Will this do?"

"It might." She darted off into her office, and returned immediately brandishing a much more powerful one with a little light on it. She proceeded to ensure it was lighting up. "This is a better one. Come on."

Isla must have left work immediately as she'd arrived just before them, standing in the doorway awaiting them like a sentinel. "You better have a good reason for this impromptu visit, Keira, for you've done me out of a freebie meal. One of my colleagues had just invited me to dinner."

Keira zapped her car locked, and then strode forward to link arms with her sister, leaving him to dawdle after.

"Fear not, sister dear." Keira's grin was infectious. "If my suspicions are correct, we are going to dine very well tonight, and I'll pay for all of us!"

Keira was still acting weirdly but he loved her enthusiasm; forgave her for leaving him to trail behind. There was something big about her behaviour that was appealing and intriguing.

David Drummond was also amused by the whole affair. He even allowed himself to be persuaded up into the loft when Keira protested she didn't want him left out of the action.

"It looks just like we left it after we did our clear-up. If any thug rifled around in here, he was very tidy." Isla's declaration came as she finished the climb of the retractable steel ladder, and joined them in the middle of the loft space. It was high enough to stand up, but wasn't a huge area. "So why the mystery, big sister?"

Keira slid her fingers over a few of the crates and stacked boxes. She came to one particular cardboard box and lifted it clear of the rest. "The burglar was definitely very tidy if he looked at these things. Nothing seems to be disturbed, but let's see."

Some of her animation suddenly disappeared. "Oh, God. I hope I'm not wrong about this, or I'll have got you all up here for nothing."

Teun clutched her hand and squeezed. "You know, I'm not so sure your dad would have shown me the loft on a guided tour of his house. It's great to see every little bit, but put us out of our misery. Explain why we're here."

Keira turned to Isla. "Do you remember what we packed in this one?"

Isla didn't look too sure. "Some scarves and stuff, shoes and bits and pieces?"

Keira jostled her sister's arm. "Not bad. Stick with the accessories. Dad, I'd like you to open the box and pick out something that's champagne-coloured satin."

"Shiny material?" David was just checking.

"Yes."

Teun held his breath as David rummaged around inside. Like a conjuror, he pulled out a piece of material which looked like a cream silk handkerchief.

273

"Keep going, Dad. It's the right colour, but this time, find something that's really shiny, and has much more material."

Teun realised Keira wasn't even looking at her dad. It was as if she was too scared to look at what he was doing.

"Now I know what you want him to find." Isla whooped, dancing around in the small space.

David pulled out a wide belt. "This thing?"

Keira turned to look and jumped forward to grasp him.

"Yes! Yes! Yes!"

Her dad and sister grinned like mad, but he didn't understand why. There was never going to be any complaint, though, about her hugging him so enthusiastically.

Isla came closer to him, laughing apologetically. "Sorry about this. My sister's usually the sane one of the family, but I think this search has done in the few brain cells she ever had."

Down in the dining room, Keira had them sit at the table. She placed the belt flat down and put a photograph on each side. Then she carefully, and precisely, put the magnifiers down on the printouts. One was of Martine in her wedding dress, and the other was the photo of the three sisters, from Jensen.

Teun thought Isla's squeal might have shattered the windows.

"It's the same!"

He felt Keira's arm snaking around him. "Can't you see it?" She prodded him in the ribs.

Teun could see the belt looked the same but couldn't drum up the same enthusiasm for a bit of material.

"Teun. You're not thinking. What did the letter from Martine to Zelda's grandmother say?"

The surge of excitement he felt surprised him when he recalled the words of the letter. "Something about telling Neela to keep her wedding gown and her accessories?"

Keira surprised him with a smacking great kiss. "That's another thing I love about you! You have a great memory for details."

Teun knew she was so wound up she probably didn't really realize what she'd just uttered. She loved… that about him?

Keira slowly recalled the part of the police interview which referred to the letter from Martine, to bring her dad and sister up to speed.

Isla was peering at the printouts while she was speaking. "So, you think Martine hid something in one of her accessories? This mystery object?"

Keira beamed alongside him. "I do."

Teun had to agree it was what the letter implied. "But what makes you think this belt-thing has something to do with it?" Lifting the magnifier, he scanned the photo again. "It looks the same, but isn't it maybe just what was typical women's fashion of the time?"

"Good thinking, Teun." Keira was still beaming like a light bulb. "But there's something which makes me very sure this is part of Martine's wedding dress."

Teun was stumped. David just shook his head.

Isla slowly transferred her gaze from the photo of the three sisters to the one with the wedding dress. "The lace has the same sort of Indian design, doesn't it? That pear drop, teardrop sort of shape?"

"Well done, sis!" Keira left the table to rummage around in a drawer in a cabinet nearby.

Teun looked at the object in her hand. A tiny pair of scissors. She lifted the belt and felt along its edge then handed it to him.

"Feel it!"

He let his fingers squeeze along its length. The belt was a band of separate panels, a firm rod like a divider between each one. It was stiff in his fingers and obviously padded.

"It's firm?" He wasn't sure what kind of answer Keira was looking for.

"Yes. But it's also so well padded there could be something in the padding."

The enormity of what she'd just declared hit him.

"Are you going to strip it?" Isla's voice was a hushed gasp.

Keira felt along each panel. One by one she moved along till she reached the centre. "The padding is different here!" She couldn't keep the excitement from her voice. Teun could see her hands shaking so much he feared she'd cut herself.

"Here!" It wasn't unexpected when she thrust the scissors at Isla. "Slit it at the back. I'm too excited."

Isla turned the belt over, and then pushed it away as if it had burned her.

"What's wrong?"

Keira looked ready to faint.

Chapter Fourteen

"Someone has re-stitched this." Isla's whisper was in direct contrast to her earlier squeals. She pointed to the different sizes of stitches on the back of the panels.

Teun sensed Keira's excitement plummet. The blood drained from her face, her difficult swallows visible. He wanted to help but wasn't sure how. "Do you want me to make the slits?"

One nod was enough. He took the scissors and made a cut from top to bottom. Fibres from the sheep's wool wadding wafted out, and floated on the air. He carefully felt inside. There was something hard right in the centre, but he wasn't sure what. Carefully retracting it, he pulled free a greaseproof-wrapped package. It sat against his fingers, a faded coffee brown wrap. He placed it on the table. And looked.

Everybody looked. Hardly anyone breathed.

"Open it!" Isla nudged him as three more heads bent over it.

He turned the thin oblong package over. There was no seal. The only thing holding it closed was its sharp folds, and age.

A chain dropped out when he un-wrapped it.

Isla picked up the gold chain and held it to the light, squeaking right in his ear. "That's exactly like your chain, Keira. The style of the links is just like yours."

Keira loosened the clasp of her original chain then laid her chain down the length of the table. Isla did the same with the one from the belt. They were identical. But what did it signify?

"This chain's broken." Isla stated to no-one in particular as they all gaped at the gold chains. She pointed out one end.

The link was intact, but it didn't have a catch ring. The other end did have a catch. "This is meant to be…" She didn't finish her sentence. She swooped up a magnifier and studied the photo of the three sisters. Pointing to Tanja, she started to jabber. "I thought something about this chain was familiar when I looked at it a few moments ago. Look, Keira! She's wearing your chain!"

The photo and magnifiers were passed around. The chain did look the same, yet what did it mean? Teun studied Tanja again. "If Tanja's chain is the same one as you've been wearing, Keira, then it must have been deliberately separated."

Keira's excitement rose. "That maybe means the painting in the *repoussé* frame is in this house. If I've been wearing half of the chain for the last ten years, then where's the frame?"

Isla nodded and clucked at the same time. "Mum gave you your chain for your sixteenth birthday, didn't she?"

Teun absorbed Keira's smile before she slid her arm into his, her topaz eyes twinkling at him. "Isla thought it was a boring present for me to get, but I liked it, and wore it from that day onwards, almost constantly."

David appeared to come to life. "I'm remembering when you got the charms for your chain. The first one was the key; your mother got that one. And then I was with your mother when we bought the second. That was a horseshoe. And at the next celebration, we bought your four leaf clover." David gave Keira's free hand a little pat. "You were eighteen then. I remember buying the four leaf clover because you already had a key and didn't need another eighteenth key."

Isla jostled her dad. "At first I was miffed that big sister got a gold chain and then ornaments to put on it but…" All three of them laughed. "I persuaded Dad to buy me a proper microscope when it came to my sixteenth birthday, and then a computer. And for my eighteenth, I got a real, proper, telescope."

Teun grinned. "Once a scientist, always a scientist. I can

278

easily empathize with that."

Keira hugged her dad. "Did you go with mum to buy me the chain?"

As soon as she said it, Teun looked at the broken chain on the table. As did the rest.

Keira licked her lips. "Mum didn't buy it."

Isla's voice was low. They were all still staring at the chain. "*Oma* Neela's last birthday visit was for your sixteenth birthday, wasn't it?"

Three Drummonds thumped down onto the chairs. Keira's head bobbed. "It was just after that she fell and broke her shoulder, and never came back to Scotland. We went there instead, when we could."

"She brought the wedding belt, and gave you the chain."

David sounded quite bemused. "But why would she break the chain and give you only a bit?"

"Dad!" Isla's voice held grinning censure. "Keira was old-fashioned, but not that old-fashioned."

"Excuse me!" Keira pretended outrage.

Teun was glad the banter kept it from being too serious, and too tense. "Could it have been some sort of weird change of use of the jewellery?"

Everybody looked at him as if he had two heads. "I mean if the chain and picture thing had been hidden away for decades, could Neela have decided she wanted someone to benefit a little from wearing it?"

Keira and Isla agreed it was exactly the kind of thing Neela would do.

"Does that mean your wife knew some of the story?" Teun looked to David to answer.

"I never knew anything at all, Teun. My wife maybe did, but she was always loyal to her friends, and if Neela asked her to keep a secret she'd have done it gladly. She loved Neela like a mother."

Coffee was produced since they had some thinking to do.

***

"I remember my sixteenth birthday, now. I'd forgotten all about it." Keira looked at her dad. "We'd been out to dinner, and mum went and got my present when we returned home. You were sitting in your usual chair, and *Oma* Neela was on the opposite side of the fire. Mum was standing and the rest of us were on the couch."

She turned to Teun to explain. "Gabriel was with her that time, but he died the year after. Mum gave me the present and I opened it. I can remember the chain slithering out of the tissue, since it's so heavy." She looked to Isla, but guessed she didn't remember, which wasn't surprising since it hadn't been her birthday. "*Oma* Neela called me over then, and said she had a little gift for me, too. It was Neela who gave me the key charm." She looked at Teun and grinned. "Neela said something like '*this little key will unlock the secrets of your past. Hold on to it always since it is your future too.*' I just thought it was an old lady kind of thing to say but didn't question it."

"Till now?" Teun's eyes glimmered. She could tell that analytical brain of his was working full steam: no surprise when he launched in.

"Here's a scenario. Neela is given Tanja's chain hidden in that belt. She keeps it for years knowing it has something of great value in it, but that it must stay hidden." Since everyone was following his theory, he surged ahead. "Who can she give it to that she can trust to keep it secret?"

Isla was the one to pipe up. "Not Ineke. I don't think *Oma* Neela ever got on with her daughter, Ineke."

"Mum?" Keira whispered. Teun's theory was sounding so plausible.

Teun continued. "Neela brings the chain over to your mother, but has decided you would like to wear it."

"Not the full length. Nobody wore real chains of that length." Isla's tone was scornful as she pointed to Tanja's

280

dangling chain.

Keira was impressed with his theorising. "Neela breaks it in half. Your mother takes it to a local jeweller to have a new catch put on it, since they decide to use it for your birthday gift." It all sounded so right. Keira squeezed his arm to get on to the end. "For some reason, they decide to put the broken chain back into the belt, and they conceal the painting bit somewhere else."

Isla's analytical brain was just as good as Teun's. "That's because the painting is the important and most precious part."

"Have you heard this story before?"

Isla chuckled. "No. It's all logical, so far." Isla flicked her head in Teun's direction. "He's a keeper, sis. If you don't want him, can I have him?"

"No, you can not!"

Teun looked as if he was thoroughly enjoying himself. "Back to my story, ladies, if you don't mind. As Isla has pointed out, they conceal the important bit, but… Neela gives you the key to finding it."

Teun wore a self-satisfied expression. But it still sounded so right.

Her dad seemed like the dormouse in Alice in Wonderland as he chipped in again. "You're thinking there's a little box somewhere in this house that Keira's tiny key will unlock and inside there will be a…"

He didn't get a chance to finish. Keira's voice was only one of four. "…painted brooch with a tassel."

"We searched the house already, Dad." Isla remonstrated with David, who wanted to launch into a search.

"Do you think the burglar found the thing?"

"No!" Teun's shout was nearly as loud as Isla's. Keira knew her own matched quite well. No-one wanted to believe it.

Keira screwed her eyes shut, hating the prospect, but it had to be done. "It has to be somewhere in the loft."

"It's definitely not in the box where we found the belt." Isla was convinced of it.

They decided to have dinner first, but it was a waste of the Indian meal they'd had delivered since no-one was particularly hungry. Everyone was on edge in the same manner she was. Unresolved mysteries were so demanding. She covered over the uneaten food and left it for later.

It didn't take very long with four of them looking: they at least had a target this time. It had to be a very small box, since her charm key measured less than a centimetre.

Isla called her over when she came to the fretwork box which held their mum's knitting patterns. She'd lifted out the pile of folded paper patterns and had uncovered some bits and pieces on the bottom. "I don't remember the box being like this. Keira?"

Keira looked at the base. She didn't recall it either, but the box was always squashed full of patterns so why would she remember it empty?

The base wasn't totally flat. In the centre was a removable baize flap, held in place by two brass flip clips, the kind you used to see on old picture, or photograph, frames. In a little concealed dent was a small gilt box, beautifully inlaid with what she guessed was ivory. Even better was the tiniest little lock.

"Oh, my…"

Her legs were so shaky she couldn't climb down the loft ladder without the steadying hand of Teun at her backside, his arm remaining tightly wrapped around her as they trooped downstairs.

In the dining room she reverently placed the box on the table beside the chains, almost too nervous to use the tiny key.

"Go on, sis. You can do it… and I can't contain myself any longer. If you don't hurry up, I'll be taking a crowbar to it!"

That was so laughable since it was a tiny, but solid little box.

Keira couldn't get the minute key to turn. Almost crying with frustration, she gave it to Teun. "You try."

Teun grinned, teeth white against his tan. "I never told you about my nefarious past, did I?" He looked so endearing when he teased. "John and I learned how to open Grandma's locked desk drawer with a hairpin. She always had a little stash of chocolate in it we'd pilfer. What we didn't learn until much later, from Adam, was Adam and *Oma* Marijke always had a bet going about how long it would take us to open it."

Though his fingers were much larger, after a few jiggles and twists, he had the lock clicking. Keira took the box, when he insisted on handing it over.

Inside the box was a miniature painting – a woman in a Victorian setting in a drawing room. The outside of the frame was delicate gilt scrollwork, or maybe real gold? She couldn't tell. A heavy tassel of fine chains hung below. Definitely the one Tanja wore in the photograph.

Two days later the Amsterdam police station was almost becoming Keira's favourite place to visit. They'd dumped their surprise package – the golden box – on Detective Golder's desk the previous day when they'd high-tailed it back to Amsterdam. And now they visited once more. The policeman beamed from ear to ear. Such a change from his usual staid demeanour.

"You are a winner, Miss Drummond." He proceeded to open the gilt box. From inside, he removed the painted brooch. Keira gasped: it wasn't the same painting. "You are correct. It is not the Victorian painting." Detective Golder handed it over for her to look at closely.

The detail was so tiny but it was a miniature painting of another woman, but more of a head and shoulders portrait. The era was much older than Victorian: she guessed at least a couple of hundred years older.

"Underneath the Victorian image was the image of a dancing Indian goddess, Lakhsmi. And underneath that was concealed an even more priceless image. This is what was underneath. Take a good look now, because it may be the only time you ever get to hold such a valuable item close to you. Have you any idea who may have painted this?" Detective Golder's voice was reverent.

Keira shook her head. Alongside her, Teun peered at it. "It's very old, isn't it?"

Detective Golder was delighted and couldn't conceal it. "It has still to be authenticated by another expert, but our resident specialist at the university in Amsterdam believes this to have been painted by Lucas Horenbout, or if not him, his father. They were very successful miniaturists back in the 1520s and 1530s, here in Holland, and also in England."

"This is what Alto Tiedman stole? Why would a jeweller steal a painting?"

"It was, I'm told, quite common to have the best jewellers set the paintings in beautiful frames."

Keira was shattered. She'd thought the day before they were just returning the chain and painting in the frame to the rest of the collection. None of them had expected this.

It was too fantastic for words. Another fantastic thing was that Golder expected Zelda Drost to be facing a sentence of a minimum of fifteen years, her cohorts with appropriate amounts depending on how heinous their crimes had been.

***

"What are you doing?"

Teun wanted to picture Keira. It was incredible how much he missed her. It had been a whole month since they'd parted in Amsterdam, but she'd been booked to go back to Edinburgh, and he'd headed back to San Francisco. Reality, and work demands, had bitten hard.

"Finishing the last of the Italian translation I told you about. I've worked the last four days almost non-stop to get it finished."

He knew how much of her work had got into a logjam when they'd been trekking around on the emerald quest. His backlog wasn't much better. Payback was always a bitch, in some way or another, so he'd put in twenty hour days since his return, especially to ensure the Boston lab's data was fully restored.

"How's Jan?"

Just one of the many things he loved about her was that she was so caring and supportive.

"Not so good. I told you a few days ago I was heading out to see him as soon as I could swing a trip, didn't I?" Keira's sympathy kept him going. "His doctor called earlier today. Dad's condition has been deteriorating very swiftly after another major stroke this morning. I've a flight booked out of San Francisco in two hours. I'm packing as I speak."

The best part of a day later, Teun sat in the room which had been his father's. Jan had been still alive when he arrived, but hadn't been able to respond more than to open his glazed eyes. Teun wasn't sure, but he hoped Jan knew his son was the one holding his hand as Jan slipped away. It hadn't all been bad, though, it had given him a long time to think about the good times they'd had together. Although Jan couldn't respond, and he didn't expect him to, Teun had felt good recalling their fun times aloud. The do-you-remembers were peppered with lots of wasn't-that-funs.

And now he was sitting by the vacant bed, his father's body having been removed to the funeral home. He'd asked the staff to dispose of his father's effects, but was waiting for Bobby to come with Jan's possessions that had been locked in the Nursing Home's main safe.

"Here you go, Teun." Bobby handed over a small padded envelope.

He emptied the contents out onto the stripped bed. Forty-five dollars, some loose change and a watch tipped out. There was a small framed photo of his mother and his father, together and happy a long time ago. And another with him as a toddler flanked by both of his parents. There wasn't one with Jan and Grace together. Teun found that heartbreaking.

And a little red velvet box, the velvet ancient and scarred, almost furred to white in places.

A chuckle escaped. It couldn't be.

Keira and Teun were present – along with all the living progeny of Geertje, including Anna who'd returned to Holland – when Detective Golder gave over guardianship of the Tiru collection. The policeman made quite a fete of the handover, having organised a laying-out of all the pieces which had been hidden from daylight during the legal proceedings. Even though he only had them spread out on a wide table, the congregated items looked fabulous.

"They're all yours. When this exhibition opens, I'll be expecting a couple of complimentary tickets."

A wink went Jensen's way, and a brimming smile met the rest of them as Teun lifted the cereal box ring from the table and turned to Keira, taking her hand to move her a little way away from the assembled company.

"Will you marry me, Keira Drummond, and accept this as an engagement ring?"

Her laughter made everyone's heads turn towards them. "I've been married to you for nearly two years already, Teun Zeger. What dumb fool question are you asking?"

"I know it's a bit late for this." Teun grinned like mad as he held out the golden-brown stoned ring. "I wanted so much to give you this way back then, even before I had to hand it over to Detective Golder. It had been in my pocket for days, burning a hole, and me desperate to ask you to marry me, though hesitant because of our situations. I thought at the time that there was only one woman on this earth who should own this ring. You."

They'd got married a month after Jan Zeger's funeral. It had

286

been a very quiet wedding, and they'd only marked it with the neat gold wedding band that was on Keira's finger. No engagement period. No engagement ring.

"This can only ever be your ring, Keira," Teun said as he held the topaz stone up to her eyes. A second later it was on her finger next to her wedding ring, his lips stealing her breath.

One week later, Jensen mounted the exhibition of Tiru jewels. Many experts had been involved; pouring over documentation till sufficient evidence had been uncovered to prove the jewels had legally been purchased from the temple by the Koopman family in Amsterdam. Back in 1815, realising the interest in the collection, the Koopmans had capitalized on it and had, genuinely, sold the collection to the Hoogeveens of the time – charging them double the price. The Hoogeveens then took it out of circulation, fearing it might be stolen. It had simply disappeared, though Geertje had come by the collection legitimately, her descendants likewise.

The painting of a four-armed dancing Lakhsmi in a simple gold frame – the image a match for the gold enamelled bangle – was displayed with the bangle as a matching pair. The painting of the Victorian drawing room in the gold tasselled *repoussé* frame was included with half of the chain worn by Tanja. The cousins had decided Isla should receive ownership of it after the exhibition was finished, since she was the only female who had none of Geertje's jewels. The emerald pinkie ring Teun found in Jan's envelope, after his father's death, joined the rest.

Twenty items on show, though only the family knew what was not on display.

The Horenbout had not belonged to the Tiedmans, and was still in safe storage in some police vault that was unknown to the descendants of Geertje. It was unclear who the owner had been – and, indeed, who the item belonged to now. That situation was immaterial to the mounted collection, since it wasn't part of the original Tiru Salana set. Absolutely no information regarding the Horenbout miniature reached the press.

Teun had refused to let Keira add her half of the long gold chain, claiming she needed it to anchor her charms. He jokingly claimed her nerves wouldn't stand it if her chain wasn't around her neck to fiddle with – and he wouldn't be able to live with a nervous wreck.

When the exhibition was declared officially open, a particularly splendid cereal box ring was worn by a woman with matching, twinkling, topaz eyes.

THE END

Fantastic Books
Great Authors

Meet our authors and discover our exciting range:

- Gripping Thrillers
- Cosy Mysteries
- Romantic Chick-Lit
- Fascinating Historicals
- Exciting Fantasy
- Young Adult and Children's Adventures

Visit us at:
www.crookedcatpublishing.com

Join us on facebook:
www.facebook.com/crookedcatpublishing

Made in the USA
Charleston, SC
23 September 2016